Ann –

Welcome to
your inner
zombie –
I hope you enjoy
the Burning Z !
o

Chris

ALSO BY CLIVE RIDDLE

Dorris Bridge
dorrisbridge.com

The Burning Z

CLIVE RIDDLE

HealthQuest Publishers

HQ

HealthQuest Publishers
www.healthquestpublishers.com

Copyright ©2013 by Clive Riddle
Cover design by Ellen Dykes

Publisher's Cataloging-In-Publication Data
(Prepared by The Donohue Group, Inc.)

Riddle, Clive, 1958-
  The Burning Z / Clive Riddle.

   p. : ill., map, music ; cm.

   ISBN: 978-0-9854920-4-5

   1. Zombies--Nevada--Black Rock Desert--Fiction. 2. Burning Man (Festival)--Fiction. 3. Meteorites--Nevada--Black Rock Desert--Fiction. 4. Retired military personnel--Nevada--Black Rock Desert--Fiction. 5. Black Rock Desert (Nev.)--Fiction. 6. Fantasy fiction. I. Title.

PS3618.I39 B87 2013
813/.6

Printed in the United States of America.

For Marshall, Sarah and Sasha

"If aliens ever visit us, I think the outcome would be much as when Christopher Columbus first landed in America, which didn't turn out very well for the Native Americans."

Steven Hawking, April 2010

"Far more Native Americans died in bed from Eurasian germs than on the battle field from European guns and swords."

Jared Diamond, Guns, Germs, and Steel: The Fate of Human Societies (New York: W. W. Norton, 1999).

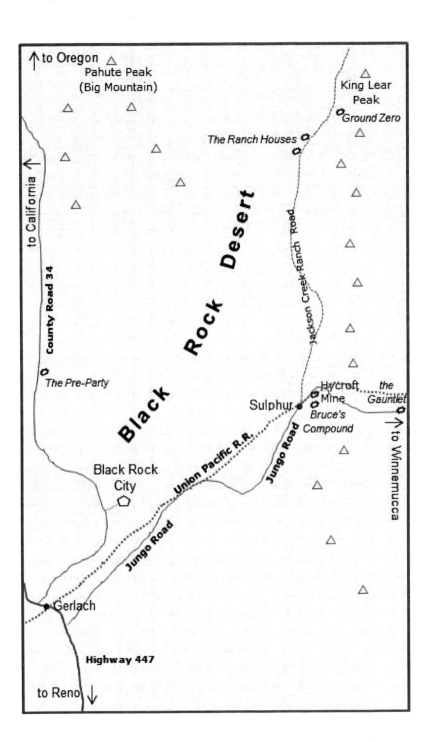

I. Sulphur

Thursday Friday Saturday Sunday Monday Tuesday Wednesda

Shooting Star

They strolled from first base, across the pitcher's mound, heading toward third under the desert's emerging night sky. The two men continued, angling past the cyclone backstop, leaving the Black Rock field of dreams behind them. They proceeded past the large, modular storage shed to the shadowy, old ranch house that lay in wait.

Bruce convinced Conner to follow him up the paint-stained aluminum ladder, onto the roof. Conner voiced concerns they would crash through the decaying structure of the weathered and abandoned two-story home, but Bruce provided assurance he had traversed this passage on numerous occasions. They found their way to the second story roof's dust-covered crest, straddling their legs on each side, settling down to take in Thursday's twilight view.

Just ahead, in the hazy foreground, Conner could make out Bruce's double-wide Fleetwood mobile home and Bruce's office trailer to the east. In the distance, across the playa to the northwest, he could distinguish the silhouette of the Black Rock range. "What's the peak of those mountains called?" he asked, pointing.

"Big Mountain," Bruce replied matter-of-factly, in his deep, radio announcer-like voice, carefully opening two bottles of Miller 64 beer he had produced from his sweatpants pocket.

Conner chuckled. "Now, that's original."

Bruce carefully handed a bottle of Miller's to Conner, first letting go of the family-size bag of Crunchy Cheetos he had been clenching in his left hand, ever since they climbed up the ladder. The unopened Cheetos bag started to slide down the eastern slope of the roof. Bruce instinctively lunged forward a few inches, before deciding the better of it, worried he might slip off the roof, or worse still, spill his beer. The Cheetos came to a stop halfway down the roof, blocked by a shingle that had become slightly raised and out of position. The bag was soon forgotten, becoming the latest addition to the old ranch house.

Bruce returned his thoughts to Big Mountain. He went into docent-mode, as he had numerous times since the early afternoon upon Conner's arrival. "Well, its actual name is Pahute Peak. P-a-h-u-t-e. But I never hear anyone call it that. Now off to the right here, just northeast of us, across the playa, are the Jackson Mountains. That's Sugarloaf Knob out in front, and the tallest of the peaks behind that is King Lear. Reaches about eight thousand nine hundred feet in elevation. But, I suppose, there's not a lot of there, there, at King Lear Peak, or our big nearby city of Sulphur for that matter." Bruce paused mischievously. "Alas, Conner, nothing will come of nothing out here."

"Huh?" Conner replied, a bit perplexed; but then wrinkled his nose. Even mentioning the name of the once-town of Sulphur reminded Conner's nostrils of the pervasive odor that occasionally wafted by with the right breeze.

The two sipped their beer silently and took in the enveloping desert darkness as the breeze continued to whisper past them. They began gazing at the moonless night sky, both shivering slightly as the night continued to cool down.

"This kind of reminds me of Parker Creek," Bruce observed, bringing up their home town as he pointed up to the stars. "Nights were just as clear and as high-def back there, back then. But now, you can't beat this HD screen above us."

"Yeah, for reals, but after all I have been through, the past ten years, I'm just happy to be here, breathing this air, if you know what I mean," Conner responded, taking in a deep breath, partly for effect. He enjoyed occasionally using the slang of someone half his age – like *for reals* – also for effect.

Bruce took that to be close enough to a toast, giving his beer bottle a clink against Conner's. "Amen to that." He held up his bottle, chugging it in a couple of gulps, while his left leg twitched continuously. He fished around to place the empty back in his sweatpants, exchanging it with the one remaining full bottle from his large right pocket. "Want to split this last beer while we take in the stars?"

"No thanks," Conner chuckled nervously. "One beer is definitely my limit these days."

Bruce grimaced, remembering their conversation on that topic from the afternoon. "Oh, yeah." He opened the last beer, deciding to change the subject to their upcoming fantasy football draft. "I know you were making fun of me earlier, about how old school this football draft is going to be, but you're going to get into it. You just wait and see...when you get back from your little rendezvous with your Facebook friend."

Conner and Bruce were certainly the two best known alumni of their generation from Parker Creek. Their lives had followed similar trajectories. They had not seen each other in years, when they bumped into each other recently at the Reno Costco near the airport, catching up on what the past decade had laid in their paths.

Both men had moved on to a new chapter in their lives in Nevada. Before their Costco encounter concluded, Bruce convinced Conner to join his fantasy football league, and spend some time with him out in the desert, sandwiched around Conner's upcoming liaison with his once and future lady friend.

"Know what I feel like now, after this beer, and after we crawl back down to the ground?" Bruce asked mischievously, loud enough for any critters in the distance to hear.

Conner chuckled again. "Something tells me I'm about to find out what that would be."

"Lemon meringue pie," Bruce stated matter-of-factly.

"Huh?"

"I would like a slice of lemon meringue pie," Bruce repeated. "I just happened to buy one in Reno and it is waiting for us in the refrigerator."

Conner tilted his head sideways. "Now doesn't that make you stop and wonder?"

"What?"

"Well...about why some things are fine in a pie, and other things aren't? I've been thinking about this lately. I mean, like, everyone eats apple pie, but not a pear pie. Pears are sweeter than apples, why don't you find them in a pie? And I realize there are recipes for pear pie, but really, how many people out there have ever had a bite, or even seen a pear pie?"

"Conner, are these the deep thoughts you've been thinking?"

Conner gestured with his hands, even though Bruce most likely couldn't make them out in the dark haze. "So, take your lemon pie, for example. If we're talking citrus, why do we eat lemon pies, or key lime pies, but not orange pies? We eat orange marmalade, why not an orange pie? And it doesn't count that somewhere there's a recipe for that too. I'm saying you don't see pear pie or orange pie at any Marie Callender's pie shop, and I'm wondering why that is?"

Bruce laughed and was about to tell Conner he was welcome to go forth and bake an orange and pear pie, when he noticed the shooting star descending from overhead. "Would you look at that?" he exclaimed excitedly, grabbing Conner's right shoulder and pointing directly above them.

Conner immediately spied the streaking bullet of light. "Whoa," he slowly gasped. "Doesn't it seem to be slowing down?"

A shooting star should flash by in almost literally the wink of an eye. This lasted seconds. They watched it descend until it blacked out somewhere beyond Sugarloaf Knob, perhaps at the base of King Lear Peak. Bruce thought to quote 'time shall unfold what plighted cunning hides' after the shooting star disappeared in the distance, but decided it was a bit much, and his audience wouldn't appreciate it anyway.

Thursday Friday Saturday Sunday Monday Tuesday Wednesdc

The Drone

Alan Gorman took the call on his Blackberry from a very excited fellow meteor observer. Alan was active and respected in the meteorological associations both men belonged to—observers with the American Meteor Society, and members of the North American Meteor Network, and the International Meteor Organization. Gorman wasn't an astronomer by trade; he was a retired Air Force physician with connections, it seemed, to everyone that mattered.

The man at the other end of Gorman's call stood next to two companions under the endless desert night sky, hollering excitedly at Alan from his Verizon iPhone. Meteors had become the man's passion since his retirement from the Bureau of Land Management in Winnemucca.

Alan was away from his Palm Springs home, spending the night at a Best Western in Auburn. Before the man could explain the nature of his call, he patiently endured listening to Alan rhapsodize about the day spent with old friends, golfing at the Beale AFB Coyote Run Golf Course, followed by skeet shooting at the Beale Air Force Base Rod & Gun Club.

Alan, seated at his motel room desk, tapped his pen on the Best Western stationary while the man explained that he drove his visiting brother and adult nephew on Jungo Road in his Ford F-150, several miles east of Winnemucca to a nice, open spot clear of the town's artificial light. The man mentioned that although their timing precluded the major meteor showers — the Perseids concluded weeks before and the Kappa Cygnids were done as well – he was still optimistic they might see something special on that night.

The man detailed to Alan how, equipped with his IMO Chart and Nikon Digital Single Lens Reduction system, he set up shop, scanning the skies with his two apprentices. The man equated to Alan that just like a river fisherman landing a trout on an opening cast, he felt an adrenaline rush, pointing out the descent of a fireball to his brother and nephew within minutes of their arrival.

The man proceeded to bombard Gorman with enthusiasm about the just-witnessed-fireball, as well as his dutifully recorded relative measurements: the field-limiting magnitude, phi (latitude), lambda (longitude), time and duration of occurrence, and the fireball magnitude, which he estimated at minus 10. The man shared with Alan that he was convinced it was not of cometary origin, and produced a meteorite fall. Above all, the man told Gorman he was stunned by the anomalies. The speed of entry seemed slower than the typical cometary showers he was used to observing, which helped support his case for a fall. But, it visibly slowed in descent while still lit.

Alan agreed with him, the expected outcome would be that somewhere around fifteen thousand to eighteen thousand meters up, the remnants would decelerate to the point where ablation (vaporization of the meteor, generating light while stripping away the outer surface of the object) ceases, thus causing the visible light to cease as well. This would mean that the object would "go dark" for the remainder of its journey to impact. Yet, the man swore to Gorman that it remained dimly lit as it continued to decelerate, virtually all the way to the ground, and more amazingly, that its rate of deceleration was quite significant.

Had Alan not known the man for years, he would have discounted this narrative to typical amateur enthusiasm, misinterpretation and exaggeration. Instead, Gorman ran him through a string of questions trying to rule in or rule out various scenarios that might have some plausibility attached to them. Gorman couldn't persuade him that it was anything but a meteorite fall, and the man was hell-bent to check it out right then and there.

Alan jotted down the man's estimated coordinates, based on observation and notes of the trajectory. Gorman found no fault with the man's logic on the potential point of impact, but Alan objected that it could wait until morning, given the difficulty of spotting the exact location – if any – at night. Alan failed to persuade his caller otherwise – the man announced they were going to set out in his Ford F-150, given his BLM career knowledge of the terrain. Gorman elicited a promise from the man to call Alan first thing in the morning and provide a rundown of what he did or did not find.

Alan plugged in his Blackberry to recharge, setting it down on the desk. He turned out the desk light, heading back to bed to read the Thursday *Sacramento Bee*.

While Alan pursued his slumber, the man and his two companions set out on their late-summer's night dirt road drive down Jungo Road, over forty miles past the Hycroft mine to the nonexistent town of Sulphur, then turning north on Jackson Creek Ranch Road for about fifteen miles, finally venturing east on a side road. The man stopped before the road veered south toward Black Canyon. A couple of hours after his call to Gorman, they were at the base of Navajo Peak, with King Lear Peak looking down at them, six kilometers to the north.

The night was unusually still. Although the evening was windless for the moment, the chill seeping through the open windows was pervasive. The man pulled out two fifteen million candlepower portable spotlights for his brother and nephew to scan the area. He inched his double cab Ford F-150 forward north, off-road, careful to stay focused on the many obstacles and elevation changes ahead.

Twenty minutes later, the man thought aloud about circling back. His nephew jumped at the opportunity to agree, having lost interest in the adventure. Five minutes afterward, the man did just that. Halfway into the slow return trip, his brother shouted excitedly that smoke or steam seemed to be rising fifty meters to the east.

The man tried not to mount any optimism, given the number of hot springs in the area, although he didn't recall one at this location. A deep gully ahead prevented any further advancement, so they stopped to walk the last twenty meters uphill, spotlights in hand. Steam or smoke indeed was rising behind the large reddish boulder concealing their quarry.

All three men broke into a trot, angling north to gain a view behind the boulder. The man gasped loudly as they beheld a fifteen-foot, shallow impact crater. He advanced a meter, his brother and nephew cautiously following a few steps behind at each side. The spotlights revealed a remarkably globular-shaped object, less than a meter in height. Its surface was blackened, which the man explained to his companions was most likely a fusion crust from the ablation during its descent, and the object itself might be another color underneath.

The man stepped up to the edge of the impact crater. He turned around to discuss with his brother and nephew the procedures and measurements they should undertake with their find. He did not see the upper half of the object rise several centimeters and initiate spinning. He only heard the soft whir behind him and witnessed his nephew drop the spotlight quite suddenly. He then heard crackling sounds reverberate, as hundreds of small projectiles shot from the object in all directions, a number scoring direct hits on the three amateur meteor observers.

Conrad Zimmerman

Conner Zimmerman you would notice in a room full of people. He stood six-foot-two, neither thin nor fat. His hands were large, his feet were large and his nose was quite prominent. His brown eyes exuded sadness, punctuated above by dark eyebrows and below by slightly darkened circles. His short brown hair failed to conceal his longer-than-normal ear lobes. His muscular face and neck falsely created the impression that Conner must have played football or some other contact sport at some point in his life.

Conner took some measure of pride in how easily and chameleon-like he adapted to each of the series of lives he occupied during his forty years on earth. He endured his small town loner-geek preadolescence to become a happy, optimistic and well-adjusted teenager in Parker Creek, the small, isolated town in Northern California that both he and Bruce Kepner grew up in. Conner ran cross-country and track, starred in the school play and played a mean saxophone.

Conner hadn't known Bruce that well in Parker Creek. Bruce was a couple of years younger and their paths didn't cross often. Conner remembered the young Bruce as an odd kid who seemed far too at ease talking to teachers and the other adults populating Parker Creek.

Conner created no expectations from his parents, siblings, friends, or Parker Creek teachers that he would excel once he went on to college. But after enrolling at California State University, Chico, he morphed into what his friends otherwise would have viewed as an oxymoron: the serious academic business administration student at Chico— still known back in the day as the California party school of choice.

Conrad Zimmerman could rarely remember being called by his real name – perhaps just by his mother whenever he suffered some major transgression, by a minister on his wedding day, or when he approached the podium during his high school and college graduations.

At Chico, Conner graduated Summa Cum Laude, with a concentration in Operations and Management, plus a minor in Economics. During his senior year he worked part-time in the accounting department at Enloe Hospital, taking an interest in the business of health care. His social life assumed third position behind school and work. Conner left Chico without experiencing a serious relationship, hangover or citation from officers of the peace.

Conner was accepted and enrolled that fall into UC Berkeley's Graduate School of Business Administration, which had just been renamed the Haas School of Business, with a new building soon to be constructed for the program. Conner sailed through the Master's program, again graduating with honors. He also interned for a one-year stint in administration at Alta Bates Medical Center. In his downtime, he fell in love for the first time since a crush in high school. Conner was deeply enchanted and smitten by a brown-eyed brunette seated one row back in his first business law seminar.

Soon after graduation at Berkeley, Conner was married in style. His bride came from a comfortably well-off Marin County family. He landed a Sacramento-based strategic planning position for the regional office of PhyNational, the giant publicly-traded hospital company. Things happened quickly for Conner at PhyNational. He was promoted three times in his first thirty months at PN, relocating to their corporate offices in Los Angeles. Conner held a rare mix of talents – he was a spreadsheet and numbers whiz; he held a spot-on ability for identifying specific strategic market trends and opportunities; he was a keen assessor of talent and charismatic leader of his growing department; and most importantly – he could schmooze effortlessly with doctors and PN executives.

Conner soon had the attention of PN's CEO, who took a liking to the deferential, polite, but highly confident young

Zimmerman. Conner guided the company toward acquisition and consolidation in key markets, while shedding their hospitals where they couldn't achieve a dominant presence. He developed subsidiary companies involved with such ventures as physician practice management, hospital group purchasing, ambulatory surgical centers and geriatric outreach centers in retirement communities.

Conner began tagging along during the "road shows" for investment analysts in conjunction with quarterly earnings reports. It wasn't long before he was an integral part of the presentations. Conner's compensation package rose as meteorically as his career, fueled by stock options.

At twenty-eight, he became the toast of his hometown Parker Creek, his proud parents dutifully forwarding his national trade journal press clippings to the local weekly paper. For the high school's one hundredth anniversary week celebration, Conner was asked to come home to give a speech and be honored alongside Bruce Kepner, as co-Alumni of the decade. Even the *Sacramento Bee* Superior California section ran a small article on the dual homecoming of the health care wunderkind and the dot com darling.

Conner's marriage stayed strong, despite the demands of his corporation, because his wife was also invested in her own career. Then they decided it was time for children. Conner lay awake at night trying to reconcile how he would adjust his career to become a father.

After announcing his wife's pregnancy to his delighted parents, his folks packed their bags on a whim to pay a surprise visit. They were killed in a horrific multi-vehicle accident involving a big rig on Interstate 5, outside Coalinga, while Conner was still in Sydney, Australia wrapping up acquisition talks for a small group of hospitals to join PN's growing international division.

Two months later, while Conner was en route to speak before the medical staff of PN's flagship hospital in South Florida, his pregnant wife contracted a hyper-aggressive streptococcal bacterial infection. Not understanding the gravity of the situation, she told Conner not to worry when they spoke over the phone shortly before his speech. When Conner returned home, his wife and unborn child were dead, PN's premier Los Angeles Medical Center and infectious disease specialist unable to save them. Her cause of death was listed as toxic shock syndrome produced by the bacteria, similar to Jim Henson's (of Muppets fame) demise years earlier.

Conner took a leave of absence from PN within days after the funeral. He never returned, instead diving into the abyss.

Thursday Friday Saturday Sunday Monday Tuesday Wednesday

Where is Everyone?

Conner pulled into the circle driveway of Bruce's compound. He stepped out of his tan Toyota 4Runner, glancing across the playa toward the mountains. During his short time in the Black Rock, he had noticed an almost perpetual presence of a small whirlwind or two somewhere on the playa. But now he could sense the full-on afternoon dust storm gathering force in the distance.

Bruce's compound was nestled on the opposite side of the playa from the big peaks of the Black Rock Range and Jackson Mountains, in the more diminutive foothills of the Kamma Mountains. The barren desert playa ended just before the old railroad tracks. The land leading up to Bruce's compound was thick with varietals of sagebrush and bunchgrass. Conner eyed the distant wall of dust and wondered if it would reach Bruce's structures or if they were safely far enough off the playa.

Conner had been listening to his iPhone playlist through the car stereo, causing him to now wonder what soundtrack would go with the approaching deluge of dust. Kansas' "Dust in the Wind"? Too cliché. Woody Guthrie came to mind, perhaps because Conner had driven to Bruce Springsteen's cover of "This Land is Your Land" sometime during the past half hour. So Conner settled on Woody Guthrie's "Great Dust Storm Disaster" from his 1940 album, *Dust Bowl Ballads* that Conner remembered being exposed to during his Chico college years.

Conner returned to Bruce's compound late Sunday afternoon, elated and exhausted. His past days in Reno could not have gone any better, from his point of view. From the moment Conner picked up his rekindled love at the Reno Airport in time for lunch on Friday, he sensed he had stepped into another life—or at least had rebooted his own.

Conner didn't know if he could or would describe to Bruce how transforming it was to have existed so numb and alone for years, then so swiftly have someone flood a void he wasn't even fully aware existed. A memory from the movie *Excalibur* flashed in his thoughts. Conner had been too young to see the R-rated movie when it was released, but viewed it on several occasions in hotel rooms on HBO or similar channels. Conner mouthed the line he had committed to memory, from when Percival finally brings the Holy Grail to a decrepit Arthur, who after drinking from it, rejuvenates, exclaiming "I did not know how empty was my soul...until it was filled."

When she and Conner bid farewell earlier Sunday afternoon, he experienced a jolt of déjà vu. The last time they said their goodbyes, decades earlier, it was possibly for all time. The déjà vu sensation subsided quickly. She gave Conner a long kiss, after firming up their plans for dinner, before her flight home on Labor Day. She then stepped out of Conner's 4Runner, grabbed her luggage, hopped in her girlfriend's van, ready to shop for provisions and head off to the annual Burning Man festival in the desert, where they would be joined by almost sixty thousand other devoted attendees.

Bruce bound out of his mobile home to greet Conner, after hesitating momentarily at the screen door, taking in the invading armada of dust headed their way. Bruce conversely felt the past day could not have gone worse. He seemingly tried to fit about two hundred words in sixty seconds as he described his day to Conner, the moment they met in the driveway.

Bruce's two buddies from Reno had recently arrived. Bruce and his two friends had been tossing a softball around in Bruce's ballpark, past the old ranch house. Now the two were getting settled in the single-wide mobile trailer that Bruce used for an office out back. But Bruce's four friends from Winnemucca were long overdue for the fantasy football party and draft.

Worse, sales from his two roadside vendors, on the reservation in Nixon, and at the northern end of Gerlach, were well below last year's. No one had attempted the Jungo Road "shortcut" from Winnemucca to Burning Man during the past several hours. Bruce's roadside sign advertisements in the Sulphur area, directing visitors to the side road leading to his mobile home for last-minute purchases, had no audience to appreciate their clever slogans.

Shortly after purchasing his property outside of the ghost town of Sulphur, Bruce encountered the exponential surge in traffic on Highway 447 as Burning Man approached. While many reservation vendors sold Indian Tacos, Nixon vendors and the non-reservation Gerlach vendors seemed to have a lock on the impulse hard-good items. Later, Bruce tracked them down, striking a deal with a friend from his overseas days to provide some on-demand inventory that Bruce could broker with the vendors for a cut. This year, he decided to retain a very small residual assortment of goods to sell direct from his home just off the Jungo Road "shortcut" to Burning Man from Winnemucca.

But his inventory check with his two vendors early in the day indicated the goggles, dust-masks, bandannas, glo-sticks, and sun-tan lotion sales tailed off prematurely. His idea to direct sell in Sulphur, after having his "shortcut" promoted in emails and on the web, laid a big goose egg during the afternoon, despite some promising sales in the morning.

What's more, Bruce's landline had gone down several hours earlier. Given they were out of range for cell phone coverage or Internet service, they were effectively cut off from communicating with the outside world. They could view the world, given Bruce did subscribe to basic Dish satellite television service, but Bruce held no interest in subscribing to satellite Internet. Bruce had bought an old CB radio to converse with tourists out in the playa or some of the folks associated with the Hycroft mine, but it quit working back in June, and he hadn't done anything about it.

"It's like someone put up a big brick wall somewhere up Jungo road," Bruce complained to Conner, standing with his arms crossed at the base of the steps to his mobile home. "And they're not letting the eastern division of our fantasy football league through either."

Conner stepped forward to pat Bruce on the shoulder. "Hey Brucemoose, things will work themselves out. Give it a day. It'll be okay. You know, tomorrow I have to leave for a lunch meeting with the people at Humboldt General Hospital in Winnemucca. But I'll stop by on my way back to Reno, and I bet you'll be swimming with business."

Bruce shook his head. "I don't know. I hope you're right. Now look behind you. We better get inside. I think this dust storm is going to reach us. See, today couldn't be any worse. There goes our four-on-four softball game, all up in a cloud of dust, with one team a no-show. " Bruce motioned out towards his 'field of dreams.' The infield was all-dirt, leveled and faithfully shorn of any vegetation at least once a week. The outfield also had once been clean-shaven, but now sported a variety of desert stubble. The cyclone backstop had a slight rightward lean, from when Bruce's Winnemucca friends visited some time ago, accidently running their pickup into the backstop as they tried to provide night game lighting with the vehicle's headlamps. The unique charm of Bruce's field lay in the inverse base paths. Bruce had laid narrow sidewalks just below ground level around the bases, then installed thick, all-weather padding over the sidewalk, and topped it with green synthetic turf.

"Hey, we can play a short game tomorrow morning, once everyone is up", Conner suggested consolingly, as they proceeded up his mobile home steps.

"I guess so," Bruce whine-moaned, in an Eeyore tone of voice. "But I still don't get it," Bruce grumbled, pausing to open the screen door. "Where is everyone?"

Bruce Kepner

Bruce Kepner had a difficult time sitting still. When seated, his right foot arched on his toes, his leg vibrating steadily.

He fidgeted with whatever small object was within reach of his right hand – pencils, utensils, remotes, knickknacks – none escaped his deployment. If absolutely nothing else was available, his sunglasses were removed from his nose and twirled between his fingers.

Bruce sported a neatly groomed goatee, which revealed streaks of gray that appeared somewhat ahead of their time. His jet black hair, much shorter than in his dot com days, was also conceding occasional territory to their gray cousins. His wiry 5'10' frame was taken out daily for a 5k run, a habit that continued from his high school cross-country and track days in Parker Creek.

Bruce always looked up to Conner during his years in Parker Creek, even though Conner did little to acknowledge Bruce's existence. He became a runner in junior high because it was the sport of Conner Zimmerman. Later in life, Bruce could never quite put his finger on why he idolized Conner, other than perhaps because Bruce had no brother of his own, and Conner lived just down the street.

Bruce's adolescence in Parker Creek was not all that joyful. He left town days after high school graduation, rarely visiting his parents until he returned to bask in the glory as the triumphant dot com mogul. Bruce's parents, lacking the funds to send him to a name college or even pay for a dorm room, arranged for their son to live with relatives in Modesto to attend California State University Stanislaus in nearby Turlock.

Stanislaus, back in the day, sold tee shirts from the bookstore sporting a turkey donning a graduation cap, bearing the slogan "Turkey Tech." Bruce, however, was very satisfied with his education in computer sciences, where he developed the reputation as an extraordinary whiz kid. Gallo Winery scooped him up in their Information Technology department immediately after he received his undergraduate degree.

Bruce became enamored of html code as soon as he became aware of it, during his last semester of college. He badgered his supervisor at Gallo to put it to use, but was repeatedly informed it was premature to invest company resources along those lines. Bruce took it upon himself to develop his own projects at night.

Vinopalooza today is a wine, food and music festival in the Texas hill country; Vinopalooza.com is now one of thousands of web sites that simply offer sponsored links and ads from a single home page. Back when Bruce conceived Vinopalooza.com, he envisioned it as a site dedicated to the wine community that would catch the eye of his employer and provide an opportunity for advancement.

Bruce, as it turned out, had a flair for graphic development and web page layout, in addition to taking advantage of available applications for site functionality. He also discovered a talent for recruiting content. Via email, he lined up a stable of respected wine reviewers and stimulated significant web forum discussions on wine topics. Vinopalooza.com became an "eyeball magnet." In the early days of the web, the site stood out, gaining national attention.

Gallo executives, however, weren't amused. They formally requested Bruce to remove references to Gallo he had placed throughout the site, mistakenly thinking his employer would be impressed by his promotion of their products. Eventually, their concerns about his conflicts of interest between his day job and the website led to escalating documented disciplinary actions and his eventual termination.

Fortuitously, Bruce was recruited by a conference company to speak in San Francisco at a seminar for Internet website entrepreneurs. After presenting, he was approached by a partner at a venture capital firm. Their discussions progressed rapidly, and soon Vinopalooza had relocated to San Francisco with a fifty-page business plan, a management team, and fifteen million in first-round funding.

The website exploded. At Vinopalooza, one could browse extensive databases on wine ratings, retail prices, and food parings. Reviews, articles and forum discussions abounded. An extensive calendar of wine tastings and festivals was available for browsing. Much more significant, round two financing followed, with major national media advertising, including network television.

Bruce's duties diminished as the company quickly grew, but he remained the public figurehead. He became a multi-millionaire after Vinopalooza went public on NASDAQ. Unfortunately, Vinopalooza experienced significant obstacles with its revenue model that centered on sponsor advertising and wine sales e-commerce. The company never did produce a profit, collapsing shortly after the more publicized demise of pets.com, as the dot com bubble burst. Nearly all of Bruce's net worth was tied up in company stock.

Undaunted, Bruce resolved to launch a new, more modest dot com enterprise that would not be dependent on venture capital for initial development. Bruce decided to pursue a business model focused on his passion, the running community. He drew in family and friend investments. Soon joggen.com (German for jog) debuted with $500,000 in angel funding. In the dot com post-apocalypse environment, Joggen's path was perilous. Revenues were near nonexistent. A second round of angel funding yielded another $250,000. Six months later, Joggen closed its doors.

Bruce promptly packed his bags, moving from San Francisco into a self-imposed exile.

The Dirt Roads to Redemption

Three weeks into a leave of absence with PhyNational, Conner Zimmerman exercised all eligible stock options. He resigned a week later, despite the protestations of his CEO and mentor at PN. Armed with the stock proceeds, a sizeable portfolio, and his wife's life insurance policy payout, Conner sat on a considerable nest egg. The egg grew as he sold their Redondo Beach home on the Strand. The nest egg funded Conner's downward spiral.

Conner first decided that he would find purpose in life through teaching high school. He found himself back in Chico, working towards a credential, but dropped out in the middle of his second semester. Conner's siblings and past friends continuously prodded him to seek counseling or support groups, to no avail.

Next, Conner flung himself into religion. A chance encounter at a fundraising event, for the Methodist Health Care Missions in Mexico, drew Conner into a twelve-month administrative volunteer assignment accompanied by a sizcable donation. He found no joy in his vocation and left without any fanfare at the end of his commitment. What Conner did find during his long empty nights shuttling between the Mexican towns in the Northern Sierra Madre, the Mission administrative office and the sponsoring Methodist congregations, was an affinity for Stolichnaya vodka.

Conner's remainder of the first decade of the millennium and beyond was a blur at best: apartments in various towns scattered throughout the west; assorted hospital consulting gigs, but mostly idle time, television, books and Stoli; no meaningful relationships; and various visits as a patient to emergency rooms of single story rural hospitals.

A DUI in Boise didn't break Conner out of his Stoli funk. Waking up in motel rooms with damp, urine-stained sheets didn't do it. Neither did totaling his aging Lexus RX 300 in an unreported single car accident outside of Spokane, or the nineteen stitches required after a bar fight in Coeur d'Alene. Instead, it was an unreliable old blue Dodge Dynasty sedan from the 1990's that set Conner on a new path.

Conner acquired the used Dynasty shortly after the Lexus fiasco. The vehicle possessed a variety of eccentricities. A gas gauge needle stuck near full until the car was close to running on fumes was one such quirk that endeared Conner to the old beast; until he ran out of gas, on an unpaved county road near Elko, Nevada.

Instead of calling AAA from his cell phone, Conner decided on a whim to jog, not walk, the seven miles to Elko to purchase and fill a gas can. Although he was exhausted and arranged a ride back to his vehicle, he had rediscovered his love for running. Stoli promptly exited his life, replaced by Nike running shoes.

Within months, Conner became active on Facebook at the urging of newfound running buddies, so they could connect to schedule group runs among other things. Leveraging a contact from prior freelance consulting gigs, Conner jumped back into the full-time professional world, landing a position as Director of Strategic Business Development for a health system in Reno.

Within twenty-four hours of updating his Facebook profile with a new picture and employment status, he received a request to friend his first crush back in Parker Creek. They had been inseparable from the start of their freshman year in high school until she moved with her family to Southern California, mid-sophomore year. Conner was devastated at that time, and didn't put forth much of an effort into finding a relationship until he met his wife-to-be.

Conner's reconnection with her eventually led him down Jungo Road to Sulphur, Nevada and the unnamed dirt road to Bruce Kepner's compound.

After the collapse of Joggen.com, Bruce quickly connected via the Internet with a persistent recruiter, who succeeded in convincing him to pack his bags and move to Mumbai, India. Bruce proceeded to spend years there instructing and supervising twentysomethings in html and related coding for TriDecaware, in Mumbai's Millennium Business Park.

Bruce was unattached when he became a dot com star, and enjoyed staying so while serial dating during his high-roller days. Out in Mumbai, he eventually became lonely and entered into a serious relationship with the daughter of a TriDecaware executive. The father, not wanting a foreigner in the family, transferred Bruce to TriDecaware's Chennai campus. After Bruce persisted with visits to Mumbai whenever off days permitted, the father arranged for Bruce's termination.

Bruce gave up, both on the relationship and on the high tech world. He responded to a flyer he received from a recruiter in Seoul, South Korea, who convinced him to locate there and teach English in an afternoon private school. Bruce fell in love with downtown Seoul; the clean and efficient subway system, Korean barbecue cut with scissors instead of knives; the courtesy and kindness afforded to Americans; and the ever-affordable soju that could leave a nasty hangover if you let it. About the only thing Bruce didn't fall in love with in Seoul was a woman. Perhaps it was the sting of his Mumbai affair, but the best he could do was return to serial dating.

Finally, the passage of time led to restlessness, then homesickness. Bruce couldn't put his finger on why he wanted to return to the states, but the thirst became unquenchable. Armed with a decent stash of savings he accrued while living frugally in Mumbai, Chennai and Seoul, he returned to San Francisco without a plan, other than his desire to live as "off the grid" as much as he could for a while. His guilt and embarrassment over losing his friends' and family's money when Joggen went south, drove this motivation.

Bruce's research into cheap, isolated real estate took him to a number of strange venues, but none quirkier than the old abandoned ranch outside Sulphur, Nevada. Bruce fondly remembered driving once with his father through the Black

Rock Desert as a child. The disfigured mountainside of the nearby Hycroft mine didn't discourage him from signing the papers to purchase the plot of land from a family trust.

Bruce drove down the dirt road to his new home to be, resolving he would somehow, little by little, engage in less risky business schemes, in order to pay back his long estranged family and friends, at least part of the money that evaporated with Joggen.com.

In the Beginning

In the beginning, there was Lake
Lahontan. The Black Rock playa
once carpeted its floor. The Great
Basin region, now encompassing

western Utah, most of Nevada, south central Oregon and far
northeastern California, back in the day sported two crown-
jewel lakes that could have competed with today's American
Great Lakes. Lake Bonneville occupied a good portion of the
eastern side of the Great Basin, while Lake Lahontan weighted
down the west end.

During the middle-to-late Pleistocene glacial period, both
were pluvial lakes, meaning their levels fluctuated dramatically
during the course of time due to climate change and
precipitation patterns. Another way of putting it is the lakes
were old souls that reincarnated repeatedly over the course of
many thousands and thousands of years.

Lake Lahontan, during the peak of its last incarnation,
around 12,700 years ago, possessed a surface area of 8,600
square miles, reaching a depth of 500 feet in the Black Rock
playa. (It reached 900 feet deep in what is now a surviving
remnant – Pyramid Lake.)

Climate change marked the end of the Pleistocene era —
first an extreme cold period known as the Younger Dryas,
followed by a warming and drying trend 11,500 years ago that
carried into the modern era. This change led to the gradual
decline of Lake Lahontan; by 9,000 years ago, it separated into
numerous small lakes and marshes, divided by changes in
elevation. Man first found his way into the Great Basin around
11,000 years ago, and the Northern Paiutes laid claim to the
area close to the time of Christ.

Today, situated in the high mountain desert Great Basin,
the Black Rock Desert covers about 1,000 square miles,
stretching from Gerlach to about 100 miles east. Elevations
run from about 3,500 feet at Gerlach, to 4,000 feet at the

north and eastern Playa boundaries. The desert is separated into two arms by the Black Rock mountain range, with peaks including Pahute Peak (Big Mountain), at 8,508 feet and King Lear Peak at 8,910 feet. The arms join at the playa.

The playa, in one word, is flat. A list of top five words for the playa might also include dry, wilderness, dusty and barren. Those unvegetated regions, often in the late spring through fall, bear miles of small polygon-shaped surfaces, as the clay sediment shrinks while it dries out. The elements convert a generous portion of the dried out mud into dust. This alkaline playa dust is pervasive, and after a heavy rainfall can create a formidable pasty mixture for anything that attempts to tread through it.

The areas with vegetation typically consist of saltbush and greasewood, sagebrush and noxious weeds such as Russian thistle (tumbleweeds). The Black Rock also contains many pockets of diversity – hot springs, marshes, the Quinn River, and countless odd formations dating back to prehistory.

So the ghost of Lake Lahontan remains to this day. The Black Rock Playa is a testament to its floor, concealing the deep-water silts and clays from the lake bed beneath its surface. The surrounding mountains bear witness to the carved coastlines, natural structures and caves of the Lahontan waters. Somewhere, prehistoric fossils from the once-teeming Lahontan-life lay patiently awaiting rediscovery.

Thursday Friday Saturday Sunday Monday Tuesday Wednesday

Fantasy Football

The Western Division of the Black Rock Fantasy Football league, by unanimous decree, determined the Eastern Division was not going to show. The draft would be held without them. The Eastern Division players would just be assigned by Commissioner Kepner. The landline was still down, so there was no way of knowing what had happened to Bruce's friends from the Winnemucca area.

This was the second year of the Black Rock league. Bruce organized the league with his drinking buddies who he connected with during his typical weekly runs to Reno on Sundays and Winnemucca on Thursdays. Being Bruce was loyal to one bar in each town, it didn't take him long to accumulate camaraderie with the recurring patrons in either location.

Bruce's motives seemed fairly apparent to the guys he guzzled beers with. He held a .400 or so batting average hooking up with the assorted females who haunted the establishments, ending the night at local hotels he was equally loyal to.

The previous year, Bruce convinced his two most erstwhile drinking companions in Reno—Dax and Jason—to form the league along with his four amigos from Winnemucca. Bruce technically stuck with his pledge to stay off the grid, Internet-wise, but in typical Bruce-style, he fudged his pledge by proxy. Dax registered everyone via espn.com, printed out the player rankings for draft day, entering the selections after the draft was held. The draft itself was conducted at Bruce's compound using the printouts. Each week, during the season, Bruce would check in with Dax during his Reno visit; Dax entering the online roster moves Bruce dictated after reviewing the sports pages. Bruce won the first annual championship pot of seven hundred dollars, determined by the head-to-head playoffs, after their regular season of head-to-head matchups.

With Bruce's recruitment of his high school friend Conner, the upcoming season allowed for an eight-team league, meaning no byes were required. From shortly after seven p.m., until the agreed-upon deadline of eight for the Eastern Division to show, Bruce, Dax and Jason attempted to educate Conner on the many intricacies of the espn.com league.

Conner learned there were sixteen NFL players drafted to each team, with nine starting each week, including a quarterback, two running backs, two wide receivers, another either running back or wide receiver, a tight end, a kicker and a team-defense/special-teams. You could release current players on your team, picking up unclaimed players throughout the season. Conner grasped that, but wasn't quite sure he got the scoring formulas for each position or what strategy made the most sense for drafting available players. Conner was sure of one thing – he wouldn't be seeing any return on his one hundred dollar entry fee.

Conner also learned the verses to "There ain't no hair on a billy goat's balls" as performed by Dax and Jason.

Conner sparingly sipped his one Miller 64 throughout discussion before the draft and during the draft itself. Being Bruce was assigning players to the Eastern Division teams, each round sailed along. The draft officially ended a few minutes after nine.

Dax and Jason resumed lobbying Conner to join in on the festivities. Conner had a difficult time remembering which one was Dax and which one was Jason. They had a similar look – thick, dark black hair with scruffy beards and moustaches, slight beer bellies, blue jeans, cowboy boots and black collared shirts with some product logo Conner hadn't quite deciphered. The goateed Bruce nearly always addressed them jointly – "DaxandJason," Bruce would call out to them.

There Ain't No Hair on a Billy Goat's Balls

There ain't no hair on a bil - ly goat's balls and

that's why they're so shi - ny but I know where there's

lots of hair on the girl I left be - hind me

"So, Conner, we know you must be watching your girlish figure," Dax started in. "You've kept yourself to sixty-four calories in two hours." Conner raised his empty Miller 64 proudly above his head in response.

Jason took another shot. "You know, you don't have to feel it's your personal responsibility to keep the alcohol level of people from Parker Creek down to manageable levels. What you don't know, is Kepner here has blown the level through the roof so many times in Reno, you'll never get the number lowered even a decimal point." Bruce raised his half-full Miller 64 proudly above his head in response.

"Come on, Conner, what do you say we play some flip-cup or at least some beer pong?" Dax prodded. Conner shot a glance at Bruce and just smiled, hoping Bruce would come to the rescue.

Conner didn't volunteer that he had given up alcohol, other than an occasional single beer. He didn't share that he had somehow survived and emerged from a lost decade. But Bruce, who Conner had confided in the past few weeks, felt it was sharing too much personal information, to tell DaxandJason to lighten up, because Conner had struggled tremendously with alcohol in the past. To Bruce, the fact that Conner had a beer each of the times they had gotten together also muddied the waters.

Still, Bruce felt obligated to say something, so he blamed Conner's newfound love. "DaxandJason, go easy on the Connerman, he's just hooked up with a long lost love and she doesn't want to be with someone who drinks. Give him credit for having a beer."

"Credit?" Dax hollered incredulously from the sofa. "Credit? Conner here doesn't get any stinkin' credit. He's got to grow some balls and have a real drink with the Western Division here."

"Yeah, Conner," Jason joined in. "Otherwise we're going to have to report this invisible lady friend of yours to the authorities, and you don't want to be responsible for her doing time."

DaxandJason paused, waiting for someone to ask a question. Conner obliged. "And do I want to know what she would be guilty of, gentleman?"

"Testicular manslaughter, Conner," Jason replied immediately, obviously having used the line before. "The prosecutor isn't going to reduce the charges based on our testimony." Jason arose from the reddish-orange sofa he and Dax had been encamped in for some time. "Tell you what. Let's just keep it simple for now. I have just the thing for the fellow members of the Western Division, which will help clear anyone's better half innocent of all charges." Jason walked over to unzip the backpack he had placed behind the sofa. He removed a half gallon green bottle of Jägermeister and a shot glass with an Oakland Raiders helmet. "This is what Doctor Jason has prescribed just for you, Conner."

Jason stepped over to Conner's recliner chair, filling the shot glass carefully, without spilling a drop. Conner didn't ponder about temptations, consequences or resolute convictions. On impulse, he grabbed the shot glass, swallowing its contents in an instantaneous gulp. Bruce's expression sank, while DaxandJason collectively shouted encouragement.

Conner grimaced at the cough-syrupy taste. He had been a Stoli man and wasn't familiar with Jager. As moments passed by, he discerned no ill-effects from the shot. So he had another. By the time the Western Division downed the bottle, the effects were apparent.

The alcohol certainly affected their reaction to the cattle stampede. The first ranch up Jackson Ranch Road near the Quinn River, at the base of the Black Rock Range across the playa, leased rights for a small herd of cattle to graze during the summer and fall through Bruce's surrounding property, and also paid a fee to the BLM for similar rights on public land in the foothills. The cattle were often the only spectators in

Bruce's occasional softball games with his Reno and Winnemucca friends.

The cattle noisily sprinted past the old ranch house, through the softball field, within a stone's throw of the two trailers. Bruce, Conner and DaxandJason exited to the back porch of Bruce's doublewide trailer upon hearing the commotion. They spectated in stupefied amazement, as the fast-moving parade of cattle whipped by them in the dark of night. The four men proceeded back inside as if such things routinely happen out in the Black Rock, while DaxandJason produced a second bottle of Jager from a backpack.

Sulphur

Visitors to Bruce's compound, a short distance from Sulphur, were consistently confused as they drew closer to his residence. Road maps  were the source of this state of perplexity. The official state map issued by the Nevada Department of Transportation correctly refers to the unmarked road between Winnemucca and Gerlach as an "other" (unpaved) road, and to Sulphur as a "site" and not a town. But most maps – including Google maps — list Jungo Road, the aforementioned unpaved road to Sulphur, as State Route 49 and give Sulphur the same distinction as any very small community. Bruce's visitors kept looking for where the state highway and the town of Sulphur had gone to. Both disappeared about the same time. The last residents of Sulphur vanished in the 1980's. Jungo Road lost its status as State Route 49 in 1976.

Jungo Road, for the most part, runs parallel to the Union Pacific railroad tracks. It was established by the Western Pacific Railroad in 1909, which led to the founding of Sulphur. Sulfur and other mining operations flourished in the area for decades, and ranching activities had matured as well, generating the demand for the railroad. The town of Sulphur grew out of the resulting railroad station.

Shortly afterwards, Sulphur swelled to eighty-plus residents, but slowly declined in the ensuing decades. The lack of adequate potable water and the harsh winter cold spells did little to aid in development of the community. In its heyday, in addition to mining and railroad employment, the town boasted a hotel, school, post office, saloon, general store, boarding house, telegraph and then telephone service, constable and justice of the peace.

The gradual decline hastened in the 1950's with the closure of the railroad and the sulfur mines. Eventually a graveyard of abandoned old automobiles remained as the largest testament to the once town of Sulphur.

The mines that predate the town of Sulphur boast perhaps the most interesting local history and folklore. Mining initiated in the area in 1875. The first significant sulfur mining operation involved a claim by F. J. McWorthy and J. W. Rover. After several years, Rover was accused of murdering an employee. He was eventually found guilty after several retrials, and was hanged. Legend has it that McWorthy, who was the main witness at Rover's trial, was the actual murderer, but ended up assuming sole possession of the claim. Legend also has it that the mine became haunted by Rover and the slain employee.

After the series of companies operating the nearby sulfur mining and refinery ceased operations, open pit gold and silver mining initiated at the site. This too ceased in 1998, due to a fall in gold prices. Today, the mine is owned by the Allied Nevada Gold Corporation under the name of Hycroft, with operations resuming in 2008. The Hycroft open pit gold site, with its recent expansion, increased in size from 2,172 acres of surface disturbance to an approved total of 5,895 acres, and a total project boundary of 14,753 acres. Employment is expected to increase from around 200 to a projected staff exceeding 530, after the expansion completes full implementation.

Even at the 200 staffing level, Hycroft commissioned four buses daily to and from Winnemucca to transport workers, and the once primitive Jungo Road was bladed and smoothed significantly from Winnemucca to Sulphur to accommodate the bus traffic.

Bruce Kepner became aware of Allied Nevada's pending expansion, which influenced the purchase of his nearby property, in the hopes that significant mining development would spur related support opportunities that he might capitalize on. Recently, Bruce held two tracks of discussion with Hycroft management: one with human resources regarding contracting to provide a food truck concession in the project parking lot; and one with the CEO office regarding leasing Bruce's water rights to Hycroft.

Allied Nevada's CEO was quoted as saying, "Hycroft has the potential to be among the largest gold mining operations in the world." Bruce waited on these words hopefully. During Bruce's years in India, he witnessed first-hand, society's insatiable demand for Au, the seventy-ninth element in the periodic table, driven by culture, religion, emotion and greed. Bruce knew well how the emerging Indian middle class was driving this demand, how predatory gold loans were giving access to even the Indian poor. While the American and European markets on the their own would have long ago popped the gold bubble, the emerging Indian economy, as well as China and a number of other Asian markets, were helping to shield the gold bubble for a significant extension of time.

Bruce knew eventually the gold bubble would burst — India or no India. But he was counting on his friends in the East to prop up the prices long enough to keep the Hycroft mine rolling full steam. Bruce's dream of paying back his one-time dot com investors depended on it.

Thursday Friday Saturday Sunday Monday Tuesday Wednesday

Z Hangover

Conner woke possessing a throbbing headache. He lay in bed on his side, eyes shut, feeling the rhythm of his pulse twitching his left ear on the pillow. Beyond his bedroom, he could hear the television blaring away. Conner became aware of his cotton-mouth; he tried to salivate to bring respite to the parched desert surrounding his teeth. He then realized how badly he needed to pee. Still, he lay motionless in Bruce's guest bedroom.

Conner's thoughts rewound to the previous evening, allowing another wave of guilt to wash over him. He had, on his own, emerged from a ten-year-drunken-funk, only to piss it all away in a few short hours. He now remembered waking momentarily sometime in the night to throw up in the toilet. He had just reconnected with his soul mate, confessing to her his past losing battle with vodka. What would she think of him now, taking a tumble right back to square one? His head pounded even more painfully, as he considered how another downward slide with the bottle could cost him his new love, his rejuvenated career and his new sense of purpose in life.

Conner mused that a long, cleansing run might strip away his sins. After all, it was such a run that set him on a sober path when his faithful Dodge Dynasty died outside Elko. He tried mightily to will himself out of bed, to gather up his running clothes but could not make it happen. Conner attempted to guess what time it was. The sun was already beating through the window and must be fairly high in the sky. He recalled they had gone to bed late — very late.

Conner heard footsteps in the hall; the bathroom door shut. Bruce must be up, or perhaps Jason or Dax had come over from the other trailer. The television volume was relentless. Conner tried to make out what was being said or shouted.

After thirty seconds or so of listening, he was fairly certain it was an infomercial for some type of weight loss smoothie. This caused Conner to return his attention to his cotton-ball mouth. He groaned, pushed himself up from his pillows, emerging from bed in search of a glass of water.

Conner wandered out of the bedroom in his Oakland Raider boxer shorts, squinting from the assault of sunlight invading the trailer. The bathroom was still occupied, so he headed to the kitchen. Conner stopped in his tracks, doing a double-take as he passed the living room.

Sitting on Bruce's reddish-orange sofa were three men he had never seen before. One, a stocky man in his thirties with unkempt brown hair and a slight beard, wore a ripped dark blue sweatshirt with "Lowry High School Buckaroos" emblazoned in yellow lettering, along with a logo of the aforementioned buckaroo. Another man was small, thin, mostly bald, and wearing no clothes. The third, a redheaded young man in his early twenties, seemed to be covered in bite marks, tattoos and hickies, wearing only a pair of brown shorts and sandals. All three were transfixed in front of the television, staring obediently at the buxom blonde woman in teal spandex leotards, extolling the many virtues of Vitagizer Smoothies.

Conner then noticed the stench. The odor surrounding them evoked the aroma of an overused porta-potty. There was enough sunlight in the room where Conner's attention was next drawn to the color of their skin. All three were pale – very pale – but somehow, their tone was almost light gray. They all had various visible sores. Conner continued standing silently to their side, watching them watch TV.

The front door was not shut. The screen door was propped open, evidently having been so since DaxandJason exited in the wee hours to pass out in the office trailer. Now Dax burst in excitedly, exclaiming to Conner, "There's some people wandering through Bruce's compound. I didn't really get a good look at them. They seemed—" Dax stopped mid-sentence, noticing Bruce's three new houseguests. He glanced at the still silent Conner and back at the Buckaroo alumni from Lowry High School.

"Well, I'll be. Our eastern division finally shows up, a day late and a dollar-fifty short. But where's your car, man? And are those people out there with you?" Dax directed his question loudly at the Buckaroo from Lowry. The three sofa mates continued staring at the television, oblivious to Dax or Conner. Dax finally noticed that one of the Buckaroo's couch-mates was buck naked. "What the f---?" Dax yelled, turning back to Conner, seeking an explanation. Dax wrinkled his nose. "And what the f--- is that smell?"

Conner retreated several steps away from the sofa and towards the kitchen. Something was obviously not right. He motioned with his head for Dax to follow him, almost tip-toeing as he headed there. The three men on the sofa continued to be enraptured by Vitagizer Smoothies.

Conner waited until Dax reached him at the kitchen counter. They both leaned against it. Conner whispered to him. "You know these guys?"

Conner had forgotten from the night before, how rapidly Dax's attention span could shift. Dax grinned, ignoring Conner's question. He lightly punched Conner on the shoulder, responding loudly, "You da man, Conner! You were an animal. Who knew what really lurked inside the Connerman until a little Jager let him out to play." Dax laughed, shaking his head. Dax glanced down at Conner's Oakland Raider boxer shorts. "And a Raider fan at that. Who knew?"

Conner shushed him, quietly repeating his question. "Dax, *who* are these guys?"

Dax paused, lowering his voice to just above a whisper as well. "Well, the one guy is Bill, from Winnemucca. Or Brad or Ben. Bob maybe? Actually, I'm not sure. It has been awhile. And I don't have a clue who the redhead or the old nude dude are."

Conner rubbed his forehead. He didn't feel well at all. "Dax, something is really wrong with them. I mean, *really* wrong."

Dax grinned again. "I'm guessing they did some mushrooms. Bruce's friends there smoke the ganja. We had quite a time with them last year playing softball out in Bruce's field and doing the ganja. That was the last time I smoked some pot. But this has to be shrooms."

Conner frowned and leaned forward. "Dax, you said there are other people outside?"

Dax's face finally returned the worried expression he wore when he entered the trailer. "Yeah," he paused, glancing out the kitchen window, seeing no one, "that is a bit odd. I saw, I don't know, six or seven at least, from a distance, wandering way out back. "

Conner rubbed his forehead again. He stepped back towards the sink, no longer able to put off his need to get some water into his mouth. He took a big slurp directly from the faucet, without benefit of a glass. On impulse, Conner lifted the wall phone to the right of the sink, placing the receiver to his ear. There was still no dial tone for Bruce's land line. "Dax, even if all four Winnemucca guys are here, then who are the others? And there's no car out there? And Dax, they don't look right. Did you look closely? Something is really wrong with them."

Dax relaxed a little. "Aahh, think about it. The most I've ever done is pot. But I've heard if you take some shrooms, or something else pretty nasty, you can go whack out of your mind, or look gorked and comatose like those three in there. And maybe you lose control over your body functions, cuz I think one of them shit their pants and I sure hope it wasn't the nude dude. So I'm guessing our friends ran into these other fellas somewhere, drove out this way with them last night, pulled over nearby to do the shrooms, got stoned out of their mind and eventually wandered over here by foot."

Conner shook his head, which felt like a brick was shifting around with each motion. "Dax, I don't think that's all it is. I say we need to get Bruce out of the bathroom and see what he thinks."

Dax grinned one more time. "Oh, let me look at 'em. I guess we better make sure they're not actually comatose or dead even." Before Conner could caution Dax that he didn't think that was such a good idea, Dax had already bounded back to the living room sofa.

Conner followed Dax into the living room, but continued on until he reached the entrance to the hallway. Dax stood in front of the television left running from the night before, still beaming Vitagizer Smoothies through the forty-two inch LCD flat screen mounted on the wall. Dax smiled, bellowing to his audience less than five feet in front of him, "Hey gentleman, what's happening?"

No response. The three men sat, eyes wide open, mouths partially open, transfixed on the Vitagizer Smoothies appearing on the screen. Belly fat would start falling off within the first seven days of Vitagizer, they were told.

Dax leaned forward, placing his hands on his knees to get eye level with them. "Guys! Talk to me here. Are you okay? Are you hearing me?" Again, no response.

Conner wondered why Dax couldn't see this was a problem better dealt with at a further distance than Dax's current five feet. The thought that the three men had some kind of disease came to mind, as Conner studied their odd skin color, running sores, and took in their odor even from where he stood.

Dax stepped forward, plopping himself in between Lowry High and the nude dude on the sofa, seemingly putting on a show for Conner, his audience. Conner drew in a gasp. "Dax, give them some room. Get off of there," he warned loudly, with a hint of pleading.

Dax ignored him, seeming indifferent to any peril his new couch mates posed. Instead, Dax smiled at Conner, providing commentary. "Well, they are breathing. And their eyes are blinking. But they are not noticing me here. Watch this," Dax taunted, snapping his fingers first in Lowry High's ears, and then the nude dude's. Still no response.

"Dax, I'm going to tell Bruce what's going on. Why don't you go see if you can find where those people are outside?" Conner suggested, feeling a wave of nausea coming on. As Conner started to step backwards down the hallway towards the bathroom, Dax felt the need to keep his audience engaged a little longer.

"Wait, Conner. Watch this!" Dax exclaimed, obviously pleased with himself for some reason. Dax started poking Lowry High in the ribs, and then nude dude, in repeated fashion. "Wake up here, party boys. It's time to come back to earth."

"Don't do that," Conner barked at Dax. Dax laughed defiantly at Conner, poking Lowry High even harder. Then he poked nude dude and Lowry High a couple times more while making what he perceived to be kung fu movie sound effects.

Lowry High turned his head toward Dax, emitting a groan. Dax pumped his fist in the air. "He speaks! He has returned!" Lowry High groaned again, now gazing at Dax, just as transfixed as he was moments ago with Vitagizer Smoothies. Nude dude's spell with the television broke as well. He too groaned, fixing his attention on Dax. The redhead joined in, slowly rising from the sofa.

Dax laughed nervously as his couch buddies continued groaning. Then, a look of panic struck Dax's face. "Conner," he yelled, attempting to flee the sofa. Lowry High and nude dude both latched onto him, pulling him back onto the couch. Lowry High grabbed at his face; nude dude yanked at a flabby section of Dax's stomach as if both were trying to rip the flesh right off of him. The redhead piled on with his head lowered, proceeding to bite hard into Dax's right calf.

"Dax," Conner screamed, his eyes darting around the room searching for anything that might possibly be used as a weapon to subdue the three men.

"What the hell!" Bruce shouted, bolting out of the bathroom wearing nothing but boxer shorts covered with red hearts.

Trying to rip open a human without any sort of knife or tool is difficult to do. That is, until an opening is made — kind of like trying to get through a thick-skinned orange until the first piece of rind is penetrated. Dax was underneath the three of them, desperately trying to break free, screaming his head off, hoping not to become that orange.

Conner settled on the thirty-inch metal candlestick situated on the narrow display table next to the wall. He grabbed it, bolting toward to the sofa. Conner noticed Bruce right behind him. He hesitated, turning to Bruce. "Do you have a gun?"

Bruce shook his head; they both charged ahead.

The sofa men found their openings into Dax. Lowry High inserted his fingers into Dax's mouth, yanking hard on the right side, which was starting to tear. Dax screamed in agony while he kicked in every direction. The nude dude found his way underneath Dax's blue jeans, tugging on Dax's genitals which caused Dax's scream to shift into a guttural wail. The redhead continued to sink his teeth into adjacent portions of Dax's right calf.

Conner clocked Lowry High across the head with the candlestick. Conner expected the force of the impact to level the man. Lowry's head tilted, displaying a nasty wide-open gash across the right side of his face and back side of his head, with grayish-thick-oily looking fluid oozing out where red, runny blood should have been expected. But Lowry High continued undaunted. Conner clubbed the redhead in the back of head, prying him loose from Dax's calf and onto the floor. The redhead slowly rose to his knees.

Bruce pulled at the nude dude with all his might. The nude, older man lost his grip on Dax's crotch, but compensated by grabbing onto Dax's left leg. The nude dude pressed his face into Dax's rib cage, proceeding to bite fiercely, while Bruce continued attempting to separate them.

Conner took a step back for leverage, then swung away cleanly at Lowry High's forehead, scoring a direct hit. The force of the impact knocked Lowry loose of Dax, onto the small glass coffee table, smashing it into pieces, and collapsing the table legs. A curved gash, like a crescent moon, appeared on Lowry High's forehead, down across his nose and right face, again leaking the gray fluid. Other than that, Lowry High was unfazed, leaping right back onto Dax, proceeding to sink his teeth into Dax's nose. The redhead returned to Dax's right calf. All three were grunting wildly, sounding like agitated pigs at the county fair.

But by shifting their positions to bite into Dax, Dax was able to regain some leverage. Aided by Conner and Bruce pulling on the sofa men, Dax kicked himself free. Terrified, he bolted for the screen door, followed by Conner and Bruce. Bruce slammed the front door as he exited, and then shut the screen door. Lowry High, the redhead and nude dude remained inside, groaning and pushing on the front door, apparently unaware of how a doorknob functioned.

Thursday Friday Saturday Sunday Monday Tuesday Wednesday

Up on a Rooftop

Dust covered everything outside, remnants of Sunday afternoon's dust storm. Bruce and Conner steadied Dax, while they all raced to the office trailer. When they reached the steps, Jason bounded out, wearing blue jeans, tennis shoes and no shirt. "What the—" Jason started to say.

"Where are your car keys?" Bruce demanded of Jason. Seeing that Conner was in boxer shorts like himself, Bruce realized both their keys were inside the main trailer with the three crazy men.

Jason searched his pockets. "I don't have them," he said apologetically.

Bruce turned to Dax, who was gasping for air and not processing what was going on very well. Bruce raised his voice, as if Dax was deaf. "Do you have you guys' car keys, Dax?"

Dax just looked at him, perplexed. Bruce reached over and felt Dax's pockets. "He doesn't have them," Bruce concluded out loud in a frustrated tone.

"I can search this trailer, guys, but I'm pretty sure they are back on your kitchen counter," Jason offered hurriedly, staring at Dax's wounds. "What the hell is going on?"

Conner responded. "Your Winnemucca friend and two other guys, one of them buck naked, went nuts. They were just sitting on the sofa, and bam, they attacked Dax. There is something seriously wrong with them. We need to get moving."

"We gotta get in the car and go," Bruce agreed. "But we're going to have to get back in that trailer to get someone's keys." Bruce paused, seeing if anyone disagreed. Bruce turned and looked back at the trailer. "And those guys still haven't come outside. This is surreal."

"Where do you keep your guns?" Jason asked.

Bruce shook his head. "Don't have 'em." He kept his eye on the main trailer. "I don't have any guns."

"What?" Jason exclaimed incredulously. "You live out here in the middle of nowhere and don't own a gun? What's the point of living in Nevada in the desert all by yourself, if you're not even going to own a gun, man? Me, I would have a freaking arsenal."

"He says he doesn't have a gun, and let's not get off track." Conner shot back as he held on to Dax, who seemed to be getting woozy. "We need to get some kind of weapons. What do you have outside that we can use, Bruce?"

Bruce didn't hesitate. "The shed out by the ranch house. It's full of crap we can use. Nice, pointy bladed medieval stuff we can take the trailer back with." Bruce started running toward the modular shed. Everyone followed, Conner helping Dax stumble along.

Conner called out to Bruce. "Dax said he saw a bunch of people wandering out back. We better watch out for them. They might be like the guys inside."

"What did they do to Dax?" Jason yelled back to Conner, who was bringing up the rear with Dax as they ran.

"They were sitting there like they were stoned, and then they went nuts and bit him...tried to rip him apart. And I think they look diseased," Conner responded in between breaths as they ran barefoot through the dust and sagebrush.

They reached the shed. Bruce stopped and stared at the door. "Crap," he screamed. "I must have locked it. I never lock it. Damn it, the shed key is on the ring with my car keys." Bruce picked up a rock and threw it at the white, modular metal shed.

Conner and Dax caught up to them. Conner asked, "Any way to break into it, or do you have anything else we can use somewhere?"

"Aaaugh" Dax moaned loudly, raising his right arm and pointing behind Bruce and Jason. They turned to see seven people scattered in Bruce's field of dreams, one near the raised pitcher's mound, the others distributed throughout the outfield. The entire group started walking briskly toward Bruce and his friends, in almost a drunken-like manner. One was naked, just like the man on the sofa, a couple were dressed in some sort of work uniforms, a lady was wearing some type of clothing ripped into tatters, and their other three Winnemucca friends rounded out the group. None were talking, but grunting could be detected, even from a distance.

"Damn, they look just like those basket-cases in the trailer," Bruce exclaimed. "Come on," he commanded, taking off toward the old ranch house. Everyone followed, Conner helping Dax along.

Bruce stopped at the paint-stained ladder they had climbed earlier in the week. It led to the roof of the single story addition of the ranch house. From there, the roof ascended to the two-story remainder of the structure. Conner gasped. "Bruce, no! This is a bad idea. You can't be serious."

Bruce started up the ladder. "We have no choice, come on, get Dax up and I'll help him from the roof."

"But we could outrun these people easy." Jason argued.

Bruce hollered back, already at the top, "Not with Dax like this, we can't. Now help him up, quick!"

Conner turned back to see the group closing in on them. He knew they were painted into a corner, with no choice but to climb the ladder and hope this crowd was as inept with ladders as the three men in the trailer must be with doorknobs. Dax mounted the ladder, with Conner right behind him. Conner could see Dax's smears of blood mixed with dust on every rung as they rose. Jason screamed at the two of them to hurry up, because the grunting people were almost upon them.

Bruce reached his hands over the roofline, helping to hoist Dax, while Conner pushed Dax's butt and thighs upwards. After that, Conner and Jason joined them on the roof rather quickly. The surprise was that one of their pursuers was right on their heels coming up the ladder. Somehow, Bruce had just assumed this group was somehow incapacitated enough to be incapable of doing so. His initial thoughts, when leading his friends up this path, were that if these weirdoes did start up the ladder, Bruce and company would have the high ground and could just knock them back to the ground.

But that didn't happen. Bruce, Conner, and Jason all lightly stepped across the small single story portion of the roof to get to higher ground, pulling Dax along with them as they progressed. They gingerly scaled the short second story peak, next sliding along the crest of the dust-covered roof, taking care as they scooted along, given its aged and decrepit state. They were too far along and out of position to offer any resistance when the grunting, gray-skinned man pulled himself onto the roof. He wore a tattered, striped uniformed shirt with some name embroidered in a circle on the left side of his chest.

Unlike Bruce and company, the man took no care where he put his weight as he boldly bounded forward on the roof. He followed them up the second story ascent, slid a couple of steps, and in correcting his footing, he crashed through the shingles, east of the crest. He came to a stop several feet down, as he struck the second story ceiling, his head and shoulders still visible above the roof, his arms and legs below. He grunted loudly and rapidly, his grimy, unkempt black hair blanketed with dust.

Bruce crawled forward a little to check things out, sensing the man wasn't able to advance any further. Bruce observed the man was not only stuck, but had a broken support beam lodged into the back right side of his torso, protruding partially out the front. Thick, grayish-oily fluid slowly oozed outwards from the areas of impact.

Bruce, feeling he was safe at this point from the Man-In-The-Roof, scooted forward to gain a vantage point of the ladder below. A number of the others were in various states of either attempting to climb up the ladder or tugging and pulling at it. The ladder came crashing down to the ground on top of them.

Bruce pushed himself backwards, relaying this news to his friends. Now, their immediate concern was what to do with the Man-In-The-Roof, who continued to grunt fiercely. Bruce, Conner and Jason's eyes were all fixated on the support beam ripped through the man's chest, seemingly causing the man no additional discomfort. He appeared only agitated, not in pain; frustrated that he was unable to pull Bruce and company within his grasp for a quick bite.

Bruce, Conner and Jason each sat straddling the crest of the roof, arguing over what course of action to take next. Dax, perched between Jason and Conner, remained in a daze, occasionally chiming in with an affirmative audible moan when Jason would make a point. The Man-In-The-Roof continued to snarl, toss and turn, unable to dislodge himself from his predicament.

A consensus was finally reached that they should try, at least for several hours, to wait out the small mob. Perhaps the group below would eventually come down from whatever high they were on or settle into a more docile and almost catatonic-like state with time, just as the three inside Bruce's trailer were, when first discovered.

No sooner had the agreement been reached, than Dax moaned, leaned left, and began vomiting small quantities at a time. The others turned the other way, trying not to listen to the repulsive sounds. After just more than a minute, Dax ceased. Jason looked him over. He decreed that maybe Dax might feel better now that he puked.

As Jason gazed at the trail of vomit down the eastern slope of the roof, he noticed what appeared to be a large, dust-covered bag several feet north of the vomit. Jason squinted, and made out the familiar coloring of an unopened Cheetos bag, under the thin layer of dust. "Hey, breakfast!" he announced. The bag appeared to be just out of reach, but

Jason was undeterred. At first, Bruce admonished Jason to disregard the Crunchy Cheetos that Bruce and Conner had forgotten on the roof several nights earlier. Bruce soon relented, deciding a distraction might be a good thing for the moment. Soon Conner was hanging on to Jason's ankles and shoes, while Jason inched forward through the dust covered shingles on his stomach toward the orange twenty-ounce bag with the yellow Cheetos logo.

Eventually, the Cheetos were snagged, opened and handed out a few at a time. Dax put one in his mouth, but then spit it out. Jason continued consuming the Cheetos at a four-to-one ratio compared to his roof mates. Halfway through the bag, Jason stopped, examining his now bright orange hands, but not able to see his now-orange mustache. Unaware of his own orange facial hair, he laughed upon seeing the ring of orange residue around Bruce's goatee. Jason glanced at the Man-In-The-Roof. He scooted a few feet to the right of the crest. Jason, with the bag of Cheetos gripped in his teeth, worked his way beyond Dax, past Conner in his dust-covered boxers, and finally, to the other side of the also boxer-clad Bruce.

"What are you doing?" Bruce asked, a little incredulous, as he watched Jason scoot by.

Jason didn't answer, continuing forward until he was just six feet in front of the Man-In-The-Roof, who was aroused into a frenzied state, as Jason tantalizingly approached close to his reach. The man's head lunged forward, then side to side as he tried to free himself, unsuccessfully, from his dilemma. His groans grew loader and more shrill.

Jason opened his mouth, dropping the bag of Cheetos into his lap. He reached in, grabbing a single, long Cheeto, dangling it back and forth, while staring the Man-In-The-Roof in the eye. Jason used a voice one might use when talking to a dog in front of your friends. "Want a Cheeto? Want this Cheeto? Do you want the nice crunchy Cheeto?" The Man-In-The-Roof stopped grunting for a moment, seemingly staring back at Jason. Jason opened his own mouth wide, held the Cheeto up high, dropped it, and caught it with his mouth. "My Cheeto," Jason yelled triumphantly back at the Man-In-The-Roof. The man resumed grunting wildly.

"Jason!" Bruce hollered in a scolding tone at his friend. "Stop that. What if you get him so worked up, he breaks free?"

Jason ignored Bruce, pulling out another Cheeto and repeating the ritual several times. The Man-In-The-Roof quieted momentarily each time the Cheeto was dangled almost within his reach.

Conner grew a bit curious with the proceedings. "Hey Jason," he called out from behind Bruce. "See if he'll actually eat one. Toss him a couple and see what he does."

Jason was only too happy to oblige. He resumed his doggy voice, asking the man if he liked Cheetos. Jason tossed the fried orange objects one at a time at the man's mouth, missing but getting closer each time. The Man-In-The-Roof began snarling at a Cheeto that bounced off his nose and landed on the plank of wood protruding from his chest. While the man groaned, Jason scored, landing a smaller Cheeto in the man's open mouth. Jason, Conner and even Bruce, all emitted triumphant yells. The man stopped groaning or gyrating momentarily. It appeared he had swallowed the orange snack.

This only encouraged Jason to try more. Cheeto by Cheeto, the bag began to dwindle, landing all around the Man-In-The-Roof after bouncing off his face and arms. Finally Jason scored again, Conner and Bruce celebrating briefly one more time. This time, after a second or two of the man silently staring back at them, he spit the Cheeto out, resuming his grunting in a lower, more menacing tone that sent a shiver up the spines of Bruce, Conner and even Jason. Jason, without saying anything more, packed up his remaining Cheetos and slowly scooted back across the crest of roof, until he resumed his previous spot behind Dax, who did not look well. The group fell into silence. Considerable time passed.

Jason finally broke the quiet, offering speculation as to what on earth was wrong with Bruce's Winnemucca friends and the others with them. "Look," Jason opened the debate, drawing circles with his index finger in the layer of dust in front of him, "I'll just say what you all must be thinking. These guys are zombies." Jason paused to measure everyone's reaction. Bruce and Conner both lowered their brows skeptically, Dax seemed a bit glassy eyed, and the Man-In-The-Roof seemed indifferent to the z-word.

"Jason," Bruce started to rebut in a condescending tone, but Jason interrupted.

"No, Bruce, I'm serious. If it looks like a duck, smells like a duck and quacks like a duck, then by god, it's a freaking duck. A zombie duck. And no offense, Bruce, but your fantasy football friends from Winnemucca and the crowd they brought with them, they look, smell and quack like freaking zombies. I don't care how stupid that sounds, that's what they seem to be to me."

"There's no such thing a zombies, Jason, and you know it," Bruce shot back. "Let's get serious and try to figure out what's really wrong with them."

"No such thing?" Jason raised his voice, irritated. "You look over at the Man-In-The-Roof over there, with that piece of wood sticking through his chest like it's no big deal, just a splinter or something, and gray ooze coming out instead of regular blood? And Dax here gets bit and attacked by them and now he's looking sicker than a dog? And all of them are just grunting and growling and aren't smart enough to get out of your trailer or put the ladder back up to get us? What does that sound like to you, Bruce? Jehovah's Witnesses here to sell *WatchTower* magazines?"

"Jason, let's get off the zombie talk," Bruce countered. "I'm sure you've heard of accounts of people on PCP or meth where they seemed to have super-human strength, getting shot by police and still coming at them and seeming to be out of their freaking gourd? Wasn't that what I heard Dax saying, before he got attacked? That they must be on drugs?"

Jason and Conner look at each other, without responding. Bruce turned to Dax, hoping for some agreement, but Dax seemed not to be listening. Bruce then pleaded with Conner. "Conner, help me out here. You were right there with those guys on the sofa. You had to see they were high on something."

Conner shook his head. "I don't know about zombies, but I do know this is something way more than drugs, Bruce. I looked at those guys on the sofa up close, and I'm looking at the Man-In-The-Roof here, and they are seriously diseased or something. I'm worried about Dax, because they bit him; bit him badly, and Dax doesn't seem to be doing so well."

Bruce and Jason fell silent. Dax cleared his throat, before speaking softly. "I'll be okay. But I feel lousy. Maybe we should go to a doctor." Bruce, Conner and Jason looked at each other uneasily. The Man-In-The-Roof even stopped grunting. Quiet fell over the rooftop.

The pause allowed Conner's thoughts to drift back to his prior predicaments. It dawned on Conner he was going to miss his scheduled Monday afternoon business meeting at the hospital in Winnemucca. His guilt from drinking, plus anxiety over what that meant for his new relationship, weighed into his thoughts. He realized his head no longer ached. The rush of adrenaline must have caused his hangover to subside. His attention turned to the fact he still hadn't peed since he rose out of bed. Now that the need to pee entered his stream of consciousness, every other thought was quickly drowned out.

Conner tightened his muscles, crossing his legs closer together. The fact they intended to wait things out, possibly several more hours, was entered into the record of his internal argument with his bladder. Conner scanned his silent friends. He tried to think of other things. He again considered his failure with drinking, of possibly losing the love he had just re-found, and decided thinking of pissing all over the place was better than thinking of that. Conner sat fully upright. He began scooting from the crest of the roof down to the roofline.

"Conner," Bruce called out anxiously, "what are you doing, man?"

Conner replied matter-of-factly as he carefully scooted down the roof, "I am going to take a leak. I'm sorry, but I cannot hold it any longer. Not a moment longer."

"Conner!" Bruce pleaded, but didn't continue, as Conner had already reached the roofline, rose to his knees and pulled down his Oakland Raider boxer shorts.

Conner looked below. The group on the ground must have heard or seen him progressing to that point, because they were all gathering directly below. Conner hesitated a moment, seeing them all glaring up at him open-mouthed. Conner sighed. "Fine," he called out, exasperated, to the group below, "have it your way." Conner felt an instant sense of relief as the yellow urine streamed to the ground.

Conner's jaw dropped in amazement, as the group all raised their arms, seemingly in joyous rapture, moaning in a higher pitch instead of grunting or growling, looking up directly into the yellow spray misting them all. The naked man, sporting a tattoo of a large oak tree on his back, seemed especially appreciative of Conner's precipitation. The man opened his mouth wide, catching the spray as best he could.

There are times, when after awaking from a night of drinking, that a man can urinate for seemingly an eternity. This was such a time for Conner, and he shook his head both at the apparently endless supply of urine he now possessed, and at the one pleasure in life it seemed to bring the strange beings below. Even the Man-In-The-Roof wanted in on the act. He began groaning loader and more animated than ever.

Finally the golden shower concluded. The group below seemed quite agitated that it ceased. Conner proceeded to scoot back up the roof, wanting to get out of their line of sight. Jason laughed loudly. Bruce shook his head at the sight of his friend making his way back up to them in dust-covered boxer shorts, until he remembered he was similarly attired. Bruce's eyes darted down to his own boxers, the red hearts now obscured by smudges of dust throughout.

Conner reached the top, drew in his breath, and sighed. "This day is just too weird for words," he commented, staring at the black-haired, uniformed Man-In-The-Roof, who was snarling at no one in particular.

"Amen to that," Bruce responded, brushing off his boxer shorts.

Conner studied the roof-man: his gray-tinted skin, his strange, raised facial wound, his impaled torso that seemed to bleed sludge. More than that, Conner was taken with his eyes. Even from a distance, Conner sensed the man's eyes seemed strangely disconnected from rational thought. Conner mused that if eyes were a window to the soul, this man's panes were so soiled and streaked that sunlight couldn't penetrate them.

"We have to make a different plan — and no more joking around – this could be life and death serious," Conner announced to his roof mates. "Like Dax said, he needs to get to a doctor. We need to figure out how and do it now." Conner, Jason and Bruce all turned to observe Dax, who didn't respond. He was slumped forward slightly, once again seeming not fully there.

The Man-In-The-Roof transformed the tone of his snarl to an even deeper growl. Jason turned his attention to the man, or least what he could see of him – a head, neck, and one shoulder. "What are we gonna do about this dude?" Jason asked Bruce.

Bruce rubbed his forehead, studying roof-man as well. Bruce hadn't noticed the persistent presence of the mid-day sun beating down on them, while his thoughts had been preoccupied. He wiped more sweat off his brow, before replying to Jason. "I guess we just leave him be, until we get everything else settled, seeing he doesn't seem to be going anywhere."

Jason poked at Dax next to him. "Hey, hang with us, buddy. We're gonna figure something out and get you out of here." Dax just shrugged a little, so Jason poked at him again.

Suddenly, Bruce rose to his knees. "Alright, I suppose the thing to do is get over to the Hycroft mine. They are just a few miles away, and they have Internet and satellite phones. I know they shut down this week, that's been the big talk, but they're supposed to keep a few security staff round the clock, I'm sure. Conner and I are runners. Jason, you stay here with Dax, and we'll sneak off the single story roof when these guys below are wandering around elsewhere. It looks pretty plain to me that we can outrun them easily enough. We can get to the mine, get some help, and come back for you."

Jason shook his head. "You're going to outrun them in your bare feet? I don't know if you checked, but you and Conner are dressed in just your boxer shorts and nothing else. I don't know that you're gonna pull that off barefoot. I think I need to do it. I'm the one wearing tennis shoes."

"Hey," Conner called out. "Look at that! Look way out down Jungo Road. Coming around the bend by the mine." Conner pointed toward the main road, miles before the turnoff to Bruce's compound. In the distance a moving trail of dust meant a vehicle was coming their way.

Conner, Bruce and Jason all stood and started pointlessly hollering at the distant vehicle. The excitement seemed to stir even Dax. Dax started to stand, waving his arms. He then grew dizzy and blacked out. Dax fell over, sliding rapidly down the west side of the roof. Jason, Bruce and Conner watched helplessly as he plunged over the roofline, landing suddenly into a three-foot-high rod of rebar anchored in a crumbling patch of cement, all that remained of a once-cement shade wall on the west side of the old, abandoned ranch house.

From above, the three men could see the rebar exiting below Dax's left shoulder blade. Dax twitched momentarily, before going limp.

Alan Gorman

Alan Gorman, as a young boy, dreamed of someday becoming an astronaut. His safety plan was to become a doctor or perhaps both.

Alan grew up one of three sons of high school teachers in Atwater, California, his father a Marine veteran of the Korean War.

After high school, Alan attended Fresno State, taking a pre-med track, receiving an undergraduate degree, Summa Cum Laude, in biology. His junior year at Fresno, Alan came to the realization neither he nor his parents had the means to enroll him in medical school, even with student loans. Between his upbringing near Castle Air Force Base and his father's core belief that military service was a point of pride and honor, Alan didn't flinch at pursuing the military as his means to a medical degree. The branch of service to pursue was obvious to Alan, given his boyhood dreams.

While Alan was an upperclassman at Fresno, Alan's father leveraged a friendship with Castle's deputy base commander, to mentor his son on the process to apply for an Air Force sponsorship to attend the F. Edward Hébert School of Medicine at the Uniformed Services University in Bethesda, Maryland.

When the time came, between the Castle connections and Alan's own merits, including acing the MCATS, Alan was sponsored and accepted. He distinguished himself at USUHS, and pursued assignments after graduation as a commissioned Second Lieutenant, hoping that might advance his consideration as a serious applicant to become a NASA Mission Specialist.

Alan Gorman, five feet ten inches with a thick head of straight black hair, an athlete's build, twenty-twenty vision, a medical degree in internal medicine, an Air Force officer's commission, and his whole career in front of him, was the object of many a young woman's attention— while he was stateside. But soon, stateside he was not.

One week before the Challenger Space Shuttle disaster, Gorman found himself starting a six-month rotation at Ramstein Air Base. Just a few days into his stay in Germany, Gorman was accompanied by several of his new colleagues into K-Town, the adjoining city of Kaiserslautern. Just seated for a late night supper, a young couple burst into the small corner restaurant, begging in broken English for Gorman's table to go outside and calm down the angry American out in the street.

Gorman stood up, racing out of the room before his fellow diners had processed the request. Outside he encountered a drunken, young USAF support personnel brandishing a large knife, bleeding from the neck and screaming obscenities. Alan hesitated momentarily, before advancing into the street, both hands raised head high. Alan called out that he was a doctor. The man stopped screaming, tilted his head sideways, dropped the knife and collapsed.

Alan reached the man sprawled in the narrow avenue. Dr. Gorman knelt down on one knee, assessing the man's vitals. Alan removed his own scarf, using it to compress the wound at the base of the man's neck and right collarbone. He could see the steam rising into the frigid January air from his own breath, as well as the man's shallow gasps, just as a silver, Mercedes-Benz SL screeched around the corner, running over Alan's lower left leg and foot.

The man with the knife survived, requiring only suturing. Alan ended up losing his left leg below the knee, and with it, his NASA dreams. Alan was initially pressured to step down due to his injury, but would not acquiesce. Alan, even in his twenties, had commanded a skill at networking, and with his connections, he managed to be fitted with a state-of-the-art, lower extremity BK prosthesis, and retain his once-again stateside position.

During ongoing evaluations, Alan was determined to possess the functional ability for prosthetic ambulating at an athletic level. Over the years, this allowed Alan to upgrade his prosthesis more than once with the latest technological advancements, supporting running and other mobile activities.

Soon thereafter, Alan married, raising a son and daughter through a number of relocations. Despite several promotions, he chafed at the increasingly guidelines-driven practice of military medicine. However, he reveled in the camaraderie developed over time with not only his peers but contacts he had developed with officials in military operations and even NASA as well.

One of his colleagues was a Researcher at the NASA Meteoroid Environment Office, who years earlier had convinced Alan to take up meteor observation as a hobby. Alan did so, with gusto, becoming increasingly involved in the formal organizations surrounding the activity.

Colonel Gorman's twenty-five year retirement, so he could relocate back to California, produced perhaps the best-attended and talked-about parties for a non-general in the history of the medical corps. Alan Gorman proceeded to settle down for a life in Palm Springs with a freshman and sophomore in college, a wife in real estate sales, a golden retriever, a library of three stooges videos, a safe full of pistols and rifles for target shooting, golf clubs, periodic locum tenens gigs at area urgent care centers, and a downstairs office dedicated to his consuming hobby of meteor observation.

Thursday Friday Saturday Sunday Monday Tuesday Wednesday

The Wandering Z's

Alan Gorman spent a second day in a planned reunion of sorts with old colleagues who had settled in various parts of northern California. Friday was a repeat of Thursday, replete with golfing, target shooting, cigar smoking, calls home to the wives, and an evening martini – Bombay Blue Safire up, with a twist of lemon, served chilled so that an ultra-thin layer of ice adorned the top.

Unlike Thursday, however, Alan wasn't relaxed and appeared distracted throughout Friday. There was no word from his Winnemucca friend about the meteorite find. Gorman progressively grew worried, but restrained himself from calling back, figuring the man might have spent the night and still be out in the desert, out of cell range, searching fruitlessly for his meteorite.

Saturday morning, Alan woke at six hundred hours as usual. He proceeded with his routine, despite being cooped up for two nights in the small Best Western hotel room in Auburn. Gorman checked his Blackberry for messages. Finding none, he stretched, watched CNN, and launched into sit-ups and push-ups. He shaved, showered, downed two cups of decaffeinated coffee, and stared impatiently at his Blackberry.

There was still no word from his Winnemucca friend. At seven hundred hours, Alan broke down and started calling him, to no avail. Although Alan had planned to check out first thing in the morning to head back to Palm Springs, he hung around instead, becoming increasingly concerned. He wandered down the street to a local diner, ordering an egg-white spinach omelet with grapefruit juice. He read the *Sacramento Bee* cover to cover, trying twice to reach his friend.

Finally, at eight hundred thirty hours, back at his hotel, he strode up to the office, sat at the desktop computer provided in the lobby, Googling until he located his friend's home address and phone. No one answered the home land line. Alan was hardly surprised, knowing the man was divorced and living alone. He Googled street addresses sequentially close to his friend, looking for names and phone numbers and started calling them. Several minutes later, he scored someone willing to check and see if anyone was home, and call Alan back. The return call reported that no one was home, with the pickup gone that was usually parked in the driveway. They noted there was an out-of-state car parked out front.

Alan Gorman next Googled and called the Winnemucca Bureau of Land Management office, to inform them one of their retired staff was missing out in the Black Rock desert. Alan still had the estimated coordinates, where he was sure his friend headed, unless his vehicle broke down. The BLM staff on the other end of the line was quite dismissive, complaining that Burning Man was about to be in session with up to sixty thousand plus people to manage, and suggested that Alan call the Humboldt County Sheriff's office.

Call the sheriff's office is exactly what Gorman did next. Once they determined Alan wasn't a relation or from Winnemucca, they replied there wasn't the requisite time elapsed or enough cause for concern to take any action. They reminded Alan they had Burning Man to contend with. They suggested Gorman try to reach some relatives and check back in if the man couldn't be located in another twenty-four hours. They also suggested Gorman try calling the BLM.

Alan stewed a few more minutes in front of the hotel computer, Blackberry in hand. He racked his brain for ideas on anyone else he could contact in the Winnemucca area that could check on the man. He considered the possibility that his friend was fine, doing who knows what with his companions, maybe in Reno on a lark with their cell phones dead or turned off.

Finally, Alan mentally rewound the man's excitement in his phone call from the night before. Alan pondered on the man's passion for meteors that was evident from their many past emails, Internet chats and couple of seminar meetings they had both attended. Alan concluded that his friend would not have walked away from this meteorite quest; that he assuredly should and would have called Alan to check in some time ago; that no one else was connected enough to him or concerned enough at this point in Winnemucca to do anything about it. Alan Gorman was going to have to travel to the Black Rock desert on this day and search for his friend at the coordinates jotted down on a piece of hotel stationary after the cell phone call the night before last.

So Alan Gorman did exactly that. He checked out of the Best Western hotel, first phoning his wife in Palm Springs, to inform her of his change in plans. Gorman headed north in his white Cadillac Escalade on I-80, dialing his Winnemucca friend every twenty minutes or so, in hopes they would connect so he could turn around to head home. Instead, he found himself three hours, forty-five minutes later, turning off Nevada State Highway 447 just before Gerlach, heading out Jungo Road in search of a meteorite that might know where his friend was.

It was eight miles or so beyond Black Rock City, the site of Burning Man, that Alan noticed a disparate group of people out his driver's side window in the distance to the north. A half dozen or so were wandering – staggering it seemed – out on the desert playa. Gorman laughed out loud, figuring they had something to do with Burning Man, as they were headed back in that general direction.

Equipped with the maps purchased earlier in the day in Reno, Gorman turned north at the Sulphur junction up Jackson Creek Ranch road. Several hours before, Alan called back his Winnemucca friend's neighbor. After determining that his friend still hadn't arrived home, Alan confirmed the make and color of his absent vehicle. Heading up Jackson

Creek Ranch road, Alan didn't feel overwhelmed by searching for the needle in the haystack that fell from the sky the night before last. Instead, he was looking for a white double cab Ford F-150 pickup truck. The pickup would be somewhere accessible to a SUV like Alan's, while a meteorite might not. The pickup was also a whole lot larger and above-ground.

Alan was soon both pleased with himself and perplexed. He spotted the white pickup truck close to one hour later while casing the side vehicular trails off of Jackson Creek Ranch road. The truck was off-road a ways up the hill but still accessible. Vexing Gorman were the two other vehicles parked close by. As he approached, he could see that one still had the rear passenger door wide open. The scene was deserted and windswept.

Gorman parked his Escalade behind the last vehicle, the four-door SUV with the rear passenger door open. Alan rolled his windows down before exiting, wanting to learn if there were any noises outside that might alert him to anything unusual. The only sounds dominating the landscape were the relentless whistle of the desert wind and the rhythmic deep-voiced barking of a dog from the back of the vehicle in front of him.

Alan puzzled over why a dog would be barking from inside the car when the rear door was opened. He exited his Escalade, approaching the SUV cautiously. After a few steps he could see the dog was inside a carrier in the way-back, where the third row seats were folded down. Gorman peered inside the rear tinted window to see an Australian Shepherd watching Alan anxiously from inside the carrier. A large clear water container was fastened to the carrier with a metal straw device for the dog to sip from, but the bottle appeared empty. The Aussie Shepherd didn't appear threatening and seemed a bit sluggish and dehydrated.

Gorman opened the driver door to find the keys still in the vehicle. He noticed a large unopened Chrystal Geyser water bottle in the front drink holder. He grabbed the keys and the water bottle, before walking to the rear of the vehicle. He unlocked the rear tailgate, reaching in to open the carrier. The Aussie Shepherd stopped barking and was now whining softly. Alan noticed an empty metal dish lying next to the carrier. He opened the water bottle, set the dish inside the carrier, filling it to the brim. The dog bolted to the dish and began lapping up the water. Alan sat with the dog for a moment, before deciding he should check out his friend's pickup.

Alan trotted over to the White Ford F-150 truck, with his slightly unusual gait, due to his left BK prosthesis. The driver door was unlocked. The key was nowhere to be seen, but a quick inspection of the cab yielded his friend's wallet, two cell phones, a briefcase, a small ice chest in the back seat, and various personal items. Alan stepped out of the truck, surveyed the other two vehicles between him and his Escalade, shook his head and muttered out loud several times about how peculiar the whole situation was.

Alan's thoughts turned back to the dog. He wondered how long it had been cooped up, abandoned on its own. Gorman had a weakness for certain breeds beyond his own pet Golden Retriever. He had always been quite fond of Australian Shepherds. Gorman circled back to the rear of the SUV, the dog lying, panting in front of the once again empty metal dish. Alan picked up the water bottle he had left on the tailgate, filling the dish again. The Aussie seemed a bit more responsive as it quickly lapped up the second dish. Alan poked around through a zippered sports bag next to the carrier, locating a small box of Milk-Bone biscuits. He offered one to the Aussie, who politely snatched it up.

Alan sat on the tailgate for another minute. He told the Aussie that something was very peculiar indeed, asking the canine what he knew about it. Receiving just panting for an answer, Gorman stroked the dog's head several times, deciding he would need to take the dog back with him after checking out the area. Momentarily, he fantasized about what his wife and

Golden Retriever would do if he brought the Aussie home to stay.

Gorman jumped up, deciding it was time to get to the bottom of things. He began speaking out loud to the Aussie as he paced around the vehicles. What had happened to the three cars' occupants? Was there a crazed sniper nearby who took them out and then disposed of the bodies? Was there a meteorite find so fantastic that they had left with authorities back to Reno or elsewhere? Was there something toxic about the meteorite, and Alan would soon find a slew of bodies lying near the point of impact? Alan cursed that his cell phone was out of coverage range, wishing he still possessed a satellite phone, as he had for some of his tenure in the USAF.

Gorman decided to search the area, as opposed to driving back to Burning Man, Gerlach, or on to Winnemucca to report what he had seen, and return with help. He strode quickly towards the gully in front of the Ford F-150. He sensed a presence, turning to notice the Aussie was on Alan's heels, tail wagging.

For close to fifteen minutes, Gorman and the Australian Shepherd scoured the desert hillside, the wind biting at both of them. Alan found random personal effects in various spots: a San Jose Sharks cap, an almost empty water bottle, a map caught under a grouping of sagebrush.

The Aussie grew quite excited, barking loudly and repeatedly, sprinting towards a large boulder. Alan tried to keep up, but was more than ten meters behind the dog. The Aussie stopped just beyond the boulder, continuing to bark at something beyond Alan's view. Alan heard a mechanical whirring sound, followed by what almost sounded like bullets – unaccompanied by the discharge of any gun — whistling through the sparse landscape that lay in front of him. The dog let out one long high pitched yelp and fell over.

Alan instinctively retreated back towards his vehicle, not knowing who or what was waiting behind the boulder. In less than a minute, he traversed the gully and was back at his

Escalade. He opened the rear tailgate, dug his keys out of his right front pocket, unlocking his TruckVault magnum two-drawer firearms storage container.

Alan brought four guns with him for target shooting at Beale: the Beretta 92FS 9 mm pistol (his favorite), a Smith & Wesson .22 Long Range Rimfire pistol, the M16 Colt .22 Rimfire rifle and his Winchester 101, 20 Gauge Skeet rifle. Unsure of what safe distance would be required to get a vantage point on what lay beyond the boulder, he grabbed the M16, a couple of magazines, and locked the container. He paused, considering if anything else was needed. He pulled his Bushnell binoculars from their case lying on top of the TruckVault firearms container, stringing them around his neck. He grabbed a tan windbreaker that might blend in with the surroundings. He quickly ran his arms through the sleeves, placing the M16 magazines in the windbreaker pockets.

Gorman eyed the boulder from a distance, deciding to approach from the southern side, so he wouldn't be cut off from returning to his vehicle. He reflected on the dog's distance from the boulder before the whirring noise triggered, estimating ten meters or so. He decided a one-hundred-plus meter buffer could provide a much better distance to observe from. Alan picked a spot with several meter-high rocks grouped together, to take cover behind. He then set out at an angle that would take him sixty or so meters even further south from the rocks, limping slightly as he darted in that destination. He worked his way back to the rocks, doing his best not to kick up dust or call attention to himself.

Panting, Alan crouched amongst the rocks, M-16 in tow. He rubbed the magazines in his pocket with his left forefingers. He lifted his Bushnells, working the focus. He held the vantage point he was seeking, but needed to adjust the zoom lever on the binoculars to gain the perspective he desired.

No one lay behind the boulder in wait. Instead, a small impact crater housed a globe-shaped meteorite. Not far from the dead Aussie Shepherd was a dead animal, probably a large jackrabbit. He spotted various personal effects scattered around the area – most prominent were two yellow portable spotlights. The occupants of the three vehicles, including his friend, were nowhere to be seen. Alan bit his lower lip, studying the crater awhile longer. He concluded that the Aussie dog had spared him whatever fate the persons before him suffered.

Gorman wasn't about to approach any closer to the object. Instead, he determined it was high time to flee to Winnemucca and alert the local authorities as to what he found, and then make some higher level calls of his own. He rushed back to his Escalade, just in case there was someone out there in cahoots with the object. After he reached his vehicle and stowing his rifle, he paused, deciding to gather some items from each of the vehicles, including cell phones and vehicle registrations, which might assist the BLM or the sheriff's office. As he returned to his Escalade, Alan had second thoughts – what if they returned to their vehicles and their phones were gone? Gorman laughed to himself, remembering there was no cell coverage in the area, so he wasn't causing much of a hardship. But just in case, he grabbed a piece of blank paper from his briefcase in the Escalade, wrote his name and cell number down, before trotting back to his friend's F-150 pickup truck, placing the paper under the driver side windshield wiper.

Moments later, Alan was working his way back to Jackson Ranch Road. It occurred to him that he should try to call the BLM or the sheriff's office now, as opposed to the considerable time the drive would take. While he had no cell coverage, he remembered seeing a ranch on the left shortly before he had turned right on the trail that led him to the vehicles. Surely there would be a land line at the ranch he could use, and perhaps they might have some other useful information. Perhaps his friend and the others had even taken refuge there.

In less than ten minutes time, he pulled into the ranch's circle driveway full of vehicles, and beheld the late Saturday afternoon z-inflicted carnage.

Urine Diversion

After Dax fell, Jason was silent, dumbfounded for ten seconds or so. Then Jason erupted into a wail, alternating between blubbering Dax's name and unintelligible moaning. Bruce and Conner looked at each other, unsure of what Jason would do next or what they should do for him.

Jason shifted into an expletive laced tirade at the Man-In-The-Roof. He scooted almost within arm's reach, calling the impaled man a litany of profane insults. Finally, Conner inched forward in his dust-covered boxer shorts, just behind Jason, reaching out to place his right hand on Jason's bare shoulder and gave it a squeeze.

Jason brushed Conner's hand off without looking back. Jason wiped his own sweaty, dusty face, examining his hand afterwards, streaked with the orange residue of Cheetos, moisture and dirt. He began carefully sliding down the western side of the roof, a foot at a time, towards Dax's body.

"What are you doing?" Bruce called out to Jason.

"Maybe he's still alive, after all," Jason screamed angrily back at Bruce, not turning around to face him. "I'm going to jump down and check him out." Jason's voice trailed off. He was growing hoarse.

"Jason, this is a two-story roof. You'll break something when you land, and then these guys will come around and get you, too," Bruce countered authoritatively at Jason's back.

"Well, what do you want us to do?" Jason rasped out in his depleted voice. "Leave him for dead?"

"Jason, he is dead," Bruce replied in a softer tone.

Jason finally turned around, carefully shifting his position to prevent slipping further down the slope of the roof. He squinted his eyes from the relentless sun now directly above their heads. "You don't know that, Bruce." Jason argued, tightening his throat muscles to elevate his volume above a whisper. "We won't know that without going down there to check him out."

Bruce shook his head, looked down, and instinctively began wiping his own dust-ridden boxers. "Jason, we get down there, somehow, and those people are going to be all over us, and what good are we going to do Dax, even if he was alive?"

Jason sighed. He fell silent. Even the Man-In-The-Roof grew quiet. Momentarily, only the soft, accelerating Monday afternoon desert breeze emitted any sound. Then, some moaning wafted up from the folks on the ground on the eastern side of the house. Bruce repositioned himself, to better see what they were up to.

Conner paid no attention to the people below, or Bruce, Dax or the Man-In-The-Roof. Conner was concentrating on the cloud of dust that trailed the far-off vehicle approaching from the horizon. Only now, a mild dust storm seemed to be gathering in the distance. Conner soon lost track of their supposed rescuer. Conner cleared his throat loudly. "I can't see that car out there anymore guys. I don't know what happened to it."

"That's just great," Bruce whined.

"Hey, we don't know if it was going to stop here, anyways. Or maybe it was just some dirt devil whirlwind and there was no car. Maybe that was just wishful thinking,'" Jason half-whispered. "We have to take matters in our own hands now," he declared defiantly, staring at Bruce. "So, I've got an idea." Jason paused, seemingly for effect. Bruce and Conner exchanged glances again.

Jason seemed to find the reserve tank in his vocal chords. "I can crawl past this asshole in the roof, and get down to the single story part of the house. From that height, I can jump down easy enough without hurting myself. I can sprint over to Dax, pull him up, and get him back to the little trailer, lock the door and do what I can for Dax there."

"Jason, you, or we, would never have time to get Dax off that rebar and drag him back to the trailer without these guys hearing us, seeing us and catching us." Bruce argued, dismissively.

Jason was undaunted. "Yeah, well, I've just been pondering that. You and Conner will stay on the roof and make a diversion to keep them occupied while I tend to Dax. Once I'm back in the trailer and get him situated, I can search the trailer. There's got to be things in there that will work for weapons. Then I'll come back out for you. We can take care of these guys. After that, we'll fight our way back into the big trailer and get our car keys. Then we grab Dax and get out of here. Or if that won't work, we can hole up in the small trailer, and I'll run over to the mine, like we talked about before."

Bruce raised his voice. "Jason, even if Dax is somehow alive, which he isn't, and you do all these other things you said, which you can't, how in hell's name are Conner and I going to make some kind of diversion that will keep these lunatic bastards occupied? I'd venture to say they have the attention span of a tweaking meth-head with A-D-D. And weren't you the one who just said they were zombies?"

"Piss on 'em," Jason said matter-of-factly.

"No, we can't just say 'piss on em.' They seem to be able to get ugly and mean on a moment's notice and we're going to have to do something about them," Bruce rebutted.

Jason grew impatient. "That's why you're going to piss on them," he replied slowly, annunciating each syllable.

Conner broke in. "Bruce, he means like I did a while ago. We get up, pee over the edge at them, and keep them occupied while Jason sneaks off down the south side."

"That's right," Jason agreed.

Conner and Jason fell silent, awaiting Bruce's response. Bruce grimaced, reflecting for a moment. "Okay, but Conner, you just went not too long ago. And I went right before all hell broke loose. So what happens if we go dry while you're just starting out?"

Jason felt it was all worked out. "You just go down the other side of the roof a ways, like Conner did before, only at a vantage point where you can see where I'm going to jump from. Then yell and make noise to get their attention, while I get down to the lower roof. I'll wave my arms to signal you. All you need to do is pee long enough for me to jump and get around the corner. Then keep yelling at them."

Bruce visibly displayed skepticism. "So what if we don't have them occupied enough by yelling to get them in peeing distance, and they're down by where you want to jump?"

"Then we wait and I don't wave my arms, and you save your pee. Sooner or later, it will work, and it will be sooner, not later," Jason shot back.

"Fine," Bruce relented and sighed. "I suppose I have enough left in me to spray them for a few seconds at least." Bruce paused, peering down below at Dax's head and torso. "But, Jason, you have to listen to us after you jump. If we see them chasing after you, you sprint back to the office trailer, and come back for Dax after you make a new plan from there." Jason started to respond, but Bruce cut him off. "Now listen, Jason, assuming you get the chance to check Dax out, you do it quick. If you can't sense a pulse or breathing, you cut your losses and head to the office. And if they cut you off from getting to the trailer, just run away until you know you're safe. You can outrun them, like you said a long time ago. You leave us here, and we'll make a break for it, later on.

"Nobody is leaving anybody, Bruce," Jason replied, his raspy tone returning rapidly. He started scooting south towards the single story portion of the house, staying on the western slope, out of reach from the snarling Man-In-The-Roof. "Dax is still going to be breathing, I'm going to get him out of harm's way, and I'll come back for you with whatever I can find in that little trailer of yours..." Jason paused and then raised his voice as best he could, "since you didn't deem it worthwhile to keep any guns on the premises."

Conner broke his gaze from the dusty haze in the northeast to begin working his way down the eastern slope of the roof with Bruce. The two scooted several feet down the old decaying shingles in just their dusty boxer shorts. They both stopped a couple feet from the edge. The group below was scattered, pacing in different directions along the eastern side of the house.

Bruce placed two dirty fingers in his mouth and emitted a piercing whistle. He smiled at Conner and repeated whistling a couple more times. Both men broke into screaming loud, random phrases. Bruce chose from a menu of insults to direct at the crowd below, while Conner selected what little Spanish he had picked up on during the past couple of decades.

At first their tactic seemed successful. Five of the six, down below, headed directly underneath Bruce and Conner. With outstretched arms, they moaned and snarled upwards at the two men. The sixth man below wasn't buying into the racket coming from up above. He was fixated on Jason, who was in his line of sight. Conner caught the problem as he monitored the far end of the ranch house.

While Bruce continued jabbering at a high decibel level, Conner pushed upwards to the crest of the roof, then to the eastern slope. He slid forward on his now-ripped boxers, beyond the impaled Man-In-The-Roof who growled menacingly as he passed by. A couple of minutes later, Conner aligned side-by-side with Jason, who seemed to understand Conner's plan without conversing. Conner continued down to the roofline, dangling his feet over the edge. The man below, wearing an embroidered uniform matching the Man-In-The-Roof, jumped up and down trying to grasp Conner's bare feet, which were tantalizingly just out of reach. The uniformed man was somewhat small and thinner than his roof mate. His upward lunges at Conner's feet only cleared the ground by a couple of inches.

Conner proceeded to work his way north, staying near the roofline, the man below following along. Soon Conner reached the second story level with the Man-In-The-Roof just ahead. He yelled at Bruce to assume commanding the uniformed man's attention, while Conner returned to the eastern side to get around the roof-man.

While Conner disappeared from view of the uniformed man below, Bruce decided to dangle his feet over the edge, as Conner had done. While he was one story higher, and thus one story safer from the reach of the half dozen people below, the group didn't seem to fully grasp the spatial relationship. They jumped up and down, reaching at the dirty, now-splintered-feet, ten yards above their outstretched arms.

Two minutes later, Conner rejoined his friend and added two more feet over the edge. Conner checked out Jason, who was frantically waving his arms. "That's our cue," Conner told Bruce with a wide open smile, unaware of how dirt-smudged his teeth now appeared. They both rose to their knees, just above the roofline, dropping their boxers.

Conner, after a couple of seconds of straining, could only produce a small, piddly trickle that soon turned into sporadic dribbles. The immediate whiff of the small amount of spray still frenzied the half dozen below. Then Bruce finally let loose with considerable stream, producing the same rapturous response that Conner had evoked earlier in the day. Momentarily, both Conner and Bruce forgot about Jason, Dax, the Man-In-The-Roof and the weirdness of it all, as they observed in fascination, the childlike response of the group.

But when Bruce ran out of urine, the group turned nastier than ever. Bruce began imitating the mangled-haired lady at the front, giving her the stinkeye and snarling out of the left side of his mouth. Conner cast a glance to the south end. Jason was nowhere to be seen.

Jason reached Dax and knelt to feel for a pulse. He detected none, but was undeterred, realizing he might not know a good pulse if one slapped him across the face. Panting from his sprint around the corner, he placed his ear near Dax's nostrils, which were facing the ground. He tried not to be unnerved by the splattered gore from Dax's descent into the rebar. Jason couldn't detect any movement of air, but realized his own labored breathing and near-state of panic didn't allow for a very clinical assessment.

Jason stood back up and looked around, beyond the crumbling retaining wall that concealed him, half-expecting to see the group on the ground fast upon him. But the coast was clear. Jason paused to listen. He could hear their faint murmur from the other side of the ranch house. More distinct was the hollering from his friends on the roof.

Jason stood, hands on hips, looking down on the mess that was Dax, trying to decide his next course of action. He recalled Bruce's instructions that if Dax wasn't showing signs of life, to abandon him and make a run for the office trailer.

Jason shook his head. He couldn't leave Dax there, when he wasn't one hundred percent certain if Dax was dead or not. He reached down to pull Dax up off the rebar, but hesitated. Jason thought about how moving Dax would damage him far worse.

Jason exhaled loudly. He decided that leaving Dax alone, with this group of zombies or whatever they were, was a less preferable option. Even if these zombie people left Dax alone, lying exposed in the desert sun, impaled by rebar, was not a great alternative either. Jason cast a glance nervously in every direction, then bent down on his knees to try to pull Dax off the rebar.

At first, Jason gingerly attempted to lift Dax an inch at a time, trying to minimize the internal damage he must be causing. Jason thought he might have noticed from the corner of his eye, a twitch in Dax's left foot, but he wasn't certain if it wasn't just movement he caused from the lifting. Jason's forearms soon began to tremble from trying to support Dax's weight, inches off the ground. He realized at this pace his arms would give out long before he could finish raising Dax up.

Jason felt painted into a corner. Lowering Dax surely would cause further internal havoc for Dax, if he was indeed alive. Jason thought he noticed Dax's entire left leg twitch. Jason decided to go for broke and lift Dax all the away, as quickly as he could.

Jason cleared Dax two-thirds of the way off of the rebar, when he could feel Dax's muscles tense up. He clenched Dax tighter, grunted and freed him from his impalement. Jason bent down to gently lower Dax to the ground so he could catch his own breath, before helping his obviously-still-alive friend to the trailer.

As Jason set Dax down, Dax's eyes opened. Dax exhibited a blank, jaundiced stare. It was then that Jason noticed an absence of any running red blood around Dax's wound or on the rebar. Instead, there was the thicker, grayish ooze, the same borne by the Man-In-The-Roof. Dax raised his head and emitted a sickening, gurgling moan. Jason instinctively retreated, tripping over the same rebar that had imprisoned his friend until just moments before.

Jungo Road

The twenty-page Burning Man Survival Guide mailed to each ticket holder, two months before the festival says this about Jungo Road: "...visible on a map, it is a very rough dirt road with easy-to-miss turns, mining vehicles, a couple of treacherous dips and is likely to cause a flat if not worse. Please don't try this route."

The once-state-route 49 runs from in between Gerlach and Empire off of Highway 447, to Winnemucca. Upon entering the road from Highway 447, a brown, wooden BLM mileage sign informs travelers the distance is forty miles to Sulphur and ninety-six miles to Winnemucca, with no services until Winnemucca. An accompanying taller white metal sign post says this: "SLOW DOWN! PLEASE DRIVE CAREFULLY & SOBER. JUNGO ROAD TAKES LIVES."

Heading east, the road sticks to the eastern side beyond the playa, often running along the hillside within a mile parallel to the Union Pacific Railroad tracks. Desert vegetation dots the hillside landscape, continuing down past the tracks where the old lakebed playa begins. One or more dust-devil whirlwinds can almost always be spotted out on the playa from the road.

The road immediately deploys strategic travelers' Darwinism. The dirt road may appear deceivingly smooth for long stretches, but in fact possesses millions of small razor-sharp rocks tightly embedded into the packed dirt, waiting for unsuspecting tires not up to the task.

Abandoned, shredded tires periodically lay partially buried on either side of the road, rubber grave markers leaving testament for long-forgotten incidents in the lonely desert sun. Occasional dips are partially concealed by deep accumulations of drifting powdery playa dust. Other stretches provide large, jagged, loose rocks ready to ricochet into unprotected undercarriages upon request.

At the start of the eastbound route, horse droppings are amply evident. Closer to Sulphur in the foothills, cow pies, along with their makers, may be found. A couple of retaining ponds with surrounding vegetation appear close to the roadside as the Hycroft mine approaches.

Cell phone coverage is lost within miles of Gerlach, and not regained until the road takes the turn a good distance after the Hycroft mine. From Gerlach to Sulphur, weekends find the road frequented by a vehicle every fifteen to thirty minutes or so during daylight hours, with traffic much sparser during weekdays or wintertime. The Hycroft mine, however, generates considerable assorted traffic, including the four employee buses traveling the route at the beginning and end of shifts.

The road from Hycroft to Winnemucca takes on a much different character. Heavy-duty graders periodically patrol that portion of the route, maintaining a relatively smooth surface for the mining traffic. Speed limit signs appear for the first time, setting the maximum speed at 45 mph, which is easy to attain after the mine.

Travelers headed west on Jungo Road from Winnemucca have perhaps a more difficult adjustment. After the relatively smooth sailing from Winnemucca, past the ghost town of Jungo, travelers reach the main entrance sign for "Allied Nevada Hycroft Resources and Development" and encounter the yellow highway right turn sign instructing traffic to remain to the right on Jungo Road and not veer up the Hycroft entrance. "Burning Man" has been spray-painted in white, on the black highway sign arrow.

From that point, the westbound traffic, typically sailing along at forty-five miles per hour, begins to experience the much more primitive road that those dispatched from the Gerlach side have already endured. So while east-bound travelers' Darwinism weeds out those early-on with inadequate tires, exposed undercarriage components, low clearance, or a propensity to travel at unsafe speeds; west-bound Darwinism takes its victims comfortably far into their journey.

The Bureau of Land Management negotiated and arranged for the Hycroft mine to suspend operations for nine consecutive days, during the duration of the current Burning Man, so that the BLM could better assess the singular impact of Burning Man on the Black Rock desert, while minimizing potential overlapping factors from Hycroft operations, including the Hycroft Jungo Road traffic. Given Hycroft operates primarily on BLM-administered public lands, it was not difficult for the Winnemucca District office to obtain this concession from Allied Nevada management.

Hycroft and Burning Man are the two high-profile regional private projects overseen by the BLM. Both generate significant BLM fees – Burning Man alone yields in excess of a million dollars annually for the BLM. Yet there are significant pressures and scrutiny from all sides and stakeholders regarding the related permit study and assessment processes. The Burning Man Special Recreation Permit (SRP) and Environmental Assessment have become increasingly complex and contentious, ever since the population limit was increased beginning in 2012 and a multi-year process provided in the 2012-2016 Assessment. BLM decided that factoring out Hycroft activities during Burning Man for the current year would provide the most accurate annual review of compliance with the Burning Man SRP conditions and stipulations and environmental assessments going forward.

After the Saturday shift finished at five p.m., the four buses and support personnel vehicles headed east down Jungo Road to Winnemucca, not to return until the day after Labor Day, leaving behind a just a skeleton security and maintenance crew of four daytime and two nighttime personnel, working twelve-hour shifts, that would carpool down Jungo Road during suspension of operations.

Thursday Friday Saturday Sunday Monday Tuesday Wednesday

The Lost Weekend

Alan Gorman pulled his white Cadillac Escalade over to the right, steep shoulder of Jungo Road. Alan had commenced hallucinating from lack of sleep, answering an imaginary ER triage nurse about suturing the teenage Caucasian boy who had suffered a nasty skateboarding accident, his laceration splitting the tattooed serpent down the middle on his left forearm.

Alan had more or less been without sleep since waking up in his Auburn motel Saturday morning, except for a couple of five minute catnaps during the past two days. He shifted the Escalade into park, shaking his head to clear his thoughts. He checked his Blackberry, plugged into his car charger, for any signal strength. This was perhaps the hundredth time he had futilely summoned the Blackberry since escaping.

Alan rotated his gaze clockwise from his driver window all the way to the passenger window. He turned around suddenly to make sure no one was approaching behind the car, or had slipped in the back seat. He had pulled over or slowed down to repeat this ritual every few minutes since he broke loose from the two respective ranches on Jackson Ranch Road. Gorman had been trapped in the bloody basement hellhole of the first ranch since late Saturday afternoon.

After winning his freedom, he pulled into the next ranch down the road, again looking for a land line. This time he was more prepared for what came next, and was only waylaid hours, instead of days. Now he was following Jackson Ranch Road back to Jungo Road, where a recently erected road sign informed him he could dust-storm-proof himself for Burning Man just two miles ahead.

Alan knew he was in a sleep-deprived state of post-traumatic stress, which was making it seemingly impossible to focus his thoughts on a rational plan of action. He put the Escalade back into drive, idling forward at five-miles-an-hour while he debated if he should turn around and head to the mining operation he observed just behind him; push on to Winnemucca; stop at the upcoming residence advertised in the road sign, to attempt a land line call – risking an onslaught of more of these zombie people – or step on the gas and head to Gerlach.

Gorman hit the brakes again, placing the Escalade into park once more. He instinctively repeated his clockwise scan of the area. He reached under the driver's seat where he usually left a bottle or two of Chrystal Geyser water. Finding a half-full container, he opened it to take a swig of the warm, stale liquid. He then held the bottle above and let it empty down on his forehead, hoping the sensation might startle him into a clearer state of mind.

Alan thought of his wife back in Palm Springs. The only specifics he had provided her was that he would be gone an extra day to check on a friend near Winnemucca. Gorman was now over twenty-four hours overdue. She'd likely made some calls, but he hadn't told her enough details to pin any hopes of a rescue party already being en route.

Suddenly the solution stepped forward. He would turn around and try the mining operation, and if there was no one there, reverse course again and drive to the residence. Alan reasoned that if he drove straight to authorities in Winnemucca or Gerlach and attempted to explain exactly what had transpired the past forty-eight hours, he risked a very uncertain outcome. They might spend many hours going over his story. If he held back parts, because of their implausibility to anyone that hadn't been there, surely holes in his story would surface. They might determine him to be mentally unstable. They would eventually make the drive to the locations he specified, and then determine him to be a person of interest after discovering a multitude of bodies.

If instead, he simply made the phone call from out in the desert that there had been a rash of murders, they would be compelled to come out and investigate pronto. Then he could move on to make his own contacts to authorities in higher positions through his Air Force connections.

Alan reached for the gear shift once more, shifting the Escalade into reverse. He completed his U-turn, navigating the steep dusty shoulder. After idling forward ten meters or so, he once more hit the brakes. He realized he needed a plan for when he pulled into the upcoming mine — or the residence after that — in case there were more of these zombie people milling around. He was running low on ammunition. Alan glanced over at his loaded shotgun and pistol lying on the front passenger floorboard. Two days ago he would have been mortified at such a breach of safety.

Looking out the rear view mirror, Alan braced himself for the brief dust storm that was about to catch and pass him, whipping across the nearby playa floor. Alan could hear the soft crackling as the dust granules whipped into his rear window. For some reason, he thought of the sound of Rice Krispies, after the milk was added to the bowl.

Soon Alan arrived at the turnoff to the mine entrance. He noted the "Allied Nevada Hycroft Resources and Development Main Entrance" sign and crept forward. The complex in front of him was much larger than he would have imagined, encompassing a series of buildings, a large parking lot and various trucks and heavy equipment. The open pits in the mountain above, with their white and tan colorations, were massive. His spirits lifted. Surely an operation of this magnitude would have satellite phones, Internet, and significant security.

Gorman's spirits sagged as he entered the parking lot. Where were all the employee cars? Outside of the company trucks and equipment, he spied only two private vehicles. As he slowly approached the two cars, his spirits sank further. The rear passenger door of the tan, four-door Subaru wagon was open, with the grisly remains of some poor soul hanging out. A pair of some type of raptors – Alan wasn't an expert on birds — bounced up and down on what remained of the man's carcass, picking away at the exposed, rotting intestines.

Alan pulled forward to find a second corpse sprawled face down in the cinder-gravel lot. The man's clothes had been ripped off, and were strewn around nearby. His torso, arms and legs exposed bare skeleton with only shreds of flesh and organs remaining, while his head seemed fairly intact; his work boots were still laced on his feet. The surrounding cinder and gravel possessed a darker coloration from the pool of dried blood.

Alan spied at least four of the zombie people advancing from the northernmost building, across the parking lot toward him. Gorman reached for his guns. He considered how many more of these creatures might be lurking about the complex. "Screw this," he muttered out loud, spun his Escalade around and retreated out of the parking lot and back to Jungo Road. He would head to the residence.

Then, out of the blue, the scene flashed back in Alan's mind from Saturday, a couple of miles before he first turned up Jackson Creek Ranch road looking for his friend's vehicle and the meteorite. Alan recalled catching out of the corner of his eye, a small group wandering from that direction out onto the playa. Gorman shuddered as he thought of the close to sixty thousand inhabitants that would be occupying nearby Burning Man.

The Savior of Sulphur

Jason's screams reverberated around the ranch house, the same time as the momentary dust storm whipped through the compound. Bruce and Conner helplessly witnessed the group of six below bolt towards the south end of the ranch house in the haze of dust, working their way toward the source of the deep wails.

Conner and Bruce both scurried around the Man-In-The-Roof, to determine Jason's fate. By the time they made it over the eastern crest of the roof, Jason's anguished tones had already grown lethargic. Below they witnessed Dax kneeling on top of Jason, next to the rebar, Dax's left knee pinning Jason to the ground. Jason was bathed in blood, writhing and twitching. Dax alternated between biting deep into the flesh of Jason's right bicep, and reaching in to gash away at the right side of Jason's neck with his incisors. Dax's backside displayed a visible wound where the rebar had protruded just a couple of minutes before, but blood did not appear to be seeping from the spot. Instead, Dax bore the same thick, grayish ooze that seeped from the Man-In-The-Roof.

Conner and Bruce made their way down to the single story roof, coming to Jason's aid. But while standing at the edge of the single story, looking for a landing spot, Conner felt Bruce's hand on his right shoulder pulling him back from the edge.

"It's too late," Bruce said slowly, shaking his head, gesturing toward their partially obstructed view of Dax and Jason. The other six had joined in. Jason was silent now, his remains being devoured rapidly by the entire group. The group below was wildly reaching into Jason's opened torso, grabbing whatever they could grasp in their now-slippery hands, and then pulling the bits of blood-soaked flesh and organs to their mouths. Bruce sat down cross legged in his tattered boxer shorts, buried his head in his hands, and began to sob in between spurts of profanities.

Suddenly, Conner knelt down and began shaking Bruce. The dust storm had already passed. "Look," Conner shouted, pointing to the circle driveway where a white Cadillac Escalade entered and was now accelerating across Bruce's property directly towards the ranch house.

The Escalade skidded to a stop, followed by a ten-foot-high trail of dust. The driver door swung open. Bruce and Conner witnessed the five-foot, ten-inch Man-In-Sunglasses with shortly cropped black and gray hair and an unusual gait, emerging from the vehicle with some kind of rifle strapped around his left shoulder, and a pistol clutched tightly with both hands. They watched the man take measured steps forward as the seven zombies — including Dax — left Jason's grisly remains, surfacing from behind the retaining wall to close in on their assailant.

Bruce and Conner silently took the scene in with awe, as the man calmly began dispatching his attackers with a shot to the head each. One by one, they went down. First, the naked man with oak tree tattoo collapsed backwards with a single shot. Next, one of Bruce's Winnemucca friends wearing in an old, faded 'I'm with Stupid" tee shirt and gym shorts took a shot to the left eye, but continued advancing. The next shot struck an inch higher and sent him down as well.

The tattered, wild-gray-and-black haired lady went down next, followed by the uniformed man who landed on top of her, a single shot dispatching each.

By this point, Dax and the two remaining Winnemucca friends were almost upon the Man-In-Sunglasses. He began retreating as he shot, at roughly the same pace as the three zombies were advancing. The first shot missed completely. The next two shots, both to the head, brought Dax down.

One of the Winnemucca friends with a shaved head lunged at the Man-In-Sunglasses' feet, as the man's next shot fired into the ground. The Winnemucca friend missed his attempted tackle of the Man-In-Sunglasses, landing on his stomach. The sunglasses man then discharged a shot into the back of the skull of the zombie on the ground as he retreated. Oozing gray goo from the back of his shaved head, the Winnemucca friend rose to his knees, unfazed.

The Winnemucca friend dived at his assailant's legs, grabbing the Man-In-Sunglasses' left ankle, proceeding to take several bites. Unfazed, the Man-In-Sunglasses reached down, pressing his pistol into the Winnemucca friend's temple, blowing a new, well placed hole in the shaved head.

The last Winnemucca friend, wearing a red Hawaiian shirt, blue shorts, and no shoes, was face to face with the Man-In-Sunglasses, taking a swipe at the pistol. The Man-In-Sunglasses fired point blank into the z's hand. The zombie paused to examine his right paw with three digits dangling by threads, before lurching forward. The Man-In-Sunglasses fired a shot into the zombie's skull also at point blank range. The zombie fell forward into the Man-In-Sunglasses, both collapsing on the ground. The man fired one more shot into the zombie's skull for good measure, and then arose.

The Man-In-Sunglasses exhaled loudly, then raised his pistol and directed it to the roof of the old ranch house, where he caught a flash of movement. He steadied both hands to take careful aim, cognizant that he had only two shots left in his magazine. Voices from the roof called out to him. Alan Gorman lowered his pistol, removed his sunglasses, and introduced himself to the two men standing on the roof. He asked if any more of these people were lurking about, and was told that there was just one stuck in the roof with them, and three inside the main trailer.

Alan inquired and learned neither of the men above had been bitten. Alan was told that it looked like he had suffered some bites to the leg. Alan Gorman politely lifted his left pants leg and pointed to his prosthesis, before heading over to where they informed him the ladder still lay in the dirt so he could join them and dispatch the Man-In-The-Roof.

Thinking Outside the Z-Box

Alan Gorman laid his rifle, and now-emptied Beretta pistol, on the dusty roof, plopping himself down next to them. He sat upright, supporting himself with his arms behind his back. Bruce and Conner introduced themselves after Alan executed the Man-In-The-Roof, using both remaining bullets. Alan surveyed the surroundings from the rooftop, doing a double-take when Bruce's softball field came into view.

"Guys," Alan started in, "I'm sorry for not getting moving here, but I have been up for two days and I just have to sit with you for a minute, to rest and collect my thoughts. I'm a bit ringy."

"Don't you apologize," Bruce replied, forgetting Alan's name already. "You absolutely saved us." Bruce sat down with Alan.

Alan breathed in and out, heavily, several times. "I need to use your phone. Or is it only in the trailer, where you said the other three are still inside?"

Bruce rubbed his forehead. "Well, the bad news is, that's exactly where the phone is."

"The bad news?" Alan half-laughed. "Is there good news?"

Bruce sighed. "The good news is it wouldn't matter. Our phone has been down since yesterday."

"Now isn't that a funny coincidence?" Alan responded sarcastically. "You'd think these events might be related or something." Alan turned to see Conner still standing, not smiling, instead looking somewhat shell-shocked.

"I'm sorry, but we should go right now. Let's get in your SUV, drive over to the mine, get some help and call the sheriff," Conner pleaded with Alan.

Gorman sighed. "I hate to tell you guys, but I just came from there. They've been overrun by these things."

"Oh, God," was all Bruce could reply to this news. Conner sat down next to Bruce and said nothing.

"So, fill me in. Tell me what happened here, and then I'll spill the short version of my last two days," Alan offered.

Bruce spoke up first. He shared what transpired since he rose out of bed to find Conner and Dax interrogating the three guys in the trailer. Bruce then paused, letting silence sweep over the roof for a good minute. He then turned to Alan. "Now, I think Conner and I are hoping you have some answers, here. I don't have many buddies, and I have just watched almost every friend I have in Nevada die. I have a friend left in that trailer who has become one of those things, and I've got Conner here, who has known me since we were kids. And we are-so-wanting some answers about this frickin' freak show of day we're having here."

Alan Gorman shared the story of his meteor-friend, the meteorite-site with the abandoned cars, and the Aussie dog that surely saved his life. Alan then recounted his visit to the first ranch on Jackson Ranch Road late Saturday afternoon.

"There were three bodies lying in the middle of the circle driveway when I pulled up. They were the most grisly things I think I've ever seen, and I was an Air Force physician, mind you. There wasn't much left of any of them, pretty much like your friend you pointed out down below there. So I grabbed my Beretta here and a magazine, and I proceeded carefully into the house. The front door was wide open. I remember seeing dried blood smeared on the tile floor." Alan stopped to wipe the sweat off his face, for the first time noticing the relentless rays of the sun. He yawned, his grogginess almost overwhelming him.

Gorman continued, "I walked past a half-bath just off of the entrance. One of them was kneeling before the toilet, his head in the bowl. I could hear him slurping from out in the hall. I entered the large family room, filled with ten or so of them. You could tell most of them hadn't been with each other until coming together at this place. There were some Hispanics that looked like ranch laborers, a man and woman dressed in tattered formal evening wear – don't ask me what that was all about—and other assorted characters. They were all just sitting there – some on the sofa, some in chairs, the rest on the floor. They were just how you described the three guys when Conner first found them on the sofa. You could tell by the smell, some of them had defecated themselves. It seems in some ways they were not beyond a baby – they don't seem to be potty-trained. Their eyes were open, but they were really non-responsive. I figured out later, that's basically their version of sleeping."

Mentioning the word sleep induced Alan to yawn again. "At the time, I thought maybe someone had drugged them all. So with my loaded pistol in one hand, I picked the lady in the torn black cocktail dress to examine. Her pupils were dilated, her eyes seemed jaundiced. I snapped my fingers, started shouting at her, she just sat there. Then I hear a woman call out, asking 'who was there' and crying for help. I turned, and the formal-wear lady rose, all of a sudden, snarling and advancing toward me. Then another one of them stood up, and another."

Alan paused, gazing east at the bodies strewn around on the ground below. "Then the shit hit the fan. I followed the woman's voice, which led to stairs off the kitchen going down to basement. Who the hell builds a basement out here? It isn't like land is such a premium that you can't just add on a room next door. So, all these people from the living room are now up and coming at me, and they're freaking me out. Right at the top of the stairs one lunges at me, so I shot him. I shot him in the chest and he kept coming. I shot him several more times from close range, including what should be a fatal heart shot. It didn't faze him. That's when I knew we had transcended anything we'd ever known or dealt with before." Alan stopped, almost too tired to talk. He glanced upwards at the silhouette of the now still, silent, Man-In-The-Roof.

Conner leaned forward. "Go on. What happened next?"

Alan coughed from inhaling the dust on the roof. "I retreated down those basement stairs, with all of them stumbling all over each other trying to follow me down. After wasting a number of shots, I managed to take one of them out with a direct shot through the center of the frontal bone of his skull. Then I made it to the basement, where this woman was holding the door open for me. She slammed it shut and I bolted it. We listened to their scratching, clawing and grunting from the other side. The basement was a large pantry and supply room. There were these little six-inch windows near the ceiling on two sides, but there was no way out of there except back up those stairs. There were nine of the zombie creatures left and I only had five bullets left in my magazine."

Alan coughed again. "So, the woman didn't speak much. I think she used all her energy calling out for me, and guarding the door when I came down the stairs. She had been bit in several places, just like what you described with your one friend. I examined her. She had one nasty laceration that I was able to suture with a sewing kit I found next to a sewing machine in the corner. I even found some Neosporin ointment in the supply shelves and applied it on her wounds. She was a young, black woman in her twenties, in hiking boots and gear. Why she ended up there, and what her story was, I'll never know. I only got a few words out of her. I didn't even find out her name. She started retching. She expelled a high quantity of vomit, even through her nose. I was worried about dehydration and found water bottles. She took some water, but not enough. I struggled to get it down her. While we sat there for hours into the night, listening to the endless clawing, scratching and moaning, she'd lapse in and out of consciousness. I paced the room, and searched through every inch of supplies in the shelves. I'd check her vitals every so often. I found Tylenol and gave her a large dosage, but at some point in the night she wouldn't ingest anything, not even water. While it was still dark, I was checking her, and she just gave out on me. Her breathing stopped. There was no pulse. I tried to revive her with chest compressions, but she was gone. There were blankets in the supply shelves, so I covered her up. Without her to think about, I resumed pacing the room, trying to come up with a plan, all the while listening to those relentless idiots on the other side of the basement door. Time passed, well less than ten minutes, and the blanket started moving."

Conner and Bruce's thoughts both went back to seeing Dax revived, feasting on Jason. Alan again yawned, before continuing. "I must say I was dumbfounded. I stood there, doing nothing, watching this woman start to flop around underneath the blanket. So, it appears, after she passed on from the infection, in layman's terms, a reboot occurred, completing the transformation in her neurological, nervous, circulatory and other systems. It sounds like the same thing happened to your friend who was bit, only earlier-on for him, because he died from the fall from the roof." Alan paused once more. Conner noticed him rubbing his left thigh. Conner got a closer look, as Alan repositioned himself, at Gorman's lower left leg prosthesis — a pretty expensive appearing one at that.

Alan resumed. "Finally, she rose, casting the blanket aside. She took one look at me, and rushed forward. She was totally reenergized, like she'd had a good night's sleep. The doctor in me, produced hesitation for just a moment, thinking 'what if' she is okay, and some true miracle occurred. But it was clear she had become just like the others, and by the time she was in my face, and I thought about the bites she had borne and would now inflict on me, I didn't hesitate to put two slugs into her forehead."

Alan cleared his throat. "The noise from the other side of the basement door certainly perked up after the gunshots. I was down to three bullets. I decided that sooner or later, these creatures would return to the state I found them in, and I would just wait them out, until things became quiet. So, with time on my hands, I took to examining the black woman. The grayish-thick-oozy blood you guys told about with the fellow stuck in the roof up there? That's what leaked out of the woman's gunshot wounds. I found a straight-edge razor down there, plus some latex gloves, so I performed some dissections.

It turns out their blood coagulates exceptionally well. I'm not sure if it turns that color on contact with the air, or if somehow it managed to change color internally, but I'm voting on the former. Anyway, that's what allows them to keep going, after you shoot or injure them without bleeding to death right away. That and they obviously are completely impervious to pain. So physiologically, the rapid viral transformation involves the blood system, a disconnect of the pain signals in the nervous system, a cessation of much of higher brain function, and a primal urge to ingest all things human – normal standard-issue human that is."

Conner interrupted. "Do you mean, on top of eating a live person, that they like our pee?"

Alan let out a chuckle. "Yeah, I remember what Bruce here said about that. That's probably what the guy I saw with his head in the toilet was interested in too, as opposed to the water. But, you know, they need liquid. They might not have the sense to take a drink of water, but their body is mostly made of H_2O, just like ours. They can get some from digesting a human, or as you said, drinking pee. But, sooner or later, they are going to need some liquid to keep in the game. It helps that they don't seem to perspire much at all; at least I didn't see any of these zombies sweating. And I saw a number of them close up."

Alan looked Conner straight in the eyes. "But where was I? It might seem like I digress, but there is a point. Another day passed. After waiting long enough down in the basement, things finally did grow quiet. It took long enough; it was sunup this morning when I decided to give it a go. I slipped something under the door to see if it would provoke a reaction. It didn't. So I opened the door a crack. There were two of them lying on the stairs. I recognized them as two I had shot when I descended. At first, I thought I'd try to sneak by them, but on closer inspection, they were clearly gone. They must require a certain level of blood circulating, just like anybody else. That grayish-gooey blood was all over them. It seems their blood coagulates and slows the bleeding way down, but if the wound is bad enough, eventually they will bleed out. That's what these two appeared to do – very slowly bled to death, at least a zombie death."

"Wait a minute," Bruce interrupted. "You're saying zombies sleep, need to drink, they poop their pants, and they can bleed to death?"

"And that's not all. I get to the top of the stairs, lying on my stomach, peeking around – there's nobody there. I tiptoe to the front door and see them milling around in the driveway and my Escalade, amidst the three bodies that were strewn around when I arrived. I sneak to the back sliding glass door, which was open. There's a one of those kid's inflatable pools in the middle of the back patio, but it's a big one, filled over almost a meter deep. One of the zombie people, a frail-looking elderly gentleman, is hunched, bobbing his head, focused completely on the pool. I'm going to have to get around him in one direction or the other to sneak the back way to my car. I remember when examining the cocktail dress lady, when I first entered this place, that she was breathing heavy in her sleep-like state. So I figured, if they need to breathe like anybody else, they can drown like anybody else. I only had three bullets left, and I didn't want the noise to attract the others. The guy didn't look that difficult to handle. Then I saw a shovel propped up against the patio wall, next to the sliding glass door. So, I grabbed it, dashed over to the man bobbing his head in the pool, and got behind him using the shovel handle for added leverage, to keep his head down in the water. I saw what had attracted him there. At the bottom were the grizzled remains of a dismembered forearm in the pool. Someone must have been walking around gnawing on it, after they yanked it off one of the bodies out front. So I kept his head underwater while he struggled. He was a lot stronger than I would have thought. I think he would have set the underwater record, because it definitely took ten minutes to finish him off. But he finally went limp. No more bubbles were surfacing. So I left him there and circled back around towards my Escalade."

Alan paused. Bruce chimed in. "Now wait a minute. This isn't right. Zombies are supposed to be able to survive anything but a shot to the head. And they aren't supposed to need anything, like air or water or sleep. They just are supposed to try to eat people and that's it."

Alan chuckled. "There are rules for zombies? And these guys broke the rules? Look Bruce, you've been through a lot here, but there is a difference between zombies from the movies, and these guys we met here and now, and we're just going to have to think outside the box a little about them." Alan laughed harder. "The zombie box. We're going to have to think outside the zombie box, because they evidently already have."

"Well, that all sounds like a good thing," Conner opined. "They could die off on their own, out here in the desert, with no water, not a lot of people to eat, and an opportunity to eventually bleed to death if we're lucky."

"Yeah, they do seem to have some planned obsolescence." Alan replied, again yawning. "It would appear to be intelligent design at work."

"What do you mean?" Bruce snapped sarcastically. "That God created these things? That you think this is the wrath of God being directed upon us?"

Alan shook his head. "Heavens no, Bruce. You forget about what happened out at the meteorite site. We're not dealing with a simple spillover virus from some animal reservoir host. We're looking at the origin being an artificial viral transmission from an extraterrestrial source. This is, in my opinion, a designer virus delivered by projectiles from a motion-sensored drone sent from some far-off alien race, wanting to wipe us out, using us as weapons against ourselves, before they come to borrow our planet for a while. And if they designed too indestructible of zombies, they would have to deal with the annoyance when they arrive in their spaceships from who-knows-where."

Bruce tilted his head in disbelief. "I don't buy that. Wouldn't it make more sense if this was some germ warfare launched at us by terrorists, or the Chinese, or someone else on this planet?"

"Bruce," Alan countered, "even an object that small, launched into US airspace from another country, or this country for that matter, or even from satellite orbit, would have been tracked, and we'd be surrounded by a response team. They just wouldn't necessarily be able to track something that small coming from a trajectory originating beyond earth orbit, and that's what my friend observed and relayed to me over the phone. The object that shot the dog in front me when I first approached it? It was extraterrestrial and intelligently designed to infect not just one patient zero, but as many who would keep wandering by it. And evidently it was efficient enough to take down three carloads before I arrived and who knows how many more since then."

Silence ensued while Bruce and Conner took in Alan's revelations. Finally, Bruce spoke. "I don't know. I still don't know if I buy it. Why zombies? If some aliens wanted to launch germ warfare, wouldn't there be a more elegant solution than this? That doesn't make sense. Anyhow, would they even think of a virus that induces zombies?"

"I don't know," Alan argued. "A virus sounds pretty elegant to me that seems to leave all other species unaffected, causes the infected to proactively and aggressively seek out others to infect, has an incomprehensibly and seemingly impossible rapid rate from point of infection to fruition, allows for the infected to consume a good number of their victims, reducing the number of corpses left to dispose of, and has some built-in obsolescence to help weed-out the infected when our aliens finally arrive to start cleaning up the mess."

Bruce didn't have a response. Conner slowly seemed to be buying into Alan's zombie logic, but asked, "Okay, but how would they even think of zombies, with so many other possibilities out there? And what kind of coincidence is it that we just happen to have zombie mythology already?"

"Who knows?" Alan sleepily drawled out. "Dumb luck? More likely they've been observing us. They had to be, to decide to launch a drone at us." Alan chuckled. "Perhaps they caught transmissions of something like 'Night of the Living Dead' and we gave them the idea."

Bruce frowned again. "It still doesn't make sense. If these things are zombies, why is it they devour some of the people to shreds, and end up only biting most of the others? Why aren't they just devouring everyone? I would think if they are zombies, they wouldn't be multiplying like this, spreading the infection, because they'd be eating all their victims."

Alan raised his eyebrows. "I gave that some thought when I had all that time to kill down in that basement, and then I saw it come into play at the next ranch down the road. I think it's as simple as they get full, and then they just take to biting whoever else is around. You ever go to SeaWorld or the Monterey Bay Aquarium, and see all the other species of fish swimming around unmolested in the shark tank? They keep the sharks full, and they don't bother their cell mates. I think the same concept might be at work here, until these zombies get hungry again or agitated enough."

"Hey," Bruce interjected, still somewhat skeptical of Alan's theories. "You didn't tell us about the next ranch down or finish telling us how you got out of there."

Alan's replied, even more slowly. He was clearly running out of steam. "Yeah, that. I trotted away a good distance, where I felt they wouldn't see or hear me. Then I circled back until I had an angle on my car that could allow for sneaking up behind some obstacles as I approached. They didn't notice me until I was almost upon the Escalade. I managed to get inside, spending my last three bullets to do so. They had the vehicle surrounded. I fortunately still had the keys in my pocket. I ran over several of them backing out at full speed. I could see them in the rear view mirror, trying to rise and walk on their broken bones after I ran them over. I stopped, once I was enough of a distance away to safely set up my rifle. Then I took out four or five of them with head shots before they got close enough that I decided to vamoose. I never did get to try using their phone. So, I arrived at the next ranch down. They also had a group of zombies running the place. This time, I arrived prepared. I spent most of my ammunition, but I mowed down every one of them in a couple of hours' work. Once I had the place cleared, I got to their landline phone, but there was no dial tone, so here I am."

"Well, I for one am thankful that here you are, too. And I'm glad to hear these things have built-in flaws and landed out here in the middle of nowhere, so they just might end up starving to death or dying of thirst," Conner announced, rising to his feet, feeling it was time to wrap up the conversation.

"Conner," Alan rebutted, "I hate to tell you this, but I don't know that they might starve to death. Short-term, there is no shortage of people to eat."

"What do you mean?" Conner asked, clueless.

The answer clicked with Bruce. "Burning Man."

Conner's face went ashen. His thoughts went to Cassie, somewhere in that sea of people. On that note, he sat down again with Alan and Bruce. Then Conner could hear Alan snoring.

Cassandra Barton

Cassie only lived in Parker Creek during junior high through the middle of her sophomore year of high school. Her father moved his family from his Orange County law practice, back to the guest house at his parent's ranch outside of Parker Creek, when Cassie's grandparents could no longer care for themselves. Her grandfather passed away during the winter of her freshman year, her grandmother the following summer. Cassie's dad took measures to sell the ranch and resume his practice. By spring, all the Bartons were back in sunny Orange County.

Cassie's best friend at the start of high school was a boy – Conner. They both ran track; they exchanged one old Isaac Asimov or Robert Heinlein paperback after another; they watched MTV together in the afternoons; they had six out of seven classes together their freshman year. They were each other's first true kiss of any duration.

Conner was much more despondent than Cassie after she moved back south. The letters exchanged diminished from a flood to a trickle by the summer after their sophomore year. Cassie remained in Conner's daily thoughts, but Cassie let go of Conner as she immersed herself in her new life.

After graduating from UC Irvine with a degree in Economics, Cassie moved to San Diego to assume an analyst position with a niche market research firm. Her boyfriend from her senior year of college had been accepted at the UC San Diego Medical School. They married before he started his residency in Internal Medicine at UC Davis. Their daughter was born several months later. The young family moved back to San Diego when Cassie's husband joined the Sharp Community Medical Group. By their daughter's seventh birthday, they were divorced. Cassie remained in the San Diego area, resuming a career in market research.

Cassie's friends remarked that she looked even better in her thirties than she did as a twentysomething. Her sleek, five-foot six-inch physique bore evidence that she worked out daily and didn't suffer from overindulgences. Her short, dark brown hair complimented the light freckles that graced her face. She often bore a radiant smile that testified to the teeth whitening sessions at her dentist's office. Cassie was generally happy, optimistic, and saw no need for a steady man in her life until her daughter was off to college.

Cassie was introduced to Burning Man by two moms she met through her daughter's club soccer. They had gone to the Black Rock Desert for the week leading up to Labor Day for several years. They insisted that Cassie join them, helping make arrangements for Cassie's daughter while they were gone. Cassie was hooked into Burning Man from the jaw-dropping start. One of the moms moved to New York the next year and fell out of touch, but Cassie and her other friend attended Burning Man faithfully.

A couple of years slipped past. Cassie found herself on Facebook, with Conrad Zimmerman suggested as a friend. Cassie and Conner's Facebook relationship evolved from generic, one or two line exchanges, to strings of supposedly clever one-liners, to private messages, to daily chats. Perhaps a month later, the phone calls started. Facebook, Skype and cell phone conversations soon occupied a sizeable portion of each evening. At some point, the plan was made to take each other for a test drive. They agreed to hook up for a few days in Reno to celebrate her fortieth birthday before Cassie went off with her friend to Burning Man.

By the time Conner bade her goodbye, as she joined her friend to buy provisions on Sunday afternoon for Burning Man, Cassie for the first time, when en route to BM, wasn't enacting the adult version of an impatient child on Christmas Eve. Instead, she was envisioning Conner meeting up with her, back in Reno after Burning Man concluded, before she flew back home.

The two ladies embarked on the late Sunday afternoon drive to queue up for the long winding Burning Man arrival wait. They talked about the sweet deal they had with their theme camp, pulling extra shifts manning the bar, but relieved of the duties that brought their camp mates out on Saturday for BM approved early setup.

After they turned off I-80 at Wadsworth, bearing north on Highway 447, Cassie stared out the window, obsessing on all things Conner, while her friend drove. She started planning his visit to San Diego. She wanted Conner to meet her daughter. She wondered how well her mom and dad would remember him. She thought about Conner's long struggle after his wife and parents died, which he eventually shared with Cassie. She thought about how their lives had zigged and zagged and now intersected.

Then she paused, turned to her friend, and commented how all sense of time would be suspended this week. Even Monday evening – in twenty-four-hours-time — might seem both an eternity and a mere few ticks of the clock away.

Winnemucca or Black Rock City

Alan Gorman turned to his side on the creaky, dusty roof. The sun shone directly in his eyes. He heard voices in the background and rose up in a panic. Disoriented, he glared at Conner and Bruce, reaching around for his pistol. He then remembered that he emptied it on this roof, and that he knew the two men in front of him. "How long was I out?" Alan asked the both of them.

"I'd say fifteen minutes or so," Bruce answered.

"We were just debating when to wake you," Conner added.

Alan rubbed his eyes, trying to decide if the sleep had done him any good. While he knew a full sleep-cycle of ninety-plus minutes would certainly have been better, that was not an option. He decided that waking before he fell into a deeper sleep-stage was preferable in the short term. His mind did seem a little clearer. "You know, if all of this just doesn't blow your mind, I don't know what would," Alan announced. "I may have spent a career in the service, but until this weekend, I just treated people, not shot them or run them over. I guess I should be thankful I haven't turned into a melted stress-sicle yet."

Actually, Alan had shot someone once before, during the previous decade. Gorman was stationed at Maxwell AFB, Alabama, serving with the 42nd Medical Group, when a severely depressed patient with PTSD entered the Internal Medicine clinic — armed to the teeth — seeking out the nurse who recently broke off their relationship. The man grazed her, then after briefly terrorizing the staff, he mortally wounded the first security policeman to the scene. Coming around the corner, Alan found the now-deceased member of the 3800th Security Police Squadron's 37mm firearm lying beside the expired lawman. Alan retrieved the weapon, traced the screaming patient's voice back into the medical records room, where Alan was greeted by two shots piercing the first records cabinet, a couple of feet from Gorman's head. Alan calmly retuned fire and dispatched the man. The incident was swept under the rug as much as possible and managed to stay out of the Montgomery press.

Alan was about to segue his conversation with Bruce and Conner into a discussion of what they needed to do next. He then recalled the Maxwell, Alabama incident, wondering how on earth it had escaped his thinking. He paused, trying to formulate how to explain that his boast of having never shot someone before, wasn't entirely accurate. After a moment, he just shook his head once, deciding it wasn't worth the time, and that these two men he had just met had indulged enough of his storytelling for one day.

Instead, Alan stretched his arms, returning to the business at hand. "Well, we have much to do, gentlemen. How are you fixed for guns and ammunition?"

Bruce and Conner exchanged awkward glances. "We aren't," Bruce replied apologetically.

"What do you mean?" Alan asked, assuming there must be some misunderstanding.

Bruce cleared his throat. "I hate to tell you this, doctor, being you seem to be an expert marksman and all, but I don't own any guns. Not a one."

Alan scratched his left thigh, his limb now throbbing above his prosthesis from inattention. He had difficulty absorbing this news. "Bruce, you live out here, of all places, all by yourself, and you don't own a gun of any kind?"

"I don't, and you're not the first person to give me that look or that question today," Bruce responded, sheepishly.

Alan sighed. "Well, I wasn't thinking clearly when I spent my last two bullets with my Beretta on this fellow in the roof here. I guess I was worried he might collapse through the attic and still be a problem, but that's all spilled milk, anyways. I do have one magazine left with my M16 here," Alan patted his rifle, still strapped to his shoulder, "which has thirty rounds, but that's it. After that I'm done. I spent most of my ammo at that place up the road from you. So, I'm figuring we leave those three fellows you left in the big trailer alone, and we all get in my vehicle and head toward Winnemucca to get within cell phone range. Hopefully, we won't run into too much, and this magazine will be enough."

Conner and Bruce looked blankly back at Alan, obviously not in agreement with his plan. "You don't think it would be wise to put down the three in my trailer? Our car keys are in there, and regardless, they might break loose at any time," Bruce countered.

"Au contraire, gentlemen," Alan responded, still itching his left thigh. "You need to think through the end game here. At some point, we are going to have to have law enforcement pay a visit here. There is a considerable body count below, and I am not going to be present. This is your property, and you're going to be the person or persons of interest. Now, if you keep those three tucked away in the trailer, the officers are going to see exactly what the problem was here. But if we put them down, as you said, then they are just additions to the body count that you are going to have to explain to an unsympathetic audience."

Alan paused to shift his weight as he sat, his limb becoming increasingly uncomfortable. "But more so, being a doctor and having killed almost every one of these things I've come across, I'm feeling compelled to leave a captive few alive for a research team. They sound like they are contained inside the trailer, we can barricade your exits, leave a warning sign on the door, and it is probably a matter more important than our convenience or safety that we have some of these things captured to be examined by some experts, don't you think?"

Conner jumped into the conversation. "Dr. Gorman, since you've brought up the subject of more of these things heading down or already at Burning Man, I have to get there right now. There is someone there who means more to me than I could possibly explain, and I have to get her out of there, stat. So we need our car keys to do that, unless you plan on driving us there."

Alan turned to Conner, then to Bruce, shaking his head. "Gentleman, now that I'm thinking a little more clearly, let me explain. First, we don't want to go into that trailer because you can't predict or control what might happen when you open that door. A rifle in close quarters isn't the same as my empty pistol here. One of us could easily get bit before we take all three of them down. Second, as I said already, we might lose the last chance of keeping these things in captivity to be tested, and that probably outweighs any other argument. Third, also as I said before, you can't win, trying to explain something 180 degrees from normal to law enforcement. You don't want to be stuck explaining this mess, and keeping these guys alive will back up your story."

Alan cleared his throat and continued. "Now, Conner, let's talk about saving someone you love at Burning Man. I'm repeating myself, but you need to think about the end game. You go up to the entrance... and say what? 'Head for the hills, the zombies are coming, the zombies are coming?' Seriously, I want you to think about what possible scenario you are going to run by persons of authority, at that entrance point, that doesn't end with you being taken in for questioning without being able to contact anyone inside. You must know there are no tickets available, and they don't let anyone but law enforcement in without a pass. Trust me, gentleman, I have spent my career dealing with persons of authority. It would be a lose-lose situation, unless you're dealing with authorities you already know. And know them, I do. So, the quickest, most effective way you can help this person you love so much at Burning Man, is to come with me toward Winnemucca, until I get within cell phone range. Let me make the calls I need to make, and then sit back and let someone in real power come down here and take control of the situation."

Conner shook his head and raised his voice. "Hey...I totally agree that you should head toward Winnemucca and make your calls. But I am going to go to Burning Man and find Cassie and get her out of there. I failed her last night, and I will not fail her again." Alan wrinkled his face, unsure of what Conner was referring to.

Alan countered, "Look, if I take you to Gerlach afterwards, we could email your girlfriend from my Blackberry, and she'd get the message. I know cell coverage isn't available out there, but wouldn't some parts of those Burning Man camps have arranged some wi-fi that she might be logging into?"

Conner shook his head. "Well, Cassie told me some camps have some spotty private wi-fi setups. But she is off the grid. She said she was turning off her iPhone and leaving it in the glove box. And I couldn't think of another email address to send a message to, could you Bruce?"

Bruce rose to his knees, glancing at the shed on the west side of the ranch house. "No, and it isn't like I'm set up to Google us an address to send some message in a bottle to, either." Bruce paused, wincing as he surveyed the bodies below one more time. "Sir, Conner is my oldest remaining friend, and wherever he goes, I am going. And it sounds like that isn't with you. But I would think that would be a good thing, because we offer a contingency plan. If for any reason you are not successful in calling in the Calvary, you're going to want to have a plan B, and we will be that. Now, I agree going to the Burning Man entrance won't accomplish anything, but what I'm talking about is sneaking in the back way, after the sun sets. Once we're inside, if the place is calm, we'll just find Conner's girlfriend and get out. If there are signs of trouble inside, we should be able to convince some lawmen that we experienced these creatures outside and share what we know before we skedaddle out of there."

Alan did not appear pleased. His face pursed, his voice tightened. "Guys, I think...no...I know, that you underestimate the difficulty in persuading the authorities inside the fences of our plight. You engage them, and they are going to either blow you off, or more likely, they will incarcerate you. Then you'll be truly helpless if these things get traction and critical mass. I could use the backup, driving up this road to Winnemucca. Who knows what is lying in wait between here and there? Look what happened at the mine just up the road." Alan paused, his eyes widening. "Now, I tell you what, I'll make you a deal. Come with me so I can make this call, then I'll drive you to Burning Man myself. Or I can take you to Gerlach, where we could talk to a bunch of folk, and I read there's shuttle bus every few hours that would have passengers coming and going from Burning Man."

Bruce responded without hesitation. "Doctor, I happen to know that Gerlach shuttle bus doesn't start service until Wednesday, and you driving us up to the gate won't be any more helpful than Conner and I driving up to the gate. But I think I have a plan that will work for you. We leave those creatures in the trailer like you said..." Conner broke in, but Bruce cut him off. "We pursue a plan B like I said. If you can spare a bullet, and you're as a good a shot with that rifle as you seem to be, you can shoot the lock off my shed behind us here, which will have some things of use to all of us. Conner and I both are runners. We can grab some clothes and extra shoes out of Jason and Dax's bags in the office trailer, and then we will have a much better chance sneaking in the back way on foot. There'd be no way to sneak in by car, anyway. It would be close to sixty miles if we had to double back near Gerlach by car, but on foot, as the crow flies, it would be closer to twenty-five. Now what I'm asking for, Doctor, is you drive us five miles down the road where there's a good cut-off we can take from there. I'm pissed off enough that you're so adamant you can't shoot the three dudes in the trailer, so we could just collect our car keys, but so be it. I sort of halfway understand. But you gotta agree to take ten minutes out of your time and drive us that far. You spent at least that much sleeping on this roof, here. Then we would have a good deal less than a marathon in the afternoon desert sun. So what do you say? You might have it all taken care of by then, Doctor, sir, but just in case, we'll be headed there to find Conner's girlfriend." Conner smiled with approval.

Alan rose up to his feet, clearing his throat. He stepped toward the ladder. "Well, I respectfully disagree, gentleman, but I don't want to waste any more time arguing. If you two want to tilt at windmills, I guess you can be my guest. I'll even shoot this lock off, and I don't like it, but I'll drive you five miles east, but no more, because it's slow going on these roads out here. Now, do you really think you'd have anything useful for me in that shed or in your other trailer? Can you get creative and load me up with some improvised weapons to supplement my rifle here and part with a few water bottles? Then we'll be on our way."

Bruce ascended from his knees to his feet. "We have a deal then, sir." Bruce gazed back towards Jungo road. He shook his head once. "Well, at least I now know."

Alan, who had almost reached the ladder, stopped in his tracks. He cast a perplexed glance back at Conner, who now was also on his feet, stepping towards him. Conner just shrugged. "What do you mean? Know what?" Alan asked, confused.

Bruce emitted a half-sigh. "At least I know where everyone went and why I'm not getting any customers."

Thursday Friday Saturday Sunday Monday Tuesday Wednesday

The Gauntlet

Alan flipped a U-turn, next to the old Union Pacific Railroad tracks, heading back east toward Winnemucca after dropping off his two passengers. Bruce and Conner exited the Escalade; each donning old day packs that had been stored in Bruce's shed. Both packs were filled with water bottles from Bruce's office trailer, along with an extra pair of shoes and socks. The tennis shoes were a particular concern, as they came from Jason and Dax's bags and were not a perfect fit. Alan bid them a quick goodbye, before watching them gradually fade in the rear view mirror as he accelerated away.

Conner and Bruce had argued one last time with Alan about his destination, when selecting provisions from Bruce's shed and office trailer. They pleaded that Empire was about ten miles closer than Winnemucca from Bruce's compound. The point Bruce and Conner didn't emphasize, was that continuing the drive toward Empire and Gerlach would shave off a significant portion of foot travel that awaited them. Alan was adamant that he was heading east. He should be within cell phone range thirty miles before Winnemucca, so he probably would be able to place his calls sooner by traveling in that direction. But more importantly, Winnemucca was where the BLM, the Humboldt County Sheriff's office, and other resources were located. Bruce countered that the Pershing County Sheriff's office in Lovelock had the jurisdiction over Burning Man, so Winnemucca wasn't important as a destination, but Alan's mind was made up.

Jungo Road diverged southeast from the railroad tracks for a dozen miles or so, then headed west from Sulphur. The straight line from Bruce's compound to Black Rock City stayed with the railroad tracks for close to five miles, before the tracks veered south to eventually meet up again with Jungo Road. It was at that point that Gorman dropped Bruce and Conner. Alan drove off-road in both directions, next to the tracks.

Gorman finished the last sip of the Red Bull that Bruce procured for him from his office trailer. Alan had never experienced one before. He whispered to himself that he was not a fan, as he threw the narrow blue and silver can down to the front passenger floorboard.

Alan eyed the provisions strewn in the front passenger seat that his two new friends hastily arranged for him. Two additional water bottles and another can of Red Bull lay underneath a Homelite eighteen-inch gas chainsaw, a thirty-two ounce bottle of Kingsford charcoal lighter fluid, a box of matches, a large cutting knife from Bruce's barbeque kit, a thirty-five inch aluminum baseball bat, a crowbar, and a hammer. Alan shook his head at the scavenger hunt collection in the seat next to him, and hoped the magazine left in his rifle would suffice.

After meeting back up with Jungo Road, Alan struggled with determining the proper speed to maintain. He instinctively kept pushing the envelope with the gas pedal, but was concerned about drawing a flat tire or worse. He impatiently continued the bumpy, jarring ride at a speed that accentuated the gyrations. Alan decided the rough ride was a blessing in disguise, as it seemed to help reduce the drowsiness that might otherwise set in on a smoother road.

Alan scanned his Sirius XM news channels. Political hacks were arguing on top of each other's voices about immigration on CNN. HLN was focused on a breaking story involving a NASCAR driver's motor vehicle accident with a police car in which the driver had an expired driver's license. Fox News featured an author of a new book on the demise of American unions, discussing why the upcoming Labor Day holiday no longer holds meaning. There was no mention of anything happening in northern Nevada on any station.

Alan passed the Hycroft mine entrance again, wary that the zombie people would be waiting for him along the roadside. He saw no sign of them. The road instantly became smoother. Gorman accelerated considerably. He made the turn past the pillared rock formation beyond the mine, as the road veered right. He navigated the twists in the road through the foothills, with the railroad tracks running parallel to his left, and a sagebrush-filled ravine in between. Alan emerged into another valley. According to his calculations, and from what Bruce told him, he should encounter cell phone coverage within another five miles.

The gauntlet of vehicles appeared less than two miles ahead. Alan slowed to a crawl one mile out from the gauntlet, the sun's reflections off the vehicles catching his eye. He stopped his Escalade, placing it in park, wondering what on earth was now placed in his path. Once again, he checked his Blackberry, only to see the familiar symbol for no service. Alan turned around to fish through the car pockets behind the driver's seat until he produced his Bushnell binoculars. He inched forward, one hand on the wheel, the other holding the binocs firmly against his eyes. He studied the distant string of vehicles that lay in the road. He continued advancing cautiously, barely more than idling, for five minutes, stopping when he made it within a half-mile.

There were no obstructions between him and the gauntlet, or on either side. The landscape on both sides of the road was littered with sagebrush, greasewood and rocks. Alan satisfied himself that no zombie creatures could be lying in wait, close to his vehicle.

At the eastern end of the gauntlet, nearest him, Alan noticed a silver pickup crashed into a downed telephone pole, which also caused the next pole to lean substantially toward the road. He couldn't see the actual phone lines from that distance, but it was clear to Gorman, the cause of the loss of landline reception lay directly ahead.

After the pickup and downed telephone pole blocking the road, Alan counted over a dozen other vehicles, including an AT&T service van, an old VW van covered with hand painted murals, a number of SUVs, and several other pickups. Alan couldn't read the letters from such a distance, but the pickup near the end of the line appeared to be a regulatory vehicle. Perhaps it was BLM, he thought. Alan also noticed two motorcycles lying in the road. What he didn't see, was any sign of life, except a single grisly corpse lying behind the bikes.

Alan resolved to steer a wide path around the gauntlet. Using his binoculars, he visualized the route he would take, free of obstructions, keeping a half-mile distance from the collection of recently abandoned vehicles.

Gorman scanned the gauntlet one more time. He thought about Bruce's mention of friends from Winnemucca that Alan had executed, except for one still in Bruce's trailer. Alan imagined this is where they somehow met their fate, then stumbled west, eventually finding Bruce's compound. Alan wondered aloud which rig in the gauntlet was their vehicle.

Alan froze his binoculars on a Jeep Wagoneer not far back in the line. He swore he saw movement inside the vehicle. He studied the Wagoneer for a good minute. He convinced himself there was someone moving around slowly inside, but making no attempt to exit. Alan's first impulse was to gun his Escalade forward to come to the rescue. No sooner had he put the vehicle in drive, than he hesitated and placed the Escalade back into park.

Alan had been wondering why Bruce's Winnemucca friends wouldn't have simply been consumed on the spot, like what happened to what remained of the corpse behind the motorcycles, unless the zombies were too full at the time. Seeing the movement in the Wagoneer, he realized a likely scenario would be a vicious cycle. Someone drives up, to find a person or persons behaving strangely inside a vehicle ahead of them. They open the vehicle to find out what is the matter, only to be attacked and bitten. But the attackers move slowly and the persons are able to escape back to their vehicle. Within a very short period of time after the bites, they become disoriented and aren't able to start their own vehicle, or drop the keys in the confusion. So they lock themselves in, eventually expire from the infection, only to reanimate shortly thereafter, without the mental capacity to know how to exit the car. The attackers, meanwhile, having been freed from their vehicle, probably wander off in the desert.

Alan wondered, with all that vast expanse of desert to choose from, how did Bruce's friends select the direction leading to Bruce's compound? How is that the creatures he found in the two ranch houses managed to find their way to those dwellings? Why did the group he initially spied, before Alan understood the problem, wander directly toward Black Rock City, as opposed to any other direction? Could their transformation have equipped them with any enhanced senses that could guide them towards their prey?

Alan realized he was still exhausted, allowing his thoughts to digress, instead of focusing on the person in the Wagoneer ahead. But he realized there was a method to his taking the time to reason through the scenario that likely caused the gauntlet. Alan assuredly would join in the cycle of victims if he opened the Wagoneer door. The occupant had to have already reanimated into one of those creatures. Alan determined he would leave any investigation of the gauntlet for possible survivors to the authorities after he connected with them. He needed to stay on task and get within cell phone range just a few miles ahead to make his calls.

Alan placed the Escalade back into drive, turning the steering wheel hard right, heading off-road for the detour he mapped out with his binoculars. Out of the corner of his eye he caught an approaching trail of dust due east. Another unsuspecting vehicle was making its way to the far end of the gauntlet.

The Zombie Paradox

Bruce knew the location across the playa of the orange perimeter fencing for Burning Man. He served as navigator, while Conner and he progressed from the last vestiges of vegetated soil out onto the playa. Bruce marveled at how soft the playa surface was, how deep in spots the layer of dusty powder accumulated over the surface.

Bruce stated to Conner that yesterday's dust storm, like the summer's countless preceding ones, were a testament to the condition of this year's playa. He told Conner how he longed for the packed surface bearing an endless jigsaw puzzle of small polygon shaped, parched clay tiles that had lined the landscape just last year – a wetter year.

They had decided not to run in the heat of the Black Rock late afternoon. They needed to make progress, but agreed there was no point going much more than halfway before nightfall, not just because of the desert heat, but more importantly because the BLM would be scanning the nearby playa for those trying to sneak into BM without a ticket, and the cover of darkness would be essential. While the BLM could spot vehicles on the distant playa relatively easily, traveling by foot hopefully would allow them to go undetected even in daylight, until they grew closer.

They periodically ventured into their daypacks for water bottles. The dehydration from the previous night of boozing, combined with the considerable time on the roof, left them both continuously parched.

The first part of their journey passed mostly in silence. Both were shell-shocked by Jason and Dax's deaths, let alone trying to wrap their heads around the carnage that ensued, Bruce's loss of his Winnemucca friends, and the concept that zombies were amongst them.

On top of that, there were the clothes. Bruce and Conner, after spending hours on the rooftop in just boxer shorts, adopted Jason and Dax's garb from their suitcase in the small trailer. They commented early in their journey, how bizarre it felt wearing the smaller-sized tee shirts and baggy gym shorts owned by two friends who passed away in front of them. To add insult to injury, the tennis shoes were starting to cause both Conner and Bruce some discomfort, even though the trek was just in its early stages.

Eventually, conversation emerged. Bruce began second-guessing their decision to sneak into Burning Man by foot. Bruce couldn't shake the whiney-tone out of his voice, making his case while they strode along the playa. "Conner, we should have just propped open my trailer door, and then ran back and waited for those three to come stumbling outside. Even if that doctor didn't want to use his bullets, we could have taken them out in the open, with all the stuff we found in my shed. Then we would have had our car keys. We could have driven to Gerlach, made some anonymous calls, then drove beyond Burning Man, stashed the car and hoofed in the back way."

"Spilled milk, Bruce," Conner simply replied, shielding his eyes from the relentless sun. He did wish he had his sunglasses that were hanging from the rear view mirror of his Toyota 4Runner. He cursed himself for locking his rig in the middle of nowhere. He cursed himself more for not going with the flow of where the day had headed – he wished he had smashed his driver window, in order to procure his shades.

"Spilled milk?" Bruce shot back, gesturing with his hands as he stepped forward rapidly. "All you can say is 'spilled milk' when we're talking about trying to get *your* girlfriend out of harm's way, on the most freakin' weird day the world has ever known? Come on Conner, we gotta re-evaluate our plan, here."

Conner kept silent for half a minute as they advanced. Then he stopped suddenly. Bruce turned around to see that Conner was standing still. Bruce came to a halt as well. "Bruce," Conner replied harshly, "I appreciate you coming with me. I really do. Believe me, I appreciate that this day is the mother of all train wrecks, and we're probably too stressed to comprehend just how surreal it is and bad it could become." Conner rubbed his head, which was once again throbbing. "You know, the day started on a bad footing. We got plastered last night. If I was trying to reboot my life, I think I just left an application running – the drunken app – that won't let the system close and restart. Here I am talking about trying to save Cassie, when I apparently can't even save myself. I must, somewhere deep inside, secretly want to sabotage the best thing in my pitiful life. So, if anything needs to be re-evaluated, it should be me. Why anyone would want to have anything to do with me is beyond me, right now."

Bruce stepped back to Conner, standing side-by-side. He switched his tone to apologetic, "Conner, I'm sorry. I—"

Conner interrupted, while squinting from the oppressive sunlight. "Bruce, maybe it's a leap of faith, but I see the logic in the path this Alan Gorman set us on. There's no point in our making any calls from Gerlach, because Alan Gorman has made those calls by now, and it would seem he's better connected. The more I think about it, the only way we're going to reach Cassie inside Burning Man, is to sneak in at night and find her. At least I know the name of the camp she's staying in. I think we're okay on the plan, Bruce. The plan doesn't need re-evaluation. I do. I'm the biggest screw-up to ever come out of Parker Creek."

"Bigger than me?" Bruce half-laughed. "I doubt that." Bruce playfully punched Conner in the arm. "Come on, Connerman. Let's get to hoofing it again." Bruce turned and resumed a brisk pace. He decided to switch to small talk, to pass the time. "You know, all the years I lived in Parker Creek, I never once visited Mount Lassen National Park even though we were well under an hour's drive away. So now that I've lived in the Black Rock for some time, this is the first occasion I've had to actually set foot all the way across the playa since I've moved here."

"Yeah, but look what it took to get your butt onto the desert floor. A zombie apocalypse," Conner retorted with gallows humor in his voice.

"Zombie apocalypse," Bruce repeated, laughing, but then they both fell silent for almost a minute. "Conner, do you think that's possible?"

"What?"

"A zombie apocalypse? Here? Now?"

"Bruce, I thought you weren't buying into these things being zombies."

Bruce stammered. "I'm not... I mean, I wasn't. But now... I just don't know what to think. I'm just pretty speechless, clueless, whateverless, about the sum of this day. But whatever it is we're talking about, do you think it's contained pretty much to what crossed our path, and the doctor's path, or do you think this is going viral?"

"Viral? That's what Dr. Gorman said, it was viral. Transmitted primarily by biting."

"No," Bruce clarified, "I mean viral more like social media viral. Viral viral. Is this virus thing, whatever it is, going to exponentially go mainstream, to all corners of the globe, or is this just some weird unexplained phenomenon that will never make its way out of the Black Rock?"

Conner's face erupted in a mischievous grin, pursuing more gallows humor. He remembered how much Bruce liked quoting Shakespeare. "Well, that's it. That is the question."

"What?" Bruce grew confused at Conner's expression.

"To z... or not to z..... That is the question."

A tiny whirlwind that had been minding its own business several hundred yards off suddenly decided to pick up steam and sail directly toward Bruce and Conner. Both men stopped in their tracks, trying to decide if and how to sidestep the gathering dusty micro-twister. The whirlwind denied them the opportunity to think through alternatives as it whipped through them. Eerily, it stayed with them, leaving them in the eye of the hurricane even as they decided to advance, for a good thirty seconds or so, before changing direction.

Conner spoke up after the whirlwind wandered away, his voice accelerating with each word. "Actually, I don't know, Bruce. I'm praying this thing is just local. And if it is, and we get to Burning Man and nothing is going on, and everything's fine, Cassie will take me for a hysterical lunatic. We'll probably get busted for sneaking in. She'll really take me for a loser, and then we'll return to your place where the law will find all those bodies and no one will believe us. We'll be accused of being leaders of some Charlie Manson or terrorist desert cult. We'll be on the cover of *People Magazine*, and not in a good way. We'll spend the rest of our lives in prison, where at least the cell phone coverage is probably better than it is here. Oh yeah, and I'm AWOL from a work meeting as of now, and I haven't even started to think about how I'm going to explain that to my boss.... But despite all that, I'm still praying it's local."

Bruce stopped walking and faced Conner. "So you're saying, the only way we come out of this looking good, is if we're on the tip of a zombie apocalypse?"

Conner stepped backwards until he met the stationary Bruce. "Well, I hadn't really thought about it that way, until this epiphany just now... but it would seem to be a distinct possibility. I mean, consider that we've already flown the coop from the scene of a crime. If we've already made it through the brunt of zombie fever here, next thing you know, we'll be in our suit and ties, squirming on the witness stand while the prosecutor grills us, trying to explain why we ran off into the desert without alerting any authorities, after aiding and abetting an alleged mass murderer physician that executed countless people that we mistakenly believed to be, of all things, zombies. You might have moved to Sulphur to get off the grid, but if I—if we—over-reacted somehow to all of this, and there are no more zombie people wandering around in the desert mist, we could be in the headlines, in a bad way, for the next decade or more. We could be this century's Charles Manson and friends."

Bruce tilted his head sideways in thought. He then dropped his worried expression, and became more animated. "Oh, you know, they would find those three guys we left in the trailer, and see what really happened. They'd do tests on all those bodies. They'd see that Jason was cannibalized by all of them. We'd be in the clear, once they did forensics."

Conner half-laughed. "So now you're glad those three things are still in your trailer, breaking all your dishes?" Bruce stammered, unable to produce a clever retort. Conner continued, "Bruce, if this zombie thing already ran its course, and the authorities swoop in on your compound, they're not going to want to buy into any zombie stories, any more than if we claimed Bigfoot took up residence in the Black Rock. They're going to go to extreme lengths to explain it away, and some scapegoats would go a long ways in advancing their version of events. And if I was them, I'd be thinking Bruce and Conner would make excellent scapegoats."

Bruce resumed stepping forward at a slow pace. Conner followed suit. After several moments, Bruce cleared his throat. "So let me get this straight. A few minutes ago you were saying you were gung-ho for this plan to abandon my compound, walk across the desert and sneak into Burning Man, and I was arguing against it. Now you're saying by following through with this plan, we're going to end up the most infamous criminals of the digital age?"

Conner emitted a joyless laugh. "Not quite, Brucemoose. I said we'd go down in infamy if there are no more zombies out there, and I'm praying for no more zombies to be out there. But I don't think my prayers are going to be answered."

Bruce grunted in a resigned tone, nodding his head. "Fine and dandy. So I guess the point is we're walking into a zombie paradox."

Conner slapped his own knee enthusiastically. "Damn straight...a zombie paradox."

The two fell silent again, trudging forward for several minutes without words spoken. Bruce spotted two circling birds a hundred yards ahead. The birds kept repeating a cycle — circling, swooping in for a landing, returning to the air after less than thirty seconds on the ground. Bruce commented that birds were quite a rarity out in the middle of the playa.

As they approached, they could see an object that the birds were obsessed with. It appeared to be a log. After they closed the gap to fifty yards, Bruce noted that the birds were sea gulls, of all things. Another ten yards forward and both Bruce and Conner stopped in their tracks. The gulls were picking at a human carcass that had been ripped to shreds.

After they both gave pause, they spontaneously erupted into a sprint. They hollered at the birds, trying to shoo them away, to no avail. As they came upon the rancid remains of the significantly devoured corpse, it was clear there had been a great struggle. Large strands of torn clothing were strewn everywhere. Contents of a daypack were scattered about, including some sort of journal, colored pencils, a large retro pink iPod, a bikini, several water bottles, smashed granola bars and various wadded up paper and wrappings. There were imprints in the ground everywhere around the body.

Conner paced around the site. He stopped and kneeled five yards from the corpse, calling Bruce over for a look. A dismembered hand with a man's wedding ring lay near other assorted debris. It didn't belong to the nearby corpse. The corpse, with nearly intact feet and facial features, was Caucasian, and assuredly female. The hand, severed at the wrist, was large, undoubtedly male, and black.

Conner wondered out loud where the hand's owner was now. Bruce offered the opinion that he and Conner probably no longer had to worry about being brought to trial or being tagged the Charles Manson family of the digital age. He decided to produce another quotation that Conner wouldn't connect with. "Hell is empty," Bruce exclaimed, "and all the devils are here."

II. Black Rock City

Burning Man Through The Decades

Cassie was barely a teenager when Burning Man was conceived. Her daughter was almost a teenager when Cassie was indoctrinated as a virgin burner. In between that span of time, Burning Man grew up and went viral.

Because Cassie posted about BM so frequently on Facebook, and worked it into at least one conversation every day, she was constantly requested to translate its meaning to her multitude of friends who otherwise considered her 'normal.' Cassie's replies typically went along the lines of "you can't explain Burning Man. You experience it." The Burning Man website states that "trying to explain what Burning Man is to someone who has never been to the event is a bit like trying to explain what a particular color looks like to someone who is blind."

Burning Man was born, not in the Black Rock, but in Baker Beach, San Francisco, in 1986. Founder Larry Harvey, born in 1948 and a San Francisco transplant in 1978, inherited his girlfriend's prior tradition of honoring the summer solstice with a bonfire on the beach, but transformed the small gathering, by building and burning an eight-foot wooden man. Each year, the man, the size of the crowd, and the meaning of the event, grew in size and stature.

In 1990, the annual Baker Beach crowd swelled to almost eight hundred, but Larry Harvey and friends were confronted by the San Francisco police, who had become aware of the event. After initially demanding the crowd disperse due to lack of a permit, it was negotiated that the man could be erected, but not burned. Afterwards, the forty-foot-high man was dismantled and stored in a vacant lot. Through San Francisco Cacophony Society connections, the plan was hatched to take the man to burn in the Black Rock desert during an upcoming Cacophony outing into the desert wilderness. Unfortunately, the vacant lot holding the burning-man-in-waiting was turned into a parking lot before the Cacophony trip, and the man was chain-sawed into moveable pieces. But Larry Harvey's roommate reconstructed the man in time to accompany him on the trip to the desert, and the man transitioned from childhood to adolescence in his new Black Rock home.

Black Rock participants were just 250 in number in 1991 for the now weeklong event leading up to the Labor Day-eve burn, but combusted to 8,000 souls in 1996, the last year the event had no perimeter fence and the first year the man ventured beyond forty feet in height (adding another ten feet to his frame with a pyramid base.) By this point, the event began feeding off of the newly burgeoning Internet and mass media interest. Law enforcement slowly began to take a less confrontational approach to the visitors who were dropping dollars into the local economies.

1996 witnessed a rash of accidents stemming from unrestricted vehicle traffic through the event, causing Burning Man to move from BLM managed land to a private site in 1997. The current pedestrian-bicycle traffic only scheme was introduced, with exceptions for event entrance and exit, and "mutant vehicles" – registered art concept vehicles – limited to five miles per hour. Burning Man moved back to its current BLM Black Rock site with the perimeter fence in 1998 with fifteen thousand participants.

Growth spurts and BLM concerns forced Burning Man – which celebrated participatory freedom from societal encumbrances — to accumulate increasing vestiges of civilization during the annual experiment in temporary community. The BM Department of Public Works and current semi-circular city grid were established. Various safety restrictions were enforced. As the Black Rock City population swelled to twenty-five thousand in 1999; thirty thousand in 2003; forty-seven thousand in 2007 and fifty-two thousand in 2012; so the requisite rules, requirements and infrastructure multiplied with the population. Ticket prices to the event also jumped to support the infrastructure: from $35 in 1996 to $80 in 1998 to $380 in 2013.

The population of Black Rock City is not static, even within each year's event. The legion of weeklong burners is invaded by masses, wanting to party and experience the burn, over just the Labor Day weekend. Starting in 2008, these peak crowds, there to witness the man burn the night before Labor Day, got to witness a structure incinerate that reached one hundred feet in height from ground to top.

Resentments began to sporadically bubble up between experienced burners, the virgins, the growing armies of RV campers, and the weekend party-crowds. Intense squabbles surfaced in 2012 over a change in ticket distribution and pricing policies, which potentially threatened to disenfranchise many long-time burners from obtaining a ticket to attend. The ticket policy returned to first-come, first-served in 2013.

Despite the conflicts, and necessary evolution to facilitate the transition to Burning Man's adulthood, core elements of BM remained remarkably recognizable: the extensive palette of theme camps; the "another-planet vibe" immersed in art – performance, sculpture and everything in between; the mantra of radical self-reliance required for a week of survival in the harsh desert environment; the ability for visitors to gain a sense of community somewhere within the confines of the orange perimeter fence; the ban on overt commercialization; the ethic inherited by most visitors to be good Black Rock citizens, and endeavor to 'leave no trace' upon their exit; and most of all, the almost irresistible gravitational force compelling citizens to experience BM through participation.

Burning Man published this about itself on the home page of its web site: "Black Rock City is a kind of Petri dish. Theme camps cling in fertile clusters to its latticework of streets, artworks tumble out of it, like pollen on the air. These nodes of interaction mutate, grow and reproduce their kind, only to effloresce and spread across five continents."

Little did Cassie and the other tens of thousands of current burners realize, the degree of a metaphor that they were about to embody.

Thursday Friday Saturday Sunday Monday Tuesday Wednesday

The Pre-Party

Cassie had looked forward the past several years, to reuniting with the two young ladies from Redding. In their mid-twenties, the two younger ladies effortlessly took in the chaotic, pulsating din of Burning Man nights, getting by on cat naps throughout the heat of the day. They donned elaborate body paint and exuberantly rode in the annual "Critical Tits" topless ladies bicycle parade.

They became the youngest members of Cassie's camp; everyone drawn to their boundless, reckless enthusiasm for all things Burning Man. Cassie nicknamed the brunette and red-headed duo Thelma and Louise, during their first year in camp. Their playa nicknames stuck, with many in camp not knowing their true identities. The ladies took a shine to their new monikers, donning them as their registered usernames in the eplaya website.

Cassie grew concerned when the two ladies announced in July they had signed on with a private Saturday Night pre-party that a couple of BM men-friends connected them with. The invitation Thelma and Louise forwarded to Cassie billed the event as the "Third Annual Black Rock Blo-Out", with a sub-header "vision quest in the desert." The invite stated that "with law enforcement in Black Rock City seemingly now present in every nook and cranny, the Blo-Out provides a safe alternative, providing a mind-altering experience on private land the night before Burning Man, and even an extended extra night under the desert stars for those not lucky enough to score tickets to the Burn."

The invitation emphasized that you needed to sign up now, with PayPal accepted, as just like Burning Man, attendance was capped at the Blo-Out — "Hurry! Only a limited number of spots are available!" The actual location of the Blo-Out was not to be disclosed until the day before the party, and then by cell phone message.

Cassie counseled her two young friends that this sounded like a scam — they might never get the actual message with the location or see their registration fees again. But the ladies insisted it was legit; the two guys they had hooked up with at last year's Burn had friends that had gone, who were adamant that the pre-party outdid the week in Black Rock City.

Cassie appealed to Thelma and Louise that taking some heavy drugs out in the middle of nowhere, with a bunch of people they either barely knew or had never met before was most unwise, let alone Cassie's position on taking drugs at all. Cassie's two friends confided that they had never done anything more than an occasional joint themselves, but they had recently decided, on a hot summer Saturday Redding afternoon, to assemble their bucket list of one hundred things to do before they died. Doing some real drugs, just once, was number thirty-seven on the list.

Cassie could not persuade them otherwise. Now it was Monday morning in camp; Thelma and Louise were nowhere to be seen, and long overdue. Cassie rode her bike down to the Burning Bell Message Center in Center Camp on the slim chance there was some word from or about her friends there. There was not.

Thursday Friday Saturday Sunday Monday Tuesday Wednesday

Saturday afternoon, Thelma and Louise drove east from Redding on Highway 299 through Alturas, then Cedarville, until the Nevada state line was reached and the pavement ended. They proceeded cautiously, as the road grew rougher through the desert pass, until they turned south on County Road 34. Well before sunset, they spotted the paper plate markers with a big letter B that guided them onto some ranch land near the edge of the playa, a dozen miles north of Black Rock City.

There was no building structure on the acreage bounded by decaying barbed wire fencing. A few cattle converged lazily in the distance near a large gap in the fencing where several of their cowpatriots had wandered beyond them out into the open range.

The two ladies pulled their Subaru to a stop behind the other haphazardly parked collection of cars. A large, big-bellied, mustachioed Hispanic man in a cowboy hat appeared from nowhere, squeezing through a narrow gap of vehicles in front of Thelma and Louise, smiling, bidding them welcome, checking off their names on his clipboard, announcing he would need to collect their car keys until the following morning.

Within five minutes, the two women found their men-friends amongst the fifty-plus partiers already assembled around the large RV, situated beyond the first row of parked vehicles. Like tailgaters who remain in the stadium parking lot after the ball game was underway, a number of the crowd had no tickets to attend Burning Man the following night.

Underneath the RV's extended canopy rested a large speaker column at each end, with a short, pencil-thin Hispanic young man serving as DJ, offering a non-stop selection of techno-pop.

Soon, the music stopped. The mustachioed cowboy grabbed the microphone from the DJ assembly under the canopy, addressing the small crowd that had now grown to the allotted sixty party-goers. The man introduced his DJ son as his co-host. He mentioned another friend would be joining them to serve as caretakers when the crowd embarked on their wild ride. He pointed out the facilities: the sleeping monkeyhuts assembled out of tarps with PVC pipe ribs, behind the RV; the tubs full of water bottles; the tub filled with apples, oranges and granola bars; the two porta potties to his right of the RV. He advised his guests to go heavy on the water provided, but lighter on any alcohol or joints they may have stuffed into their daypacks – the main event would be unveiled after sunset and he promised it would pack a pleasant, potent punch.

As the twilight dwindled, Thelma, Louise, their two men-friends and the rest of the crowd were shepherded some fifty yards out in the field, with the instruction to sit cross-legged in a giant circle, marked by dozens-after-dozens of ninety-seven-cent solar ground lights. The mustachioed cowboy, his DJ son, and a leather-faced silent friend dispersed sheets of blotter paper. The cowboy, shouting so he could be heard, instructed everyone to wait until he finished talking before they partook.

He conveyed they were taking slightly more than 300 micrograms of acid – LSD – then he spelled it out: Lysergic Acid Diethylamide, horribly butchering several of the syllables in their pronunciation. He mentioned the blotter paper might be slightly thicker than they had experienced when embarking on any previous trips. He encouraged all to stay in this designated area, and take in the desert night sky to enhance their experience.

He compared taking an acid trip to going onstage for group hypnosis at a county fair – your experience was going to be a lot more pleasant and memorable if you were positive and open to suggestion. He then led a group countdown for the sheets to be placed under everyone's tongue. Someone shouted far across from Thelma and Louise to "let the Wild Rumpus begin!"

Within a half-hour, the three men had their hands full, trying to keep track of a group of sixty. Last year, their crowd was almost half the size. They realized they were seriously understaffed. But with frantic perseverance, they managed to poke and prod their herd of partiers to stay within manageable confines as the trips accelerated into full swing, a little more than two hours after sunset.

Thelma had heard ahead of time from their men-friends, the drug of choice this year would be LSD. Thelma and her circle of Redding friends could not claim knowing anyone who did anything more potent than a periodic joint or had any street knowledge of the drug world. Thelma had spent the night before Googling LSD and acid. She came to learn that everyone's experience could be unique, and was disappointed that over two hours in, she seemed to be only on the periphery of the new dimension that everyone else, Louise included, seemed to have entered.

The harder Thelma tried to relax, seated under the stars next to Louise, the tenser she seemed to become. Louise, on the other hand, had already made love in public with one of their men-friends, and was now blissfully taking in the endless parade of alien rocket ships above while humming cartoon songs from her childhood, sitting cross legged on top of her abandoned clothes.

Right about then, five shadowy figures came into view of the cowboy. They were wandering into the field through the gap of the fence where the cattle had previously been parked, before the cows settled off to sleep out in the open range, away from all the strange goings-on inside their familiar surroundings.

These five were making loud, unintelligible sounds as they stumbled forward. The cowboy seemed perplexed as to how they had obviously escaped monitoring for some time. His son had walked by just five minutes ago or so, confirming the head count was one hundred percent. The cowboy rose up from his folding captain's chair, calling out to his silent leather-faced friend, who was guiding three giggling men back to the solar-lit circle. His friend quickly joined the cowboy, leaving the gigglers behind. They both quickened their pace out into the field.

The five approaching men were nonresponsive to the cowboy's queries, called out across the distance. In less than half-a-minute, the cowboy and his friend were face-to-face with five wild-looking, dust-covered men who clearly weren't part of their party customers. The cowboy wondered if any of his group had somehow arranged and snuck off to the fences, slipping some of the blotter papers to these men-in-waiting, because they seemed to be on some sort of trip themselves.

The closer the five became, the less the cowboy liked what he saw. The odor surrounding them was putrid. He informed the five men they didn't belong here, they were on private property, and needed to turn around and leave now. Instead, the five continued advancing, reaching out and grabbing at the two. The leather-faced friend pushed back at his closest assailant, a young black man with a shaved head and a gooey mess oozing over the wrist area of his missing right hand. A bearded man, wearing a tattered daypack with hiking boots and khaki shorts stepped behind the cowboy's friend, bear-hugging him as he sunk his teeth into the leather-faced man's neck and then face, while they fell to the ground.

As his friend screamed, the cowboy jumped on top of the bearded man, trying desperately to disentangle the man from his friend. Then, the other four were on top of the cowboy. The cowboy screamed loudly for his son, several times. His friend's external carotid artery had already been severed. Blood was seemingly splattering everywhere. The cowboy's friend gripped tightly at his throat, gasping helplessly, as the bearded man continued biting, gouging, shredding away at the softer parts of his body.

The cowboy could feel teeth sinking into his abdomen and leg. The four men on top of him continued to wrestle for control. He managed to rise to his knees, swinging away at the four men, clubbing at them with his fists. He connected several massive blows to the head of a couple of his assailants, which after brief pause seemed to not have registered.

He then felt hands wrapping around his head, hands grabbing his right arm into submission, sharp teeth sinking into his own neck. He felt a thumb reach into his right eye socket, gouging away until his vision went dark. His upper body collapsed back onto the ground as he softly called out for his son again.

The cowboy's son had been selecting a playlist at the RV, deciding it was time to bring some music back into the party. The DJ sprinted out into the field upon hearing his father's curdled call for help. Wearing an LED head lamp, the young man could see the grisly scene unfolding ahead. He turned around, sprinting back to the RV to find his father's pistol. He scooted past the mostly-seated party-goers, who seemed unaware of what was going down.

Inside the RV, the son hurried to the bedroom safe, installed in the custom closet floor. After a couple of frantic, failed attempts, he opened the small safe, procuring the pistol and magazine sitting on top of a couple of sacks of cash. Arming the pistol, he sprinted back to rescue his father. He found a chilling sight in view of his head lamps as he sprinted forward. Five blood-soaked animal-like men were kneeling over his father and friend, tearing away at their torsos, shoving gobs of flesh and organs into their mouths.

The son stopped at six or seven yards out, steadying his stance. He fired away at the bearded man with the daypack. He missed wide-left; the five men seemed uninterested and continued their bloody feast. The son decided to close his range a few steps. He tried, with no avail to stop his hands from shaking. He squeezed the trigger, this time missing wide-right. Taking two steps closer, he connected on the third shot, hitting the one-handed man with the shaved head square in the right shoulder. He fired again, connecting into the man's abdomen. He fired again, this time hitting the bearded man squarely in the jaw.

The one-handed man and bearded man did not fall over after the direct hits. Instead, he merely got their attention. They both looked up, seemingly annoyed. The one-handed black man rose, then the bearded one, now bearing an unhinged jaw. They stepped over the carcasses they had been feasting on, advancing toward the son.

The sight of two blood-covered, grisly humans with seemingly supernatural bullet-defying powers sent the son into panic. He turned to race back towards the RV. He decided to fire away at his assailants while he retreated. As he clinched his pistol mid stride, he felt a shot go off.

The son dropped to the ground in searing pain, the pistol dropped out of reach as he collapsed. The accidental shot had struck his femoral artery in his right thigh. He clawed at the ground, trying to rise back up, but the pain was all-consuming. Within moments, the one-handed man and bearded man descended upon him.

Thelma heard screams, then the series of shots. Her own trip, while somewhat a disappointment, was finally gaining intensity. Still, she knew that her hearing had not betrayed her. Something was wrong. Thelma rose up. Despite Louise's plea to stay and behold the rocket ship show above, Thelma advanced toward the source of the noise. She stumbled as she attempted to step around her fellow partiers and the solar lights that had somehow grown into neon candles several feet in height. Thelma stopped after progressing past the lights, shaking her head, realizing she was succumbing to visions. She couldn't be sure to trust what was real or imagined.

She could hear the grunting noises in the distance. Thelma stepped gingerly in the darkness, tripping and falling more than once. She was drawn to a flashlight of some type at ground level, shining out further into the field. As Thelma approached, the flashlight allowed the surrounding fuzzy objects to come into focus, she could make out two bloodied men, a black man with a shaved head and a bearded Caucasian man wearing a daypack, kneeling over what was left of the DJ.

The DJ's head lamp shone out towards the field, where she caught a glimpse of three more shadowy figures kneeling over some bodies on the ground. The DJ was torn apart. The two men continued to gouge away at his opened torso, the man with the shaved head only using his one hand to do so.

Thelma tried to scream but couldn't. She tried to move but couldn't. Sleep paralysis dreams from her youth came to mind; she hoped this was just part of her trip and wasn't real. All sense of time slipped away from her. Thelma tried to relate how long she remained in this state, fixated on the bloody ghouls dining in front of her, but could not hazard even a guess.

Suddenly she snapped out of it. Someone bumped into her from behind. Thelma turned to see two men her age, heavily tattooed, wearing only swimming trunks, strolling casually past her toward the solar-lit circle, chatting in high-pitch voices, blissfully unaware of the ghastly scene little more than ten yards away.

Thelma began to back away slowly towards the circle. Doubts surfaced again, as to if the carnage behind her truly existed. As she glanced around the circle, a cavalcade of colors streaked across her field of vision. She sighed, relieved and certain that she had just imagined the horrific cannibalism beyond the circle. Thelma headed back towards Louise, who lay naked in front of her on the desert ground, still gazing upwards into the desert night sky.

But a resonating cry of pain brought Thelma's attention back in the other direction. The two blood-soaked strangers, whom Thelma had just dismissed as imaginary, rose up to wander out towards the crowd. The one-handed man and the bearded man — with open wounds oozing a thick-grayish material instead of normal blood — both grabbed hold of one of the swim-suited tattooed partiers, planting a deep bite into both swim-suited men's arms and chests.

Thelma glanced back towards where she had spied the bloody men before. A human carcass bearing the headlamp remained. The fuzzy outline of bodies further in the distance, at the receiving end of the headlamp's beam remained. The other bloody strangers previously huddled over those bodies, however, were now advancing toward the circle as well.

But the party-goers, for the most part, took the cries of pain and the bloody, biting men as merely an elaborate turn in the path of their trip. One by one, they began to rise up and join the freaky ritual occurring in the center of the circle. The five zombies, satiated with their feasting on the party hosts, instinctively swarmed from one victim to the next. After a simple bite or two, the z's lost the desire to attempt to gouge and devour any flesh, instead moving on to the next available moving body. Many of the party goers began to mildly bite each other as well, assimilating what they assumed to be all part of their hallucinations.

Thelma shook her head, hoping to clear her mind even ever so slightly, as she tried desperately to reach Louise with haste. Unfortunately, her perceived speed was considerably faster than the snail's pace she was actually progressing at. To her benefit, the five zombies were keeping more than busy, as their victims continued to eagerly come to them.

Finally, Thelma reached Louise, still sprawled on the ground, transfixed on the rocket ships in the sky, oblivious to the goings-on around her. Thelma pulled aggressively on Louise's left arm, hurting her a little, lifting her upright. Louise began to voice objections as Thelma began tugging her toward the parked cars. The one-handed man caught up to them, scratching Louise's right arm and planting a painful bite into Louise's right breast. Louise gasped, moaned, but didn't scream. Thelma reflexively stepped forward and pushed the man backwards. He fell over another partier who was sprawled on the ground, transferring his attentions to them.

The bearded man with the shot-apart jaw was close behind. Perhaps aided by adrenaline, Thelma was able to drag Louise along, outpacing the bearded man all the way past the first rows of vehicles, back to their Subaru, which they had left unlocked. Thelma opened the passenger door, shoved Louise inside, slamming the door shut, circling around the front, entering the passenger door just as the bearded man reached the passenger side. He began moaning and beating on the passenger window.

Thelma reached across, locking Louise's door, then remembering she had automatic locks, pressed the button to lock all the doors. She reached around for the car keys, growing frantic with each passing moment as they eluded her.

Louise, who seemed unfazed by the bloody stalker just outside her window, calmly reminded Thelma they had surrendered their keys to the cowboy when they first arrived. Louise informed Thelma, that all of a sudden, she did not feel well at all. The bearded man, with grayish blood dripping down his chin onto his red-blood soaked shirt, still sporting his torn daypack, continued to pound away with the base of his right palm at the passenger window. Suddenly, the black man with the shaved head, appeared at Thelma's driver window, thumping away with the stump of his wrist, seemingly unaware one of his hands was missing.

Thelma grabbed Louise's left hand with her right, silently stared straight forward, intent on not seeing the grotesque men in either window. She tightly squeezed Louise's hand. "Are we getting away, now?" Louise asked in a weak, groggy voice. "It feels like we're moving."

Mapping BRC

The Black Rock City grid has been a constant from year to year, although situated on rotating portions of the designated playa floor. Cassie figured out the lay of the land easily enough, her first day in Burning Man, years ago.

The city is laid out in a circular design within a pentagon-shaped boundary on the playa, with Burning Man at the epicenter. The core, surrounding the Man, is non-residential, housing myriad sculptures and other BM art installations spread generously throughout the center.

Designated "streets," lined by "lampposts," emanate from the Man, marking the axis of the city. These four lanes originating from the center are called the Promenades, and mark the clock-inspired three o'clock, six o'clock and nine o'clock radial "streets." (The promenade opposite six o'clock is not formally named twelve o'clock, as the radial streets don't cover that portion of the clock – that area, and the core combine to form the open playa.)

The open playa creates a playground in which the mutant vehicles, burner bicycles and those hoofing it on foot randomly romp. The traffic inside the open playa makes little effort to stay within the confines of the promenades, electing instead to meander wherever the moment inspires a given direction.

The street grid beyond the core is an intersection of each clock-named radius, with alphabetically named rings growing from the central core. While the core only includes the promenade streets, a full grid starts at the boundary of the central core, with the circular Esplanade. After that, the circular "ring" streets in the camp are named in alphabetical order, like on a cruise ship. Each year these streets bear a different thematic name – in 2011, Anniversary, Birthday, Coming out and Divorce marked the inner rings of the map; in

2012 these inner streets were named Alyssum, Begonia, Columbine and Dandelion and ended with Lilac.

Actually, even these official map naming of the streets matter little, the intersection signs throughout the center provide different names for each circular street at almost every radial, albeit all remain consistent with the first letter of their name. The radial streets are named by every fifteen minutes on the clock: 6:00, 6:15, 6:30 etc.

The alphabetical ringed streets do not go full circle. They stop at 10:00 and 2:00, with the open playa in between. Center Camp, the hub of activity, is a circular plaza situated starting at Esplanade and 6:00, surrounding by a circular drive cutting through the grid entitled "Rod's Road," named after Rod Garrett, who designed the Black Rock City grid, and passed away in 2011. Smaller circular plazas are situated in four other locations.

After taking the BRC exit from County Road 34, coned lanes winding through thick playa dust continue for one and a half miles, to the entrance "gate." On Sunday night and Monday, all lanes often experience gridlock, as each vehicle awaits inspection for stowaways or prohibited items. The queue diminishes as the week goes on.

After finally clearing the gate, each vehicle must drive more than a mile, to reach the greeters who provide the current map and the "what, where, when" program paperback book that details all the repeating and one-time events throughout the week in 160 or so pages. From there, the outer "L" road is another one fifth of a mile away. The traffic coming from the greeters enters BRC at around the 6:00 mark.

After each vehicle finds its way to a desired camp, the vehicles are required to remain parked until exiting BRC. The only means of transportation while encamped is via bicycle, by foot, or by hitching a ride on a mutant vehicle. Most burners bring bicycles to BRC, but a fleet of community bikes are available to anyone for one-way use. The community bikes are painted green, but for some reason are labeled and referred to as the "yellow bikes."

Mutant vehicles are repurposed or custom-created motor vehicles decorated and reshaped to bear no resemblance to a standard vehicle. They are required to travel at a very slow rate of speed, pick up any pedestrian desiring a ride when room is available, and must be registered with the BRC Department of Mutant Vehicles (DMV.)

The entire BRC pentagon occupies around four and half square miles. From the Man at the center, it is about twenty-one hundred feet to the Esplanade, and between seventy-three hundred feet to eight hundred plus feet to the outer pentagon fence points.

Walk-in camping is provided from 5:00 to 2:00 beyond the outer road. No motor vehicle traffic is allowed in this area. The temporary BRC airport is situated further out from 5:00, beyond the walk-in camping. Theme camps, and villages comprising multiple theme camps, are generally located between the Esplanade and G streets, Loud, 'big sound" club camps are generally situated closer to the 10:00 and 2:00 edges. The outer streets, from H on up, generally house the individual campers unaffiliated with a theme camp.

Cassie's theme camp is more unique, situated at the start of the calmer "suburbs", at 7:30 and "I," where the nighttime roar and hubbub from the inner rings tones down to a somewhat more ambient level of noise, although no part of BRC can truly be called quiet, calm or mellow at night.

Monday Morning, Black Rock City

After Cassie left the Burning Bell Message Center in her fruitless quest for word on her missing two younger friends, she wheeled her bike in Center Camp over to the Café. The Café is one of only two types of venues in Black Rock City that accept cash transactions, the other being the ice stores in Center Camp, 9:00 Plaza and 3:00 Plaza.

Cassie made it a point to turn off and leave her iPhone in her glove box upon arrival, not only because the playa dust was not kind to technological devices – but more because she loved being off the grid for a week. Cassie spent most of her stay each year in BRC having no clue what the exact time was or caring for that matter. Based on the sun sitting a quarter of the way up in the sky, she was content to know it was mid-morning.

She had been up late Sunday night, getting their cabin tent situated in camp, unpacking, catching up in conversation with old friends. The previous day's afternoon dust storm was a major topic of conversation. The storm had blasted through the city, wreaking havoc throughout Cassie's camp, while Cassie was still waiting in the comfort of their car to clear the gate.

Cassie had awoken to the surround-sound of sledgehammers pounding rebar stakes in every direction, as late night and morning arrivals set up their tents, monkeyhuts, and various shade-apparatus. Only various playa virgins set up their camp with the little six inch stakes provided with camping tents. Those who knew the uncooperative playa soil, as well as the ferocity of the periodic winds, chose to tie down anything that mattered with rebar stakes, preferably two feet or even more in length.

While individual camps were still being erected throughout BRC and would continue to proliferate throughout the week, the city's infrastructure was up and running from the moment the gates were opened Sunday at six p.m. Those responsible for the large art installations had been toiling away in the playa for some time. Even those setting up theme camps obtained Saturday entry passes. Thus, BRC was good to go when the gate opened for general admission Sunday night.

Cassie strolled through the Café, already crowded to near-capacity. The Café was constructed like a huge, tall, circular desert tent, with lengths of different colored canvas secured to the ceiling radial support beams of pipe, adorned with flowing decorative cloths dangling from the pipe supports. Huge rally flags flew above the center of the roof. Rugs covered almost every square inch of the café floor.

Acro-yoga partners crowded the café center, lifting each other into the air with one limb, stretching, bending, and sometime intertwining with each other. Huge sofas, many red-colored with white hearts, provided audience seating for the small music stage, and the poetry-comedy stage, separated by a display area of framed artwork. On the other side of the tent was the massive café counter, with over a dozen lines queuing up for morning beverages.

Cassie made her way to the back of a line that almost stretched to the central yoga area. She glanced around the tent. A musical act was already into their second number. Cassie marveled at how nice they sounded – an odd collection including a bassoonist, violinist, ukulele-lead singer, drummer and Casio keyboardist. The sofas were filled with an appreciative audience – at least those who were awake. Many who party the night away in BRC find their way to the Café once the sun starts beating down, hoping to steal a nap in the breezy-shaded shelter.

Cassie seemed not to notice the various topless ladies in line. While nudity at Burning Man can be a big topic with those who had never been, nudity seems to just blend into the scenery for those in attendance. Actually, the number of less-than-clothed people was not a significant portion of the population. The women in state of undress were almost without exception just topless. Many of their breasts were adorned with pasties. Men were the true nudists. Cassie found amusement in how much some of these men wanted to be the center of attention. The only ones that bothered her were the ones insisting on riding the community bikes sans underwear or the smirking man she saw earlier that morning wearing an apron with a large hole cut through, complete with a black circular border, so he could display his genitals for all to see. Actually, Cassie was curious if he bothered to put suntan lotion on his dangling apron appendage, or if he would be experiencing a painful sunburn at the end of the day.

Cassie soon found herself near the front of the line, studying the menu board above, which offered hot and iced coffee or tea, lattes, espresso, hot chocolate and lemonade. Her volunteer waiter, greeting her with one arm in a sling, welcomed her to his church of caffeine. After she ordered an iced coffee, he inquired what Cassie's favorite sexual position was, so he could work the answer into the announcement when her order was ready, as opposed to just calling out her name. The young man in front of her didn't come up with a reply; his hot tea was announced as Mr. Boring's when it was ready. Cassie decided spontaneously to state her favorite position was weightless. Her server seemed pleased with the response; a minute later he bellowed that ZeroG's iced coffee was ready.

Cassie slowly angled her way back to the music stage sofas, plopped herself next to a couple in their late sixties, and absorbed the soft, soothing original music. She pulled out the "Burning Man What When Where" paperback program guide from her daypack for amusement while she sipped her drink. She randomly browsed the guide, stopping to read Monday happenings in various theme camps that caught her eye, including: *Belly Dance and Playa Performance –starting at 1:30PM; Quinceanera Party - 5PM (put on a frilly dress & celebrate your inner 15 year old. Unleash your desert princess & inner playa queen); Eyebrow Dancing and Other Offbeat Human Tricks - 6PM; 80's Metal Big Hairball - 8PM; White*

*Russians & The Dude: The Big Lebowski Party - 8:30PM; and
Fire Baseball - 9PM (Baseball is so much more exciting with
fire! We have mitts and leather gloves, but bring your own if
you can, and wear fire-safe clothing!)*

After ten minutes or so, she finished her drink, rising to
head to the one of the elevated receptacles with four rebar
stakes above a drainage cylinder, where you could spear your
paper cup onto one of the rebar rods for later collection. While
everyone had to take out their own trash from Black Rock City,
with zero garbage cans provided, an exception was made in the
Café for disposal of the paper café cups.

Cassie exited the Café tent, searching for her bike in the sea
of bicycles parked in the wooden bike rack stalls outside. She
located the beat-up beach cruiser another camp mate brought
every year for her, plus another for her friend. She smiled at
how perfect everything looked in every direction, wheeled her
purple bike out of the stall, and headed out past the Esplanade,
to check out what art was on the open playa this year.

Cassie wasn't disappointed during her hour-long solo
bicycle stroll to take in the 240-plus art installations. Some of
her favorite items had returned, and a number of clever new
creations lay in wait. She enjoyed riding up to the shipwreck,
and checking out the man's head and arm protruding out of
the playa floor, his hand holding a large sculptured fish. This
year, the 3-D block lettering spelled out "F-A-T-E;" the past
years displayed "E-G-O" and "L-O-V-E." In a semi-enclosed
exhibit, she turned a crank to activate an apparatus that
displayed an act of kindness she must perform for a stranger
next to her. She was instructed to share a treasured treat.
Cassie pulled off her small sports-daypack, grabbing a bag of
Mini-Oreo cookies that were nestled in between her water
bottles and sunscreen lotion, and presented them to the
Australian couple next to her.

Cassie's journey took her to the Man in the epicenter, where
she entered the pedestal, climbing the three flights of stairs to
take in the view of BRC. She rode from there out to the

Temple, where a large group was meditating intensely, it appeared. The pagoda-style temple structure was intricate and impressive. Most of her friends enjoyed the Temple burn on the last Sunday night much more than the Man burn on Saturday the night before.

Many of the mutant vehicles seemed to be out, randomly testing their playa-legs. Cassie made way, as she rode along, for motorized chattering teeth, a sofa-mobile, a recliner-chair scooter, several pirate ships with awesome sound systems, an aardvark, an anteater, several dragons, a traveling tiki bar, a mechanical octopus, and some seriously tricked-out double-decker buses.

Cassie grinned as a large group strolled past her, all caked in a fine layer of playa dust. Everything around her, it seemed, was given a nice gentle dusting – people, camps, vehicles, gadgets, bicycles, packs – nothing was immune to what was referred to as playafication or being playafied.

Cassie decided it was time to head back to camp to check in with her tent mate. She smiled as she negotiated her purple cruiser back around a rather large puddle of dust, wishing Conner was there to experience Burning Man for the first time. She wiped her face, now bearing a foundation layer of playa dust, wondering what Conner was doing right at that moment.

At the Gauntlet's Gate

Alan Gorman gunned his Escalade off-road, wide-right of the gauntlet, closer than he had originally planned. A sizeable trail of dust followed in his wake. He began honking his horn as he drew even with the first vehicle – a wrecked pickup accompanying the telephone pole in the road. Alan wanted to draw the attention of the driver of the white pickup truck, who was slowing to a stop at the other end of the gauntlet.

The honking either was to no avail, or drew the driver outside. Gorman witnessed the young man, clad in a BLM silver-tan shirt and chocolate-brown cargo shorts, exit the vehicle, and stand momentarily with his hands on his hips. He stared intently at Alan, as Gorman sped toward him. The man turned abruptly as something caught his attention in the two-tone Jeep Wagoneer, a couple of cars ahead. The young man trotted towards the Jeep, while Alan continued honking as he pulled up opposite the BLM pickup.

Alan opened his door as he screeched to a halt, yelling "Wait!" as loud as his voice would allow. The shout was all for naught. The young man reached the Jeep and opened the driver door. Alan grabbed his loaded rifle from the passenger seat, bolting out of the Escalade into the gauntlet.

The young BLM employee retreated from the Jeep, shouting expletives, leaving the driver door open. He stumbled backwards, as he reached for his satellite phone from its holster. He awkwardly fumbled with the phone buttons, while backing away, so he could keep an eye on the horrid thing emerging from the vehicle.

BLM man came crashing to the ground as a hand reached out from underneath the second vehicle in line, a black 1980's Dodge D-50 mini-pickup. The hand firmly grasped his ankle,

143

causing him to immediately lose his balance, landing on his back. BLM Man's phone went flying in the other direction, towards the Jeep, as he hit the ground.

Alan Gorman raised his rifle, standing just three meters behind the Dodge D-50, ready to dispatch the tall-blonde-female-bikini-clad-zombie, bounding out of the Jeep. She stared blankly at Alan and the freshly-fallen BLM man, tilting her head while she moaned in a deep voice. Several open-gray sores dotted her face, rib cage and abdomen.

Alan hesitated, as he saw not one, but two different sets of arms emerging from underneath the Dodge D-50. He could hear the grunting sounds as they scooted out from underneath the pickup. Looking ahead, he could see yet another one crawling out from underneath the Jeep. It occurred to Gorman that evidently these zombies must prefer the shade to the hot sun when they were resting.

Alan lacked the time to get off a shot. He raced forward to grab at the young BLM man's arms and pull him up to safety, in a tug-of-war with the zombies lying on their stomachs, still half underneath the D-50, yanking at his feet.

Just as BLM man kicked free, Alan looked back, hearing grunting noises behind them. Yet another two zombies – where did they come from? – were now in between Alan and their vehicles. Gorman had lain his rifle down momentarily to pull BLM man free. The two zombies were now just three meters away, with the rifle closer to them than to Gorman.

Alan sized up the situation as the zombies closed in from all sides. "Come on," he barked at BLM man, yanking him back towards the D-50 with the two zombies still half-underneath. Alan pulled on the driver door, which fortuitously opened. He pushed BLM man into the cab, before hopping into the driver's seat. He locked the door, ensuring BLM man did the same.

Alan gambled that the car keys would be in the ignition, or at least be lying in plain sight. He looked outside at the now-five upright zombies surrounding the black mini-pickup. He spied the BLM sat phone prominently positioned ahead in the road; he turned to spot the rifle patiently waiting for him on the ground in the other direction. What Alan did not see, was the D-50 truck keys.

Alan Gorman wondered out loud to BLM man, how many more zombies were napping away the late afternoon underneath the vehicles. BLM man, severely freaked-out, demanded to know what was going down. Alan did his best to share a two minute drill of the past two days, while he scoured the cab for car keys.

BLM man wasn't entirely satisfied by Alan's story. He wasn't sure about Gorman's sanity, or if perhaps he was safer on the other side of the truck door. But the snarling faces in the windows, particularly the grotesquely disfigured bikini-clad blonde, kept BLM man inside the pickup.

He shared with Alan that he was a Range Technician. His day had been slated for monthly report preparation, but a BLM volunteer, last reported en route to the Hycroft mine that morning, disappeared and was unresponsive to sat calls. More troubling, Hycroft Mine had not returned numerous calls made to see if they had contact with the volunteer. The Range Tech, typically a desk jockey, had been tasked with riding out to Jungo Road as far as the Hycroft mine to check things out.

Alan asked sarcastically if the Range Tech saw the volunteer amongst their new friends surrounding the D-50. Then, Alan did a double-take at one of the zombie-men peering in, pressing his mouth and gray tongue against the Range Tech's passenger window.

"No way," Alan blurted out loud, in disbelief. He stared intently at the zombie man cycling through a ritual of banging his head against the window, pausing, pressing his open mouth into the window, stepping back to let out a long, pitiful moan, and repeat.

Alan had met this man on several occasions in years past, and remembered him well. Gorman harbored no doubt it was his friend from the American Meteor Society, for whom Alan had set out on his quest two days prior.

Patrolling the Playa

The conversation turned to women. Conner's ill-fitting shoes were starting to blister his feet, so he welcomed the distraction while they plodded along in the playa late afternoon sun.

Conner brought up a memory from Parker Creek, when he was a high school freshman. "So, Cassie wanted to ride ten speeds all the way to Lake Almanor this one Saturday in May. She had this friend from back in Orange County staying over for the weekend, coming along too. Cassie was lecturing me on the phone before we met up, instructing me to be nice and make lots of conversation with her friend, so she didn't feel like a third wheel. So I did. Her friend was cute, as I recall. Real cute, and a flirt, too. So we're chatting it up about everything — I'm trying to sound more sophisticated than a kid from Parker Creek – we're offering up opinions on Tiananmen Square, Salman Rushdie's *Satanic Verses* and who knows what else. I look behind and Cassie had fallen a good quarter mile behind us while we were climbing a grade as we neared the lake. We waited for her to catch up, and she wouldn't speak to me for the rest of the way there." Conner paused to chuckle. "So this weekend, I'm asking her about her bicycle situation for Burning Man, because I know she rides a bike there all week, but I didn't know how she was getting one there. She explains someone in her camp brings one for her, and then we start talking about bicycles and the next thing you know she's bringing up that Lake Almanor trip, and I can tell she's still mad about it decades later."

"Do you think Cassie remembers me? After all, she left right before I entered high school... I bet she doesn't remember me at all," Bruce announced loudly, answering his own question.

"Actually, we talked about you several times this weekend. She remembers you, Brucemoose," Conner reassured Bruce. "She says she's not sure why you stuck out in her mind, when she's forgotten half the population of Parker Creek, but she said always knew you would do something big in your life."

"Do something big..." Bruce repeated, kicking the playa surface as he spoke, creating a small trail of dust behind them. "Yeah, I did something big alright. I fleeced all my friends and relatives out of all their money." Bruce wiped the sweat off his face, stopping as he turned to Conner. "Now, I thought you and I, we were like...two peas in a pod from Parker Creek, having it all and losing it all." Bruce paused, licking his chapped lips. "But that's not it. I didn't really lose anything, not that matters anyway, and you lost everything. And yet, here you are, back with the woman you were meant to be with, you've just rebuilt your life and you're throwing it aside just trying to make sure she's safe." Bruce paused again, scanning the playa around them. "Now what's wrong with me that I can't connect with someone, find a woman in my life that makes me want to march across the desert for her?"

Conner felt the moment needed a little deflation. "Well, buddy, you're marching across it for me, aren't you?" Conner started walking again, and nudged at Bruce to do the same.

Bruce emitted a semi-chuckle. "I guess you're right. Although it's pretty pathetic." Bruce halted again.

Conner sighed. "What?"

"Well, that my best remaining friend in the universe right now is a buddy that I didn't keep in touch with or ever know that well over the years.... And I never had a woman that I wanted to be with the rest of my life because I'm some kind of timid idiot. The woman I thought would be the one...in India...I turned and ran at the first sign of any fight from her father. I'm nothing like you, Conner."

Conner again started slowly moving forward, patting Bruce on the shoulder to prod him along. "Bruce, don't kid yourself. You don't want to be like me. I turned and ran on a ten-year drunk when my world turned upside down. And then I find Cassie again, and I probably pissed that away in a pool of Jägermeister last night, so don't go trying to play a game of 'top me,' because I'll win. Nothing you can come up with about any women woes is going to top a ten-year drunk, and then falling off the wagon after just getting on it."

"Aww, crap, fine. We're both losers, then." Bruce laughed nervously, resorting again to gallows humor as a distraction while stepping up his pace. "But, then again, having nothing, nothing can he lose."

"What?"

"Oh, just a quotation for us losers. We are losers, aren't we Conner?"

"Losers? Hells yes." Conner paused, before hollering out into the empty desert at the top of his voice, "We are losers from Parker Creek!"

"Now, I don't suppose I'm going to meet any women wandering around out here with you, loser?"

Before Conner could respond, their conversation was cut short by the sound of helicopter blades above, coming from the northeast. Bruce and Conner both craned their necks, watching the chopper sail on past them.

Conner tried to make light of the situation. "You never know, Brucemoose. Maybe she was up there in that copter."

Bruce stopped again. His tone changed. "Conner, this isn't good....Chances are we've been spotted."

The two further hastened their pace. Conner spoke up. "So, what happens now?" Conner's answer soon appeared before them. In the distance they both saw a trail of dust approaching, led by a white pickup.

Bruce turned to Conner. "Okay, so let's just follow their lead. If they bring up anything to do with these zombie creatures, we can spill the beans, because they won't think we're crazy. But if they don't say a word about it, then neither should we. Agreed?"

Conner nodded his head. "I'm fine with that."

Within a minute, the white BLM Ranger Dodge Ram pickup was upon them. The ranger pulled in front of them, as to cut off their intended route. Conner and Bruce stopped. They watched the no-nonsense ranger step out of the pickup; speak a few words into his hand held radio, sizing up the two of them as he slowly made his way over. The ranger, probably in his thirties, was wearing brown BDU pants, a khaki short-sleeved shirt, sunglasses, and sported a flat top brown haircut accompanied by a neatly-trimmed moustache.

"Gentleman..." the ranger began, standing five feet in front of them, "identification, please?"

Conner and Bruce exchanged glances. Bruce spoke up. "Sir, we didn't bring anything with us. I live on the other side of the playa, in the Sulphur area, and my friend here is visiting me."

The ranger studied them silently for a moment. "Names, please." They provided their names, which the ranger then relayed over his radio. The ranger then asked the question suggested by his superior, relayed in by the dispatcher. "So where do you live, exactly?"

"The old Hanford family trust. I get BLM visits there from time to time. I have a double wide and single wide on the property; their old ranch house is still standing, although someday it's probably going to have to come down."

The ranger repeated this information over the radio. He paused, listened intently to his superior, responding with one-word answers occasionally, before finally putting the radio in a holster on his belt. "So what brings you out here today, gentleman?"

Bruce attempted to pry more out of the ranger, before divulging further information. "Is there a problem, officer? Is there anything going on out here?"

The ranger cracked a small smile. "Well, yeah. Burning Man. And we've got more than the usual nonsense to tend to right now. You should know, living out here, we have to keep a safe zone for quite a radius. And you gentleman, are strolling, it would seem with no purpose, inside my radius."

Bruce assumed they had not encountered anything zombie-like, or the ranger wouldn't be talking about just Burning Man. "Well, the truth is sir, my friend has never been out here on the playa flats, and we were just hiking for the exercise until dusk, and then turning around."

The ranger turned to Conner. "Is that so, Mr..." the Ranger paused to recall Conner's last name, "...Zimmerman, are you just hiking through this god-forsaken dusty playa, in those clothes, to get some exercise?"

Conner smiled as reassuringly as he could. "Sir, we didn't really have anything appropriate for the hike to wear, so we just threw together what we could."

The ranger stood silently, staring at the two men. Bruce remembered the adage he learned years ago from a sales manager at Gallo, that when you're looking to close a sale or get the information you want, create an uncomfortable silence, and whoever speaks next loses. Bruce bit his lip slightly, hoping that Conner was still plugged into following his lead.

Thirty seconds or so went by without a sound. The ranger finally spoke up. "Well, I'm going to have to ask you now to both to get in the pickup with me. So, let's get you secured, and then we can move on."

Z Migration

They were all heading south. The first group from the previous Thursday night at ground zero made their way to Jungo Road gauntlet, east of Sulphur. There, they increased in number – some staying – some wandering west to the Hycroft mine and Bruce's compound. The next two groups from ground zero worked their way down Jackson Ranch Road, picking off a few hikers, tourists and ranch hands on the way, before settling in at the two ranches nestled on the east side of the road, where Alan Gorman found them. As their numbers grew, some wandered off, following the southeastern foothills beyond the edge of the playa, making their way toward Black Rock City. A couple of more groups, having stumbled across ground zero after Alan Gorman's visit, also followed the southeast path skirting the edge of the playa.

Their enhanced sense of smell and hearing helped pull them southward; ambient sound and light in the distance, helicopters, the occasional train on the Union Pacific tracks. Randomly, others in a group would follow someone rising up to wander out in pursuit of a sound, light or smell, and the small herds would gather and continue on their way.

An initial feeding frenzy might develop when a normal person was stumbled upon, but often the groups' appetites would subside enough so that instinctive biting, of anyone within reach, would suffice and occupy their waking moments. Catatonic-like naps for extended periods of time helped fill their daily calendar. With each passing day in the hot desert sun, lacking proper hydration, their energy was slowly being sapped – their naps typically grew longer and more frequent. Along with their lethargy, their appetites were somewhat diminished, many seemed happy to take a bite or two out of someone instead of devouring them from limb to limb.

Of the original Jungo Road group and their progeny, a formidable number remained at the gauntlet. Of those who broke off from the gauntlet on Sunday to head further west down Jungo Road, a small portion remained at the Hycroft Mine, including the remaining skeleton crew they overran. Of the contingent that continued past the mine, most perished at Bruce's compound at the other end of Alan Gorman's pistol. Three remained in Bruce's double wide trailer, spending their time bobbing their heads in the two toilets, stumbling around walking into windows, breaking most every knick-knack left on display, and parking themselves on the sofas, beds or floors to nap, usually in front of the television, which was still being broadcast into Bruce's living room.

Alan Gorman had noticed a half dozen or so persons traversing the playa after entering the Black Rock desert early Saturday afternoon. Their actual number was five, and he was unaware at the time that they were zombies.

Saturday morning, two z's encountered a couple hiking by themselves westward across the playa. The unsuspecting couple spotted the two z's behind them, staggering in the desert heat. The couple backtracked until they reached the two, worried there was something wrong with them, only to be mauled and bitten immediately upon their encounter. The couple both broke free, running westward together. Within a minute, the virus took hold, their speed gradually slowed to a standing crawl. The couple became disoriented. The zombies behind them were relentless in their staggering pursuit. The scene played out as a slow motion chase.

Finally, the slender young lady in the pink Tek tank top and tight blue shorts collapsed on the ground, her husband stopped behind her, trying in vain, to lift her upright once again. Exhausted, he too collapsed. Minutes later, the zombies were upon them. She struggled, trying to crawl away as they grabbed at her, ripping her clothes, pulling her daypack off in the process; her prized possessions scattering with the desert wind. Her husband valiantly fought to come to the rescue, crawling to push them off of her. They devoured her in short order, pushing him aside with each futile attempt to stop them. Finally, the two blood soaked zombies were satiated, even though they had not completely consumed her.

They turned their attention to her sobbing black husband with the shaved head, who was attempting to scream, but his voice was too hoarse and weak to emit little more than a whisper of a wail. They worked and gnawed at his hand, finally severing it. The husband passed out, never to regain consciousness as a normal human again. His blood loss helped accelerate his decline. The two zombies sat near the fallen couple in the playa dust and power napped. Not long after they finally rose up again, to trek further westward, the now one-handed husband expired and reanimated. He eventually noticed the remains of his once-wife, nibbling away where he could. He soon sensed the two zombies in the distance. He abandoned the partial corpse beside him, setting himself in motion to follow after them.

Eventually they met up. Hours later this trio encountered two more zombie-friends. By late evening, the pack of five encountered the Burning Man LSD pre-party at the edge of the playa north of Black Rock City. After over-running and feasting on the three chaperones, the zombie-five made quick work of infecting the sixty hallucinating party-goers. Evidently, the higher concentrations of hallucinogenic drugs in the bloodstream sped up the timeframe for an infected person to perish, and then reboot. An entire zombie herd was produced in record time. Only two of the entire wacked-out party managed to avoid infection. A young man had entered one of the two porta-potties to pee, early in the ensuing chaos. He was too far gone to figure out how to open the porta-potty door after locking it upon entry. He spent the next number of hours sitting on the toilet seat talking to the not-too-real firemen he imagined outside the unit, there to rescue him.

The other uninfected partier was Cassie's friend — nicknamed Thelma — from Redding, trapped inside her

Subaru with her bitten friend. She remained frozen in the driver's seat, still feeling the effects of her own subdued trip, for some time while the one-handed zombie and another z pounded incessantly on the windows. They eventually became distracted, vacating to pursue other tripped-out members of the party.

Shortly thereafter, Thelma tried to coax her friend into leaving the keyless vehicle and flee the area on foot. Her friend – nicknamed Louise — by this point bore the ravages of the virus accelerated by the impact of her acid trip. Louise slipped into unconsciousness. Thelma stayed, trying to wake Louise with bottled water, screaming, tapping, even shaking. Finally, unsure if Louise was even still bearing a pulse, Thelma decided to risk sprinting to the RV to search for her or anyone else's car keys.

Thelma's plan went well enough after exiting the Subaru, until she reached the RV to find the entrance blocked by one of the zombies sitting on the steps in a trance. A couple of the party crowd staggered in front of him, already zombiefied. These two took after Thelma, moaning wildly in pursuit. She could hear someone talking loudly from one of the two blue porta-potties. Panicked, as the two zombies were almost upon her, she bolted for the outhouses, opening the door to the unoccupied one, and locked it from the inside.

The two new zombies started pounding on Thelma's porta-potty. The commotion eventually drew the first five zombies over to check things out. The young man hollered from his porta-potty, trying to engage whoever was producing the racket outside. This caused the zombies to bash and shake his stall as well. Soon enough, they managed to tip both outhouses over. Thelma's porta-potty landed with the door on the ground, trapping her safely inside, to contend with the spilled sewage seeping everywhere. The young man wasn't as fortunate; his landed, sideways, the door facing westward. The door opened upon impact. He crawled out to be greeted in a rugby scrum of seven zombies.

The zombies' motor skills were discombobulated by the LSD still in the bloodstreams of their victims, as they bit their way through the stoned-out party-goers. One-by-one, they fell into zombie-trance naps. Hours later, the Sunday morning sun rose fully in the sky. The entire party, save Thelma trapped in the porta-potty, was zombie-ready.

Sixty-plus z-partiers wandered aimlessly through the encampment, including Louise; her Subaru door had been left open. A helicopter in the distance soon attracted several to walk in that direction. A chain reaction ensued; the herd headed southward, concealed in the foothills, their path inevitably leading toward Black Rock City. Their route was circuitous, like the cartoon path taken so often by the boy in the Family Circus comics. But over the course of the next day, the path veered nearer and nearer to BRC.

They were not alone. Behind the party zombies were additional victims from ground zero after Alan Gorman's visit, along with those not put down when Gorman raided the second ranch home. In front of the party zombies were previous ground zero groups and their progeny, who never stopped with the others at the ranch houses.

These lead zombies focused on heading southbound, working their way through the edges of the western foothills more rapidly than their trailing party zombie friends. They passed near the pre-party site before it was rocking. The same Sunday afternoon dust storm that hit Jungo Road, making such an impression on Bruce and Conner, first struck the northwestern end of the playa with a vengeance.

This smaller group of lead zombies was undeterred by a little dust or a lot of dust. With the cover of the dust storm whiteout, they headed out into the playa, arriving at the doorstep of Black Rock City.

Thursday Friday Saturday Sunday Monday Tuesday Wednesday

The Trojan Horse

The giant sundial was the last art project to be installed on the outer open playa. The original sundial sculpture had been damaged in transit; the replacement pieces hastily re-constructed back in San Francisco, just arrived early Sunday afternoon, hours before the public opening of the Burning Man gates.

The sundial sculpture pieces were delivered in a white, Ford F-650 Cargo Box Truck, which parked just outside the northern BRC orange perimeter three-foot-high fencing. Only mutant vehicles were allowed on the open playa at this point, but the sundial was to be situated just inside the fence, so they could be delivered easily from the outside. It helped that the sculpture pieces were light and easy for two people to move around and situate.

After the sundial placement was completed, the truck driver walked westward to talk with the project group buttoning down their small faux theatre, also near the perimeter fence. The driver's companion climbed the small stepladder used to navigate over the perimeter fence and headed back to the Cargo Box Truck to close the cargo doors. He planned to hop back over the fence and catch a ride into the city on the next mutant vehicle to buzz the far reaches of the playa, as the vehicles were all stretching their legs on their initial voyages.

The Cargo Box Truck had an overhead rolling cargo door that had been customized with an overhead garage door opener unit. It could be automatically opened or closed with the remote opener, which the helper held in his hand, or with a switch from inside the cargo bay. As the driver's companion neared the truck, he caught sight of a wall of dust rapidly approaching. He spontaneously decided to jog to the truck in order to hop up in to the cargo bay and wait out the dust storm from there.

The dust storm arrived with a fury. His last several steps toward the truck were made in whiteout conditions. He pulled down the retractable ladder to step up into the bay, making his way to the refuge. He headed to the back of the cargo bay, debating if he should pull out the remote from his cargo shorts pocket and close himself inside until the storm past or just leave the door open, since not that much dust was working its way inside the bay given the angle the truck was parked at.

The lead zombies in the coming zombie migration stumbled along in the dust storm whiteout, riding it out like body-surfers on the beach. They walked right into the side of the Cargo Box Truck. They felt their way to the back, where they smelled the driver's companion up in the bay. The six zombies bounded up the truck step ladder one-by-one.

The confused companion didn't know what to make of the crowd joining him inside the truck. He assumed they too were seeking shelter. He found out differently as they approached him; hideous smells wafting throughout the truck, their skin a strange pale-almost gray pigment, several of them adorned with grotesque gray gashes and lacerations.

The six zombies had been traversing just beyond the edge of the playa for some time. They were dehydrated, even for zombies. The hot sun beating on them also zapped some of their energy and altered their appetite. In their weakened state, the best they could do was pile on top of the driver's companion, gouging a number of deep bites, sucking and licking away the blood for moisture as well as sustenance. They lacked the will or energy to rip the man to shreds. As they groped him, the remote was inadvertently pressed; the cargo overhead door dutifully shut, the companion's screams muffled by the shut cargo door and the howling dust storm wind.

Fifteen minutes later, the storm dissipated. The driver, who had been taking shelter at the faux theater, headed out to the truck. From a distance, he could see the cargo door had been closed, but could not spot his companion anywhere as he scanned the open playa inside the fence. The driver assumed his companion already caught a ride with a passing mutant vehicle.

The driver found the fence stepladder left for him, traversed the fence, and then took the stepladder with him back to the cargo door. He cursed as the remote control for the door wasn't left on the tailgate as agreed upon, and the retractable cargo ladder was left out. He pulled up and pushed the ladder back into its storage slot. He toted the stepladder up into the cab. He shook his head, thinking he had heard grunting sounds from somewhere, but decided he was just hearing things.

The driver started up the truck, wheeling it back around the perimeter of the fence, to reenter through the staff entrance, so he could park the rig in the designated truck parking area inside the perimeter. With his iPod cranked up through the auxiliary jack of the truck's CD player, he was oblivious to the bodies being thrashed against the cargo walls with each turn as he maneuvered his Trojan Horse inside Black Rock City.

The First Kiss

The evyening started and ended unexpectedly. Conner piled into someone's older brother's decade-old Honda Accord, six of them crammed  into the vehicle with only five seat belts. The passengers were on Parker Creek's junior varsity track squad, having concluded the opening home meet of the season just hours before. Now, they were scurrying to the town's lone cinema, not even aware or caring what movie was playing that Friday night.

In the lobby, arming themselves with popcorn, Milk-Duds, Good 'N Plenty, and sodas, they bumped into a female contingent of the J.V. track team filing through the door. Minutes later, they were all seated together in the upper balcony of the old movie house. Cassie found herself next to Conner at the end of the row, next to the wall. They paid little attention to a forgettable movie. They whispered commentary to each other – one-liners making fun of the dialogue or adults they spotted in the rows below. They poked at each other, shared a bag of popcorn, and as the movie progressed, found their legs and feet intertwined under the seats.

The movie finally concluded to the credits, the lights came up, adults made their way back out the lobby – a number of older ladies giving disapproving glances at the un-chaperoned, giggling pack of freshmen still seated in the upper seats. Finally, the small herd filed outside, finished with grazing their popcorn and candy.

As the crowd headed east down Parker Creek's Main Street, Cassie stopped, pulling on Conner's arm, so that the two of them fell behind the others. She informed him she would need to call her mom at some point soon to get a ride back to her grandmother's ranch outside town – and suggested they might take a stroll until then.

Cassie's braces were invisible to Conner. Her pink shirt emblazoned with "Parker Creek" in block letters on the front and "Track Diva" on the back also went unnoticed. He was intoxicated with the light perfume fragrance he had never noticed before. He was spellbound by her hazel, intense eyes, her dreamy laugh and the subtle freckles that outlined her face.

Conner had been smitten with Cassie since first spending appreciable time with her in class the previous year in junior high. He was far too tongue-tied and uncourageous to ever ask her out. Now they were slowly ambling down Third Street, the rest of their assemblage still parading noisily down Main Street, blocks away. Conner made small talk about how cold it still was outside and no one seemed to have received the memo that spring had arrived. Cassie slipped her right hand into Conner's left as they slowly advanced. He struggled to find any intelligible words to fit the moment.

Finally, after silently progressing a block, hand-in-hand, Conner suggested she could call her mom from his house, and maybe they could sit out in his parent's car for a few minutes to get out of the cold air before going inside to make the call. Conner felt confident his parents would be lying in bed — reading the morning's *Sacramento Bee*, and *San Francisco Chronicle* – and be oblivious to Conner's stealth mission into their unlocked Chrysler Le Baron parked outside the house.

To Conner's shock, Cassie tilted her head back, laughed lightly, exclaiming that she would like very much to see the inside of his parent's car.

Soon they were in the back, stretched across the bench seat, laying almost side-by-side, self-discovering what French-kissing was all about. Time seemed to stand still. The windows began to fog. Conner kept trying to find new places to set his hands, only to have them repositioned by Cassie back around her waist.

Both gasped and froze when they heard Conner's squeaky front gate creak open and creak shut. She had been at Conner's home enough on school day afternoons, to recognize the sound instantly. Conner's dad was whistling loudly just outside the car.

Conner put his fingers to his lips; he then pointed down and rolled to the floorboards. Cassie angled herself uncomfortably on top of Conner, her head level with the base of the rear bench seat. They could hear the jingling of keys. The driver door opened, Conner's father started up the Le Baron, still whistling as he turned the defroster up full blast and fiddled with the radio dial. He turned the vehicle around, heading for Main Street. Conner's mother had complained of a terrible headache, with no aspirin to be found and Conner's dad was now on a mission to the Shell Station Mini-Mart at the end of Main, unaware of his two stowaways.

Conner and Cassie traded smiles, their faces separated by less than two inches. Cassie boldly planted another long kiss on Conner's lips, fighting the urge to laugh as Conner's dad whistled along to the radio, which was blaring much louder than when Conner's mom accompanied her husband.

Thursday Friday Saturday Sunday Monday Tuesday Wednesday

Monday Afternoon, Black Rock City

Cassie and Tess dusted off Space Ghost as best they could, but remnants of playa remained in his hood and cape. Cassie's good friend Tess had heard so much about Conner during the past twenty-four hours, she renamed Space Ghost as Conner, holding forth a conversation with the costumed manikin about his exploits with Cassie over the weekend.

Cassie and Tess joined the Space Ghost Bar and Lounge Theme Camp a number of years back when they found themselves parked in the bar every afternoon anyways, and the invitation was extended to join the fans of the cartoon hero-turned-talk-show-host. Their camp was supposed to number thirty-five Space Ghosters this year, but Cassie and Tess's two younger friends Thelma and Louise still hadn't shown, which was a major topic of concern for the camp.

Monday was the gala opening for the bar, which would be available for patrons each afternoon through Sunday, from five to seven p.m.. The bar served a different short selection of free drinks that started with the same first letter of the corresponding day of the week, with Mojitos, Martinis and Margaritas being offered on Monday. Setting the drink selections for the other evenings was much more challenging.

The camp, situated at 7:30 and I, was the most remote theme camp in terms of distance from the Esplanade. The bar crowd was a little older, mellower, and local – mostly only those in the nearby suburbs frequented the joint, as opposed to the bars and clubs near the center of the city, which drew patrons from all sectors of BRC. Cassie and Tess felt at home with their camp mates and daily bar crowd.

The public entrance to Space Ghost Bar and Lounge was adorned by a large archway, with the camp name lining the top of the lighted arch, appearing in "Space Toaster" font, a custom font first created for the Cartoon Network's *Space Ghost Coast to Coast* website. Painted flying saucers and rocket ships dotted the wooden curved façade that fronted the archway.

The bar was situated directly behind the archway, underneath a large homemade shade structure. Between the bar and 7:30 were a dozen small sofas, also shaded by homemade structures, available for patrons and camp mates. Two camp RVs were parked immediately to the left, which also served as anchors tethered to the archway and shade structures. Just behind the bar was the large elevated throne housing Space Ghost, a manikin modeling a purchased adult costume including his black hooded mask and undergarment, that facially revealed just his eyes, and everything south of his nostrils; his yellow cape (purists argued over the color of the cape, depending on which vintage Space Ghost cartoons they identified with); red arm bands and belt; and white suit and boots. Blip the space monkey clung to a pole helping to erect the bar's shade structure; Blip being a stuffed monkey doll donated by Cassie several years before.

The camp was launched by a relatively wealthy widower in his early sixties, who served as the major benefactor underwriting the daily drinks. All camp mates also were expected to annually donate a set amount to the kitty to help fund the ice, mixers, bar and camp supplies, as well as several camp-wide meals.

It was less than an hour until the gala opening, with Cassie and Tess the Co-Chief Bar Officers. They were responsible to set up and staff the bar each night, and were spared other duties shared by their camp mates. They were, in typical style, amply prepared ahead of time. All supplies, including chests full of ice, were present and accounted for. The bar inventory was set. All that was needed was customers, so with time to spare, the two ladies ducked back to their cabin tent, all the way back to almost J Street, to freshen up. They strolled through the common area of their camp, dotted with folding chairs, makeshift tables, and speakers tied in to the central sound system.

The sound of sledgehammers striking rebar could still be heard in the distance, as campers continued to arrive throughout the day. Situated in the suburbs, Cassie and Tess could see the individual camps being erected behind their theme camp in every direction.

The camp's trailers, RV's and tents circled around the common area like a pioneer's wagon train at night. Cassie and Tess's six-foot high cabin tent resided at the back end of camp, with a few individual campers situated between them and J Street.

As the two ladies approached their tent, the call of "ice cream... free ice cream..." caught their attention. The two young men from Sweden, camped just southeast of the ladies' tent, decided to offer a plastic bucket of vanilla and a bucket of chocolate that had been stored with dry ice. The two were scooping the ice cream into cones for an increasing clientele showing up on J Street via word-of-mouth for the impromptu offering. Cassie wandered over, snagging a small vanilla cone for her and for Tess.

Ice cream cones in hand, Cassie and Tess relaxed in their tent's folding captain's chairs, enjoying the slight breeze from their battery operated fan, taking in the eclectic mix of songs wafting from their retro boom box, via Burning Man Information Radio 94.5 FM. Several camps operated their own specialty low-power FM stations during BM, but the ladies preferred listening to the official broadcast, which combined event announcements, weather updates, disc jockey chatter and whole lot of offbeat music.

While Cassie and Tess conversed, they missed the DJ's warning that potent high winds, to be followed by a major thunderstorm with heavy precipitation, was predicted in the late evening. They also missed the plea to locate three physically and mentally ill campers who were considered to be highly dangerous to themselves as well as others.

Tess eyed the Tupperware snack box resting on their makeshift coffee table in the center of the tent. She debated with Cassie if they should nibble on any of the Wheat Thins, peanut butter crackers or fruit cups stacked neatly in the Tupperware. Both ladies knew they should have something in their stomachs before they began tending bar, because they tended to imbibe during the process. The problem was, the Black Rock sun seemed to sap their appetites. The best each could do was a couple of Wheat Thins, and generous swigs from their water bottles.

While seated and chatting about nothing in particular, both women found themselves brushing the playa dust off whatever objects were within reach. They had purchased a mass quantity of baby wipes, and had already almost blown through their first box, between wiping their hands, arms and faces, and wiping down anything inanimate in their field of vision.

It was too hot to nap in the tents, despite the shade structures strategically located around camp, which helped shield most of the tents, trailers and RVs. Some of those with RVs or trailers with generators were more fortunate, running the air inside their confines for a period of time, while they stole an afternoon slumber. But many of the Burning Man population simply trooped forward through the week in a sleep-deprived state, staying awake much of the night while there was way too much going on, then spending the day drifting back and forth between lucid thought and a blurry haze, interrupted by an occasional nap when the elements would allow it.

Cocktail hour arrived. Cassie and Tess changed into costume in their tent just before heading back to the Space Ghost bar. Both were outfitted each year as "Jan," the teenage sidekick in the original Space Ghost cartoons, along with her twin brother Jace. They both wore hair extensions to sport a Jan-like ponytail, and wore a black mask around their eyes, a blue and yellow spandex outfit, long red gloves, and a red utility belt.

Their first year in Space Ghost camp, they were officially christened with the playa nicknames Jan and Jace by their campmates. Cassie was dubbed Jan, while Tess was stuck with the moniker Jace. At most theme camps, virgins announced their own playa nicknames, but Space Ghost camp had a tradition of awarding nicknames to their virgin campers.

Jan and Jace were reminded by their camp Commander in Chief before officially opening the bar, on how strict they needed to be in asking for identification for anyone that conceivably appeared under age thirty. Two years prior, the Commander himself had inadvertently not asked for identification, and served an undercover minor working in cooperation with the Pershing County Sheriff's department. The ensuing fine was eleven hundred dollars, which the entire camp chipped in to help pay.

Business was brisk immediately upon opening of the bar, as all the camp mates kicked off their cocktail hour. But soon enough, the surrounding suburbanites wandered in with their own assortment of cups, mugs and glasses – patrons were expected to provide their own beverage containers at all the BM camp establishments — presenting them to Cassie and Tess, to gift them a martini, mojito or margarita. The mojitos – a concoction of white rum, sugar, lime juice, sparkling water and mint – were by far the drink of choice.

The majority of the patrons, beyond their camp mates, were male. But few hit on Cassie or Tess, as the preponderance in the neighborhood were gay. Tess, a recent divorcee, lamented this fact out loud to Cassie, stating that Cassie needed to fix her up with this eccentric friend of Conner's that Cassie had told her about who also came from Parker Creek and lived further out in the Black Rock all by himself.

Then, a man all by himself angled through the small crowd standing in front of the Space Ghost bar, seating himself at the one open stool. He had gray stubble for hair, one large loop earring on his right lobe, and a tattoo of a sun and moon on the right side of his neck. He was shirtless, and wore tattered black shorts and sandals.

He held out a large coffee mug, ordering a mojito after hearing his choices. He looked both ways, as if to ensure no one else would hear the ensuing conversion. "So have any of you heard about all the commotion on the other side of camp?"

Cassie and Tess looked at each other, perplexed. They both shook their heads.

"Do you listen to the radio?" he asked the ladies. They both nodded their heads. "There's been nothing on the radio about anything strange going on today?" he prodded them.

Cassie smiled. "What's this about, mystery man? You tell us what's strange going on today."

The man darted his eyes in both directions again. No one else seemed interested in their conversation. "Well, I walked by the main medical clinic in Center Camp a while ago and it seemed like all hell was breaking loose. All three ambulances were going. There were lawmen everywhere. A sheriff and BLM trucks were pulling up. People were yelling and screaming. Soon they cordon off the area. Chased me out of there, chased everyone out of there. There seriously hasn't been anybody talking about this out here?"

Cassie lowered her eyebrows skeptically, glancing nervously at Tess. "Well, I guess we are really way out in the suburbs, because we sure haven't heard anything like that." Both ladies looked for something to do, to steer themselves away from conversation with the man wearing the sun and moon on his neck. Experiences like this occurred every year at the bar—lonely people bearing embellished tales, because Burning Man didn't manufacture enough urban drama.

But they didn't escape the man's attentions. "Ladies," he called out to them as they re-stocked the bar's ice buckets from a nearby jumbo ice chest. "You need to check it out. Something big is going down right now on the other side of camp."

Thursday Friday Saturday Sunday Monday Tuesday Wednesday

The Walk-In Zombies

Burning Man designates a large swath outside the last circular street, L Street — from 5:00 all the way to 2:00 — for walk-in camping. Campers in this area must park on the other side of 5:00, then cart in their belongings.

The benefit of walk-in camping is the distance from noise – generators, booming speakers, and such. The din from the center of camp diffuses into quite tolerable ambient noise in the walk-in section. The area is a sanctuary for those who highly value their sleep or want to get in touch with their inner-recluse.

The downside of walk-in camping is apparent upon parking one's vehicle. Toting every belonging, for a week's stay, by foot is a challenge. On top of that, without the wind break that exists elsewhere in camp provided by all the surrounding structures, the walk-in tents are significantly more exposed to the wind, dust, and elements. Also, if one wants to go check out what is going on around camp, the commute is a whole lot further from the walk-in area.

At the start of the week, walk-in camping is less popular. Those who arrive at the onset typically are tied into the theme camps, or if they happen to be individual campers, they desire to be closer to everything else going on. As the week progresses, walk-in campground business tends to pick up.

Thus, early Monday morning, walk-in camping was sparsely populated. Those who had set up walk-in camps tended to do so a considerable distance from the nearest camper.

The Trojan Horse Cargo Box Truck was parked in a designated area with a number of other emptied freighters and cargo trucks, southeast of walk-in camping. The trucks were unattended Sunday night; no one was around to listen to the grunts, moaning or banging against the cargo container walls emanating from the Ford Cargo Box Truck.

Like a group of monkeys placed in front of typewriters that eventually constructed a sentence at random, the Trojan Horse zombies finally won their release from the truck around six fifteen a.m. Monday, when one bumped into the customized interior button that activates the automated overhead cargo door opener. The official sunrise was less than ten minutes away as the zombies fell out of truck, one-by-one. None were cognizant enough to climb down or pull out the retractable cargo ladder. They simply stepped out of the truck into thin air, falling to the playa dust, each slowly rising up to wander out into their surroundings.

The Trojan Horse zombie ranks had increased by one; seven ultimately fell out the end of the truck onto the ground. The truck driver's companion, severely bitten by the half–dozen zombies upon their afternoon entrance, lapsed into a coma in the late evening, expired a couple of hours later, reanimating to join the group.

All seven seem to be drawn to the walk-in camping area after they rose up from the playa. Perhaps they were attracted by the aroma from the nearby bank of porta-potties. Their newest zombie member was ravenous, while the other six were weak, dehydrated and no longer capable or possessing the appetite to devour a person whole.

The newbie zombie made a beeline for the porta-potty bank, which happened to have one toilet door swinging open with the breeze, allowing the odors to waft out to appreciative approaching zombie nostrils. Newbie zombie made its way into the porta-potty, dropping to its knees, attempting to dip its head down into the toilet receptacle. Newbie was a middle-aged Hispanic, wearing a white tee shirt and tan cargo shorts. Newbie had been wearing an Oakland Raiders cap, which fell off early-on in its afternoon struggle with the others inside the truck. Now the back of its balding head was exposed for all to see, which would have mortified Newbie a day ago.

Unfortunately for Newbie, the toilet seat was down; its shoulders collided with the seat, allowing only a view of the enticing pool below. Newbie moaned loudly in frustration.

Soon the six zombie mates caught up, crowding around the open porta-potty, wanting in on the action. Their dehydrated state made the liquid they sensed from the pit of the porta-potty all the more attractive. They became frenzied, trying to crowd in to join Newbie in the toilet. One small, thin silver-haired z, dressed in work jeans and a flannel shirt, finally wiggled in alongside Newbie, discovering the urinal to the left of the toilet. The thin zombie gleefully pressed its head to the plastic urinal bowl, trying to gather what little moisture remained in the container.

The other five zombies, in their quest to maneuver into the one open porta-potty, somehow managed to shut the door. Newbie's toilet companion, grabbing for leverage as it tried to immerse itself in the urinal, amazingly grasped the interior lever, shifting the stall to occupied status, locking them in, and the other five z's out.

After the sun rose, the remaining five zombies lost interest in the porta-potties. They began to scatter around the walk-in area. Within fifteen minutes, they followed their noses to unsuspecting campers. Two of the z's stayed together to harass the walk-in campers, the other three went solo.

Their routine at each tent was similar. Just about every tent in the area was the typical backpacking variety, three or four-man tent. The z's wandered up, pawing and stumbling into the vinyl tent material, softly grunting as they pushed at the tent fabric. Someone would wake, unzip the tent, angrily announcing to whoever was outside that they were at the wrong tent. This would bring about biting, scratching, tackling, yelling, and investigation by anyone else occupying the tent, who would be subjected to the same treatment.

While ultimate death and reanimation typically required anywhere from six to ten hours after infection, barring an accident or significant blood loss, the initial symptoms –

disorientation, severe fatigue, debilitating headaches, loss of equilibrium, nausea – were almost immediate. While the zombies moved on to other tents, almost all the victims stayed behind, initially to aid a tent-mate or gather some items – a makeshift weapon, glasses or pants — but soon were too confused and ill to leave the tent. Several of the victims that did make it out, followed their attackers, while cursing them, only to collapse inside the next tent under attack.

Not every one of the walk-in tents was hit. Like the path of a tornado, the zombies cut a random swath, attacking some tents and missing others.

Two strong victims separately fled to get help, both making it to camps at the outer fringes at the K street level. They were ignored as they yelled for help, while nearby campers slept through the ruckus or assumed them to be high. They both eventually collapsed in nearby camps, one in a folding chair - the other on a tarp, underneath a shade awning.

The two zombies traveling together came across an empty, unzipped tent; its occupants never made it back from all-night partying at a big sound club down near the edge at 2:00. The campers, adverse to porta-potties, had their own small bucket inside the tent filled with kitty litter, with a toilet lid fastened on. The two zombies were fascinated by the aroma. They seated themselves in the tent, digging around in the used bucket, sniffing and tasting the kitty litter. Eventually they grew tired and settled into a zombie nap inside the tent.

The remaining three zombies finally herded together, wandering out of walk-in camping, following a few early morning bicyclists heading out into the art installations. Unable to keep up, the zombies continued in the bicycles' last known direction. Time passed as they trudged through the open playa, until they arrived at the shipwreck rising out of the sand. They wearily ventured into the lower quarters underneath the ship deck, attracted by the darkness. They reclined on the ground against the ship walls, each totally spent, falling into a deep zombie nap.

Thursday Friday Saturday Sunday Monday Tuesday Wednesday

Asleep at the Wheel

His former meteorological friend and current zombie nemesis snarled outside the Dodge D-50 window. Alan Gorman studied his graying skin, blank eyes, greasy-matted thinning hair, discolored gums, and open sore in his chest with the grayish ooze surrounding it – where a large rip in his shirt left it exposed.

Alan said to the BLM Range Tech seated next him, that his once-friend and new zombie companions reminded him of sharks – seemingly mindless, relentless, blank-eyed, pursuing their prey because that is what they do.

Alan recounted to the Range Tech his series of mistakes the past two days that kept him from the simple task of driving within cell phone range. Each stop he had made, opened up a new horror shop that extended what should have been an hour's drive from ground zero, into this two day odyssey. The Range Tech was mostly silent. He was somewhat skeptical of Gorman, and Gorman's sanity, but was more frightened by the creatures outside, so he cast his fate with Alan. He prodded Gorman for a plan.

They had already scrounged through every inch inside the Dodge D-50 cab, in a fruitless search for ignition keys or anything useful. A couple of signal flares were the best they could produce. Alan, though, was not rejuvenated enough from his fifteen minute nap on Bruce's ranch house roof earlier that afternoon. The two days of almost no sleep continued to take a toll, as he would repeatedly experience flash hallucinations as they bided their time in the cab.

Alan shook his head, announcing to the Range Tech that he was in no condition to advance a plan at the moment. Perhaps the zombie-fest outside would dissipate with time; in the meantime he had to surrender to a nap for a short while. On top of that, his stump above his prosthesis throbbed and ached. He instructed the Range Tech to wake him if anything significant or worrisome happened, and in any event, to wake him within the half-hour.

The Range Tech was incredulous that Gorman could sleep at a time like this. He started to argue about the wisdom of doing nothing for now, as he watched the zombie group continue to circle the small pickup. He received no response other than soft snoring. The Range Tech's eyes continued to be drawn to the blonde zombie lady with the neon orange bikini, snarling just four meters away. He couldn't help but speculate that she must have been incredibly hot before her recent transformation. He smiled as the thought occurred to him that until this day, she probably would never have had anything to do with him. Now, she apparently wanted him in the worst way.

The Range Tech's right leg shook with impatience. He had been told, just before leaving, that a major thunderstorm was now a possibility for that evening, likely to be preceded by high winds that would certainly launch dust storms all around. He didn't want to stick around for the complications the weather would ensue. The rain also might likely render his sat phone – still lying in the road – useless, even if there was any hope of retrieving it.

The Range Tech debated bolting from the pickup, to sprint away from the gauntlet of vehicles, leaving Gorman and the zombies far behind. He felt confident he could outrun these staggering, grunting creatures. His concern was if he could successfully traverse the first three or four meters without getting bit, given the warnings Gorman conveyed to him, that one bite was all it took. He inhaled deeply, deciding to go for it, but then turned and glanced at the snoozing Gorman. Guilt overtook his impulse to run. Gorman had stopped for him, when Gorman didn't have to. He would wait for Gorman, for now.

Thursday Friday Saturday Sunday Monday Tuesday Wednesday

The U Turn

It turned out, the BLM Ranger didn't let on to Conner and Bruce that he knew something was starting to go down in Black Rock City. After commanding them to strap into their seat belts in the back cab, the ranger took off like a bat out of hell, back in the direction of Sulphur, leaving a wide trail of dust in his wake. Conner and Bruce were separated from the ranger by a standard law enforcement back seat barrier. It occurred to Conner he had been in such a rear seat several times during the past decade.

The chatter over the ranger's vehicle radio seemed frenzied to Conner and Bruce. They listened as best they could, shifting around trying to get comfortable while their daypacks pressed into their spines, jammed between them and the bench seat cushion. It was difficult to follow the conversation, given all the jargon, but as best they could tell, they were in the midst of some kind of medical emergency involving multiple persons. After a very long minute, the ranger addressed the two men in the back of his double cab BLM pickup.

"Gentleman, I'm taking you back a good ways towards your spread in Sulphur. I've been informed you check out, so I'm not going to pursue what your business is out here today. We've got a lot going on. There is a rash of missing person reports we're dealing with. And then we've got Burning Man issues to deal with, even more than usual. So, I've got to keep this area clear, those are my orders. And you need to hoof it directly home when I do drop you off, because on top of everything else, there's supposed to be a major wind and dust storm whipping through here after dark, followed by a pretty significant thunderstorm. And you, sir," the ranger pointed his comments and gaze at Bruce in the rear view mirror, "have to know what a heavy rainstorm will do to the dust on this playa.

Nobody is going to be able to drive much of anything for hours if it rains like they say it's going to."

Bruce forced a smile. "Well then, I guess we need to thank you, because we hadn't paid any attention to any talk about a storm coming." Bruce paused, trying to sound spontaneous with his next question. "But what's this about missing persons or something going on at Burning Man. Is everything okay there?"

The ranger didn't answer for a moment. Then he turned to look back at his two passengers. "I can't really talk about that, gentleman. Unless there's something you can tell me." The ranger stared Bruce down, before continuing. "Now, at Burning Man there are always people getting taken out of there by helicopter every year. It died down the last couple of years after Humboldt General came in to help run the clinic. But I must say that it got interesting fast this year."

Conner and Bruce exchanged glances. Conner then turned to watch the ground they had covered over the past few hours revisit them, their progress becoming rapidly erased. The ranger started conversing over the radio. Bruce leaned over to Conner, whispering, "If those zombie things got into Burning Man, and they helicopter someone who got bit, to your hospital in Reno, there's going to be a lot more to worry about than saving your girlfriend."

Conner leaned back toward Bruce, intending to whisper about irony — he was supposed to be meeting with Humboldt General in Winnemucca this very afternoon, providing a service call on transfer protocols and any other issues that might have surfaced so far. Instead of passing along that thought, Conner stopped to listen to someone talking in jargon-speak that the ranger was needed immediately at some private property well north of Burning Man, off of County Road 34.

The ranger flipped a U-turn, bringing his pickup to a sudden stop. He turned around to face Conner and Bruce. "Gentlemen, I hate to strand you in the middle of nowhere, except that you were in the middle of nowhere when I found you. At least now you're closer to home. I've been summoned to a new incident. I'll leave word if anyone's back in this sector anytime soon to come give you a lift closer towards Sulphur. Now don't you be heading back anywhere near Burning Man. Remember, it's off limits this week....And watch out for the storm. Be sure to be off the playa tonight when it hits." The ranger stepped out, opened Bruce's door in the back, helping both of them out of the cab back seat. Moments later he was back behind the wheel, peeling out, leaving a dust cloud enveloping Conner and Bruce.

Conner and Bruce slowly paced themselves in the direction of Sulphur until the ranger's pickup was clearly out of sight. They both scanned the horizon, seeing no signs of another vehicle or air traffic overhead.

"Maybe we should have said something to him," Conner debated out loud to himself. "He brought up missing people; he alluded to trouble at Burning Man. And who knows what they might run into next. Maybe we should have said something to warn them."

"All true," Bruce countered patiently, "but we've both been arguing in circles about this the past couple of hours. Chances are we'd still be in the back of his vehicle if we had talked, only cuffed or worse."

Conner vented, "So instead, we're marching through this desert, forever. Gorman drives us a ways. Then we walk. And run. Then this BLM cop finds us and drives us back the way we came from. Now we walk. And run."

Bruce forced a laugh. "An afternoon in the Black Rock desert is not forever. You should try living out here for a couple of years."

Conner shook his head. "Yeah, well, this afternoon is feeling like forever. I want to be that kid in the back of my dad's car, saying are we there yet? Only the way today is going, my dad would have said, 'just for asking, we'll turn around and do this all over again'."

Bruce cleared his throat. "Forever is a funny idea. We talk about doing something forever, and yet people live less than a hundred years. The universe measures years in the billions, we measure years by decades and yet we talk about forever."

Conner was quick to retort, "Well, Brucemoose, this still feels like it's taking forever to me, and I'm just measuring time in minutes."

Bruce stopped to stretch his legs and arms. Conner appeared perplexed. "Want forever to go a little faster Connerman? Want to get ourselves into real trouble?" Bruce slyly asked, grinning nervously.

"Something tells me we're already in real trouble," Conner replied, as Bruce took off running back towards Black Rock City. Conner sprinted after him.

Thursday Friday Saturday Sunday Monday Tuesday Wednesday

The 3:15 Daily

The three fifteen daily agency coordination meeting was an annual Burning Man ritual.

The Black Rock Ranger/ LEAL (Law Enforcement and Agency Liaison) Director is responsible to host and conduct the daily meeting, pulling in representatives involved with BRC security and related functions including BLM, Pershing County, Humboldt General (in the most recent years), and numerous other entities.

The Black Rock Rangers are trained Burning Man volunteers that serve as the first-level security team inside BRC, mediating camper disputes, resolving applicable conflicts, and coordinating escalated incidents or other situations requiring intervention with law enforcement, medical teams or other appropriate on-site personnel.

Some outside agencies view the daily meetings as a requisite pain; others find the time well spent. But this year, this Monday, even the most peripheral players were in attendance, with everyone at rapt attention. The venue was changed at the last minute to the staff dining tent in order to hold the overflow crowd.

The longtime BRR/LEAL Director, whose playa name was "Ranger Rick," derived from the National Wildlife Federation Ranger Rick children's magazine – even though his actual name wasn't Rick — opened the meeting by stating that due to events of the last several hours, the more routine specific incident reports, status updates and carryover action items would be dispensed with, to be addressed by a subcommittee immediately following conclusion of the regular agency meeting. He then stated that while everyone present was now generally aware of the high magnitude issues to be dealt with, he would overview them to ensure everyone was equipped with same slate going forward and to frame the discussion that would follow, including the report from the Medical Director. He requested to hold all questions, while he provided the opening assessment.

There wasn't a public address system inside the dining area. Given the larger crowd, the idea was suggested, but dismissed because of the sensitive nature of the discussion, with the concern that ears outside the dining area might pick up on what was said. Ranger Rick chose to walk amongst the dining tables as he spoke as loudly as he could.

First, he gave a synopsis of the shipwreck incident:

"Out on the open playa, inside the shipwreck art installation, there were several early morning reports relayed to at least two BRR teams, regarding a trio inside the lower level of the shipwreck who displayed symptoms consistent with a significant adverse drug reaction, combined with dehydration and other possible medical issues, given their reported skin-coloration, open sores and pungent odor. It was reported the three were reclining against a wall, eyes-open, in a non–responsive state. Before a BRR team could coordinate with Rampart [the nickname for the main medical facility now managed by Humboldt General in Center Camp], two Black Rock citizens took it upon themselves to engage the trio."

"According to the one other eyewitness underneath the ship deck at the time, at around eight o'clock, the two men interacting with the trio were shaking them lightly, asking them if they were okay, and suggesting they get up and walk around. Reportedly, after a minute or two of these repeated attempts, the trio responded, rising up, aggressively seizing the two men, applying a series of deep bites into their flesh, ingesting a sizeable portion of one of the men's right arm in the process. The eyewitness indicated she was too terrified to intervene or yell for assistance, for fear of calling attention to her and becoming subject to attack as well. She stated that the trio abruptly left; she started to follow them out from a distance, but then returned quickly to the two men, as they were crying for help."

"No other witnesses to the attack have been identified, and no witnesses have come forward to report on the assailants' direction or eventual whereabouts in the aftermath of the incident. The female eyewitness to the attack, after offering initial care to the two men, ran from the scene towards the Esplanade until she encountered other citizens, who assisted her in obtaining BRR and then medical support. As everyone should be aware, the two men were brought to Rampart, initially treated and assessed, and transferred to Reno via chopper at around nine forty-five. As the Medical Director will elaborate, there were highly unusual abnormalities in the lab panels taken prior to transfer. The patient with the deep right arm wounds experienced significant blood loss, resulting in being given a poor prognosis for his post-transfer outcome."

Ranger Rick next reported on the two K street victims:

"A BRR team, interacting with the outskirts community in the quadrant between K and J, and 3:30 and 3:45, at around eleven o'clock, received separate reports of two men passed out in different individual camps in that area. Upon inspection and interviews, it was determined that both men were semi-conscious and relatively non-responsive, displaying symptoms of an adverse drug reaction combined possibly with a viral illness. Both men had vomited near where they were situated."

"Nearby campers noticed both men, upon waking in the morning, and handled them in a similar manner. Both were left alone for some period of time, before being engaged with gentle poking and prodding. Eventually both situations were reported and relayed to the BRR teams that investigated, summoned medical teams, and subsequently determined that no one in the immediate areas could identify either male. Neither man was carrying identification; one was dressed only in swimming trunks, the other in just pajama pants. Upon inspection, bite marks and lacerations in multiple locations were found on both males."

"After initial treatment and assessment at Rampart, transfer protocols were invoked at around twelve thirty. Again, the patient lab panels produced unusual abnormalities, consistent with the results of the previously transferred patients. Upon confirmation of these lab results with the transfer facility, Renown Medical Center in Reno, their Emergency Services Medical Director requested a delay in transfer, while he consulted with the CDC. He requested that our Rampart place both patients in isolation, and that we initiate protocols for a potential communicable disease outbreak, at least until receiving further direction from CDC, and or when the patient zeroes, assumed to be responsible for the biting incidents could be located and apprehended."

Ranger Rick followed with a rundown of the Rampart incident:

"Rampart staff improvised with available resources, arranging two isolation areas out of separate treatment rooms, although certainly not to CDC standards. Both patients lapsed into comas between thirteen thirty and thirteen forty-five. Shortly after fourteen hundred, the more frail of the two patients was determined to have expired. Due to the isolation order, no morgue transfer arrangements were initiated. Obviously, the death pronouncement proved to be incorrect, undoubtedly due to the highly unusual nature of the undetermined condition, as evidenced in the lab panels. The patient arose from his gurney, attacking a volunteer nurse, severely wounding her. Numerous lab staff attempted to restrain the patient, while calls for security were immediately placed. Given the proximity of the BRR HQ, a sizeable BRR force arrived in less than two minutes, in addition to two Pershing County deputies and two BLM rangers."

"Medical staff retreated after initial restraint attempts failed, with three staff bitten by the patient, in addition to the now-critically injured nurse. Our respondents on the scene were counseled by medical staff that a potentially serious, undetermined communicable disease might be transferred orally. Attempts to subdue the patient with Tasers proved unsuccessful. What transpired next is still subject to verification, forensics and administrative process, but this room includes witnesses who report the patient was subjected to what would be assumed to be more than adequate deadly force, but continued to advance, reaching and biting a ranger before he was finally subdued and placed in restraints."

"He remains restrained in his isolation area, and has not expired despite nine gunshot wounds in the upper torso, with at least three that would otherwise have been assumed to produce a fatal result. Our medical director will comment on the highly unique blood coloration and coagulation, yielding thick, gray ooze at the wound sites, which seems to assist in prolonging his life."

"Immediately after the incident, the other initial patient was placed in gurney restraints. He also was assumed to have expired, pronounced dead around fourteen thirty, but was placed under watch. He revived around ten minutes later, and continues to remain in a very agitated state, under heavy restraints on the gurney in Rampart."

"Each of our bite victims have been placed in separate isolation areas, basically rendering Rampart ineffective from providing medical treatment to our population for the time-being. General medical care is currently being referred to the medical stations in the 3:00 and 9:00 plazas."

Ranger Rick could no longer conceal his frustration as he next commented on communication from the Reno hospital and CDC:

"Understanding that events in real-time can overtake us, one might understand some lapses of timely information flow. But, incredibly, we now know the first patient at Renown expired and revived in the same manner that transpired at Rampart at around thirteen hundred, in excess of an hour before our incident, depriving us of intelligence that undoubtedly would have prevented the injuries and potential transmission of disease that subsequently occurred."

"An initial CDC contact was made to our medical director via email, simply restating prior directives, and that an on-site assessment was being arranged. Phone follow-up proved fruitless. The information regarding their patient incident arrived only via email around fourteen thirty. We have more recently received further CDC directives, again simply via email, that we are to continue refraining from patient transfers until CDC assessment can be made, and that staff from the CDC Carson City field office was currently being arranged for a site visit, hopefully to occur within the hour. They are on-site assessing the Reno hospital incident as we speak. We're informed they are just about to conclude, and will then directly helicopter to our Black Rock airport."

"We have been advised to review contingency evacuation plans, but we have been specifically directed to refrain from any formal actions until after CDC conducts their assessment, as something from the other end of the spectrum, i.e., quarantine, may also have to be considered if events get away from us. Certainly we have been counseled that the events are not of the scope and magnitude yet to actively engage such protocols, we've just been encouraged to dust them off and familiarize ourselves with them."

"We have been directed not to publicize these patient incidents prior to a CDC assessment, as no determination has been made regarding a potential disease outbreak, and certainly considerable more information is required. However, we have been advised to publicize and focus our attention on locating the three patient zeroes, and to pull in all the resources of the entire community to do so. It is recommended we give the highest priority to publicizing that these three men are considered to suffer from significant physical and mental illness — without providing specifics other than their physical description and attributes, and that they are to be avoided at all costs, but it is imperative that they be located immediately to ensure the safety of the community. We have a sub-group that was commissioned just before this meeting to initiate coordinating this effort."

Finally, before giving way to the Rampart Medical Director, and then opening for discussion to address immediate action items, Ranger Rick concluded with one additional tidbit:

"There is one more significant item of concern. We'd have moved aside the regular agenda just for the weather situation. As you are probably aware, the National Weather Service now advises a severe thunderstorm warning for the Black Rock region late this evening, with possibly more than two inches of rain to be produced in an intense squall, and what's more, this event will be preceded by a high wind warning that should produce intense dust storms."

"Everyone in this room is aware of the impact of this level of rainfall in that short period of time, with the record high levels of playa dust on the surface this year, particularly in the roadways between the city, the gate, and County Road 34. The streets and roadways in and out of the city will simply be impassable for up to several hours."

"We are advising our Gate Perimeter and Exodus Department to be prepared to temporarily shut down entrance to the city upon official notice, to shut off entrance from County Road 34, and to provide temporary signage outside Gerlach leading up to the entrance, warning of the potential closure. We have been through this drill a couple of times before, in years past."

"We will need to coordinate mass communication to our community regarding the weather situation, so they are prepared, and determine how to effectively manage this warning alongside our bulletin regarding the three patient zeroes. Our communications sub-group has also been tasked with this initiative."

"The good news is the weather could provide the means to effect a de facto-quarantine, if God forbid, that's how far CDC takes this thing. The bad news is if an emergency exodus is required, we could be screwed."

Thursday Friday Saturday Sunday Monday Tuesday Wednesday

All Aboard the Zombie Train

The Trojan Horse Zombies had three quite different experiences with their Monday in Black Rock City. Three of them wandered out into the open playa art installations to catch a nap in the shipwreck, before launching the major incident resulting in a manhunt for their whereabouts. Two were pinned inside a porta-potty, trying desperately to reach the contents below the toilet lid. The remaining two napped inside an unoccupied walk-in camping tent.

The porta-potty zombies were not easily deterred. Given their quarters were cramped, and the fact an exit existed was now long a forgotten memory in their zombie-brains, they remained very on-task with their mission to reach the promised-land eluding them down below. For an extended period of time, the skinny, smaller zombie was satisfied with availing himself with the urinal, but after consuming all the moisture available from the plastic receptacle, he began jostling for position at the toilet seat with the most recent inductee to the seven Trojan zombies.

Their grunting and jostling inside the porta-potty did not go unnoticed. Several of the walk-in campers, who had been spared their dawn raid and were unaware of the attack, shook their heads upon hearing the commotion when strolling by the bank of porta potties during the day. Porta-potty sex was an often-rumored occurrence at Burning Man. This was the assumption when the BRC vendor truck conducted its scheduled maintenance stop, close to noon at the walk-in camping porta-potty bank. The walk-in banks were skipped at the four and eight a.m. intervals until Wednesday, due to the lower walk-in camper density earlier in the week. Stall No. 5 was noted in the checklist as occupied for a long duration, during the noon hour servicing. The four p.m. service checklist bore the same notation; no one cross-referenced the two checklists to notice the same stall had been occupied on both occasions.

The two zombies that settled down for a long morning's nap in an unoccupied walk-in camping tent, finally arose around eleven thirty a.m. They wandered out into the intense mid-day sun, both bothered by the bright light and heat of the day. They headed directly southwest towards the city, connecting with a rental RV near J and 3:45. Attracted by the human smell and offering of shade, they wandered inside the propped-open door. A very surprised gray-haired lady in her late-fifties, halfway through washing dishes, was speechless as the two partially clothed, open-sored, stench-laden, unkempt man and woman approached. They reached her within moments, dragging her toward the bedroom at the front of the RV, scratching and biting her as they progressed. She was too paralyzed with fear to cry out.

Her husband, unaware of the intruders, entered the RV fresh from his neighborly visit, introducing himself to just-arriving campers nearby. He closed the door behind him, heading toward to the bedroom when he didn't spy his wife at the sink where he had left her. Neither made it outside after the attack. The husband's left ear, cheek and thigh had been significantly consumed. The wife made it through the initial ordeal with deep bites in numerous places, and a sizeable portion of her right breast ingested by her attackers. The two lay helplessly on the bloody RV bedroom floor in a daze, before passing out.

The closed door to the outside was too formidable a foe for the younger zombie couple. They wandered around the small RV like feral animals trapped inside a domestic setting, knocking over and breaking anything in their way, pacing wildly for extended times in front of each window, pushing at the glass to no avail. They no longer were interested in bothering their prey that lay on the bedroom floor. The loss of blood helped accelerate the older couple's demise. By late afternoon, the RV numbered four zombies, all pacing, moaning, and pawing the windows.

The remaining trio of Trojan horse zombies — after attacking the two men who woke them out of their zombie nap inside the shipwreck structure — wandered back outside onto the open playa. A woman accompanying the two men momentarily followed after them, but returned to her fallen comrades inside the shipwreck after hearing their pleas for help.

Moments later, a smaller Mutant Vehicle pulled up, a modified John Deere lawnmower tractor dressed up as a train engine with the driver seated within the full enclosure. The train engine was impressively connected to a wheeled open boxcar with seats for three. The driver sounded his custom train whistle, commenting that he was most impressed with the trio's zombie attire and make up, but the fake blood could use a little work. He called out "All Aboard!" to the trio. The zombies, still in a weakened, dehydrated state from their days of wandering across the desert to Black Rock City — despite their dining on one of the men's arm inside the shipwreck — were somehow attracted to the three boxcar seats. They stepped up onto the low-riding boxcar and seconds later were whisked away further out onto the open playa.

The train engineer hollered back a scintillating monologue to his passengers, unaware they had no comprehension whatsoever as to his witty remarks. The engineer thought he saw them nod, when he asked if they wanted to check out the best maze on the open playa. He pulled up to the isolated structure, situated halfway between the Wall Street buildings and the Temple. After the train came to a stop, the zombies sat still momentarily, eyes blankly fixed on the structure in front of them. One of the z's finally rose, stepping off the boxcar, stumbling as he landed on the open playa. The other two followed. The train engineer blew his train whistle, tipped his cap, riding off into the distance.

Black Rock City possesses many mazes every year. Theme camps construct them within their confines. During the day, they typically aren't much of an attraction, but under the cover of darkness and under influence of alcohol or mind-altering substances, they often prove quite popular. The new art installation maze took the craft of mazing to an entirely new level. The structure provided near total-darkness within the interior, even during the day. Recorded loops of drum beats blared from overhead speakers. The black heavy-duty six-foot-high maze walls, constructed with rolling sliders mounted to the tops and bottoms of each modular wall section, were shifted into new configurations every few hours. After solving the maze, a participant could repeatedly return to face a new challenge.

The z trio wandered inside, sticking close together, soon finding themselves at a dead end. After pushing unsuccessfully at the walls in front of them and on each side, they took the opportunity to quietly rest against the walls – zoning out again, into a short open-eyed zombie nap.

One of the maze art installation managers pulled up, parking his bicycle against the structure. No other bikes were situated outside. He entered, stopping to listen. Hearing no one, he called out three times to see if anyone was inside. Receiving no response, he pulled out his keychain, unlocking the stops in the floor in designated spots, allowing him to slide and shift pre-determined maze wall layouts into a planned new configuration. In less than three minutes, his work done, he exited the maze, riding off to join friends back at his camp. He didn't plan to return until late afternoon as the maze was less visited during the day; the reconfiguration frequency would pick up at night, and as the week progressed.

The new configuration created two dead spots, with no entrance or exits. The z trio was resting comfortably inside of one of them. After the maze drew in new visitors, the zombies eventually were enticed by the aroma of persons tantalizingly close by. They pushed and prodded at the maze walls, bumping into each other repeatedly in their closed quarters. Their moaning and grunting was largely drowned out by the drumbeats from above.

Six occupied, domed, backpacking walk-in tents had been subject to the daybreak attacks by the Trojan Horse Zombies. Two of these tents had single male occupants, who each were able to escape after being mauled, both collapsing in camps in the outer fringe of the city. They were eventually taken to Rampart, the source of the medical clinic incident. Their long, excruciating walk from their tents to the city, helped bring about their demise more rapidly than the other walk-in victims trapped inside their tents.

The occupants of the other four victim-tents, all couples, turned at varying points during the three o'clock afternoon hour. Three of the four tent couples had zipped themselves back in – in their immediate post-bitten delirium, perhaps somehow thinking sealing the tent doors would keep their attackers at bay, while they could still be heard stalking around the area. Now, none of the three couples were capable of simply unzipping their tents and stepping out into the playa.

The fourth victim-tent, left unzipped, found its zombie occupants rising up and out into the world. They caught sight of a small group heading from the walk-in camping area toward the city, and followed them, staggering, grunting, and squinting at the bright afternoon sunlight. As they reached the city, their nostrils caught the scent of the bank of porta-potties near the public plaza at K and 3:00. They passed up a number of Black Rock citizens while en route, but were focused on the approaching outhouses, instead of attacking those that they passed. They didn't draw stares, despite their appearance; they apparently blended in with the Burning Man landscape. A polite porta-potty occupant held the door open for them upon her exit, as they approached, expecting one of them to step forward. Instead they both entered. The door swung behind them. The lady laughed, and exchanged amused glances with two other citizens strolling by, witnessing the couple's double entry into the porta-potty. The zombie couple stayed inside their new confines for a considerable length of time.

One of the zipped victim-tents was quite sturdy, anchored by rebar. Its two new zombie campers continued to push, bang and paw away at the tent walls to no avail. Seemingly thinking very inside-the-box, it did not occur to them that they should try to stand, as the roof clearly wasn't high enough to allow it. Instead they crawled around the tent, moaning in frustration as the afternoon progressed.

Two of the tents had been anchored by simple tent stakes, which any experienced burner will strongly advise against – rebar was the anchor of choice. The couples in these units attempted to stand up inside the domed backpacking tents, poking and banging against the vinyl material and flexible curved rods that framed the structures. Eventually, they managed to stand erect, ripping or pulling free from their tent stakes; the curved rods popping out and partially disassembling. Neither tent's occupants were successful in freeing themselves from the tent interiors, despite the presence of various small developing rips and tears. Instead, they began blind journeys as walking tents, stumbling around in a circuitous route that led them towards the art installations out on the open playa. They were drawn by the sound of each other's moaning to stay within hearing-distance proximity to each other – possibly some herding attribute that seemed inherent in the Black Rock zombies.

Given the frequency of performance art occurring in every corner of Black Rock City, no one witnessing the walking, moaning tents seemed overly concerned. A Burning Man mantra is that everyone participates; evidently even if they become walking tents. A more typical reaction was bemusement – then there was the group that debated joining them in a spontaneous walking tent parade, until they considered the damage the escapade might inflict on their sleeping quarters.

Good News

It didn't take long for the
saturation radio warnings and
Black Rock Ranger inquiries
throughout BRC to produce results. While many vague leads
were quickly received, producing a few wild goose chases, the
mutant vehicle train engineer stepped forward after being told
by camp mates about the repeating radio announcements.

Ranger Rick, the BRR/LEAL Director excitedly relayed the
information to his BLM Ranger counterparts. The lead seemed
concrete – it put the train engineer at the shipwreck exactly at
the time of the attack; his description of the trio matched that
of the female eyewitness; he witnessed the three entering art
installation No. 97, the moveable maze. While the trail was in
excess of eight hours old, it was a start, and would hopefully
provide fresh clues.

A BLM Ranger tactical team of eight was assembled inside
the dining area, which continued to be appropriated as a
command center to deal with the crisis. Eight Pershing County
deputies were assigned to serve as backup. A medical team of
four was brought into the operation. The maze installation
manager, possessing a satellite phone, was quickly located as
he was about to leave camp to bike out to the installation. He
was rushed into the dining area, providing a copy of the maze
design, briefing the team on the maze layout, and leaving the
team his keys that unlock the sliding wall stops.

The BLM Ranger serving as Incident Commander agreed
with Ranger Rick that the likelihood of the trio still being
situated inside the maze was low, but they had to try. The two
CDC staff had just set up shop on-site during the past few
minutes, whisked to the Rampart clinic from the Black Rock
City Airport after their helicopter arrival. The BLM Ranger

pulled one of the CDC staff into sat phone consultation, as they quickly planned their operation.

The team discussed alternative approaches to subduing the trio without reaching proximity whereby physical contact was a possibility. One of the team would be outfitted with immediately available items that would reduce the chance of penetration, in the event that biting or other contact became inevitable. The CDC representative at the other end of the phone strongly emphasized the need to avoid killing the targets, as any hope for a medical solution for their stricken comrades isolated in Rampart, might depend upon what they could glean and attempt on these patient zeroes.

Given what was witnessed inside Rampart when the first victim was unfazed by Tasers, withstood a barrage of chest-shots, and still had not expired, the team agreed upon a plan to entrap them with heavy netting if possible – which was currently being obtained – and otherwise shoot them continually in the kneecaps and lower extremities until they were unable to ambulate.

Just after four thirty p.m., the team proceeded to art installation No. 97, a convoy of four BLM and Pershing County SUVs, an ambulance, and a small cargo box truck commandeered to hold the trio if they were captured. Minutes later, they arrived. After disembarking, the Pershing County deputies encircled the building at equal-distant intervals; a BRR ranger stationed behind the wheel of the Cargo Box Truck with the engine running; the medical team positioned just outside the ambulance. The BLM Incident Commander sent two rangers to guard the maze exit on the opposite side, with two rangers close behind. He positioned two rangers at the entrance door, and kept the heavily-padded ranger, looking like an overdressed hockey goalie, in tow. The commander and his padded companion burst into the entrance, shutting off the sound system. The commander announced he was with the BLM; this was an emergency and ordered anyone inside to exit immediately. He and the hockey goalie retreated back outside the entrance. They expected at least four persons to exit one way or the other, based on the four bicycles parked outside.

Indeed, four persons quickly filed out, three through the entrance, one via the exit. All were sized up by the rangers at the respective doors – determined not to be their quarry – and allowed to proceed safely outside the building. A fifth person could be heard hollering that they couldn't find their way out. Outside, one of the persons that had exited the maze, a young man in his early twenties, called out that his younger brother was still inside.

The Incident commander and his goalie reentered with flashlights. A sixteen year-old-boy - attending Burning Man for the first time with his dad and older brother — hit another dead end in the dark. On the other side of the walls, he could hear people shuffling around, breathing heavily. The wall shook as hands pounded it from the other side. Then the moaning started. Panic stricken, the boy backed out the way he came in.

A flashlight shone on his face as he rounded the corner. He looked up at the beam shining from above. He couldn't make out its source, but a voice instructed him to follow the light, and they would guide him out. Within one minute, he was safely outside. The Incident Commander interviewed him, learning of the sounds the boy heard behind the walls.

This news caused the commander to become quite excited. He entered the structure again with his goalie, putting his finger to his lips as they entered. They quietly stood inside the pitch dark maze, listening intently. Within moments, definitive audible moans and movement could be detected. The commander and goalie exited again, shouting loudly to their teams that the targets were likely inside. He pulled the current maze layout, provided by the art installation's manager, out of his side vest pocket. Sure enough, there were two dead areas within the maze. He hypothesized that the trio became trapped inside when the maze was reconfigured that morning.

The Incident Commander trotted back to the Cargo Box Truck, opening the back swinging door, where a number of supplies for the mission had been hastily packed, including the heavy net, lying on top of a six foot ladder. He called another ranger over to fetch the ladder. Reentering the structure, he positioned the ladder upright just inside the entrance, climbed up to the fourth rung, his head bumping against the structure's ten-foot ceiling. He shined his flashlight down into the structure, training the beam to where he expected the dead areas to be, after studying the diagram.

Within moments, the trio appeared at the other end of the beam of light. The commander called out to them, receiving no response other than low-pitched moaning. Studying them, he felt satisfied they matched the descriptions provided, and certainly displayed the same characteristics he personally witnessed inside the Rampart Clinic, when he viewed the two victims in restraints. The commander climbed down the ladder, stepping back outside, announcing confirmation their quarry was trapped within.

The commander frowned, deep in thought, as several rangers rushed forward for orders. He reconsidered their previous plan. Speaking out loud, he questioned the risks of rushing in to apprehend and transport the trio. The structure was already serving as an adequate jail. He saw no reason not to simply secure the structure, and continue to hold them inside.

By five p.m., he was back at the dining area, meeting with Ranger Rick and the senior member of the CDC public health team of two. A security team guarded the two doors back at the now-closed art installation No. 97.

The CDC Senior Public Health Advisor smiled. "Gentleman, this could not be better news, given the circumstances. The chain of events seems adequately documented, that our three patient zeroes did not infect anyone else after the attack in the shipwreck installation on the two patients now at Renown Medical Center. The initial two victims in your Rampart clinic would most likely seem to be directly tied to the patient zeroes as well. No other victims have surfaced to date inside Black Rock City, and the timeframe from infection to manifestation seems to already have passed based on the cases of the four initial victims. The probabilities would be extremely high, that if someone else had been infected prior to eight a.m., when the patient zeroes whereabouts are unaccounted for, the victim's second stage of disease would have already manifested, in which case, based on the observed behavior here and in Reno, their presence would be impossible to miss. Don't get me wrong, we have a lot of work to do here, and the outcome for the infected staff is in the balance, but I believe it may be safe to initiate arrangements for transfer of the Stage II patients to Reno, under adequately secured transport of course, where we are so much better equipped to study and deal with this now that the threat of further spread appears to be contained. Unfortunately, the Stage I staff needs to stay here because the clock is ticking, and too much time would be tied up in their transfer. I've already called in our infectious disease specialist of choice from Reno, and he is en route via helicopter."

"So you are saying the worst may be behind us?" the BLM Incident Commander asked, for reassurance.

The woman from the CDC exhaled loudly. "What I'm thinking, is this is an ugly situation, that will likely get uglier for the poor infected Stage I staff over there, and may be the most bizarre case that I am aware of in my almost twenty years on the job. Someone is going to be researching this for some time to come, but despite that, I think we really dodged a bullet here. Things could, and should, have been much worse, based on the possibilities."

Ranger Rick slapped the dining table. "Well, I am in agreement with you there. Dodge a bullet we did. Now at least we can focus on the weather, maybe return this dining area back to staff in time for a late dinner, and pray for our friends in Rampart. But any way you look at it, I'm taking this as good news. Good news indeed."

Thursday Friday Saturday Sunday Monday Tuesday Wednesday

Gauntlet Gunfight

The Range Tech lightly shook Alan Gorman. He then resorted to repeatedly poking him hard in the ribs. Alan woke in a fog, having only benefited from ten minutes or so of sleep.

"Wake up, man," the Range Tech pleaded loudly. "Someone's coming down the road. Look, they're almost here."

Gorman's head felt heavy, his thinking fuzzy. He only saw his once-meteorological-friend-and-current-zombie's face in his window, with a couple of z acquaintances milling around the Dodge D-50 pickup, and two more inside the truck bed, banging on the small rear window. Gorman wondered how they had managed to crawl up in the pickup bed while he was napping.

The Range Tech could tell that Gorman wasn't connecting with the approaching white SUV. He pointed at the vehicle closing in from the road ahead, "Look, it's right there." The young Range Tech was depending on Gorman to come up with a plan.

Gorman exhaled, closed his eyes for an instant, opened them and spotted the SUV. The first thought that came to mind was, this would be their opportunity to free themselves from Dodge D-50 prison. The second thought that came to mind was, the occupants of the SUV were about to find themselves in deep trouble if they got out of their vehicle.

Gorman drew in a deep breath, before exhaled loudly. "Okay, sir," he addressed the Range Tech with the worried face and worried tone of voice, realizing the two had never exchanged names during their time in the cramped mini-pickup cab. "That vehicle is bound to come to a stop and these creatures are likely to wander their way. We have to bolt out of here quick when they give us some distance. I'll go for my rifle;

you go for your phone, unless it's not safe. Then, run far enough to keep a safe distance from them biting you. Get in my Escalade or your pickup, and let's back up to the SUV if we can, and do what we can for them."

"What about..." the Range Tech started to reply, with questions surfacing in his mind; but the SUV pulled up twenty meters behind the Range Tech's white pickup and Gorman's Escalade. His voice trailed off, his attention now fixed on the unfolding scene. On cue, Gorman's once-friend, the bikini woman and the other surrounding zombies directed their attention to the Acura MDX that had just came to a stop. The z's staggered in the new vehicle's direction, including the two that stumbled out of the D-50 pickup truck bed. The driver and passenger of the MDX both exited their vehicle; hands on hips, watching the approaching half dozen strange looking people closing in on them.

Gorman opened the driver door, noting the distance between his rifle and the zombies was now greater than the distance from the rifle to him. Gorman took off, limping, for the rifle, a tantalizing ten meters away. The range tech froze, as he stared behind at his sat phone nearby.

Alan Gorman reached his rifle, while bikini woman made it within six or seven meters of the two men standing bewildered outside their SUV. The other five zombies were close behind. Alan positioned the M16 Colt .22 Rimfire rifle, knowing if he was going to take a shot, he must do it now. Feeling confident, he maintained his aim, squeezing the trigger. He scored a direct hit in the back of the skull of bikini woman. She dropped to the ground, just three meters to the left and three meters in front of the heavyset passenger standing outside the door of the SUV. The MDX passenger screamed an obscenity and dove back into the car. Alan took aim, felling the next zombie in line, an odd looking fellow with his head turned, the well placed bullet shattering his skull just above the temple.

The somewhat obese, goateed, balding MDX passenger stepped back outside the vehicle, having retrieved his pistol from the glove box. The man returned fire, the shot missing Gorman wide right, but scoring a direct hit on the Escalade's front driver side tire.

Alan was mentally preparing for his next shot, first focusing on next zombie closest to the MDX, who happened to be his meteorological-friend, but then chose the another target without rationalizing why. A shot from the MDX rang out as Gorman was preparing to take aim. Instinctively, Gorman lowered his weapon and dashed ahead for cover behind his Escalade. Alan could hear the MDX passenger telling the approaching zombies that everything was okay, he had them covered. Another shot was launched; Gorman could hear it zing past.

The BLM Range Tech, like a boy standing over a frigid swimming pool on a blustery day, was doing his best to force himself to burst out of the pickup towards his sat phone. He cast a glance again at the open driver door, realizing he had to do something, because anytime soon another one of these creatures could emerge from underneath or behind one of the cars in back of him. Just as he opened his passenger door, the cliché 'be careful what you wish for' crossed his mind, as he spotted two zombie-people working their way up the gauntlet, equal-distant between him and the sat phone. He wondered where on earth they just appeared from; he had not noticed them, moments earlier.

The BLM Range Tech turned to note the exchange of gunfire between the MDX and Gorman; he turned again to notice the two creatures advancing in his direction. Without pausing to think, his feet made a choice for him. He pushed the passenger door fully open, sprinting away from the gauntlet in the road, out into the playa. He did not stop.

Alan caught the Range Tech's movement peripherally, spotting the young man scamper out on the playa, two zombies slowly staggering after him, losing ground with each stride. Gorman noted no additional shots had been fired from the MDX. He poked his head out from behind the Escalade on the driver's side. Meteorological-man and another zombie had reached obese man; the three were in a tussle. Two more zombies were close behind. The MDX driver was screaming at his passenger.

Alan couldn't make out what was being said in the confusion. He hobbled up to his Escalade's driver door, opened it and hopped in, immediately locking the doors. He fished for his keys. A moment later, the ignition was started. Alan lurched forward, the flat driver side tire giving way to the gravel below. Alan could feel his rim crunching into the gravel as the tire shredded into pieces.

Thursday Friday Saturday Sunday Monday Tuesday Wednesday

Space Ghost Mojitos

Cassie and Tess continued to serve a steady clientele at the Space Ghost Bar. Mojitos sustained their domination over margaritas and martinis. As the sun wound its way towards the Gerlach horizon, a greater proportion of the citizens of Black Rock City were dressed in costume. Space Ghost Bar patrons were outfitted in Star Wars Stormtrooper outfits; ballerina tutus (male and female); evening formal wear; Samurai warriors; winged angels and fairies; marching band drum majors; Italian chefs; painted nude sculptures; and mad scientists.

Discussion around the bar touched on the whereabouts of Thelma and Louise. They still had not shown up, and many including Cassie and Tess, were quite concerned. A couple of camp members had satellite phones, calls were placed after Thelma and Louise's cell numbers were tracked down, only to go straight to voicemail. Debate ensued about what more should be done.

The conversation turned to romance. A good number of the bar crowd knew Cassie and Tess from prior years, and held semi-regular Facebook contact. Those who knew Cassie insisted on hearing about this "Conner" that caused her to change her Facebook status to "in a relationship" just before entering Burning Man.

Cassie was cautioned about throwing herself headfirst into something serious with someone she really didn't know all that well. Cassie replied that there is bond between those that grew up together in a truly small town – a level of trust – a sense of knowing what lies beneath someone's surface. Cassie mentioned how Conner had also reconnected with another friend from their hometown – Bruce – and the two were quickly becoming the best of buddies.

Tess once again announced she needed to meet this Bruce. Tess had piercing blue eyes, short, dark brunette hair, a slender figure and an effervescent personality. Tess and Cassie did not come to Burning Man to hook up with men, although friends back home often suspected otherwise. They gravitated towards the Space Ghost camp because the crowd was a little older and content to converse and have a good time. There was plenty of opportunity for hooking up at Burning Man; but for Tess and Cassie, that was not was Burning Man was all about.

Plans for the evening were being made. Many in Space Ghost camp were happy to stick around at night, partying with old and new friends, and explore Black Rock City during the day. Cassie and Tess, however, wanted to check out the open playa art after dark, all lit up. They intended to hang out at camp until there was no trace of sunset on the horizon, then hop on their bikes and take in the sights and sounds of Burning Man at night.

Two Black Rock Rangers arrived at the bar, carrying a handmade sign. Before they had a chance to explain themselves, Tess asked them to hold it up. She read it out loud: "WARNING! High Wind Advisory This Evening. Major Thunderstorm and Heavy Rain Projected Later Tonight."

One of the rangers, after Tess's dramatic reading, pulled out a roll of duct tape, requesting that the sign be displayed at the bar. He advised that the rangers were visiting all theme camps, asking them to help spread the word that the weather needed to be taken very seriously that evening. The entrance gate was going to be shut down for several hours; no one would be allowed to exit for that time period as well. The conversation turned to memorable weather events that a number of camp veterans had endured.

Before leaving, Cassie asked the ranger what they could do about their missing younger friends. He didn't offer much hope. He suggested, if they were really concerned, and being Cassie mentioned that there were sat phones in camp, that they track down the ladies' families, to let them know they had not arrived, and let the families take it from there.

Tess told the ranger that someone at the bar earlier was rambling on about big trouble at the medical clinic at Center Camp, and she wanted to know what that was all about. The ranger's smile evaporated, his body tightened up. He grabbed the arm of his partner behind him, who was quickly chatting up two bar patronettes, scantily clad with fairy wings and wands. The ranger announced to his partner that they needed to move on, then turned to Tess, responding in a low, hushed voice, "Something did happen, and there was a big concern about an outbreak, but we're advised everything is contained and under control now. But between you and me — and I wasn't there mind you — all I can say is I would keep your eyes open and be careful out there, or better yet, think about staying in tonight."

The Playa Marathon

Conner and Bruce halted at a random spot in the dusty playa for a drink of water. After leaning over, hands on knees, gasping for air, sweat dripping down onto the playa floor, they fished through their respective daypacks, reaching for what had dwindled down to one water bottle apiece. Conner felt momentarily dizzy. They refrained from conversation at first, catching their breath in between small bursts of coveted H2O.

Conner finally broke the silence, coughing before he spoke. "It seems the law has deserted us out here. There has not been a sign of anyone or anything since we took off running."

"Don't jinx us, Connerman," Bruce responded, still panting a little. "We are sitting ducks out here if another helicopter flies by, nosing around."

Conner stood straight up. He started to walk at a slow pace. Bruce followed suit.

"Well, if they do stop us again, I think we have to come clean at that point," Conner said tossing out his opinion for Bruce's reaction.

"Oh yeah? Why now?" Bruce reacted in surprise.

"Let's face it, Bruce. It doesn't sound like Alan Gorman came through, or that BLM Ranger would have said some things differently. And if we're not going to make it into Burning Man, we have to at least try and tell them what's going on. What do we have to lose?"

Bruce chuckled. "Only our current address, when they transfer us to cellblock D, or some mental institution." Bruce glanced over at Conner, who was not amused. Bruce sighed. "Look, Connerman, I'm just tagging along on your quest here. You're the boss. You want to level with the law about Black Rock zombies, I won't stand in your way."

Conner sighed as well. "Let's hope it doesn't come to that." He hesitated, scanning the horizon. "How much longer until dark, would you guess?"

"There is no darkness but ignorance, my dear Conner."

"Huh?" Conner continued to get caught off guard by Bruce's quotations.

"Two hours or so, Mr. Zimmerman."

"I would think we'll make it within range of Burning Man by then, Mr. Bruce."

"Well, the wild card is going to be what the ranger told us about."

"And what is that, Mr. Kepner?"

"The storm we're supposed to be worried about after dark. A dust storm and a thunderstorm could rain all over our plans or just perhaps be an opportunity," Bruce ventured, then broke into a jog.

"Opportunity?" Conner replied quizzically, trotting after him.

Cracks in the Dam

One-by-one, the remaining zombies inside Black Rock City began finding their way out into the Burning Man world. Four hours after the three fifteen Daily; two and a quarter hours after the five p.m. pronouncement that the three patient zeroes were accounted for and the outbreak contained, evidence to the contrary was rearing its ugly head. The cracks in the dam were all too apparent to Ranger Rick.

At six twenty p.m., the z-couple trapped inside their backpacking tent broke free. While a portion of their afternoon was spent zombie-napping, their remaining time involved pushing and pawing at the interior, light-brown tent walls. A tear in the floor seams ultimately resulted at around a quarter after five in the afternoon. A little more than an hour later, the rip enlarged enough to provide an escape route. The once attractive, twentysomething z-man and z-woman proceeded to stalk the walk-in campground; the man wearing just red pajama pants, the woman in tan shorts and a bikini top. Their now-grayish skin bore open wounds that interrupted the colored tattoos they once prized.

They came upon a middle-aged fellow, all by himself, napping in his open tent, with a paperback book nestled across his face. After half a minute or so of agonized screaming, the man fell silent, ripped to shreds, his tent and Coleman sleeping bag bathed in blood and discombobulated internal organs. The tent was distant enough from neighbors, and enough of the walk-in population was out and about, so that little attention was paid to the goings-on from the zombie drop-in visit.

However, their next encounters created more of a stir. No longer possessing the desire to completely devour their next victims, they came across a trio seated in folding captains' chairs, debating the accuracy of the prediction for a major storm that evening. The trio all rose up when they spied the couple staggering toward them, covered with blood. All three assumed the couple had been in some sort of terrible accident, rushing forward to provide aid. Within moments, the three had been bitten, gouged, scratched and groped. The resulting screams brought a nearby young, gay, male couple to the scene, who both suffered the same fate.

Within minutes, a crowd of a dozen additional walk-in campers were drawn in, all trying to subdue the tattooed zombie couple. The z-couple was finally taken down, pinned to the ground by the crowd, with all but two of the rescuers bitten in the process. One of the unbitten liberators sprinted from the walk-in campground to seek the first available authorities, telling anyone along the way there was trouble in the walk-in campground. The other unbitten man stayed behind, helping hold down the snarling couple. Within minutes, the bitten rescuers were completely sapped of their strength, became disoriented, losing their grip on the z-couple they had pinned to the playa. Now the only remaining unbitten rescuer was the one searching for help. The zombie couple was once again roaming free.

The original porta-potty zombies, the balding, middle aged Hispanic, wearing in a white tee shirt and tan cargo shorts and his smaller, skinny companion, had been trapped all day in their blue fiberglass prison. Their porta potty bank was further south in the walk-in campground, out of hearing distance from the z-couple incident. Someone, after exiting a nearby toilet in the walk-in porta potty bank, heard commotion in the stall occupied by the zombies. Thinking the noise to be unusual, they approached the stall, unsure if someone was hurt or needed assistance. They remained outside the stall for more than five minutes, asking if the person or persons inside needed help. They received no response, other than grunting and thumping against the door.

By chance, at around six thirty-five p.m., the porta potty vendor happened to be driving by on the way to service some RVs parked just outside the walk-in area. The concerned porta-potty citizen flagged the vendor down, letting him know it appeared that someone apparently incapacitated was stuck inside the loo. The serviceman was convinced to check it out. He arrived at the occupied stall, listened for half-a-minute, making his own unanswered inquires, before proceeding to pull a small special tool from his belt that unlocked the door from the outside.

The balding, Hispanic zombie and his diminutive z-companion were on top of the serviceman and the concerned citizen within seconds, chomping and gouging away. Both managed to break free, fleeing to the service truck and shutting the doors. The two zombies continued to circle the service truck, drawn in not only by their cornered prey, but also by the truck's aroma.

Close to six fifty p.m., the other porta-potty couple emerged. They had been sharing a unit in a bank of porta-potties near K and 3:00, after wandering from their open tent in the walk-in campground. Their door wasn't locked, but the groaning, moaning, bumping and banging coming from inside managed to scare off just about all potential occupants who approached the unlocked door with the handle turned to the green, vacant position. Several times, preoccupied persons opened the door only to find the couple inside, kneeling at the stall, intently focused on the sights below. Each time, the door was promptly shut, while the prospective occupant moved onto another stall, shaking their head with an 'only at Burning Man would you see that' kind of expression.

After three hours of futilely trying to obtain the elusive pay dirt at the bottom of the porta-potty, the couple stood up, pushing at each wall, quickly finding that one was a door. They stepped outside. Just as they emerged, an overweight man, costumed in a pink ballerina outfit, exited the stall next to them, trotting up to his more conventionally dressed boyfriend waiting by the hand sanitizer provided at the end of the porta potty bank. The two men strolled briskly back to the walk-in campground. The porta-potty couple was completely focused on the two men, staggering after them.

The ballerina and his boyfriend arrived at their tent, far enough away from the developing zombie ruckus at the other end of the walk-in campground, so that they were unaware of the goings-on. They were aware of the porta-potty couple's arrival, as they kneeled outside their tent, sifting through a duffel bag they had just pulled outside. Both zombies were drawn to the weightier ballerina, grabbing on and biting hard as the ballerina screamed. The ballerina's left ear was severed moments later. The ballerina's companion broke free unscathed, running to the next large cabin tent, pleading for the two couples inside to go get help. One couple returned with the companion to assist the screaming ballerina. One minute later, all three were bitten, while the ballerina's left face and upper left arm had already been consumed. Things only got worse from there.

The two walking-zombie-tents had both tripped and fallen in their trek across the open playa on several occasions. Both had been down for an extended period of time, and had fallen into zombie naps, when a Black Rock Ranger came across them on the open playa, around a hundred feet apart from each other. Neither set of tent-occupants responded to the BRR's repeated queries.

The ranger unzipped the tents; the occupants were clearly alive but quite unresponsive. He assumed a drug overdose was involved; he radioed for an ambulance. While Rampart was still off-limits to new patients, the ambulances were still being dispatched from there; transporting patients to the clinics in the 3:00 or 9:00 plazas. At 7:09 p.m., two ambulances were on their way; the 3:00 plaza clinic was notified of the impending arrivals.

The zombies trapped inside the rental RV near J and 3:45 had yet to be heard from. But at seven fourteen p.m., Ranger

Rick was apprised that all hell was breaking loose in the walk-in campground, with all available units being deployed to three reported flashpoints in that area, and that four patients with highly suspicious symptoms had been found lying inside two collapsed tents out on the open playa. The patients were currently being transported to the 3:00 plaza medical clinic.

Ranger Rick picked up his radio. The Executive Team needed to meet, stat. He wondered out loud if an evacuation needed to be ordered or if this new outbreak could be contained in the walk-in campground. He considered the impending thunderstorm that would sink the BRC streets into a quagmire. He shook his head. Speaking to no one in particular, he exclaimed, "Just when I think I have seen it all, I behold something new that makes me realize exactly how blind I must have been."

Thursday Friday Saturday Sunday Monday Tuesday Wednesday

The After Party

The BLM had been monitoring the twenty-plus cars and RV parked on private property, twelve miles north of Black Rock City, since Sunday morning. There had been no noticeable activity. The operative assumption was the site had been used as some sort of staging ground for a private party bus to Burning Man.

But around six thirty pm, the BLM helicopter patrolling the playa took a side trip to check out the site, at the suggestion of a Ranger who had driven just outside the property. The crew reported back that the site appeared unoccupied, but looked as if it had ransacked, and it was difficult to verify with any certainty, but there might possibly be two or three decaying bodies on the ground.

The BLM Incident Commander radioed the Winnemucca District Manager for direction. Initially, it was determined that a search warrant should be obtained to enter the property. After almost a half-hour was spent pursuing the warrant, the DM relented and authorized the Incident Commander to send in a team, without the warrant, on the basis of the potential sighting of several bodies.

Two ranger pickups were deployed to the site of the Burning Man pre-party. They maneuvered around the impromptu parking lot of deserted cars, including a Subaru with the driver door still open. The sound equipment, drink tubs, and drink containers littered around the site made it obvious a party had taken place. The rangers parked both vehicles in front of an RV that had been totally trashed. A generator was situated immediately north of the RV, dead, but still hooked up. The four BLM rangers inspected the RV with the front door open, floor littered with trash, debris and broken shards of RV furniture, fixtures and dinnerware. Blood stains were abundant.

The rangers exited the RV, proceeding north on foot. They discovered three grisly partial corpses and a field full of people's personal effects – purses, shirts, smartphones, wallets. The rangers chased off a lone sea gull that had been picking around the corpses. The rangers commented on how rare it was for a bird to be spotted just off of the playa, and a sea gull at that.

A report was called into the Incident Commander at seven thirty-one p.m. The rangers were instructed to probe further. Casing the property due south, the rangers came across two blue, rented porta-potties, both knocked over. One unoccupied stall lay on its side, the blood-stained door open on the ground.

The second porta potty lay face down. The Rangers approached the outhouse, two on each end, and turned it forty-five degrees so that the door faced to the left. A ranger opened the door to discover a dehydrated, delirious, semi-conscious young brunette woman, too weak to talk. A call was made to Black Rock City to dispatch an ambulance, but the request was denied, as apparently a bit of a situation was rearing its head back in Burning Man.

The woman was lifted up and placed in the back of the double cab ranger pickup; a team of two of the rangers sped off with her toward Gerlach. The remaining rangers called to file another report with their Incident Commander. The topic of conversation centered on the possible whereabouts of the occupants of twenty-five or so vehicles left deserted at the edge of the Black Rock playa.

Thursday Friday Saturday Sunday Monday Tuesday Wednesday

The Mother of All Dust Storms

Monday 7:42 PM

The wind started whipping up the dust just north of the Black Rock City, first in mild bursts, then with sporadic strength, and finally, shortly after sunset, in full force. A wicked, brownish-gray, mammoth wall of dust was sweeping relentlessly toward BRC.

Conner and Bruce were somewhat ahead of schedule as they hoofed it towards Burning Man. More than once, they had to stop while Conner gathered his bearings after a bout of dizziness. Both men commented that the BLM must have become pre-occupied, as the two advanced across the playa without incident.

As the wind first caught them, they yanked the extra shirts out of their daypacks, tying them around their faces to serve as makeshift dust masks. Bruce insisted he could navigate them forward as the dust wall built in intensity and depth. He convinced Conner that the dust storm was their ticket inside Burning Man – they should be able to walk right up to and over the perimeter fence unnoticed, if the storm continued with such ferocity. The storm proved to be a much greater struggle to proceed through than anticipated. Bruce had never experienced anything of this magnitude. Still, the two trudged forward.

Due west, the herd of sixty-five zombies from the pre-party wound their way out of foothills, crossing back over County Road 34, onto the playa. The dust storm enveloped them as well. The zombies seemed indifferent to the whistling wall of dust. Like Conner and Bruce, they slogged forward, undetected.

As a darkening Black Rock City took cover in tents, cars, mutant vehicles and art installations, the dust whistled through. Several backpacking tents without proper inside weight, secured only by six inch tent stakes, launched into the sky. Countless folding chairs, tables, signs and bicycles blew over.

A lone BLM Ranger parked outside the western perimeter fence, put down his night vision goggles, deciding it was pointless to scan the area for potential BRC illegal immigrants, until the dust storm died down a bit. Then out of the corner of his right eye, he swore he caught movement. It appeared to be a group of mind-boggling size. After letting loose a couple of expletives, he gunned his pickup forward just as whiteout conditions again took hold. Fifteen seconds later he pulled to a stop, realizing he just ran through the orange perimeter fence, a portion of which was now tangled underneath his wheels.

The ranger opened his door, preparing to exit the vehicle to inspect the damage. As the dust filled the cab, he decided to wait out the conditions. He pulled the driver door back shut, which required both hands, due to the force of the wind. He peered out the front windshield, but could see nothing. He was in the epicenter of the mother of all dust storms, with visibility ranging two or three feet. He radioed his dilemma back to the Incident Commander, but withheld mention that he may or may not have seen a group of people outside the perimeter just before he took out a section of the fence. He decided he was just seeing things in the whiteout conditions.

Had the ranger been able to distinguish twenty feet further, he would have noticed the sixty-plus party zombies trudging past. He remained unaware that their entrance into Black Rock City had just been arranged by his errant rendezvous with the fence.

Minutes later, a quarter of a mile east, Conner and Bruce pulled themselves over the perimeter fence. The two were exhausted. Their lungs and throats ached from all the dust they inhaled. Like runners crossing a marathon finish line, they collapsed immediately into the playa. In the disorienting deluge of dust, Conner shouted at Bruce that they needed to get up, push themselves forward at least another hundred yards, and then rest, so that they wouldn't be found conspicuously next to the fence whenever the storm did let up.

It seemed to require every reserve of energy remaining in their bodies, but Conner and Bruce rose up, their lips and mouths parched, their eyes bloodshot and swollen, their limbs trembling and unsteady. They sucked it up, advancing the length of a football field in the relentless dustathon, finally crashing to the ground, too tired to think or move.

Further west, the party zombies cruised into the Burning Man open playa, undaunted by the elements. Then, as suddenly as it started, the mother of all dust storms ceased.

A couple minutes later, back in the Space Ghost Camp, the cessation of hostilities from the playa dust was celebrated with resounding whoops and hollers. Cassie and Tess had taken refuge in their cabin tent, now coated with a heavy layer of fine playa dust. They unzipped the front door, emerging to take in the evening in Black Rock City.

Thursday Friday Saturday Sunday **Monday** Tuesday Wednesday

The Colonels

Ranger Rick sighed deeply, while seated in his small office at the Black Rock Ranger HQ on the Esplanade. He was determined to compartmentalize the stress, from knowing the difficulty of tasks that must be undertaken, the sorrow from seeing several bitten friends laying near-comatose back in Rampart, the sense of loss that Burning Man was about to end just when it was getting started, the frustration from being faced with fighting a situation and disease that defied logic.

The Executive Team, consisting of Board Executive Committee members and Senior Staff, had quickly reached consensus that full Incident Command System protocols must be deployed, and a rapid evacuation was required. There had been initial argument that the reported flare-ups in the walk-in campground could be contained to that area. The BLM Rangers, Pershing County deputies and Black Rock Rangers and any other available enforcement that answered the call had formed a line to seal in the walk-in area from the rest of BRC.

Then news came of an incident occurring behind the line. A lady opened the door to visit a couple in an RV near J and 3:45, only to be greeted by four of the diseased persons, who attacked her before disembarking into the neighboring camps. The count of persons reported bitten and injured from the RV assailants kept growing; the assailants had not yet been subdued.

While the total number infected at this point was probably only fifty at the most, out of almost fifty thousand inhabitants that had arrived in the city at this point, what had the Executive Team's attention was that the number had the potential to grow exponentially, and each case appeared to be a one-way ticket without hope of recovery.

All three medical clinics had now taken in bitten victims, and were at capacity. The available supply of gurneys with proper restraints had been exhausted. The new victims, if their disease progressed similarly to what was observed earlier in the day, would have to be subdued in advance, by improvised means. Plans were being finalized for a new makeshift facility to receive new victims until the evacuation could be completed.

The two victims, which had already turned, had been transported from Rampart to Reno, two hours before. Still, an ominous dark cloud hung over the heads of those still brave enough to staff Rampart. Weighing on their minds was the fact the restrained victims, from the early afternoon incident inside the clinic, might turn at any time.

Then there was the matter of the impending thunderstorm, still predicted to hit within a few hours, which could render the dirt roads useless for almost any vehicle for a number of hours. Other members of the Executive Team were still meeting, discussing the logistics of the evacuation plan drawn up long before, as a theoretical and regulatory exercise, arguing if it could be accomplished before the storm hit in full force or if the evacuation would need to be prioritized and staged over time.

The two on-site CDC staff and the recently arrived infectious disease specialist, were nowhere close to providing explanations — let alone a treatment plsn — for the baffling condition. One of the CDC staff was currently sequestered in an area of the Media Mecca, which had the best available bandwidth and technology, Skyping with superiors back in Atlanta. The two higher-ups in Atlanta were pointedly reprimanding her for not taking stronger action or red-flagging the situation sooner. She was informed that all communication and direction henceforth would be coordinated from Atlanta.

Ranger Rick dialed into a hastily arranged conference call with the BLM Incident Commander, BLM District Manager and Pershing County Sheriff to coordinate the imminent evacuation. Ranger Rick was thirty seconds or so into his opening remarks when the BLM District Manager interrupted.

"Look, I'm sorry to cut you off, but there has been a change in plans. I didn't get the opportunity when we all entered the call, but we have two additional persons on the line. I have handed over authority for the mission that you're about to be briefed on, to the Colonel and Vice Commander at Nellis Air Force Base, who is coordinating with the Nevada National Guard Joint Forces, that are currently being deployed.... Colonel?"

"Thank you and I will make this short. I will do my best to avoid military-speak and jargon. We have a lot to do. I understand this was to be a conference call to coordinate an evacuation of Black Rock City, but that is not going to happen now. We are operationalizing a quarantine of the surrounding area and.."

"What the hell are you talking about..." Ranger Rick cut in.

The BLM District Manager shut him down. "Gentlemen. I will remind that you are talking to a Colonel of the United States Air Force and it is imperative that we get through this call ASAP. Let us ensure there are no interruptions.... Sorry and please go on, Colonel..."

The Vice Commander and Colonel continued. "I was about to say, this situation is a lot bigger than your Burning Man. During the course of the past two and a half hours, I have been apprised that this contagion has sporadically spread throughout the Black Rock region over the past three days without being detected by authorities until this afternoon. We commissioned a Nellis chopper and verified the ground zero for this outbreak, which is classified with respect to location and operating details. We are in consultation with CDC in Atlanta, and have civilians under observation that are in Stage I of what has been determined to be a virus of devastating magnitude, transmitted, basically, orally via biting. We also have victims under observation in Stage II, which evidently occurs after the infected person technically expires. The Stage II cases no longer possess basic cognitive abilities, but are capable of functioning and seeking victims either to consume or simply infect. They continue functioning, even after experiencing what by definition should be fatal application of force, unless they are obliterated or receive a direct shot that pierces the brain sufficiently to permanently incapacitate them."

The Colonel paused. Several voices chimed in. The BLM District Manager again reminded the conference callers not to interrupt. The Colonel once again proceeded. "So the point, gentlemen, is that CDC advises us the best-case timeframe to develop any actionable clinical response is days, not hours away. More likely, we're looking at weeks or even months, not days. There is no precedence for a virus of this nature. The Stage II victims are invulnerable to almost anything but a military response, and in their state, they are dedicated to one thing and one thing only – spreading the virus. The potential for pandemic of something unchartered, of this magnitude, requires isolating this outbreak no matter what the cost. I understand the temptation to follow through with a hasty plan for evacuation, given the rate of infection as we speak is so small. But in discussing scenarios with the CDC, this virus is such a wild card, that if it is not contained to this area, the population of your city will be miniscule in comparison to the devastation in the general population that will ensue within a week's time. I have been thoroughly convinced of this, and have secured authorization to proceed operationally on the basis of containment, here and now. So, before we discuss logistics for the quarantine of Black Rock City, understand the intelligence we have just received, that you are likely not party to. An event, with an estimated fifty or sixty attendees based upon the vehicles present, occurred about twenty kilometers north of here, in which BLM Rangers have just discovered at least three corpses, with the remainder unaccounted for except for one survivor who we have not spoken with yet. Every indication is that this group has, in their entirety, progressed to Stage II, and our best operating assumption is they headed in your Burning Man direction, but understand, they have not been located."

The Colonel cleared his throat. This time, no one interrupted. "While I have procured an immediate response team from Nellis and supplemental forces from area law enforcement agencies, we still have very limited available personnel until the National Guard deployment is one hundred percent. Thus we will dedicate all resources toward securing the region's perimeter. No Stage I or Stage II infected can break this perimeter, or I trust you all understand the potentially catastrophic consequences. Now, I must note, our advance team, which has already set down in Gerlach, just reported that a Pershing County deputy, violating all protocol, transported a Stage I infected fellow officer at high speed, off-road across the desert floor, back to Gerlach. The officer was bitten during an incident that I understand is still ongoing at the edge of your city. The Deputy, when debriefed, indicated your medical clinics are at capacity and he did not want to leave his colleague unattended to. He intended to arrange transport to a hospital in Reno. My point is, that if your deputies are going to attempt to smuggle an infected person outside the perimeter, what makes you think the citizens of Black Rock City wouldn't do the exact same thing in a mass evacuation? Or aren't attempting to do so right now? We simply do not have the resources to inspect each passenger of each vehicle at this point in time. What we have done, is send someone to your gate to ensure it is shut down now. So, Black Rock City is being quarantined as we speak. As I said, we'll discuss those logistics in a minute."

Ranger Rick broke in again. "Now, just hold on..."

The Colonel talked right over him, raising his distinctive, authoritative voice. "Sheriff, we have already notified your off-duty deputies, residing at Bruno's Motel in Gerlach, that their services are about to be required, and we'd appreciate the courtesy of your contacting them to authorize their support in securing the southern perimeter, along with our advance team. Our Nellis 57th Wing advance team personnel and the advance National Guard team will hold the northern perimeter, and the BLM rangers and other onsite enforcement agencies will be responsible for the eastern and western perimeters. My Chief Master Sergeant, Darren Carter, is en route to your Black Rock Ranger headquarters to coordinate securing the city. He will provide detailed information regarding the perimeters, which I will remind you, are well beyond the boundaries of Burning Man."

Ranger Rick bristled, again attempting to take the floor. "Now would you just..."

The Colonel was not about to yield, again speaking over Ranger Rick. "So, Pershing deputies on-site will provide the armed security inside the city, and the Black Rock Rangers will work with them to establish a Green Zone. Chief Master Sergeant Carter will provide a briefing and will welcome your input, but the assumption would be you will start small and expand the zone as you verify the occupants and have the resources to adequately secure its perimeter. I have been provided some limited background on your infrastructure. Understand, you will need to transfer the victims out of your main medical clinic, if it is to be within this zone. And you're going to need to take control of your communications. You will shut down your media tent, take control of the private FM broadcasts and broadcast from your own station that due to a public health emergency, everyone is advised to immediately take shelter inside a vehicle and secure themselves until further notice, and that due to the impending storm, the gates to the city are closed until further notice. I'm not worried if some people manage to break ranks and sneak out on their single passenger bicycles to our perimeter. Victims in Stage I or Stage II aren't going to be riding bicycles solo. We just can't have vehicles leave the city. To even allow a limited, screened number of them through, invites all others to attempt to follow suit, and we don't have the resources to manage a mutiny on that scale. CMS Carter will work with you on plausible details. But I don't think I need to tell you that you must control the flow of information, and we must be judicious in the information we provide as to not precipitate a panic, resulting in a rush to the exits."

The Colonel paused, the conference line filled with voices. The Colonel inserted himself one last time. "Now, don't think we are opposed to an evacuation. There will be a successful evacuation in this mission, but not until we have secured the perimeter with adequate personnel to perform a controlled exit. And unfortunately that will not be anytime soon tonight. You and your citizens are going to have to work together and hunker down, tonight. Gentleman, I have to excuse myself. It is going to consume more time than any of us would like to operationalize this, and the citizens of your city are going to be on their own, and likely clueless in the immediate future, while we put this package together in real-time. You can save your questions for CMS Carter, who I understand has already cleared the city gates. In the meantime, I am going to turn this over to our advisor, who is the one person that has a trove of actionable intelligence on these Stage II cases and has been amongst them for the past three days, going back to our ground zero, which he directed us to. He is basically responsible for blowing the lid off of this and bringing us in. He will brief you tactically for a couple of minutes on how to accomplish successful encounters with these Stage II cases. He has been listening in on the call, and gentleman, I give you retired Air Force Colonel and physician, Alan Gorman."

Thursday Friday Saturday Sunday Monday Tuesday Wednesday

The End of the Odyssey

Alan Gorman was not a man to curse, but he let a series of expletives fly as he felt the rim of his driver side wheel crunch against the ground, the remnants of the tire shredding in the process. The Escalade rattled as he lurched forward. He glimpsed sideways to his right, spying the BLM Range Tech sprinting away towards the hills, outpacing the two zombies staggering after him.

Alan pulled up next to the white MDX. He noticed a Hycroft mine company insignia on the driver door. The driver, a younger man wearing a Reno Aces baseball cap, was frozen behind the wheel, terror residing in his facial expression. The bitten, balding, obese man had fought his way back inside the SUV. His attackers were pounding on his MDX passenger door.

Alan swung his own door open, planting his prosthetic foot into the gravel, positioning his rifle over his right shoulder. He had a clear shot at his meteorological friend, but hesitated. Moments later, he took the one shot still available to him, felling another one of the zombies with a direct shot through the forehead. This brought the attention of meteorological man and the other two remaining z's harassing the MDX. All three headed straight for Alan.

Alan decided to try the rear driver side door to the MDX, as opposed to his own vehicle. He slid into the middle row with rifle in hand, shutting the door behind him.

"Your friend has been bit." Alan stated the obvious, watching the obese, balding man clutching at his bleeding arm, gasping for breath.

"What the hell is going on? You have to tell us what's going on here," the panicked younger driver pleaded.

First, Alan wanted to get something out of the way. "Why did you guys take a shot at me?"

The driver glanced around nervously as the three zombies were now at the driver side windows, pounding away. His companion didn't look so good. "Hey, we're sorry, man. He didn't realize that something was really wrong with those people outside. He thought you were the bad guy, man, shooting at them....We...we...we were just sent out to the mine because the overnight crew apparently never made it back to their homes, and we seem to have lost all communication."

Alan grunted. "And they just sent the two of you? How many were on that crew? And why did they wait so long to send you?"

The driver was having trouble processing why he needed to answer these questions when the most bizarre thing in the world seemed to be going on just outside his car door. "I....I don't know. There were just two of them working nights, and four during the days, with twelve hour shifts. BLM shut us down this week because of Burning Man. And...I think....I think it took this long for their family or whoever to figure out they were missing and track down someone with Hycroft."

Alan sighed. "Well, I hate to break it to you, but these things have overrun your mine. You really don't want to go there."

Alan provided a very short version of what had gone down, not bothering to explain any extraterrestrial origin or his every encounter during the past three days. He grew quite disappointed to learn that his new companions lacked a satellite phone. As the three zombie-pests continued to beat at the driver side windows, the obese passenger in the front moaned, offering complaints in sentences constructed of four words or less. Alan weighed their options.

Gorman considered coaxing the nervous driver to maneuver the MDX down into the gauntlet to retrieve the runaway BLM range tech's satellite phone, still lying out in the road. He considered the inventory of potential weapons in his Escalade that he might retrieve to take down into the gauntlet if he could dispatch or distract the three zombies outside. Alan pictured the chainsaw, lighter fluid and matches, knife, baseball bat, crowbar, and hammer that Bruce supplied him hours earlier, all waiting for him on his Escalade floorboard. He could outfit the driver seated in front of him with this menu of potential weapons should Alan's rifle not suffice, if they ran into trouble retrieving the phone. Alan closed his eyes, trying to imagine how the sat phone rescue mission would play out.

Gorman then chuckled, realizing he was so tired that he wasn't thinking clearly. All they needed to do was turn around, drive less than five minutes or so, and be within cell phone range. As fortune would have it, his own Blackberry, with his contact list, happened to be on his person. He had placed it his rear pocket when he reentered his Escalade less than ten minutes prior after spying the Blackberry in the middle of the driver's seat.

Alan convinced the MDX driver to turn the vehicle around, so they both could make some calls. They left meteorological man and his zombie companions in the distance. Alan debated if they should go off-road to retrieve the BLM range tech, but he couldn't spot him as he scanned the foothills. Alan decided he was done with any further rescue missions and distractions.

Alan first called the BLM Winnemucca District Office, opting to go easy on the zombie talk, so he didn't get dismissed as a crackpot. He let them know they had a range tech wandering the foothills, a gauntlet of vehicles on Jungo Road, filled with crazed, diseased individuals, and the Hycroft mine had been overrun by these people as well. He put the Hycroft driver on the phone to verify that a problem existed at the mine. He advised the BLM to send some armed rangers out their way to check it out.

Alan didn't want to spend too much time with the BLM. He was more interested in tracking down his old friend, now in the leadership at Nellis Air Force Base near Las Vegas. Alan knew the ground zero meteor site would be of interest, and that Alan had sufficient credibility with his onetime patient. It took a while to connect, but once they did, events unfolded quickly. Eventually, Alan found himself in Gerlach with the Air Force advance team, courtesy of BLM transport, at the request of Alan's friend.

Once fully up to speed in his office at the base, the Colonel and Vice Commander of the Nellis 57th Wing was most concerned about keeping under wraps the extraterrestrial nature of the virus and the globe-shaped weapon disguised as a meteor. He expressed his disappointment with Gorman that Alan shared this information with some citizens he encountered. The Colonel tracked down the BLM Winnemucca District Manager, not only to discuss assuming authority for the mission under development, but to locate a certain runaway range tech, isolate him, and make sure he talked to no one until debriefed by the Colonel's staff.

The Colonel was just as anxious to locate and sequester this 'Bruce and Conner' who Gorman spent time with earlier in the day. The Colonel wasn't happy to subsequently learn that the BLM had them in their possession, and let them go, back out on the playa. The Colonel instructed his Chief Master Sergeant, Darren Carter, who had been quickly dispatched to Black Rock City with an advance team, to ensure that these two individuals were broadcast as persons of interest to all agencies coordinating under the mission.

Thursday Friday Saturday Sunday Monday Tuesday Wednesday

Monday Evening, Black Rock City

It was a sight to behold — the multi-story Burning Man platform, lit up at night on the open playa, with the star of the show standing tall on the platform, decked out in pastel, neon colored lights. The Promenades leading out to the Man were lined with streetlights. From this center of the Burning Universe, it was more than a third of a mile to get to the Esplanade; close to a mile and a half out to the perimeter fences.

Like any city of fifty or sixty thousand, the citizens in one part of town typically had no idea about what was happening at any given moment outside their neighborhood. *Unlike* any other city of fifty or sixty thousand, the BRC citizens were for the most part off the grid, unable to receive a text message, a tweet or a Facebook post from a friend across town.

So Cassie and Tess, like their thousands of companions on the open playa beyond the Esplanade, had no idea of the battle being waged in the walk-in campground or in the wake of the four zombies carving a path into the city from the neighborhood of J and 3:45, after escaping from an RV. Cassie and Tess and the other citizens out on the open playa had no idea the party zombies had broken through the perimeter fence during the dust storm and were wandering toward the big sound camps at 10:00.

What Cassie, Tess and the masses out on the open playa did know, was the dust storm was finally over, nighttime in Black Rock City had finally arrived, and the party needed to rev-up quickly, because a big thunderstorm was predicted within a few hours.

Cassie and Tess's bicycles were outfitted with battery powered pink Christmas lights, both for ambience and for safety – an unlit bike or pedestrian could easily get inadvertently wacked by a nighttime mutant vehicle. After visiting the large well-lit sights—the Man,; Wall Street, the Temple, among others—they started to randomly explore, still decked out in their Jan costumes sans hair extensions, marveling at all the structures illuminated with electroluminescent wire covering the color spectrum.

Watching the mutant vehicles cruise the playa at night was half the fun. Many were equipped with devices to shoot out flames — pirate ships, neon paper hangers, dragons, fireflies, a penismobile, a breastmobile — all on wheels, lit up, and emitting a glorious blaze in the night.

Cassie and Tess came across PlayaFighter III, the live-action video game. In a large, roped-off rectangle, a grid of cylinders released flames in various patterns and sequences. On small, elevated stages — opposite each other on the short ends of the rectangle — stood the opposing contestants, air-boxing each other from a distance. On a larger center stage, just beyond the roped-off grid, stood the MC, the scorekeeper and a trombonist. The MC provided play-by-play and randomly awarded points over a wireless microphone, the scorekeeper turned over flip-pages with a progressive point total for each contestant. The trombonist played little riffs at odd times for no particular reason.

A small bicycle parade meandered by, out-of-sync, the bikes all adorned with purple florescent lights, the riders all younger ladies in Thing 1 and Thing 2 spandex outfits, with a naked man literally bringing up the rear, attired in a tall cat-in-the-hat hat on a stingray banana seat bike.

Cassie and Tess decided it was time to ride out further on the open playa to their favorite art installation, a repeat from the previous year: Pee-wee Herman's Alamo. The two-story structure had a vague resemblance to the fort in San Antonio, only brightly lit and populated with life-size cut-outs of Pee-wee Herman, a fake basement door, a looped soundtrack of "Breakfast Machine" by Danny Elfman from the "Pee-wee's Big Adventure" movie —Cassie and Tess's favorite movie music of all time—laminated posters from the movie, and a sculpture of Pee-wee's beloved bicycle from the movie.

Just before hopping back on their bikes, Cassie reached into her small, purple daypack to grab a water bottle. In fishing around through her bag for the bottle, she realized her camera was not in the bag. Cassie was adamant they take some photos of Burning Man at night, and insisted on quickly returning to camp to fetch the camera. Tess wanted to take in a couple of art-installations that Cassie had visited in the morning, so it was agreed they would meet in fifteen-to-twenty minutes at the Alamo.

Cassie pedaled hard across the playa. She entered the Esplanade at 7:00, by the Roller Boogie Theme Camp — blaring out Donna Summers for the dozen or more bladers and skaters – then raced back to Space Ghost camp. As she approached her tent, she had more than her camera to deal with.

Thursday Friday Saturday Sunday Monday Tuesday Wednesday

Zombie Parade

Sixty-plus party zombies proceeded directly to a new party. The big sound theme camp at the edge of the BRC open playa at 10:00 and Esplanade – camp PlayaPiano — attracted the z's, the pulsating concert-level volume pulled them in, the gargantuan speakers blasting out a house techno pop mash-up.

Contrary to popular opinion, the vast majority of the citizens of Black Rock City don't do drugs, other than caffeine and alcohol, at least during the week of Burning Man, partially due to the enhanced law enforcement presence. The residents of camp PlayaPiano evidently were members of the minority.

During the dust storm, the thirty-five PlayaPiano campers plus their guests, close to a total of seventy in number, took shelter in their massive awning-enclosure behind the sound stage. The down time led to the camp raiding their stash of ecstasy, handing out the entire supply to the patrons bored by the dust storm. They weren't bored for long, although the overdosing didn't accentuate anyone's high.

En route to camp PlayaPiano, the party zombies staggered at a higher rate of speed than usual, progressing from their point of entry — the fence taken out by the errant BLM pickup. The party zombies were a sight to behold: ragged, torn clothing – four or five of them sans clothing –grayish, open wounds and sores of all shapes and sizes were sported by all, in every imaginable location; pale-gray skin tone and greasy-matted hair was the look that seemed to be in vogue.

It wasn't long before they were spotted in the dark by a group of a dozen or so citizens, recently dropped off by a mutant vehicle, near the outer fringes of the BRC open playa. Someone in the group exclaimed a nighttime zombie crawl was taking place in front of them. It was commented on how realistic the costumes and makeup looked on those in the parade.

The people spontaneously decided that even lacking costumes and makeup, it was time to join in the zombie crawl. At first, they mixed in without incident. But within sixty seconds, every member of the group had been mauled, two being consumed beyond recognition. In the dark, other citizens couldn't really tell what was going on, the screams partially drowned out by the nearby big sound camp.

The z parade left the dozen citizens in the dust. Several were just corpses. The remainder of the group was sprawled on the open playa floor, a mixture of flesh, blood and soil, only less flesh than they previously possessed. In the dark, passersby steered clear of the bodies on the ground, assuming they were alright and just having some unique experience or napping, perhaps. Some time passed until their plight was discovered.

Camp PlayaPiano welcomed the approaching zombie parade with open arms. Campers trotted up to the lead zombies to fist bump them in approval of their get-ups, complete with authentic bloodstained faces. Only two or three PlayaPiano partiers escaped unbitten from the ensuing carnage in the rattling din of the full-on techno pop medley.

Just a couple of the PlayaPianos were devoured. The remainder ranged from minor bites to losing almost all flesh from a limb. The whole episode played out within two minutes of the arrival of the zombie parade. A handful of spectators approached the camp as the attack unfolded. They were caught in the mayhem.

Having almost uniformly swallowed the supply of little white ecstasy pills, the Camp PlayaPiano patrons were not long for this world. As with their attackers from the pre-party after ingesting LSD, the Playa Piano campers and guests experienced a fatal reaction quickly after the onset of Stage I, many foaming at the mouth and convulsing near the end. This cleared the path to Stage II, allowing the party zombie population to more than double in size.

Thursday Friday Saturday Sunday Monday Tuesday Wednesday

Kayaking Through Time

They made love, off and on from late Friday night through early Saturday morning — three separate times — interrupted by some quiet conversation and a couple hours of sleep or vice-versa, the sleep interrupted by the making love, depending on how one looked at it.

After that, Conner and Cassie slept in until late in the morning. They finally rose, showered, awkwardly dressed in the same room for the first time; they then ventured out into Reno close to noon. They decided to head downtown, parking in a public garage off of Third Street, adjacent to Harrah's, the National Bowling Center, and the El Dorado Casino.

Not wanting to stuff themselves at a casino buffet, they opted for a small brunch in a local restaurant on First Street as they angled toward the Truckee River. The two emitted an aura of infatuation with each other (their waitress commented on how much they seemed to enjoy each other's company), as they nibbled on their omelets and buttermilk blueberry pancakes.

After their leisurely brunch, they strolled down to Island Avenue, taking in the sights and sounds of the small park around the Truckee River. Spur-of-the-moment, they elected to check out the Reno White Water Adventure Tour shack, just off the downtown Truckee River Whitewater Park. A quick decision was made to blow off movie plans, instead opting for a two-hour, two-person kayak trip. The kayaks were plastic, the water was slow and shallow. A small ice bag was provided, which they filled with several beers procured from a nearby convenience store.

At two fifteen p.m., the bus arrived to transport them several miles upstream with their rented kayak, which was soon launched into the Truckee. Conner sat in back, Cassie up front, as they tried to maneuver down the river with as minimal effort as possible.

Their conversation drifted as much as they did in the water. What became of whom back in Parker Creek was a big topic, along with the issues of the day in their respective professions – hospital management and market research. Cassie wanted to know all about Conner's rekindled friendship with Bruce; Conner was interested in hearing all about Cassie's Burning Man companion, Tess.

Eventually, as the kayak floated and periodically required paddling, past houses, apartments, brush, and beached partiers along the river – with the partiers' aroma of marijuana wafting from shore out into the Truckee — the conversation steered toward their current state of thinking about each other.

"I was determined not to talk too much about us, to us, so I apologize in advance," Cassie started, brushing the wisps of hair off her forehead as she finally downed the last sips of her second beer – a Coors Light. "But Conner, I have to let you know how damn nervous I was coming off that Southwest flight, minutes from seeing you in person for the first time in more than two decades... I wanted so much for everything to be good between us and was so worried that we would meet up in baggage claim and just not click; that we would try to carry on like we have from a distance for so long, but somehow, in-person, the magic might not be the same."

Conner laughed just a little, slightly sipping and still nursing his two-thirds-full first beer. "Cassie, I don't know how to explain it, but I wasn't nervous at all. I was just so happy. I dream now and then that my parents are still alive, only I didn't realize it, and I'm just getting to see them for the first time, since forever, and I am so, so happy. Seeing you at the airport was pretty much like that."

Cassie reached forward and kissed Conner's bare back; his shirt was wrapped around his waist. She blurted out, "Well, I've told you over and over, early-on, when we've talked on the phone and chatted online, how I was not wanting or looking for a relationship. And the truth of it is, I wasn't. You are something I was not planning on or hoping for or dreaming of. But now that you're here – we're here – I just feel like time is standing still, and I want it to stay this way – us to stay this way – forever."

Conner was speechless, but ecstatic. He performed some necessary paddling as they rounded a bend, the current growing a little stronger and rougher. He then simply exclaimed, "Yeah, I know."

Cassie continued. "Conner, we can change the subject and talk about something a little less serious, anytime. But I just want you to know what's going on in my head right now. I feel like we've traveled through time, that we never left each other, that we've always been connected to each other, that somehow, you and I, were just meant to be."

Thursday Friday Saturday Sunday Monday Tuesday Wednesday

Luke and Leia

Bruce and Conner lay, covered in playa dust, out in the far reaches of Black Rock City, just a hundred yards from the perimeter fence they recently scaled. Glancing around, it was almost completely dark. Only a thin band of twilight still hovered around the western horizon. They were spent, and they knew it. Conner pulled himself upright, resting on his palms, only to feel a wave of nausea and dizziness. His mouth felt like a mixture of cotton and sand.

Just then, an angel appeared before them, from out of nowhere. A young lady in her early twenties with short jet-black hair, and wearing a white see-through blouse and short-shorts approached them, her daypack in her arms. She pulled out two full water bottles, exclaiming, "Well, you survived the dust storm, but you two look like you need these more than I do." She handed them each one, smiling radiantly in the darkness.

"Thank you so, so, much," Bruce replied, still a little short of breath, as he opened the bottle, held it to his lips, letting the cool, refreshing liquid trickle through his parched mouth.

"My pleasure, boys," she replied, retreating back into the darkness. "The playa provides. Remember always, the playa provides." And then she was gone.

Bruce sat upright with Conner; the two men surveyed the city in the distance, as well as all the lit art installations in between. They were quiet as they slowly sucked down the water bottles. It didn't take long to finish them. Each stuffed the empty bottle into his own daypack.

"Now what?" Bruce asked, turning to Conner.

"Now, we look for something called Space Ghost Camp," Conner stated, although pretty sure he had repeated this bit of information more than once during their trek across the desert floor. Conner swiveled his head, scanning the lights of Black Rock City end-to-end, unaware of the party zombie invasion down at the 10:00 side. "You know, I somehow envisioned this place being more compact. It's humungous. I just thought somehow we'd be able to stumble into this camp right away. How the hell are we supposed to find one little camp in this place, when all we have is a name?"

"We've come this far, Connerman, something tells me we're going to find this Cassie that you won't shut up about, sometime soon, very soon," Bruce offered to Conner as encouragement. He stood up. Conner joined him.

They ventured no more than ten yards when a mutant vehicle approached, a white, sleek, spaceship blaring the soundtrack from *Star Wars Episode IV*, the original movie. The space vehicle pulled alongside Conner and Bruce, the driver, wearing some type of uniform, hollered from his open window, "Would you like a lift, earthlings?"

"Would you be headed back into the city, by any chance?" Bruce inquired.

"For you, earthlings, anything," the driver answered, playfully. "You shall fly to the city with us. Now climb aboard."

Bruce turned to Conner. "I guess it's true," he cracked, stepping up the ladder.

"What?" Conner asked with a puzzled expression as he followed Bruce.

"The playa provides, Connerman. The playa provides," he deadpanned, their mood lifting as their destination neared.

Conner shrugged, trying the line on for size. "For reals, Brucemoose, the playa provides."

The front of the vehicle was needle-shaped, where the driver was situated. The mid-section and back were some sort of open-bay trailers with bench seats and space-vehicle-like facades. Conner and Bruce climbed up a step ladder and took the first row. Behind them was a young couple making out. In the last row were two persons dressed in Imperial Stormtrooper outfits. Both waved.

As the spaceship slowly meandered towards the city, Conner's wandering thoughts flashed back to his youth when he saw *Star Wars* for the first time. He was too little when it originally aired, but the movie was rereleased for a short period of time just before *The Empire Strikes Back* was about to come out. His parents took young Conner to see it in a packed Parker Creek theatre.

The scene from the movie that now came to mind for Conner, as their Burning Man spaceship crept along, was when Luke Skywalker bursts into Princess Leia's cell wearing a Stormtrooper uniform in disguise. She asked Luke: wasn't he a little short to be a Stormtrooper? To which the hero replied after taking off the Stormtrooper helmet, "I'm Luke Skywalker, and I've come to rescue you."

Conner cracked a grin, wondering how his own rescue scene with his Princess Leia would play out soon, somewhere in Space Ghost camp.

As fortune would have it, when the spaceship reached the Esplanade to drop off the young couple who separated their locked lips long enough to deplane, Bruce shouted down to the driver, "Do you know where Space Ghost camp is by any chance?"

"What?" the driver called out, having trouble hearing over the motor just a couple of feet away, which was idling heavier than usual.

"Space Ghost camp. Do you know where it is by any chance?"

The driver didn't make out exactly what Bruce said over the roar of the motor, but replied anyway, "Sure, I can take you to Space Ghost Camp. I love Space Ghost Camp! Space Ghost Camp, next stop."

Bruce elbowed Conner, telling him in a low voice, "I had a hunch that some guy driving around a spaceship would know where Space Ghost camp was.

The mutant vehicle wound its way up 7:30 slowly, maneuvering around bikes and pedestrians. The spaceship was wide enough, so that there wasn't a whole lot of clearance on either side of the street. Minutes later, they arrived at Space Ghost camp. Conner and Bruce dismounted, thanking their driver profusely. Conner could not believe their good fortune, in how quickly and easily they happened upon Cassie's camp. *Maybe the playa does provide,* Conner thought, imagining that they might be able to pull off escaping Burning Man within the hour.

The two men wandered through the camp, asking about Cassie and Tess. There was some confusion, as they were instructed where to find Jan and Jace's tent, but Conner and Bruce sorted it out. They quickly found the cabin tent as described, only sans Jan and Jace.

Conner decided the best thing to do was wait. They plopped down into the dusty, folding captain's chairs outside the tent, taking in the sights and sounds of the dark and half-deserted camp. They turned on the large battery operated lantern situated next to the chairs. Time passed by slowly. Finally, Cassie arrived. She sailed in quickly on her lit-up bike, jumped off, deploying the kick-stand.

She walked right up to the tent, almost passing by Conner and Bruce, focused on retrieving her camera – still in her Space Ghost Jan costume — not processing that the two men were there or that someone had turned on her lantern. She stood dumbfounded for a moment, then shrieked, bounding forward to hug and squeeze Conner, who had risen from his chair.

"You came! You got tickets and came to see me!" Cassie could not conceal her utter delight at Conner's spontaneity. "How did you ever get tickets? And is this Bruce? Little Bruce Kepner? Oh..my..God!" Bruce rose up. Cassie gave him a big hug, and kiss on the cheek.

"Cassie," Conner spoke out in a most serious tone, "we need to talk. Right now. Can we step inside your tent for a few minutes?"

Cassie's face fell. *What on earth has happened?* she wondered. *Who died?*

Cassie unzipped the tent, forlorn, as Bruce and Conner fell quiet. Conner ducked his head, entering the tent. Bruce sat back down in the captain's chair. Cassie looked back at Bruce, settling in the chair. "Aren't you coming?" she asked apprehensively.

"I'll let you two talk. I'll join in later," Bruce responded, adopting Conner's grave tone.

Cassie's face grew ashen. She turned, entered the tent, sitting herself cross-legged on top of the two light-blue sleeping bags that resided on the queen-size air mattress, as Conner had already done.

The conversation did not go well.

Conner had a half-day to rehearse and refine exactly how he intended to convince Cassie that she needed to flee Burning Man post-haste. Instead, he rambled, blurting out startling fragments of his day, followed by having to backtrack and explain some context.

Conner did manage to impart that he slipped the night before – drinking himself into a plastered state; now realizing he could never have a drink of any kind again. His story from there found him waking to a room full of zombie-like people that attacked them, chasing them to a roof of an abandoned old ranch house on Bruce's compound, with one of his friends bitten by the creatures, becoming quite ill. Conner described the zombie Man-In-The-Roof; their friend's fall and subsequent transformation into one of the zombie creatures, their other friend's attempted rescue of their fallen comrade – leading to his demise as well. Conner worked his tale into the arrival of Alan Gorman, who shot each of their zombie attackers in the head, sat on the roof with them, sharing his own experience of the past days fighting the zombie people after discovering the source – an alien weapon disguised as a meteor. Conner closed his recap of the day's events explaining how their car keys were trapped inside Bruce's trailer with several zombies, how Alan Gorman insisted on driving back towards Winnemucca and surely must have reached some authorities by now, unless something happened to him, and how Bruce and he wandered the desert floor the rest of the day — encountering a corpse on the way — until they made it to Black Rock City, sneaking through in the height of the dust storm.

Cassie just listened, nodding, supplying an occasional "uh-huh." Her body language tightened up, she couldn't stop her face from contorting at times. She latched on to certain things that Conner said, not catching what might follow as she attempted to process what she was hearing.

Conner closed by imploring that they needed to pack and leave right now. He could tell Cassie wasn't on the same wavelength, as he studied her, sensing she was shutting down.

"I know it's a lot to take in. Too much to take in, I'm sure. But please, Cassie, tell me what you're thinking. Tell me what I need to explain better or say differently." he pleaded.

Cassie felt like her head was spinning. She glanced around the tent nervously. She was worried about saying something she might later regret.

There comes a point in many — perhaps most – sudden, intense relationships, where at least one of the partners has a blindsiding moment of doubt, where there is a realization that the person they were so infatuated with may not be everything they thought them to be, and the questions and qualms start bubbling up in a cauldron of dark thoughts.

Cassie went down this path. She was angry that Conner and Bruce had snuck into Burning Man without a ticket. She was angry that he showed up at her doorstep — her tent step — demanding, insisting that she leave. But her anger was secondary to her fear; fear that Conner was not who she thought he was, not the sweet, brilliant young man from high school in Parker Creek. Instead, he might still be an unstable alcoholic with mental illness, who had connected with an equally troubled, hermit-friend from his past.

Cassie decided the best thing to do was say little, get the heck out of there, and think this through further far away from the two men now occupying her camp. "Conner, I just don't know what to say to that. I'm sorry, it's just a bit much, and it's not like we're hearing about any of this out here. I'm sorry, but there has been no talk of anything you're trying to tell me about."

"But, I need to—" Conner started to prepare his defense.

Cassie interrupted him in a firm tone of voice. "Conner, we can talk about this later. Right now, Tess is waiting for me at the Alamo, and I've been keeping her waiting. I'm going to catch up with her, and we may be awhile. We can talk more when I get back."

Cassie grabbed her camera, bolting out of her unzipped tent, past Bruce and onto her bike. Conner scrambled after her, calling out her name, but she had scooted out of camp, and far out of sight. Conner turned around, heading back to Bruce, who had eavesdropped on their conversation.

"So, now what do we do?" Bruce asked sympathetically, leaning forward in his chair.

Thursday Friday Saturday Sunday **Monday** **Tuesday Wednesday**

The Wheels on the Bus

After laying waste to Camp PlayaPiano, the party zombies left seventy camp mates strewn around on the ground underneath the awning-enclosure behind the sound stage, as well as the dance area in front. Three in the camp had been torn to shreds in a feeding frenzy, the remainder had been bitten, gouged, and in some cases had parts of a limb consumed.

The blasting techno pop soundtrack effectively masked the screams of terror permeating the camp throughout the brief attack. The camp, having almost uniformly taken generous quantities of ecstasy, was already rapidly accelerating through their Stage I infection.

More victims lay out in the open playa, having encountered the party zombies on their way to Camp PlayaPiano, mistakenly assuming the group was an impromptu zombie parade ready for additional recruits. A handful of passersby witnessed the carnage, as it occurred or shortly thereafter. They independently sprinted off in different directions, seeking authorities.

A couple of the party zombies spotted mutant vehicles traversing the open playa. They wandered out of Camp PlayaPiano in slow pursuit of the brightly lit vessels. The other party zombies followed their lead – the herd was on the move.

Spotting a large group hoofing it past 10:00 in the hazy darkness, the driver of an articulated bus – a bright red, wildly painted and decorated, retired Mercedes-Benz Citaro bendy bus, previously used for over a decade in London – changed direction to offer anyone interested in the group a ride in the massive vehicle. The bendy bus pulled to a stop alongside the party zombies; the three sets of double doors swung open as the bus creaked and moaned while it idled.

The bendy bus, during its tour of duty in London, could hold 140 passengers. After customization and conversion into a mutant vehicle, the capacity was lowered to ninety. The bus was close to two-thirds full when it came to a stop alongside the leading edge of the party zombies. The z's flooded all three entrances; in doing so jamming them sufficiently so that none of the almost-sixty passengers could exit.

The mayhem initiated immediately. Smiles from the playa passengers at the zombie getups switched to screams of horror within seconds, as the initial entrants began assaulting the passengers. Growling, groaning, gnashing their discolored teeth, the gray-toned party zombies bathed the passengers in their own blood. Panicked passengers not immediately bitten arose, pushing and shoving into each other, clogging the aisle as they attempted to escape the onslaught.

The bendy bus driver tried desperately to close the three sets of doors from the control panel, but all were jammed by additional party zombies trying to access the new meals on wheels delivered to them. The driver gave up, deciding instead to start moving the vehicle forward with the doors open; a feat made possible during the bus's customization.

The bendy bus lurched forward, party-zombies hanging onto each other and to the retracted doors. One-by-one the zombies in the doorways began falling off into the playa, as the bus picked up a little speed. Inside, however, the twenty or so z's that made it inside were plowing their way through the passengers. Many passengers were fighting back against their attackers, but getting bit and gashed in the process. A couple of the first-bitten collapsed onto the aisle floor, to be trampled by the ebb and flow of the crowd. Within ten minutes, the repeated trampling would lead to their fatalities, resulting in new Stage II recruits. Several more passengers tried to hide from view on the floors, only to suffer the same trampled fate.

As the zombies seized the upper hand inside the bus, the attention of several z's near the front turned towards the driver. He felt teeth sinking into his back, hands grabbing at his arms. He backed off the gas pedal, tapped the brakes, and pulled the bus to a stop as three party zombies swarmed over him.

The bendy bus wasn't the only mutant vehicle to check out the party zombies. After the bendy bus pulled away with about half of the party-z's, a two-story black pirate ship pounding out Dubstep music from the upper deck, pulled up to see what was going on with this large group out on the playa. Almost everyone on board was situated on the larger, upper deck.

The remaining party zombies stormed the ship and its twenty-five or so upstairs passengers, making quick work of them. There was only one entrance to the upper deck, via a medium-incline flight of stairs, which the zombies were able to navigate. Trapped, as the zombies streamed up the stairway, a couple of passengers jumped down to the ground, but were assaulted by several of the party-z's still circling around the outside of the ship. Most of the upstairs passengers were from the same camp and had partaken of an allotment of cocaine and psychedelic mushrooms out on the playa before getting picked up. After their zombie encounter, they deteriorated rapidly.

The pirate ship did not set sail again. The Dubstep kept pulsating out of the speakers to a now unappreciative, infected audience.

Thursday Friday Saturday Sunday Monday Tuesday Wednesday

The Quest for Jan and Jace

Conner plopped into the other folding captain's chair, dejected and defeated. He placed his face into his dusty hands, breathing in deeply, before exhaling, emptying his lungs. He rubbed his forehead, casting a glance at Bruce, shaking his head.

"Bruce," Conner began wearily, "you should have seen her face. I lost her. She thinks I'm nuts. I shouldn't have rambled on about zombies or drinking or Alan Gorman shooting anybody. I should have just kept it simple, should have not thrown so much at her so fast. I came here to save her, and I failed. I don't seem capable of saving anyone, I never have."

Bruce waited through ten seconds of silence before rising out of his chair. He stepped in front of his friend, who was still seated. "Conner, I'm not giving up on you, and you're not giving up on her. Now listen, my friend, these things are still out there, and you know all hell is going to break loose around here, sometime soon. You and I have been through a lot today, and the Conner I knew—and the Conner I know — is no quitter. Now get up." Bruce held out his hand to help Conner out of this chair.

Conner remained seated, not responding to the gesture. "And do what? Get up and do what?"

Bruce raised his voice. "Go after her, you dork. Find out what the heck this 'Alamo' is she was talking about and go there and make sure she is safe." Bruce held out his right hand again. Conner shook his head again.

Bruce could see that Conner was crushed. He paused to think of the right thing to say to his friend from Parker Creek, when his attention was drawn by yelling behind the parked Suburban next to Cassie's camp. A man was shouting 'Holy crap' repeatedly from underneath some heavily secured outdoor awning next to the Suburban. Bruce and Conner looked at each other.

"I'll be right back," Bruce told Conner, who remained seated. Bruce trotted in the dark to the source of the noise.

A man with a straw cowboy hat and a protruding, gray ponytail was seated in his camp chair, listening to his boom box radio, next to a woman who was staring intently at the radio from her camp chair. A propane lantern was lit next to the boom box on a makeshift, homemade outdoor table of some kind.

"Is everything okay?" Bruce asked the man, upon arrival.

The man glanced up at Bruce. He turned to his wife, whistling loudly, before turning back to Bruce. "Man, have you been listening to the radio station here?"

Bruce shook his head, not wanting to divulge he had never heard the Burning Man station.

The man rose up, beginning to pace in front of his wife. "Man, they just said that there is some kind of public health hazard, and everyone is advised to get into their cars for their own safety and listen to the radio for further instruction. Get into our cars, man, and lock the doors. And get this – get this - they said they have shut down the camp gate – the exit and entrance. It's like the camp is in lockdown, man. They said the big storm coming will make it too dangerous to drive until hours after the storm passes." The man looked intently at Bruce. "What do you think, man, what do you think about that?"

Bruce shook his head. He was growing weary of not telling people about impending disaster, even if it didn't go so well when Conner tried it with Cassie. "I think it's a good idea. If I were you, I'd lock yourselves in the car. There is something going on out there, we've seen it."

The man stood up. "I knew it. We heard somebody telling the Swedish dudes behind us, there is like, all the law in the entire camp over by the walk-in campground, and there is something big going on down there. They said shots were fired, and all sorts of people are on the ground, and ambulances are out there with people screaming everywhere. They saw it from a distance, the law has the area off-limits, they said. So what have you seen, man? What do you know about any of this?"

Bruce hesitated, trying to decide what made sense to divulge. He cleared his throat, opting for the middle ground. "Look, I don't know exactly how to explain this, because I'm not sure exactly what is going on, but what I can tell you is this: There is some unknown disease that is causing people to become really violent and mentally incapacitated at the same time. They seem to be able to spread their infection when attacking others, and those who get infected get sick, but don't get to the full blown stage until some time passes. The infection started out in the desert, north of here, but now it sounds like its spreading inside Burning Man. That's why we came here. We saw it happening out it the desert, and my friend wanted to warn his girlfriend in your camp about it."

The man nodded his head until Bruce finished. "Jesus! You saw people getting attacked out in the desert, just like these dudes were telling the Swedes happened here?"

Bruce nodded. "Yes we did. More than once, we did."

"Holy crap!" The man exclaimed. He turned to direct his comments at his wife. "Can you believe this? Can you believe what is happening right now?"

She looked disdainfully at him, grimacing as she spoke. "Oh, get over yourself." She turned to Bruce. "Never mind him, he gets worked up over everything, he thinks everything is a conspiracy. And you're not helping any, getting him all worked up like this."

The man turned away from her, speaking to Bruce. "Don't listen to her; she's always trying to shoot down what's going on in the world. By the way, man, I'm Duke, and my wife here, she's Pearl. Duke of Pearl, get it?" The man held out his hand.

Bruce shook his hand. "I'm Bruce. I live way out here in the Black Rock, northeast of here. My friend, Conner, is here, just behind your camp. We came to talk to his girlfriend."

The woman leaned forward with great interest. "Jan? You're with Jan and Jace? He's the Conner Jan's talking about, blah blah blah, Conner-Conner-Conner, blah blah blah?" She used her left hand as a puppet, mouthing the 'blah's and 'Conner's.'

Bruce looked confused. "Jan? Jan and Jace?"

The woman shook her head. "Oh, I'm sorry. We're talking playa names – like I'm Pearl and he's Duke." She turned to the man for confirmation. "Her name is Cassie, right?" The man nodded his head.

Bruce smiled. "Then that would be us. Conner, all he talks about is blah blah blah, Cassie-Cassie-Cassie, or is it, Jan?"

"So where is this Conner?" the woman asked excitedly.

Bruce shook his head. "He's sitting over in Cassie's camp, just behind you. He's pretty down. He tried to explain this to Cassie, and she kind of freaked out. She went to some place called the Alamo, to find her friend. And we have no clue what that is or where it would be."

The woman rose out of her chair. "Well, come on, I want to meet this Conner." She made a beeline for Cassie's camp. Bruce and her husband followed.

Conner was still seated in the folding captain's chair, staring out into the darkness. The woman strode up, placing her hand on his wrist. "So you are the famous Conner."

Conner's head snapped upwards, startled. "Huh?"

"Oh, don't mind me," she reassured him. "Your friend was just telling us all about how you two showed up, spreading these scary stories my husband is so worked up about, and Jan ran off and left you to find Jace."

"Jace?" Conner replied, confused.

The woman explained again that Jan and Jace equals Cassie and Tess.

The man caught up to his wife and interrupted. "Look, Conner, I'm Duke." He held out his hand. Conner shook it while he was still reclined. "Bruce here tells us you fellows have seen some freaky stuff going on, just like we've been hearing about?"

Conner looked at Bruce for some acknowledgment of what was going on. Bruce nodded. "Yeah, we have," Conner replied weakly.

"Well, go get her then. Go get Jan and Jace then, or Cassie and Tess or whatever you're supposed to call them, and get them back here," the man advised.

"She doesn't see it that way," Conner responded, downbeat. "She told me she'd come back with Tess whenever they were good and ready to."

"Well, are they safe out there?" the man asked. Conner shook his head. "And you're supposed to be the new love of her life? Man, don't just sit here, moping." The man turned around to Bruce, who was now standing behind them. "Bruce, you said they went to the Alamo?"

Bruce nodded his head, but wanted to confirm with Conner. "Conner, she did say Alamo, didn't she?"

Conner, still seated, answered flatly. "Yeah, I'm thinking that's what she said, although my head was kind of spinning at that point."

The woman put her hands on her hips. "Well, I don't blame her for running off, if you come bombing in here unannounced, talking crazy-talk like the mayor of crazy-town himself, my husband here. But, Conner, you got to get off your rear end here, quit feeling sorry for yourself, and get back on the horse. You got to go out there and tell her what they're saying on the radio, and bring those two ladies back safe and sound. Just go easy on all the extra crazy-talk."

Conner gripped the side arm, starting to ease forward in his chair. Then, the man spoke up, in a loud animated tone, stepping forward in front of his wife so that he was directly in front of Conner. "Don't you listen to her. I mean, well, listen to her about going out there and bringing Jan and Jace back here, but you go right on telling people what they need to hear about what's really going on at the edge of this camp and out in the desert. Somebody is not telling us everything that's going on, and people need to know."

The woman rolled her eyes. "Puh-leaze... Just go Conner."

"Tell him where to find the Alamo," the man barked at his wife, before breaking away, trotting back to his camp. Bruce traded a perplexed expression with Conner. The woman proceeded to explain what Conner would be looking for, and how to get there. She repeated the directions several times.

The man reappeared with an armload of items. He dropped them in front of Conner on the ground, where the lantern provided adequate illumination. Interrupting his wife, he spoke directly to Conner. "Look, man, your friend here told us about these infected people attacking others, biting them and everything. They don't allow weapons at all in Burning Man, but take these with you." He pointed at several three-foot-lengths of rebar lying on the ground. "These were extra when I set up camp. The baseball bat we brought for a camp softball game later this week. And put this stuff on," the man continued, pointing at the other items on the ground – the plastic gear for a full-on Imperial Stormtrooper costume. "This stuff might provide a little bit of protection if they try to bite you, man. Now when you're ready, we'll lend you our bikes, too, okay?"

His wife laughed. "Poor Conner. You put this on, and you'll fit right in out there. But when you reach our Jan, your Cassie, she's going to think you're as nutty as my fruitcake husband here. She's going to run away from you all over again."

Conner pictured Cassie, Saturday in the kayak, looking like an angel gliding in the water right in front of him. Then, he pictured her disappointed face, her disgusted tone of voice, a short time earlier. He had lost her, there was no doubt. But he now realized that fact was immaterial to the task he must now undertake. He had to do one good thing in his miserable life and get her to safety, even at the cost of losing her love in the process. He also owed it to Bruce to not make their desert journey in vain.

Conner stood up. He looked at Bruce as he tried to decide how to put his thoughts into words and words into action. He turned to the man. "Hey, thanks. Thanks a bunch. All of you are right. I need to go find them. Do you have any kind of bag I could put the costume in? I'll carry one rebar, the bat and the costume with me, and if it looks like anything bad is going on out there, I'll put them to use, for sure." Conner turned to Bruce. "And Bruce, I have to ask you a huge favor. I'm thinking it will be best if you stay here, because enough time has gone by where I might miss them, and they'll end up coming back here. You can let them know I missed them, and I'll head back here too."

Bruce's eyes opened wide. He shook his head in disapproval, but the man beat him to a response. "Hey, man. We can tell them all that. You both can go. We have two bikes, and stuff here for both of you."

Bruce chimed in. "Conner, that's nuts. You're not going without me."

Conner raised his voice, looking first at the man, then at Bruce. "Thank you, sir, for everything you're doing and offering. But I need Bruce to wait here, because you all know there's a good chance — as big as this place is — that we'll miss connections. I need Bruce here if they come back without me, so he can vouch for me and tell them what I tried to say and convince them we need to get somewhere safe."

The woman laughed. "Get somewhere safe? They just said on the radio nobody is going anywhere."

"We'll figure out a plan," Conner replied to her, emphatically. He then turned and pleaded with Bruce. "But you've got to do this for me. You've got to stay here and convince her, after I failed to do so, if she gets here first."

They argued back and forth for a minute until Bruce relented. The man retrieved a bicycle and a cloth bag. Conner hopped on the lit up cruiser bike, a rebar rod and bat in his left hand as he gripped the handlebars, a cloth bag strapped around his right hand, holding an Imperial Stormtrooper outfit.

Conner set off on his quest for Jan and Jace.

Thursday Friday Saturday Sunday Monday Tuesday Wednesday

Porta-Potty-Pandemonium

The party zombie herd was
winding its way in the dark, out
into the open playa art
installations. The disparate collection of gray-toned, open-
sored, mangy-haired, torn-attired, new arrivals to Burning
Man progressed at a steady pace, perhaps at the same speed as
someone taking a very long stroll.

Some of the party zombies detached from the herd after the
group ransacked a pirate ship, bendy bus and other mutant
vehicles near the 10:00 PlayaPiano camp. These breakaway z's
were attracted by the whiff of the nearby bank of porta-potties.
Five of them headed directly towards the toilets.

They came across a bank of eight blue stalls. Every door was
closed. No one was in line at the moment. The first zombie to
arrive, a heavyset female, stopped at the closest stall,
commencing to push and beat on the door. From inside, a
perturbed young lady hollered out "Hey, someone's in here. I'll
be out in a moment. Just hold your horses, out there."

The second zombie arrived, a slender, younger woman,
pushing past the first z, taking the same tactic with the door
two stalls down. A middle-aged woman wearing a headlamp,
coasted in, with her well-lit cruiser bike, observing the two
strange looking ladies impatiently pounding on the porta-
potties. The woman in the headlamp assumed they might be
high and could use some help. She approached the slender z,
speaking soothingly as she arrived. Her nose wrinkled a little;
she hoped the odor was from the toilet, not the grungy lady she
was assisting.

"Here, it's green. You just need to pull on the handle,
sweetie." The woman with the headlamp explained cheerfully,
opening the door for the z lady. The zombie took one step
forward, turned to glance at the helpful woman, turning again

to admire the enticing aroma of the stall. The zombie seemed frozen with indecision. The woman with the headlamp patiently smiled, continuing to hold the door open.

Finally, the z took another step toward the stall, before reaching back with its right arm. With surprising strength the z yanked the headlamp woman forward with her. The door swung into the two, but the zombie had a clear path into the stall, dragging the screaming headlamp woman with it.

At the same time, the young lady inside the first stall started to exit her toilet. She was greeted by the heavyset lady z. It pushed her backwards into the stall, before plunging forward to join her in the porta-potty; the door swinging shut behind them.

The other three zombies arrived at the porta-potty bank. A burly, younger man exited the fifth stall, concerned about the nearby screams that had just commenced. "What the hell?" he exclaimed in anger and fear, sizing up the three zombie men closing in on him, while the screaming from the stalls persisted.

Assuming these three were standing guard, while someone was raping or assaulting some women in the stalls next door, he charged into them. "Get out of the way, get out of here!" he barked at them. It was the last thing he said upright, as the three pulled him to the ground, biting and gouging away. They continued to gash away at him while he fought and clawed back.

His shirtless friend, waiting off to the side, had not been paying attention at first, but sprinted to the scene as the scuffle continued. Soon the man on the ground was listless; the three zombies concentrated their attention on the newly arrived friend. Moments later, a large portion of the bare chested friend's upper right arm was bitten off, while the friend screamed in agony.

Half a dozen people ran up to the fracas, but all were keeping a wary distance. They observed the two men moaning in agony on the ground, bathed in blood; their three horrific-appearing, blood stained attackers now eyeing the new arrivals.

One of the three zombie men became interested in the aroma behind him. The zombie turned around to find a well-built man wearing a florescent pink bikini and Ugg boots, mouth agape, standing frozen in the doorway of the fourth stall, holding the door open with his right hand. The zombie charged forward like a linebacker, taking his bikini-clad quarry back into the porta-potty with him.

The two remaining zombies advanced on the group of six that just arrived. One person peeled away, sprinting back towards the camp. The zombies flanked the others, so that the z's were in between the people and the camp. The zombies lurched forward. The remaining five retreated out into the open playa, the z's in methodical pursuit.

Thursday Friday Saturday Sunday Monday Tuesday Wednesday

Chaos Squared

Chief Master Sergeant Darren Carter was a habitual gum-chomper. In his youth, he was a Copenhagen aficionado. Now, his Wrigley's was in hyper drive, in the Black Rock Ranger HQ just converted to his command center.

He had already won over Ranger Rick. Carter was charismatic and saw no need to make things difficult with the person who was the lynch-pin of intel and logistics inside the city. He kept Ranger Rick stationed in the office next to him. While still adamant that the gate remain closed to traffic, Carter acquiesced to allow the planes parked in the BRC airport to leave whenever arrangements could be made and there was no incoming military traffic — subject to adequate inspection of the passengers. Carter convinced the Colonel to pull a team of ten additional deputies from the perimeter line back into the city. Carter also gave the Ranger Rick free rein to manage the effort to warn the Black Rock citizens to lock themselves in their vehicles.

But CMS Carter was beside himself. He'd heard frequent reference to zombies in chatter over the radio during the past half-hour, he barked out an order that the z-word was not be uttered. He was even more worked up over the casualties – the Stage I infected.

"This is just like in an infantry engagement," he vented to Ranger Rick. "It's the injured, and the personnel required to support the injured, that become an albatross around your neck. We have what, five of the Stage II cases that we finally took down, out in that walk-in campground? Sure, they tied up our men a good bit, trying to isolate them enough from the citizens to take a clean kill shot, and we might have a couple still running loose in the outer camps...maybe one still unaccounted for in the walk-in area. But just those few of them, and look what they left behind. We've got close to a hundred citizens out there now in Stage I being tended to by a lot of staff. Then there was that flare up, when we transferred the cases out of Rampart, here. "

The Chief Master Sergeant was referring to the debacle a half hour earlier, when all the patients were transferred out of Rampart to the 3:00 clinic. Those that had turned to Stage II already were adequately restrained, but those in Stage I had been restrained while lethargic or even comatose; the same level of precaution wasn't uniformly applied. Perhaps it was the stresses on the patients caused by the transfer, but four 'expired,' progressing to Stage II during the ambulatory relocation – the ambulances had all been deployed. Three of the four quickly broke loose, infecting another twenty-five medical support staff and bystanders before they were finally subdued.

Chief Master Sergeant Carter continued. "So now we have the hundred new cases in the walk-in area, plus the twenty-five cases taken out to the walk-in area from the Rampart transfer infections. The two outlying clinics are well beyond capacity. We have to tie up personnel caring for them, securing them, and every person doing so is taken offline from getting this city under control. Now we're just getting reports that something has flared up at the opposite end of camp. And we're stretched, between trying to warn your citizens, and supporting this increasing number of Stage I cases. The Colonel is intractable about sending further reinforcements inside here until the National Guard and the Reno agency call-ups arrive. We're going to collapse under our own weight of required support for these cases until those reinforcements arrive."

Ranger Rick repeated his position. "If the problem is caring for all the Stage I cases, we need to reduce the potential Stage I growth. We need to at least move the people in the safe sections of the city out of harm's way. We still have a window before the rain hits."

CMS Carter sighed, clasping his hands behind his head. "Yeah, I hear you, but whether that was the right call an hour ago is one thing. The fact is we're stretched too thin without some reinforcements coming off the perimeter to support, inspect and secure those relocations. This is what it is. We have to hang in there, putting out fires until we get some more boots in this city."

"You know I disagree," Ranger Rick countered.

"Duly noted. But I tell you what we are going to do. The CDC people and the infectious disease doctor onsite recommended we heavily sedate all these Stage I cases; that would reduce the demands on our personnel the patients are creating, at least until they progress later on to Stage II. So, I just authorized that. Our advance team brought in adequate medical supplies and some additional nursing personnel to help pull it off."

"So now we're promoting drug use in Black Rock City?" Ranger Rick cracked wryly.

"It would appear so—" Carter stopped to listen to another radio report of trouble at the other end of camp. He pushed for a status report from the two deputies pulled off the 9:00 clinic security to investigate. They hadn't checked in after leaving their vehicle.

CMS Carter shook his head, playing with a pencil in his hand. "You know, I always wanted to go to Burning Man, if I just had the kind of occupation that would have allowed it. You'd be surprised to learn how many Burning Man clips I've viewed on YouTube. The chaos out there just fascinates me. And now to unleash this into that chaos, it's like we're dealing with chaos squared."

Ranger Rick allowed himself a very small chuckle. "No, I don't think so."

"What do you mean?"

"It's like infinity. Chaos is like infinity. If you introduce infinity into infinity, you just have infinity, not infinity squared. Chaos into chaos is just more chaos," Ranger Rick lectured.

"More like infinite chaos..." Darren Carter countered, cutting his comments short as the deputies at the other end of the camp reported in. The Chief Master Sergeant let loose a stream of profanities as they provided an account of widespread new Stage I infections. "Looks like we're going to need to send some nurses and whole lot of drugs out their way to put these new cases into la-la land," CMS Carter commented to Ranger Rick. "And we're going to have to sequester a new casualty collection center out there because we don't have the space or resources to take them back to your 9:00 clinic."

CMS Carter's sat phone rang. Alan Gorman was on the line. Carter put him on speaker. "Doctor Gorman, or should I say Colonel Gorman, what's up down your way?"

"I just heard you authorized morphine for all the infected cases," Alan stated, in an accusatory tone.

"That's a fact. It's now our protocol. The shots are underway as we speak, but there's a ways to go," Carter replied calmly.

"I think we should have tried that with just a trial group, not the entire infected population," Alan commented, irritated.

"I don't think we have the luxury of time for that," CMS Carter replied. "But why do you say that?"

"We don't know enough about the impact of this virus on the victim's systems to have enough confidence that there won't be any material unanticipated outcomes," Alan argued.

"Unanticipated outcomes?" the Chief Master Sergeant inquired.

Thursday Friday Saturday Sunday Monday Tuesday Wednesday

New Arrivals

The party zombies weren't the last wave of z's to head south from the ground zero region.

After the LSD-pre-party was crashed Saturday night, two small zombie groupings were behind them, bearing south, weaving through the foothills east of the playa. They were undetected by the BLM chopper Sunday afternoon and all day Monday, as the helicopter focused on the playa.

Late Sunday night, the lead z group came across two off-road campers, zipped tightly in thermal sleeping bags. Unable to extract them from the bags, they settled for biting and gouging them, before losing interest when a distant cow caught their fancy. They were unsuccessful in catching up to the scrawny cow, which sprinted away after catching their scent. The z's stopped in a shady fold in the foothills mid-Monday morning. Soon, they were drawn into a lengthy zombie nap.

About that same time, the second zombie group came upon the infected campers, who had recently turned into zombie brethren. Unfortunately, the campers were trapped inside their tightly zipped sleeping bags, encountering as much difficulty getting out, as the first zombie group experienced trying to get in. The second zombie group passed by them, roughly following the path of the z's preceding them.

The two sleeping bag zombies were determined to join the herd. They crawled along in pursuit, in their sleeping bags, eventually managing to stand upright, shuffling and hopping for stretches. After some time, the zippers worked their way downwards, the sleeping bags dropped to the ground; the two new z's were able to advance at a normal-zombie pace, in the direction those before them were last seen heading.

The second zombie group caught the lead pack, still in a trance-like nap in early afternoon. The second group, instead of bothering the nappers, settled into a trance themselves.

This allowed the formerly-known-as-sleeping-bag-zombies to catch up to the groups. They managed to disturb their predecessors, waking the entire herd. Soon the assembled, merged herd was heading south again, twelve zombies strong. After dark, they turned east, as distant noises and lights drew their attention. They advanced, making contact coming out of the foothills overlooking County Road 34, one mile north of the gate.

The perimeter line was stretched thin, waiting for the main National Guard units to arrive. They were spaced, not equidistant, but by line-of-sight, in teams of two, extending as far as they could while still able to make visual contact down the line via flashing lights. Many teams had night vision goggles, others had spotlights.

The three available choppers circled the long perimeter, scanning below with searchlights. One chopper spotted two zombies near the western perimeter, several miles above Jungo Road. The nearest perimeter team was dispatched to verify they were Stage II, before putting them down. The incident, and lack of other sightings, gave the Colonel and all of the perimeter teams, a level of confidence that the perimeters were secure for now.

The operating assumption was that the infected were within the perimeter, and the assignment was to contain them inside.

The eastern perimeter was manned by teams of BLM Rangers, plus an assortment of other agencies represented in Black Rock City. A mile north of the Burning Man gate, nestled in the foothills overlooking County Road 34, were two agents with the Nevada Department of Investigations.

The agents stood next to each other behind their car, both on the sat phones with the NDI Assistant Director, who was angry that he had been out of the loop when his agents had been commandeered for this mission. The Assistant Director vented that the agents ultimately reported to him, not some Chief Master Sergeant with the Air Force. The agents attempted to scan up and down County Road 34 and beyond, while they dutifully listened to their boss's boss ream them out. It was quite dark – the storm cloud cover had completely enveloped the sky – making it all the more difficult to spot any activity.

They were too preoccupied with the phone call, and peering ahead with binoculars, to notice the herd of one dozen zombies stagger up behind them. They were gang tackled while on the phone, the Assistant Director continuing to rant. Both calls were soon disconnected as the phones dropped to the ground with zombies crawling over them. The Assistant Director was furious that his agents hung up on him, next calling back their supervisor.

One of the agents, already bitten, managed to get one shot off, into the rib cage of one of his attackers. No other shots were fired. The zombies consumed his fellow agent, ripping his clothes to shreds; then ripping his flesh to shreds. The other agent was left next to his car, his throat slashed, while the zombies worked their way down the hill to County Road 34. Within a half hour, the agent passed on, and was soon staggering on his way to join them.

Thursday Friday Saturday Sunday Monday Tuesday Wednesday

Pee-wee's New Adventure

Cassie parked her bicycle just outside the Alamo, next to Tess's and two other bikes. She found Tess around the corner, talking about the impending storm with a couple in costume – she in a tight-fitting Catwoman outfit, he in Mexican Lucha Libre wrestling garb.

The couple decided they might just ride out the storm out on the playa, perhaps in one of the rooms in the Alamo art installation. They pointed out to Tess that while the storm was supposed to be fierce, it wasn't supposed to last for all that long.

As soon as Cassie arrived, it was abundantly clear to Tess that she was upset and wanted to talk. They excused themselves from the couple, pacing around the outside of the Alamo while Cassie, in tears, shared her sudden revelation; Conner wasn't who she thought he was.

Tess felt her role was to offer not just sympathy, but some counterpoints – so that her good friend was properly thinking things through. Still, Tess was having a tough time swallowing Conner's story as Cassie retold it.

Their lengthy conversation was interrupted as a small mutant vehicle sped by, doing well over the five mile per hour speed limit imposed throughout the city. Catwoman could be heard from around the corner, yelling at the vehicle as it passed by. Cassie and Tess look at each other, shaking their heads. Then, they heard shrieking from out in the open playa where the vehicle had come from.

Cassie and Tess rounded the corner, stepping ten yards forward, trying to make out the source of the noise in the darkness. Catwoman and Lucha Libre joined them. Lucha Libre produced a small but powerful LED flashlight, pointing it out into the open playa.

They spotted two young women joined together in a custom tequila bottle costume that sported just two visible arms and two legs shared between both of them. Their interior arms and legs were concealed inside the homemade tequila bottle, with their heads protruding on each side of the bottle's neck. They were fifty yards out, advancing slowly, screaming for help with each step forward.

Lucha Libre pointed the beam of light past them, into the darkness. More than twenty shadowy figures were about thirty yards behind the tequila bottle, staggering forward at roughly the same speed as the two tequila ladies.

As the ladies continued the pleas for help, Cassie and Tess instinctively sprinted out to them, their Jan costumes not slowing them down. Lucha Libre and Catwoman followed their lead. Moments later, the tequila ladies tripped and fell. They apparently were having difficulty getting back up.

Cassie and Tess reached them first. The tequila ladies were still screaming and quite panicked. They were babbling that they needed to get away from the crazed people chasing them, who had attacked their friends out on the open playa. Lucha Libre reached them, shining his light on the approaching horde, now twenty yards out. He let loose several expletives, before yelling that they should get out of there, now.

Cassie reached into the ladies' costume. It started to rip as she yanked at it with all her might. Tess and Catwoman joined in. Moments later, the two tequila ladies were no longer joined at the bottle. The approaching herd was now ten yards out. The ladies rose from the ground; the six of them sprinted back to Pee-wee's Alamo, outpacing their pursuers.

They arrived back at Pee-wee's pad, 'Breakfast Machine' still playing in a loop through the speakers. "Let's get outside to our bikes and go find help," Cassie shouted to Tess, Catwoman and Lucha Libre. She turned to the tequila ladies "Come run alongside us," she instructed them.

They all dashed to the left side of the Alamo to retrieve the bikes. Two of the same sort of creatures that were advancing behind them was also lurking in front of the four bikes. As Cassie scanned around, she could see the creatures had fanned out while closing in. Their escape routes were cut off. "Conner," Cassie cried out, her voice forging an alloy of equal parts fear and guilt, "why didn't I listen to you?"

"What are these things? What the hell is going on?" Lucha Libre screamed.

"Come on," Tess barked out, waving everyone back into Pee-wee's Alamo.

A Tipping Point

Lightning could be seen striking repeatedly in the distant mountains north of Black Rock City. Sprinkles of rain occasionally were felt throughout the city. The big storm was imminent.

Teams of Black Rock Rangers were attempting to patrol the camps with loudspeakers, warning all citizens to take shelter inside their vehicles until further notice. The problem was the Rangers kept getting called offline to tend to reported flare ups, or to assist transferring the newly infected to a collection point. The bigger problem was not enough people were listening to or heeding the warnings over the radio.

All hell started breaking loose around a quarter after nine.

With few exceptions, the fifty or so PlayaPiano camp casualties had already turned to Stage II by that time. After the PlayaPiano victims were reported, they were temporarily retained in the tent behind the camp's sound stage until they could be transferred to new collection point for Stage I infected being setup nearby. A dozen BRR Rangers and medical staff arrived on the scene to initiate their transfer. No sooner had the process started, when victims began turning to Stage II, beneficiaries of the reaction to the ecstasy they had partaken. All but a few completed the transformation within five minutes. They overwhelmed the transfer team, infecting every one of them.

The new collection area on the 10:00 side, it was decided, would be the site where around sixty victims of the Bendy Bus mutant vehicle had been discovered. They had already been extracted from the bus, laid out on blankets nearby, and administered morphine. Almost an equal number of victims from more isolated attacks were also collected to the site.

Evidently, the effect of drugs taken after Stage I infection was even more severe than drugs merely in one's system before the infection's onset. The timeframe for progression to Stage II was reduced to less than fifteen minutes after administering morphine to the victims. The Bendy Bus passengers and the other victims given morphine around nine p.m. soon overtook and infected all support staff in the area, except two souls that managed to sprint further out into the open playa.

These one hundred twenty morphine-accelerated zombies were soon joined by the twenty-five or so victims in the upstairs of the nearby pirate ship, who had not yet been relocated. Having done coke and mushrooms, they turned within the hour after initial infection. Altogether, the PlayaPiano, morphine-administered, and pirate ship zombies merged into a super-herd of almost two hundred zombies, pushing their way out into the art installations, following the path that the fifty party zombies had taken before them.

There were also more isolated Stage II cases reported in several flashpoints at each end of the camp. Additional infected individuals also continued to join the ranks of Stage II. Citizens recently attacked out on the open playa would stagger around or lay down – unlit and unseen – resulting with an increasing number of them meeting an accidental early demise – struck in the darkness by fleeing mutant vehicles and other such fates, yielding more numbers in Stage II.

The 3:00 and 9:00 clinics were overrun fifteen minutes or so after morphine injections were given at those sites. There was no remaining clinic support staff to handle incoming infected at the clinics; all the staff and clinic security were now in Stage I themselves. The overflow crowd of around seventy-five cases stacked up at each at the two clinics. All advanced into Stage II after the morphine, sending another one hundred fifty zombies out into the camps, half at each end. Even Rampart inside the Green Zone wasn't spared. A handful of cases taken there, awaiting transfer, were administered morphine as well. Rampart no longer had attending physicians on staff – the two onsite CDC representatives and infectious disease specialist were among the new Rampart victims, when their cases awaiting transfer turned.

The other large casualty collection point was at the walk-in campground, with in excess of one hundred fifty Stage I victims – some which had been properly restrained, along with a number of restrained Stage II victims. All in Stage I were administered morphine. As a result, all the walk-in victims were now in Stage II; close to one hundred thirty were on the loose, heading in varied directions.

Earlier that evening, one hundred unarmed Black Rock Rangers and thirty Pershing County deputies were left to defend Black Rock City, while the greater balance of law enforcement was drawn out into beyond the open playa, sealing the perimeters. As the nine o' clock evening hour progressed, only twenty armed Pershing deputies and sixty Black Rock Rangers remained uninfected to secure the city.

They were now seriously outnumbered.

Thursday Friday Saturday Sunday Monday Tuesday Wednesday

Luke, Jan and Jace

Conner was having no easy time pedaling the bike lent to him by Cassie's neighbors. In his left hand he held the three foot length of rebar and the aluminum softball bat he had been equipped with, in his right hand he held the bag containing the plastic Stormtrooper outfit — all while attempting to also grip the handlebars.

Bearing down the 7:30 radial, he almost was struck by a BRR pickup as he approached Esplanade. The distraught Black Rock Ranger driver stopped long enough to chastise Conner, who had dismounted to pick up the costume bag he dropped. "Don't head out onto the open playa. Things are bad out there. You need to turn around, get back to your camp, and lock yourself in your car. You understand?" The ranger didn't wait for a response; he peeled out, heading left into the open playa.

Conner hopped back up on his bike. He felt a few drops of rain. He positioned the bike so the LED headlight pointed out in the open playa. The art installations were all lit, making the evening appear deceptively as enchanting and carefree as any night in any past year on the playa. From his vantage point he couldn't see any sign of zombies or mayhem.

But what Conner heard — what he sensed – was a different matter. The far-off sounds emanating from the open playa were chilling. They possessed the distant, but unmistakable pitch of terror. Conner turned to see someone sprint behind him, yelling incoherently. He resolved there was no question – the zombies were in Black Rock City – and there could be a good number of them.

Conner glanced at the costume bag. He laughed at himself for just a moment, feeling stupid for even thinking about donning the Stormtrooper outfit. But then he remembered the early afternoon in Sulphur, witnessing Jason ripped to shreds by Dax and the other zombies. Conner hopped off the bike again, opting for looking stupid and possessing even a little bit of protection from a zombie bite.

Cassie's neighbor provided Conner a folded map of Black Rock City that was handed out by the greeters upon entrance. Conner pulled it out of the bag, studying the map one last time. Next, Conner suited up next to his bike, just off Esplanade, adjacent to the outdoor rink for the Roller Boogie theme camp. A minute later, he was back in the saddle – Luke Skywalker in a Stormtrooper uniform – searching to rescue Jan and Jace, formerly known as Cassie and Tess.

Conner stayed left of the brightly-lit Man at the center of all things. He placed the softball bat and rebar rod in the bag, wearing the bag's former contents, so it was much easier to maneuver the bike, although pedaling was more of a challenge when wearing a Stormtrooper outfit. He pedaled as fast as he could, crossing the 9:00 Promenade without incident.

As he started to draw even with the 10:00 edge of the camp, things changed quickly. He spied several isolated zombies hobbling towards the Man at the center. The din of screaming, yelling, confusion, moaning and even occasional gunshots, increased in volume. Conner passed the outdoor casualty collection point for that end of the camp, which recently emptied out after morphine was administered to the victims. Already there was a row of new victims, being tended to by new volunteers.

The Alamo was further out in the open playa. With each passing moment, Conner could sense the change in his surroundings. He wheeled by a crawling zombie that had been run over by a passing mutant vehicle. He came across a wave of a dozen screaming citizens, retreating from the direction Conner was heading. "Turn around and come with us," one of them stopped and implored as Conner passed by. "You're going the wrong way..." Conner could hear the person yelling at him as Conner continued on his path.

Conner slowed, scanning to get his bearings, making sure he could distinguish the other major art installations he was instructed to study on the map as his landmarks. He looked down to see a dismembered corpse, several feet to his right. Glancing around, Conner could spot abandoned daypacks, sandals, clothing, and debris of all sorts.

Conner caught a group of a half dozen zombies in his LED headlights, heading the same direction as he was — another thirty yards out. Conner veered to the right, soon catching and passing them from a safe distance. The Alamo came into view, still a quarter of a mile away. It was the largest, well-lit installation this far-out on the 10:00 side of the playa. As Conner approached, he could see that it was drawing attention. The installation was encircled by zombies, and it appeared, as he turned his handlebars to scan the area, there were more on the way.

Conner had no idea if Cassie and Tess were inside the installation. However, it seemed obvious that someone was occupying the Alamo, drawing the attention of the twenty-plus zombies swarming the exterior. Conner came to a halt, trying to formulate a plan. The installation appeared to be two stories high on the back side, so he reasoned if Cassie and Tess were there, they would be on the second floor. The question was how could he get up there?

Conner turned off his headlight, hoping to attract less attention, plus the Alamo exterior lighting illuminated the whole area anyway. Studying the back side of the structure, he spied his opportunity. From an open second story bay, a ladder was built into the exterior wall, running half way down, perhaps as a fire escape. The challenge was it stopped about eight feet off the ground.

Conner decided the thing to do, would be to ride up below the ladder, prop the bike against the wall, using the bike as a footstool to climb up high enough to reach the bottom rung of the ladder. This had to be accomplished while in the midst of zombies.

Conner resolved there was no time or point to think much about that. He strapped on the bag, holding his bat and rebar rod, across his back, with the drawstring draped around his neck. Conner raced forward. There were no zombies just below the ladder, but there were a couple of them on both sides, little more than ten yards from his target point.

Conner hit the brakes too late, wrecking the bike into the wall, the bicycle collapsing to the ground instead of leaning against the wall at an angle as he had hoped. Conner picked himself off the ground, ensuring that the bag was still draped around his neck. Glancing both ways, he could see there was no hope of lifting and positioning the bike so he could climb up it. The zombies were almost upon him. There was only enough time to do one thing – run.

Conner headed to the right, his strides slowed by the Stormtrooper costume and the bag draped around his neck. He now questioned the wisdom of wearing the costume. He wasn't outpacing his pursuers by very much, thanks to the inflexibility of the Stormtrooper uniform.

Ahead, in the darkness, Conner could see a bicycle laying on the ground, its lit headlamp pointing up into the sky. As he drew near, he could see a lady sprawled beside it, wearing a familiar looking outfit. A zombie was leaning over her, clawing at her arm, reaching in more than once to take a bite. Conner felt a sickening sensation; a wave of dread almost overcame him. As he pulled within ten feet, he could see that he had found Cassie, and he was too late.

Conner ran past her and the preoccupied zombie, so that he could turn around to face him and also see his pursuers. He reached into his bag, grabbing the aluminum bat. Without hesitation, he closed in on the kneeling zombie that had just taken away his one love and salvation. The zombie, an older, tattooed man wearing only a swimsuit, looked up at Conner, hissing out of his gray, blood-soaked teeth. Conner let him have it, clocking him on the forehead. The zombie fell over, but rose right back up. Conner wailed away at the side and back of his skull, repeatedly, until it broke open into a mixture of brain, gray goo, slimy hair and bone fragments. Conner paused momentarily to survey the violence he had just wrought, having never gone beyond fisticuffs in his forty years.

Next, sobbing, he stooped down to Cassie, who was unconscious. He screamed her name into the darkness, through his costume helmet. He then smiled, realizing his mistake, and then felt guilty for smiling. It wasn't Cassie. She looked somewhat similar, but not so much when up close. Even the costume wasn't really that much of a match. Conner thought about lifting the stricken lady up, before coming to the realization that the four zombies in pursuit were almost upon him.

Conner guiltily grabbed the woman's bicycle, hopping on it, placing his bat back in the bag, escaping just as the zombies were within arm's reach. Equipped with a second chance at the ladder, he pedaled once more to the back side of the Alamo. Although he could see plenty of other zombies at the sides and around front as he approached on the bike, no other zombies had taken the place of the four that had chased him away.

This time, Conner had the opportunity to safely park the woman's bicycle next to his previous, wrecked bike. Just as planned, he was able to step up on the bike, reach up and grab the bottom rung on the ladder. It wasn't easy going, the Stormtrooper outfit again got in the way.

Conner lost his grip, falling back onto the playa next to the bikes. Looking in the direction he had pedaled from, he could see the fuzzy shapes of the four zombies in the darkness, returning to reclaim their territory.

Conner inhaled heavily and gave the maneuver another try. One minute later, he was crawling over the open bay of the second floor, onto the five-foot wide balcony that lined the entire interior, except for two small corner rooms. Conner rose from his knees, panting to the sound of screams and Danny Elfman's 'Breakfast Machine' playing through wall speakers.

He glanced down to see a scuffed-up, life-size cut-out of Pee-Wee Herman laying on the balcony floor beneath him.

Conner caught a glimpse of a two-by-four swinging at him from the right side, at mid-level. He was able to partially block it with his arm, but the force still knocked him to the balcony floor. His arm ached from the blow.

"What the hell?" Conner yelled, pulling at his Stormtrooper helmet. After a couple of tugs, it came off.

"Oh..my...God! Conner!" Cassie shrieked, dropping the two-by-four. She dived to the floor, on top of Conner, kissing his face repeatedly. "I am so, so, so, sorry. Will you ever, ever forgive me for running out on you?" She didn't let him answer, planting another round of kisses on him, before stopping to consider his attire. She crinkled her face and smiled. "What on earth are you wearing?"

Learning About E.T.

Chief Master Sergeant Carter was beside himself. It had been his ultimate call to approve rapid deployment of morphine to all Stage I infected. In doing so, he authorized creation of an army of Stage II infected that seriously outrivaled his own personnel in numbers. After rescinding his order, he was informed it was a moot point. The supply of morphine had been exhausted.

Just as alarming was word that the western perimeter had been breached. Two agents from the Nevada Department of Investigations didn't respond to their scheduled light signals with adjacent teams or to radio queries. A Washoe County deputy, being held in reserve, was dispatched to their location, reporting back one agent deceased, one agent missing, and a sign of a struggle involving multiple persons. In the deputy's opinion, the agents were assaulted from behind, with their attackers continuing down onto the playa. Although the assailants had not yet been located, the Colonel expressed relief that they seemed to have entered the perimeter as opposed to exiting it.

CMS Carter consulted the map on his laptop. The dynamic had changed. The required perimeter had been miscalculated; the number of infected within the perimeter had been underestimated; the projection of spread of infection to the Burning Man population had been underestimated; the rate of progression from Stage I to Stage II had been accelerated. The sum total for of these factors, he concluded, added up to the necessity of serious adjustments to the mission. A new game plan and set of assumptions was required.

He invited Ranger Rick to listen in while he radioed his Colonel, who was already apprised of the situation.

Darren Carter tucked his wad of gum with his tongue up under his upper lip. "Colonel, I trust you've been briefed. Our situation has deteriorated significantly. We contributed to the equation by administering morphine to the infected. But as of this moment, we need more boots in this city, and we need to consider a different mission template."

The Colonel responded calmly with a lengthy briefing. "Son, I understand the seriousness of the problem there, and I understand your frustration. We're all frustrated. It is taking longer than anyone would like to get National Guard deployment here onsite; I still don't have a reliable estimate on their arrival. Plus, you know, we still have a perimeter breach to get to the bottom of. Now, I did pull strings, and the Commanding Officer of the Marine Corps' Mountain Warfare Training Center off California Highway 108 has a UH60 Black Hawk there on an exercise that they can spare for the night, so they're loaning a dozen armed troops. They'll be pushing off in a bit, and when they arrive, we can have them trade out for county deputies, who can vacate the perimeter and assist your operations. Realistically, ETA is well over an hour or more, depending on this thunderstorm. The Reno agency call up is going to yield forty to fifty officers; we'll need half of them to help secure the gates to your city, because you know it's a matter of time until some people start storming the exits. You can have the other half for your operations, but they are still boarding a bus – they didn't want to mess around with air transport given the storm – so they're a couple hours out. Outside of that, I can scrounge up a half dozen now who were providing support to the perimeter teams. But that's it. That's all we've got. You've got to hold it together for a couple of hours, and probably more here, son."

Ranger Rick broke in. "Sir, with all due respect, because your Chief Master Sergeant here certainly can't question you, you're signing the death warrant to fifty-two thousand people in the city tonight by not sending every one of your troops in here right now. Fifty thousand people. Dead. That's what very well might happen. And you have your men, miles off, patrolling empty desert. How is that going to look, sir?"

The Colonel didn't respond. He waited for CMS Carter to speak up. "Sorry, sir. Everyone is a little worked up right now, sir."

"I get that, son," the Colonel replied, without rancor. "Anything you all can do from your end to keep a better wrap on things is going to help us all focus on the task at hand, because the media is getting wind of this. You've got citizens sending out pictures and video from sat phones, and even laptops from the camps with some bandwidth. Taking over your Media Mecca or shutting down the aerial webcam didn't seem to put a dent in it. You make sure that everyone in that room understands, unwanted outside attention at this point in time is going to divert resources, including yours and mine."

"Understood," the Chief Master Sergeant answered dutifully, staring at the floor.

The Colonel continued, "Now, there's something I'm going to share with you, so that you can be crystal clear in your mission from this moment forward. Get on a secure line, and step outside for a moment. I'll be awaiting your call."

Chief Master Sergeant Carter excused himself from the room. Moments later he was reconnected with his superior, while he paced around on the Esplanade outside. He pressed the receiver tightly against his ear, the din of the surrounding area continued to escalate in volume and level of confusion.

"Son," the Colonel began, "this virus is extra-terrestrial. You know about the ground zero site. It was first thought to be a meteor, but it's a metallic, motion sensor-activated probe that fires off projectiles armed with the virus. We are holding the lid here on something we don't understand and has likely been designed with global catastrophic intentions. Now, we want to save as many of these fifty thousand people as we can, we truly do, but the downside if we fail to keep a lid on this tonight, staggers the mind. So I need you to keep your resolve, do you understand?"

Darren Carter stared out into the playa, almost in a daze. "Oh my God. Yes, sir, I do understand, sir."

"Good. Now son, there has to be absolute security on this information. You repeat this to no one. No one, understood?"

"Yes, sir."

"Okay, my good friend Doctor Gorman shared this information with a couple of men we're still trying to track down. He thinks they may have come to your city. You'll see their name on the lists. If you catch wind of them, they have to be secured."

"Understood."

"Now, you asked for a new mission template. Beyond securing you more boots and buying some time, you should focus on your idea to subdivide the ground outside your Green Zone into red and yellow zones. Get your infected collection sites in the red zones, clear out the ambulatory citizens into the yellow zones. Be creative to attract the Stage II infected out of the yellow and into the red. Start moving around the citizens when you need to build some separation between the zones. Okay? You ready to get on it, son?"

"I'm on it, Colonel."

Thursday Friday Saturday Sunday Monday Tuesday Wednesday

Doctor Gorman

Alan Gorman rolled over, opening one eye, spying the time on the nightstand clock. He had napped slightly more than a half hour. Alan was given a room at Bruno's Motel in Gerlach that had been occupied by a Pershing County deputy who was called back out to duty.

Alan had been flown to the BRC airport hours before, rushed down to Gerlach, and was vitally involved at first – briefing personnel on what they were facing and giving opinions on tactical options. But as time progressed, he was shuffled aside. The last request for his participation involved the requisition for the remaining medical support staff and morphine in Gerlach. After dutifully providing a physician's signature to the requisition forms, he called to register his objections to the mass administration of morphine for the infected. He then retreated to his recently assigned motel room, showering and taking a nap.

Alan stretched, yawned and decided to shave. He considered disobeying his friend, the Colonel, and phoning his wife to let her know he was okay. The Colonel imposed a communication blackout with the outside world. Alan decided his own situation was decidedly different - neither the Colonel's men nor local law enforcement had been missing for two days. Alan wanted badly to hear the sound of her voice.

Alan scrolled through all his wife's missed calls and messages on his Blackberry. The Colonel had said he would arrange for Mrs. Gorman to be notified that her husband was safe, but she had not attempted to contact him since that time. Alan debated if she knew his status or not. He decided to let her know, but not to call and end up answering questions she would ask, divulging information he had been ordered not to share. Alan keyed in his text message, advising he was safe, he hoped she had been notified; he was assisting authorities and wouldn't be able to communicate further for a while longer.

Gorman opened the luggage he had packed Saturday morning at his motel in Auburn. He dressed in some fresh clothes, grabbing his Blackberry, wallet and room key, before stepping outside. After closing the door, he stared at the room key, attached to the colored plastic oval with "Bruno's" emblazoned on one side. He wondered when the last time he had stayed at a place that still used actual keys.

Alan wandered over to the outdoor command center. The first staff he bumped into apprised him of the morphine debacle. Pressing for more information, Alan learned that the clinic physicians and staffs were all basically out of the game.

Gorman strolled past an ambulance loading the young woman found in the porta-potty out at the party site twenty-kilometers north of Burning Man. Alan examined her shortly after he arrived in Gerlach. After Gorman determined she was stable enough, one of the Colonel's men briefly interrogated her. She was suffering from post-traumatic stress – too distraught and incoherent to provide much useful information. She claimed her name was Thelma and kept asking about the whereabouts of her friend, Louise. Alan, listening in on the questioning, was sure those weren't their real names.

Alan stared down the road at the sheriff's road block, turning away any approaching vehicle that somehow had made it around the previous roadblock for the now-closed stretch of highway 447. Gorman glanced around the small command center staffed with a handful of personnel, all busy and unaware of his presence. He overheard a conversation that a sheriff's SUV was about to be used to shuttle a load of requested items back to the Chief Master Sergeant. Alan butted in, asking if he could hitch a ride.

Minutes later, Gorman was in the passenger seat racing straight across the playa, a good distance from the designated Burning Man roadway. He was on his way to become the new, interim physician in charge of the Rampart Clinic.

Thursday Friday Saturday Sunday Monday Tuesday Wednesday

Mad Dash for the Exits

With almost all Black Rock City citizenry off the grid – save those with satellite phones or the few camps that set up Internet bandwidth – conversation fills the void. As the situation began to decay around the fringes of the city, conversations were bursting with rumors.

The radio stations, the official Burning Man Information Radio- BMIR – 94.5 FM, and the low wattage stations run by a few of the theme camps, were not their normal selves. The low wattage stations had all been simply rebroadcasting BMIR for the past several hours. BMIR was still working through a playlist – but in between songs were the same dire, taped warnings about a public health emergency and the coming thunderstorm that necessitated closure of the gate, with listeners urged to lock themselves inside their vehicle until further notice.

Those considering themselves typically in the know at Center Camp, were worked up about the strange goings on – sightings of men in military gear, the closure of the Media Mecca, the inaccessibility of anyone in the Black Rock board or Executive Team. Then there were the comings and goings of the ambulances, the frantic scrambling around the clinics, the disappearance of most law enforcement or even Black Rock Rangers – tales from friends of friends who had witnessed bizarre group attacks and behavior near the walk-in campground, or out near the 10:00 sound camps and out on the open playa. The rumor mill was primed from the center of the city to fill in the blanks about these and the other escalating events around BRC. The frenzied rumors whipped their way into every corner of the community.

After all hell starting breaking loose as the nine o' clock hour progressed, an increasing number of citizens witnessed incidents first-hand. A number of the Stage II infected wandered into wide portions of city, attacking at random.

It would be difficult to say in what part of the city the first campers threw their belongings in their vehicle, leaving various items behind, peeling out to the exit roads, well past the stated speed limit of five miles per hour. But seeing one panicked neighbor scrambling to get out of 'Dodge' begat another. By a quarter-to-ten, hundreds of vehicles were heading out the dusty exit road, with thousands more vehicles being packed. A few campers, lacking a vehicle, hopped on their bicycles, heading out into the playa to escape the city. The mad dash to the exits was on.

As Chief Master Sergeant Carter caught wind of the rush to the gate, he radioed the Colonel – who had no choice but to pull his southern perimeter team forward, in their vehicles, to stem the tide.

Back in Space Ghost camp, Cassie and Tess's neighbor was arguing with his wife. He was adamant they were leaving. She was equally adamant they were staying. Nothing was getting packed. She pointed out that the radio station announced the gate was closed. Their argument was interrupted by a loud ruckus behind Cassie and Tess's camp in the intersection of 7:30 and I. After several bone-rattling screams, the couple grabbed flashlights and ran through Cassie's camp to see what was happening. They met up with Bruce when they reached the street.

A woman was wailing on her knees in the middle of the intersection. Two men were collapsed on the ground. Several bystanders were kneeling over them. Bruce and Cassie's neighbors trotted out into the intersection. As they approached, they could see the men were bleeding, their clothing torn.

The woman was trying to talk, but was hyperventilating and hysterical. Bruce knelt down with her, put his right arm around her, attempting to soothe her. "It's okay...just slow down...slow down. That's better. People are here to help. See?"

The woman took another deep breath, pausing before words finally escaped. "We were just right down there," she lifted her right arm, pointing at the porta-potties. She breathed deeply, in and out, a couple of times. "My boyfriend came out of the stall, and this horrible looking man jumped out of nowhere, grabbing hold of him. He started biting him, tearing at him. Our friend jumped in to defend him and got bit. Someone stepped out of another stall and this freak left them and ran inside the toilet. Both my guys started feeling real sick right away. We started walking up this way to tell someone about that freak, and they just collapsed right here, and I can't get them up. .What's wrong with them? And someone needs to go get that freak in the porta potty."

"We'll do that," Bruce offered, soothingly. "Now come on, let's get you up, and then let's get them out of the road." Bruce and Cassie's neighbors lifted her fully upright; the three of them escorted her towards Cassie's camp.

The rumble of thunder could be heard in the distance. The three bystanders, tending to the two men sprawled in the middle of the road, cheered; one of the men was able to sit upright. Two of the bystanders trotted over to their camp to fetch a cot they could use as a stretcher. The third strolled over to the woman, to tell her their plan.

The group standing near Cassie's camp turned around, hearing a car barreling down I street at high speed. Several in the group screamed at the vehicle to no avail. A black, rusted Mitsubishi Gallant plowed into and over the two men. A sickening thud could be heard throughout the area.

The growing crowd raced out to the intersection. The Mitsubishi continued forward at full speed for twenty yards or so, before slamming on the brakes, emitting an enormous cloud of dust. The Mitsubishi lurched forward ten feet, stopping again, then slowly backed up halfway to the intersection, before coming to a halt. Two shirtless young men, visibly shaken, cautiously opened their doors, stepping back towards the intersection, the crowd growing very ugly, hurling profanities at them.

The woman raced out to her boyfriend and his companion, Bruce and Cassie's neighbors close behind. The two run-over men were a mess. Bruce tried to shield the woman's eyes without success. Her boyfriend's legs had been driven over, leaving shards of bone jutting out of his skin, below his shorts. His companion's lower torso was ripped open — close to obliterated — intestines and other internal parts remained exposed. The blood oozing out of both of them was an odd reddish-gray.

The crowd — now swelled to a dozen — and the Mitsubishi drivers had converged. People were pushing and shoving the two young men, cursing them. Bruce ran to the woman, kneeling once more in the middle of the intersection next to her fallen comrades. She resumed wailing.

A couple minutes went by, the crowd not giving the young men a chance to go anywhere, angrily encircling them. The two men, for their part, were trying to explain that they were fleeing the camp, and everyone else should be trying to leave too. Thunder continually interrupted the exchange, the storm's intensity building each time.

Bruce, while consoling the poor woman in the road, began eyeing the companion with his guts spilling out. He knew what was going to happen next. He pulled the woman back as the companion's head rose up, snarling. The companion propped himself up with his right arm, grunting loudly. Unable to stand, he began to scoot a few inches at time toward Bruce and the woman, while emitting a low guttural moan.

Bruce stood up, quickly pulling the woman back towards Cassie's neighbors. The crowd fell silent. The two men from the Mitsubishi fell silent. Bruce stepped through the quieted, dropped-jawed crowd, now shining their flashlights at the man-who-should-be-dead, oozing gray goo out his exposed mid-section, scooting on his rear inches at a time, towards them. Bruce demanded car keys from the young, shirtless, shaken men. One meekly volunteered that they were still in the vehicle. Bruce ran to the car, hopped in, backing it up slowly, positioning it not to run over the unfortunate men in the intersection again, but angling it until the car resided on top of them. The snarling man hissed as the bumper slowly kissed his face, forcing him to lie back down as the Mitsubishi trapped him underneath along with his friend.

Bruce hopped out of the car. He tossed the keys back to one of the young men. "Sorry guys, but you're going to need to leave the car there for a while, to keep them contained." Bruce turned to face the small crowd. "Everyone should keep clear of those two under the car. Whatever you do, don't let them come into contact with you or you could end up like them."

Bruce glanced at Cassie's neighbors, motioning with his head towards their camp. The three briskly walked away, calls from the crowd hurling a jumble of questions at Bruce in his wake.

"Alright, let's leave right now. We can come back and get our stuff later," Cassie and Tess's neighbor lady exclaimed in a shaken voice to her husband.

"Did you see that? Can you believe that, man?" her husband babbled. He turned to Bruce. "You should come with us, man. Right now. Leave a note for Jan and Jace and your friend. The way things are going, they're going to have to find their own way out from where they are."

"No, that's okay, you go," Bruce responded. "I am going to leave a note, but I'm going to try to find them. So, I'm hoping you can quickly show me again where this Alamo is, and maybe you've got some pen and paper?"

Thursday Friday Saturday Sunday Monday Tuesday Wednesday

The Deluge

Bruce had to hoof it towards the playa, cautiously jogging on the far right side of 7:30, only possessing a single flashlight to illuminate himself in traffic. As he crossed each concentric street — H, G, F — the chaotic din of the neighborhoods raised up a notch. A bright flash lit up the intersection of E and 7:30; the thunderclap followed in several seconds. Bruce noticed an eerie stillness in the air. He glanced up to witness the arrival of the deluge.

Small hailstones whistled downward. A minute later, the precipitation converted to heavy rainfall. Bruce trudged forward, his shoes starting to stick in the wet cement-like clay surface. At first, he ran his fingers through his hair as he attempted to run, the shower feeling nice after all he had been through that day. A couple of minutes later, he was feeling like a cold, drowned rat, and quite miserable.

For the several hundred vehicles that had made it to the exit roadway, the slog quickly became a battle with a quicksand-like surface, in which the cars were losing. As the lead cars became bogged down and stuck well short of the gate, a chain-reaction developed behind them. A couple of heavy duty SUVs and old jeeps managed to pass the quagmire of cars to the right or left, running through the roadway barriers, but even they finally met their muddy demise minutes later.

Countless cars featured soaked passengers pushing on the rear bumpers, as the front or rear tires dug deeper and deeper into ruts in the runny, cement-like ooze. Regular flashes of lightning lit up the muddy-gridlock scene.

The dozen zombies that had surprised the two Nevada DOI agents on the perimeter, slipped out onto the playa undetected, and were quite drawn to the parade of headlamps attached to stuck vehicles. Five minutes later, the zombies had made their way through the playa, which wasn't quite as impassable as the exit roadway. They found plenty of targets as people tried to push their vehicles out of the muck. After five minutes of heavy rainfall, the roadway was now impenetrable.

Visibility during the deluge was extremely limited. Those that stayed inside their cars generally had no idea a dozen zombies were wandering down their line. Even the yells and screams of those under attack were difficult to detect from inside a vehicle with the windows rolled up and rainfall relentlessly pounding on the automobile's surface.

The deluge zombies seemed content to drag their victims to the mud, biting and tearing away at them as the people lost their footing and collapsed in the muck, but the z's abandoned them once they were fully horizontal and embedded in the mud. Minute by minute, the z's worked their way up the line. Now and then, the driver of the vehicle behind a zombie's victim would witness the assault through the rain-cluttered windshield. Occasionally, a driver would get out in the downpour to be of assistance, not to return.

The rain persisted. The streets of Black Rock City became as impassable as the exit roadway. Anyone who hadn't already attempted to exit was no longer in a position to do so.

The Southern Perimeter team, upon onset of the deluge, began a hasty retreat. They knew the rainfall would perform their job for them for the next couple of hours. By staying off the Burning Man roadway, with a more manageable playa surface, they were able to make it back to Gerlach.

Cassie and Tess's neighbors didn't even advance as far as the Greeter's station before becoming stuck in the muddy gridlock. The spouses locked their car doors, biding their time arguing and listening to the radio. A half hour later, the deluge zombies worked their way to them after the rain died down. The husband witnessed the zombies claw the shirt of the man in front of him. The husband honked his horn, trying to chase them away. He wasn't willing to step outside, despite his wife's urgings to help the man now lying in the muck.

Thursday Friday Saturday Sunday Monday Tuesday Wednesday

Bruce in the Green Zone

The temperature dropped rapidly. As Bruce forged his way to 7:30 and B, soaked and shivering, he stared at his feet, coaxing them forward through the mushy street. The bulge in his back pocket annoyed him as he trudged forward, and with every step he questioned the wisdom of bringing the duct tape that Cassie's neighbor insisted he absolutely had to take with him.

The loud banging, popping, and flashes of sparks and light — just to his right — caused Bruce to spin and turn his attention to the theme camp next to him.

The camp's main awning collapsed — some object had been tossed and stuck half way up, earlier in the day — causing a reservoir to form as the deluge began. The collapse sent water flying into the lights and other electrical, causing a short just as two persons were working with the wiring, due to a failure that had just occurred in the mid-section of their camp's public area. Both men dropped to the floor. One rose up halfway up almost immediately, stunned. The other wasn't moving, apparently electrocuted. The awning structure was strewn about, partially covering both men.

No one else seemed to be around. Bruce stepped around the side barrier to their camp, worked his way around the collapsed structure, and kneeled next to both men. One was sitting upright, dazed, the other appeared to be out cold. The rain continued to slap down everywhere without mercy. Bruce considered applying the CPR he barely remembered how to administer, but first placed his palm on the man's chest, checking for any movement from breathing or a heartbeat.

Bruce sighed in relief. He could feel the chest slightly rising up and down. Moments later he heard a momentary snore. Bruce found himself checking the man up and down for any sign of zombie molestation, but saw no evidence of such. Another man trotted up from within the camp. He knelt down next to Bruce, eying his two felled campmates. "Hey, thanks for helping them. I saw the lights flash from the car, so I jumped out and headed over." The man glanced around the area nervously.

"Where is everyone?" Bruce asked.

"Some we don't know, but most people are in their cars or someone else's car. Isn't that what we're supposed to be doing?"

"So what happened here?" Bruce wanted to know, pointing at the two men.

"The lights were flickering badly, so they got out of their car to check it out," the man answered, while patting his campmate who was sitting upright, looking woozy. His upright campmate leaned over, vomiting a small amount onto the awning lying next to him. The other campmate remained unconscious. "Look, we're going to need to get him help," the man stated to Bruce, pointing at the campmate still passed out, as the rain continued to pelt all of them.

"Hey, I have to go help some people out there right now," Bruce responded, shaking his head, pointing out to the open playa.

"Dude, you got to help me carry him to the clinic," the man insisted.

"Can't your friend here do that?" Bruce countered, pointing at the man sitting upright next to them.

"Look at him," the man replied emphatically. His campmate turned to acknowledge the attention, but appeared very pale and confused. "Now, wait right here." The man got up, ran back into his camp, returning in less than one minute with a cloth hammock in his hands. "Come on," he pleaded with Bruce. "No one else is around, and he might be getting worse by the second. You have to help me carry him to the clinic."

Bruce shook his head while he shivered from the downpour. "I can't. I have friends out there."

"Look, I'm begging you, dude. This guy could die for all we know. He needs to go now, and I can't carry him by myself." The man fumbled with the cloth hammock in his hands while he talked.

Bruce sighed loudly. "Alright, fine. But let's go now, and I'm not going to stick around when we get there.

"Just a second," the man stated. He turned to help the other stricken campmate rise to his feet, walking him to the next set of awnings within the camp, seating him underneath some shelter. He quickly returned, unfolding the cloth hammock, handing one end to Bruce. They stretched it alongside the unconscious man, before slightly lifting him onto it. Moments later, they rose up in the deluge, slowly carrying the occupied hammock down B Street toward Center Camp.

Bruce had studied Cassie's neighbor's extra map. "Isn't there a closer clinic behind us?"

"Yeah, there is," the man answered, panting, while they started carrying their patient in the hammock down B Street. "But the radio said it's closed to new patients, so I'm trying our luck at the main clinic.

Bruce audibly groaned. After trudging to 7:15 in the mucky right edge of B, they worked their way in the rain to the middle of the road, where the going was much easier. B was packed more solidly, with less fine dust to turn into impassable glop, plus the road was slightly sloped in the center, so the rainfall was running off to the sides. Their pace picked up considerably.

Still, Bruce was aggravated and impatient as they passed 7:00. He started to look for anyone he could pass off his duty to so he could return to his quest for the Alamo. He could see people as they progressed, but none in a situation where he could engage them in a plea to take over his position. Those they passed by were either frantically entangled in their own activities or ignored them.

A pickup started bearing down on them from behind. Bruce was surprised to hear the engine gunning, the headlights illuminating the whole rain and mud-soaked scene. "I can't believe a vehicle is getting through this mess," the man called out to Bruce as they veered right back into the mud to let the pickup pass.

The Pershing County deputies in their 4x4 Chevrolet 2500 Silverado slowed down to crawl, lowering their window. "Where are you taking him?" the deputy on passenger side demanded of the man, who was leading with the hammock, while Bruce followed.

"Center Camp, to the clinic," the man hollered above the rain, which was picking up. He and Bruce continued forward at a slow place while they conversed with the deputy, while the driver inched forward in their truck.

"What's wrong with him?" the deputy asked in a harsh tone, frowning.

"He was electrocuted back in our camp. He's breathing, but unconscious." the man replied, hopeful the deputies might offer some assistance.

"Has he been bitten? Does he have any wounds?" the deputy inquired, matter-of-factly.

"Huh?" The man was confused by the question. He wasn't aware of what was transpiring all around him.

"Has he been bitten?" the deputy shouted back, quite annoyed.

Bruce chimed in. "No, he's clean. He just got shocked, that's all." Bruce grew hopeful as well that they might offer some help.

Sure enough, the deputy came through. "Well, let's get him in the back, and hurry up, before we get stuck. This road may be the only workable street on this side of the camp right now." The pickup came to a halt. Bruce and the man loaded their patient in the pickup bed; the man jumped in with him. Bruce started to walk away, but the deputy yelled at Bruce at the top of his voice. "Hey, get in there with your friends. We don't have time to unload him, we're just going to give a ride inside the

Green Zone and drop you off. You're going to unload him and take him inside the clinic."

"I have to get going. I was just passing by and lent a hand..." Bruce started to argue.

"Hey, don't waste our time, here," the deputy yelled. "Get in the pickup bed now. Do you have any idea what's going on around here? We don't have time to piss away with you."

Bruce sighed and hopped in the pickup bed. The sheriff's truck spun its back tires for a moment, but gained traction and continued down B.

The man pressed Bruce for information as they steadied their patient in the pickup bed, while the rain beat down on them. "What's he talking about, asking if he had been bitten? What the hell is that all about?"

"It's a long story," Bruce replied, not wanting to launch into a long story. "But that health emergency I hear that they're talking about on the radio? That's the emergency, people are infected and biting other people. And if you get bit, you can die, it's that nasty."

"What?" the man responded in disbelief. "And what's he talking about a Green Zone for? What's a Green Zone?"

"You got me there," Bruce told the man, while shielding his eyes from the rain with his hands. Within moments, they both learned what the Green Zone was all about.

Rod's Road was a circular loop surrounding Center Camp, cutting through the curved lettered streets from D down to Esplanade, and the clock numbered radial streets between 6:30 and 5:30. The deputies arrived at Rod's Road, spoke to an armed guard at a barricade, who moved the obstacle and allowed the deputies to pass.

They turned left to A Street, and then cut across through the middle of the Center Camp Green Zone. Two minutes later, they were at the other end of the zone, stopping at Rampart. "This is it, good luck, gentleman," the deputy on the passenger side yelled back to Bruce and his companion.

Bruce and the man dismounted, gingerly lifting their patient, careful not to slip and fall in the muddy morass. Someone just inside Rampart saw them coming, but didn't open the doors for them. Instead the gentleman came outside.

"What's wrong with him?" the Rampart door monitor wanted to know. They repeated a dialogue similar to the one held with the deputy minutes before. They were allowed passage inside.

After helping the patient inside, Bruce turned to scurry out the door and find his way to the Alamo, when voice called after him. "Bruce? Is that you, Bruce?"

Half a day later, Alan Gorman looked quite different to Bruce. Now he was Doctor Gorman, clean-shaven, armed with a stethoscope instead of a rifle. Alan had been standing in the bay behind the treatment area where Bruce and his companion deposited the patient. Now, Alan was shaking his hand as if they were old war buddies. "I can't believe you made it here. You must have been through a lot, my man. I can tell you that I have."

Bruce let out a small laugh. "Yeah, I bet we both have." Bruce was ready to let loose with a stream of questions, when the man accompanying Bruce stepped forward from behind Bruce.

"Wait a minute....Wait just a minute," Chief Master Sergeant Carter interrupted. He had been paying a very quick visit to Gorman to discuss how they were shielding the Stage I victims from the rain out in the open collection areas. "Talk about dumb luck. Are you telling me this is one of the men you were with earlier today?"

Alan paused. He now realized Bruce might be in trouble, but there was not much that could be done about it. "Well, yes but we should talk about that. I don't think that—"

Darren Carter interrupted. "Doctor, I'll catch up with you in a minute, let me just take your friend here aside for a minute." Alan could be heard protesting, while Bruce was whisked away. Bruce was escorted to the Rampart double doors, where the monitor still stood at attention. Bruce now noticed the monitor was armed.

"I want you to escort... Bruce...what is your last name again, sir?" CMS Carter asked Bruce politely.

Bruce sighed. "Kepner. Bruce Kepner."

"Escort Mr. Kepner back to my office and send a replacement to take your position here on the double. Keep Mr. Kepner with you until I return," CMS Carter instructed the monitor.

"Wha...What did I do? Why would you hold me a prisoner?" Bruce yelled at the Chief Master Sergeant, indignantly.

"Calm down, Mr. Kepner," Carter replied in a flat tone. "You didn't do anything. I just have a Colonel that is anxious to have someone talk to you about today's events, and we need to keep you secured at least until that happens, and that may take a little while."

III. The Alamo

The Alamo

The Alamo was under siege. During the past half hour, zombies were drawn to the two -story art installation. When Conner arrived, there were maybe twenty surrounding the structure. Now, despite the deluge, Conner estimated the number had swelled past one hundred. Conner didn't see his own kind moving about in the area, only zombies. They seemed to get along just fine in the mucky, wet-cement-like conditions below. Conner commented to Cassie, that zombies seemed like they were made for the mud.

Conner wondered why the zombies were enraptured earlier in the day when urine showered down on them from the rooftop, but didn't seem to even notice or acknowledge the rain. He didn't comment on this puzzlement to Cassie.

The Alamo wasn't an accurate replica of the real thing. The Burning Man Alamo consisted of fifteen-foot-high outer walls, with wooden gates in the front, left open into the courtyard. Inside, the left side wall contained a facade of a mission church; the right side wall façade encompassed a series of simple rooms. Both facades were just two-feet-deep. Toward the back of the courtyard was a sign indicating "Basement" with an arrow pointing downwards. A faux wooden basement door lay in the playa dirt below in the sign. A sculpture of Pee-wee's bicycle was nearby. Behind the courtyard, in the back of the Alamo, was the second story balcony. Underneath the balcony were two rooms – one in each corner. Likewise, the balcony held two second story corner rooms. The interior and exterior were well-lit, with floodlights at ground level and track lighting along the upper walls. The entire installation was painted in a Southwestern palate, over a stucco surface.

After arriving, and nursing a nasty welt where Cassie had clobbered him with a two-by-four, Conner took stock of their situation. In addition to Cassie and Tess, they were joined on the second floor by a pair in costume – appropriately using the monikers Lucha Libre and Catwoman.

Catwoman, a well-shaped medium height brunette, nicely filled out her "Dark Knight Rises" Catwoman costume, complete with a short-sleeve, black jumpsuit with a zip-front closure, thigh-high boot tops with a stirrup bottom tucked into her black boots, black gloves, a molded eye mask with attached ears, and a molded black belt. She never took off her mask in public at Burning Man.

Lucha Libre, Catwoman's boyfriend, was her same height with a stocky build, outfitted in a lycra Blue Demon wrestling mask; long white spandex tights with a red German cross running down his outside hips and upper thighs plus a red stripe running from his crotch all the way down both inner legs; tall red lace-up boots; and a white lycra wrestling shirt with an inside pocket.

Catwoman and Lucha Libre fled up the Alamo's balcony ladders with Cassie and Tess, when the zombies first arrived. The two other ladies originally with the group — Cassie was just calling them the tequila girls without providing Conner much of an explanation – ran inside one of the downstairs corner rooms. Now and then, the tequila girls could be heard pleading for help from down below. Also upstairs was a strange man, who talked to himself, and wouldn't leave the upstairs western corner room where Cassie found him when they first set foot on the balcony.

Lucha Libre and Catwoman pulled up the ladders, so the zombies didn't have the means to climb up and join them on the second floor. Still, the z's gathered in greater numbers to loiter inside and outside the Alamo, hoping that someone from above would come down to mingle with them. The zombies made quick work of Pee-wee Herman cut-outs on the first floor. Shortly after Conner arrived, he could see every first floor Pee-wee indignantly trampled on the ground.

Pee-wee's music ceased. Danny Elfman's "Breakfast Machine" vanished. The group wasn't sure if the zombies below had inadvertently disconnected it or if it had been running off batteries and died.

Conner, Cassie, Tess, Lucha Libre and Catwoman spent their time trying to brainstorm an escape, but no big ideas were forthcoming as the surge of zombies soon had any escape route sealed off, even if they were willing to jump. The greater concern, as the z's started packing in underneath the balcony, banging into everything, was that the structure could end up collapsing, with the group tumbling down into the crowd of zombies below.

There was also the issue of the tequila girls. There were no locks on the upstairs doors or door handles for that matter. There was great debate as to if or how they had managed to keep the zombies out of their downstairs room. Different ideas for rescue attempts were bandied about, with none gaining much popularity.

Once the deluge started, the five of them moved inside the western corner upstairs room. After several minutes of the strange man's yelling at them, at himself, and at the walls, they spontaneously exited back into the soaking downpour, taking shelter in the eastern corner room. Every few minutes, Conner excused himself to quickly patrol the balcony, surveying what was going on below.

Cassie, Tess, Lucha Libre and Catwoman sat cross legged on the floor, wanting to know everything Conner knew about the swarm of z's outside. Conner shared the story of his day, commenting on the irony that he was ending it as he began, stuck on a roof, surrounded by zombies below.

Conner remained standing by the door, leaving it partially open so he could at least hear what was going on outside through the rain. Some of the downpour angled in through the opening, spraying Cassie, who was grasping onto Conner's right leg. Conner had removed his Stormtrooper costume, which lay in a pile in the corner with his bat and rebar and the two-by-fours that came with the room.

"If I would have listened to you and brought Tess back to camp right away, we wouldn't be in this mess," Cassie lamented, kissing Conner's pants leg. The group had already heard Cassie's repeated public disclosures of regret, shortly before Conner's arrival.

"If you would have listened to him, you wouldn't have been around to help us, and we might not have made it up here alive," Catwoman pointed out, smiling, "so at least I'm glad you didn't listen to your hero here, who wandered all the way across the desert for you."

Conner stepped out to scan their surroundings. Each time he checked outside, he monitored a smaller, well-lit mutant vehicle stuck in the mud a ways to the east. Seeing no activity there, he re-entered the room.

"Every vehicle is quite stuck in the mud. I don't think we are going to get rescued any time soon," Conner cautioned.

"I wonder what we did here in Burning Man to piss the Gods off so royally," Catwoman remarked, launching into a diatribe, resorting to the same gallows humor that sustained Bruce and Conner earlier in the day. "It's like, we think the Man you built this year was a little lame and doesn't please or countenance us, so we are going to stretch out our rod and strike the dust of the earth, that it may become a mighty dust storm throughout all the lands of the Black Rock, to smite you...Oh? What's that? You're still there? You're not smote? Okay, we will stretch out our rod and strike the dust of the earth, and we will send rain upon the Black Rock forty days and forty nights, and every living thing we will blot out from the face of the ground....Huh? Oh, we can't freakin' believe it. You're still there? You're not blotted? Fine, then. We will skip right past turning the water to blood or unleashing gnats, frogs, wild beasts, pestilence, boils, hail, locusts, darkness or slaying your first born. No, instead, we're gonna freakin' stretch out our rod and strike the dust of the earth, that it may become a horde of crazed zombies that want to tear you from limb to limb. We'll teach you to build a freakin' lame Man in the middle of the Black Rock!"

Everyone laughed, but not for too long. The room fell silent for a moment, the rhythmic sound of the rain and the monotonous drone of the moaning zombies below, both wafted through the doorway. The shrill voice of the crazed man in the western room across the way also worked its way through the door. Something had set him off into an incoherent, profane, outburst at the top of his lungs.

Conner decided to check it out. He closed the door behind him, dashing across the balcony towards the other room. He spotted the man standing out on the edge of the rail-less balcony just outside his corner room, arms outstretched to the sky. The man had stripped; his shorts and tee shirt lying at his feet, the rain pelting his naked, thin body. The man burst into a tirade directed at the zombies below. He reached down, grabbing his shirt, throwing into the agitated crowd, like a rock star on stage. Next, he picked up his pants, twirling them above his head, before sending them flying as well.

The man seemed to not notice Conner, instead pacing back and forth a few steps in each direction, scratching at his arms, hurling loud random insults at no one in particular. Conner shook his head, turned away and headed back to the wall outside the other room. He peered out toward the mutant vehicle stuck in the mud. Movement caught his eye.

Despite the rainfall, Conner could distinguish several people fleeing from the well-lit vehicle, back towards the city. He could also make out the fuzzy outlines of zombies, apparently in pursuit. Conner lost sight of all of them once they distanced themselves from the lit vehicle into the darkness. Conner listened intently, not detecting any new sounds at first. Then he noticed the zombies milling around the outer side wall below, starting to advance out into the playa. Unfortunately, the z's situated at the back wall – where the ladder was located – were still present in force.

Conner hollered out warnings into the rain-filled blackness. He then noticed a number of the zombies in the Alamo courtyard below, starting to head to the open gate, following the lead of the zombies outside the wall. Conner studied the gates through the rainfall, trying to determine what they were actually made of, and if they would really work. Conner glanced back outside the walls. The zombies were on the move streaming away from the Alamo in the direction that the escapees from the stuck mutant vehicle must be heading.

Conner, it seemed, now had a plan.

He bolted back into the room. "We've got to act fast," he declared excitedly. "Most of the zombies are leaving, chasing some other people who just left their vehicle. Some zombies are still in the courtyard, but not many. I'm going to put back on this Stormtrooper stuff on for protection. I'll take my bat and go after them. If it looks like I can keep the few of them left at bay, everybody come down, and bring those two-by-fours you found here, and my rebar. We'll free the two tequila girls if they're still alive, and sprint out past the gates." Conner walked across the room to his costume in the corner, while he spoke. He sat down to start outfitting himself.

"I don't think we can do much sprinting in that mud and rain," Lucha Libre argued.

"That might be, but I would think we could still outrun these zombies," Conner responded, optimistically, while fastening on his Stormtrooper pants.

Lucha Libre disagreed. "Didn't I hear you telling your girlfriend here that zombies were made for the mud? They seem to get around pretty good down there, if you ask me."

"Okay," Conner countered, "let's say you're right about that. If we can't move around well, we'll know that in the courtyard before we ever leave this place. My Plan B is that we at least close the gates, now that most of the zombies are back outside, and before who knows how many start to come back in. We can still rescue the ladies below, come back up here to be safe, but not have so many of them swarming below us."

"What makes you think those gates even work?" Lucha Libre remained skeptical.

Tess spoke up, rubbing her hands through her hair. "They do work. We've seen the gates closed before – last year, and this year too, when we first checked out the playa. I think we should go with Conner's plan, even if it's just to shut the gates. You all felt the balcony swaying when the zombies were pushing into the beams below. We talked about the balcony collapsing back then. And if we're ever going to see if those tequila girls are okay, it sounds like now would be the time."

Everyone rose up, exiting to the balcony. Lucha Libre sighed, while others nodded in agreement. Conner filed out last, now in full Stormtrooper regalia, including face mask.

"See, there's just four or five left down there," Conner pointed out, speaking loudly through his mask. He was emboldened by his previous softball bat z encounter outside the Alamo. "I'll jump down, so they don't have time to come at me. If I can keep them at bay, you guys lower the ladder and bring your two-by-fours. Lucha Libre, you decide when you get down if we can outrun them in this mud. If you don't think we can, say so immediately, but head for the gates with Catwoman and close them. Cassie and Tess, you check on the tequila ladies once I've drawn the zombies away, and then we're either running outside or going back up the ladder."

"What about him?" Tess asked, pointing at the naked, unstable man, standing outside the door to his room, muttering something unintelligible.

The thin, naked man seemed fixated on Conner. He pointed back at Conner, shaking his head. "Darth Vader," the Man yelled apprehensively. "Darth Vader is coming." The man retreated back to his room.

"I think he's safer staying up here," Lucha Libre suggested.

"Okay then, this is it," Conner exclaimed, grabbing his bat. He jumped into the muck below, landing awkwardly, falling backward after he landed. The remaining zombies turned their attention to Conner on the ground before them.

Thursday Friday Saturday Sunday Monday Tuesday Wednesday

Slipping Out of the Green

The Green Zone was sliding into chaos. Center Camp was adequately defended along the semi-circular Rod's Road, but the Esplanade side, facing into the open playa, was another matter. Once the deluge developed, there was no means to patrol Esplanade with vehicles. The stretch was too long to sufficiently secure with available personnel on foot. The downpour obscured the visual out into the open playa. It didn't take long for the zombies to slither through, little by little.

While personally checking in with his teams throughout the Green Zone, Chief Master Sergeant Carter came to the realization that his office in the Black Rock Ranger HQ, situated on the Esplanade, would require relocation. Carter decided to position his base of operations further within the Green Zone, in BRC Post Office, off the inner circle in Center Camp. He headed there directly, without returning to the BRR HQ.

Carter placed a call to his two remaining staff in the HQ to grab his laptop and other gear and double time it to the Post Office with Bruce Kepner in tow. Ranger Rick, had already vacated the premises, personally coming to the aid of a pair of rangers who radioed a plea for assistance from the edge of the Green Zone, at 5:30 and Esplanade.

Carter's two assistants stepped outside into the rain with their weapons, gear bags, laptop bag, and Bruce. Within moments, the sound of gunfire and a cry for help pierced through the night further down the Esplanade.

"Here," one of Carter's assistants barked to Bruce, "you carry this, now." He handed Bruce a gear bag and laptop bag, then started sprinting as best he could through the mud in the direction of the continued plea for help.

"Damn it, come back!" the other assistant yelled, as his comrade disappeared into the darkness. "We're under orders to report directly to the Chief." There was no response. The visual was quickly lost on his comrade. Moments later, additional gunfire could be heard. "Come on," he commanded Bruce, "let's quit screwing around and get to the Post Office."

Bruce and the remaining assistant trekked through the mud with their gear to the 6:00 portal into the inner circle. Hugging the outer rim of the circle, they started to pass the Playa Info tent. The rain, now dropping in at an angle, was soaking the sofas and first display board from the street. Bruce was not happy to be lugging a heavy gear bag or to be under some sort of house arrest. Bruce pleaded, "Can't I just carry this for you over there and then be on my way?"

The assistant chose to ignore Bruce's query, instead concentrating on each deliberate step into the slick gooey playa surface. It was Bruce who noticed the two dark figures situated on one of the sofas on the left side of the Playa Info counter. They seemed to be pulling and yanking at someone in between them. They rose up as Bruce and the assistant walked past.

Bruce poked at the assistant's soaking wet shoulder. "Hey," Bruce cautioned, "look to your left coming off of the sofas."

The assistant stopped, placing his right arm across Bruce's chest. "Halt," he commanded the two advancing towards him, "you just stay put right there." They didn't stay put. The assistant dropped his gear bag, pulled out his Beretta M9 side arm, disengaging the safety. "Stop or I will shoot." The two continued forward in the rainy darkness, now close enough for Bruce and the assistant to be fairly certain they were zombies.

The assistant, instinctively reluctant to shoot a citizen, placed shots into both their kneecaps. The question if they were zombies was settled. The two still silently progressed, limp-hopping on one foot.

"Put them down," Bruce implored.

The assistant obliged. At close range, he placed a kill shot, center-forehead, into each. The two dropped in their tracks. The assistant reached down to grab his gear bag, still grasping his side arm. Neither he nor Bruce saw the third zombie coming from behind or had any idea where it originated from.

The zombie grabbed the assistant up high while he was stooped over lifting his bag. The two went to the ground. The assistant let out a scream as the zombie bit into his shoulder and neck. The assistant raised his M9, pressing against the zombie's temple, and fired. Grayish goo splattered all over the assistant, who proceeded to spit repeatedly, trying to expunge the particles that landed in his open mouth. The zombie collapsed lifeless next to him.

"Oh my God," Bruce exclaimed, stooping down on one knee, trying to shield the assistant's face from the rainfall. Bruce could see the man was bleeding from the neck.

"Crap!" the assistant screamed. "You cannot believe how fast you feel like shit." He paused, breathing irregularly. He coughed. "Oh, no. You....just can't believe....how bad this feels..."

"What do you want me to do?" Bruce asked him, apprehensively.

"Shoot me....Shoot me, so I don't end up like one of those things. Take all this gear to the Post Office down there....Get this stuff to the Chief Master Sergeant." The assistant reached up, handing his M9 to Bruce. Bruce hesitated, but accepted the weapon.

Bruce had never owned or fired a firearm. He held the weapon gingerly, pointing it away from the two of them. "How do you put the safety on?"

The Assistant coughed again. "Shoot me...damn it...shoot me."

"Tell me how to put the safety on, first," Bruce insisted. The assistant finally obliged, and Bruce engaged the safety as he received the instructions, placing the pistol in his left back pocket – the right one already occupied with the duct tape

Cassie's neighbor insisted he bring along. "There we go," Bruce said soothingly. "Let's get you up, and I'll carry these bags and help you over to that Post Office."

"You...lied..." the assistant protested.

Bruce interrupted. "I just said you needed to tell me about the safety first. I didn't say what I'd do after that. No more talk about shooting you. I'm going to take you to your Chief Master Sergeant. You never know, maybe they'll figure out something they can do for you before it's too late."

Bruce helped the assistant up. He grabbed both gear bags and the laptop bag, strapping them around his shoulders. The load was heavy; the bags were now caked with playa mud. Bruce had the assistant put his right arm around Bruce's shoulder to steady him while they slowly proceeded forward in the rain. They had to stop once for the assistant to vomit.

"How many bullets are in this pistol," Bruce inquired, as they closed in on the Post Office.

"Fifteen rounds," the assistant answered weakly, "so you have ten shots left." It was obvious to the assistant that Bruce was going to keep the pistol, drop him off, and run off without staying in custody. The assistant no longer cared. His mind was clouding and growing confused.

They reached the Post Office. A guard was standing outside. Bruce called out to him as they approached. "Hey, your Chief Master Sergeant's man has been bit. I helped him here with all of the Chief's gear." The guard rushed forward, helping prop the assistant against the outside wall, while Bruce pulled the three bags off his shoulders.

The guard seemed unaware of Bruce's identity. "Thank you, sir," he said to Bruce, observing Bruce was smeared with mud, and wasn't military, law enforcement or a Black Rock Ranger.

"No problem," Bruce replied, "but I've got to go." Bruce turned around, doing his best to sprint through the mud. "Good luck," he hollered back to the guard. Bruce glanced around to get his bearings, before heading off to find the Alamo.

Thursday Friday Saturday Sunday Monday Tuesday Wednesday

¡No Rendirse, Muchachos!

At least one thing was going according to plan. Conner had the five zombies preoccupied while the ladder was being lowered. Unfortunately, he wasn't upright. He happened to fall in a spot where the zombies had previously paced and sloshed around the playa into an almost quicksand-like mush. His Stormtrooper costume survived the fall intact, but its inflexibility was a significant impediment toward his becoming vertical.

Two younger, naked male zombies reached him first, lunging forward at his legs. Conner could hear Cassie's helpless screaming of his name from the balcony, as one grabbed his leg and sunk his teeth in. Conner kicked furiously, freeing himself. Using the softball bat as a crutch, pumped with adrenaline, he rose up. Now, all five z's were within arm's reach, lunging forward. Conner managed to back up two steps, swing the bat solidly from his right side, connecting into the skull of the lead zombie, knocking it into two others, causing all of them to lose their footing for a moment.

Conner took another mighty swing into the skull of another z, knocking it sideways to the ground. Conner quickly retreated several steps in the rain and muck, keeping himself further than arm's distance away.

Lucha Libre and Catwoman were now on the ground, each carrying a two-by-four, behind Conner and the zombies. The mud throughout the courtyard was troublesome, thanks to the large number of z's that had been milling about earlier. They progressed slowly, their feet sinking and sticking with each step. "We're just going to close the gate," Lucha Libre yelled at Conner as they gradually passed him to the right.

Conner grimaced. By calling out, Lucha Libre drew the zombies' attention. The two females of the zombie group peeled off, heading in Lucha Libre's and Catwoman's direction. Conner turned to witness Cassie and Tess hopping off the ladder, onto the mud. He bit his lip, hoping they would not call out to him.

Conner took a wild swing into the three remaining zombies, connecting with the rib cage of the one furthest to the right. Conner took several steps further back into the sloshy playa courtyard. He glanced down at his leg, thankful that the Stormtrooper outfit had served its purpose, causing the zombie to bite only hard plastic.

The three male zombies were once again upon him. The two naked ones lunged forward, just as Conner stepped back. They both knocked into each other, stumbling, knees-first into the ground. Conner took a quick, downward swing with his bat in the back of one of their skulls, then the other. Both went completely horizontal after impact, face-first into the mud. The third zombie, wearing an oversize tie-dye shirt stepped over them, grabbing Conner's left arm, sinking his teeth into the plastic Stormtrooper outfit. Only able to swing with his right arm, Conner struck the zombies face, causing a slow, gray nosebleed. The blow sent both of them off-balance, falling into each other in the mud.

The mud-covered zombie was face-to-face with Conner in the muck. Conner watched the muddy face close in toward his exposed neck, the zombie's gray teeth snarling as the teeth zeroed in on their target.

Conner managed to turn, so that the teeth merely crunched into his plastic Stormtrooper shoulder pad. Again using his bat for leverage, Conner managed to win the race to become vertical. He began to land one blow of the bat after another, downward into the mud-caked zombie's face and back of the skull. After five swings, the zombie's skull cracked open, grayish matter oozing out onto the lifeless body.

The two naked zombies he had previously sent to the ground were now upright again, only heading in Cassie and Tess's direction. The women had discovered the tequila girls were quite alive, and convinced them to come out of their room. The four women were now standing where the ladder once was. They were all hollering up at the balcony. Conner glanced up to see the unstable, naked man finish pulling the ladder back up to the balcony, yelling incoherently at everyone below.

Conner called out to the four women to get back into the downstairs room. The tequila ladies happily obliged, but Cassie and Tess stood their ground — Cassie holding the other two-by-four – Tess gripping the rebar rod.

Conner turned around to check on Lucha Libre and Catwoman. Each had unbuckled a respective gate from the side walls; they were now dragging them through the mud toward each other, while the hinges fastened to the walls creaked and moaned. The two lady zombies were closing in on both of them.

Conner lifted his feet one at a time through the mud, while the rain pelted him sideways, washing away bits of the playa from his face mask. With each step, he could sense that he was gaining on the two male naked zombies from behind. The question was would he reach them before they reached Cassie and Tess?

The answer was no. Cassie and Tess stepped backwards as the zombies approached, until the ladies could feel the outer wall of the corner downstairs room scraping against their spines. Cassie held her two-by-four length-wise, pushing against the chest of her assailant to hold it momentarily at bay. Tess did the same with her rebar. Just as Tess's zombie started to brush her rebar aside, Conner caught up to it, unloading a hefty swing into its right temple, knocking it into Cassie's zombie, sending both z's sideways to the ground, several feet away. This allowed Cassie and Tess the opportunity to reposition behind Conner.

Conner lunged towards the two naked z's, lifting his bat, swinging downward at the closest appendage. He struck the closest zombie's kneecap, shattering it. The zombie stood up to take a swipe at Conner, but fell forward on its broken leg. Conner spun and smashed the other zombie in the face, while it was rising up off the ground. Teeth went flying in all directions. Gray goo began to drip from its broken nose. Still, it lurched forward.

While Conner had the two zombies' full attention, Cassie and Tess circled behind them. Conner inched warily toward the snarling, broken nose zombie, jockeying for a better angle to take another swing. The broken leg zombie managed to become half-upright, hobbling at Conner's left, dragging its damaged leg at its side. Cassie lunged at broken leg zombie with her two-by-four, knocking it in the back of the head, sending it, face first, back into the mud. Broken leg zombie turned in the mud, snarling up at the ladies, placing its hands at its side, so it could push itself up again.

Tess stepped up to the naked broken leg z, raising the three foot rebar rod with both hands, thrusting it directly into the zombie's throat. Gripping hard with both hands, elevating herself on tiptoe, pressing her weight with her chest onto her fists, she emitted a high-pitched grunt, pushing down hard until the rod penetrated the back of the z's throat. The rod pierced just below the base of its skull to the right side of its vertebrae, into the playa mud. Tess didn't let up, using her weight to jam the rod deeper into the playa until the zombie was pinned to the ground, flailing away wildly with both arms, kicking up and down with both legs, while the rain pounded away at its face.

Conner took a heavy swing at broken nose zombie, who lunged at the same time. Conner's swing barely connected with its right elbow, exacting no damage. The zombie's forward leap took both of them down to the ground, the zombie on top. Conner landed on what was left of a Pee-wee Herman cut-out, partially buried in the mud. Conner could hear the zombie's teeth clacking away at his plastic chest plate. Conner struggled to pull himself away, pushing against broken nose zombie's chest.

Suddenly the zombie weight was lifted off of him. Cassie scored a direct hit with her two-by-four into the side of broken nose zombie's face, knocking him several feet to the left. Conner rolled away, right into the grip of broken leg zombie's left hand. Conner turned to see the zombie's head pointed slightly toward him, the rebar rod jammed down its throat and into the ground. Broken leg zombie tugged at Conner's costume with a firm grip. Conner yanked himself away.

Broken nose zombie chose to pursue Cassie and Tess, who were both retreating toward the gates. Conner staggered up, looking for his bat. He found it several feet away, the handle encased in mud. Conner scooped it up, setting out for broken nose zombie, once again from behind.

Conner caught up after seven laborious steps in the mud. He raised his bat in the air, striking downward on the back of the zombie skull. The force sent broken nose z forward a couple feet, but not to the ground. The zombie turned around to confront Conner.

Now it was Cassie's turn. She advanced almost to Conner's side, swinging the board at the zombie's calves. She found a decent angle, tripping the zombie down to the ground. Cassie and Conner both began to wail away at the back of broken nose zombie's head until they obliterated it.

Only then did Conner realize that Lucha Libre and Catwoman had been screaming for help. Conner could see that the gates had been shut, but the two female zombies, both encrusted with mud, had them trapped in the left corner. Constant swings of their two-by-fours were keeping the lady zombies at bay, but Lucha and Catwoman were both quickly tiring.

Conner, Cassie and Tess strode as rapidly as they could through the treacherous mud. Conner reached them first, delivering a decisive blow to the lady zombie on the left side, sending it to the ground. The second lady zombie turned to face Conner, as he brought his bat around again, knocking it in the face and onto its behind. Catwoman, Lucha Libre and

Cassie all joined in the fray, whacking away at their skulls until the two lady z's ceased to exist or even be recognizable.

They all stepped up to Tess, who had been standing just behind them, unarmed. The five hugged each other repeatedly, panting. They all dropped their weapons — boards, bat and rebar — their arms were sore and tired.

Cassie started crying. "This is so wrong, what we just did. It's just so wrong."

Tess put her arm around her, crying too. "It is, Cassie. I know. I've never hurt anyone before in my life."

Catwoman walked up in between them, pressing her forehead into theirs, placing an arm around each of them. "Yeah, you're right. But we better get used to it quick, because I don't think this is over yet," Catwoman advised, wiping the rain that was falling in her face, all around her mask, hoping to clean away some of the mud. She checked out Cassie and Tess, their Jan costumes no longer recognizable. Catwoman chuckled. "Ladies, you two look like you've been in a mud wrestling contest. Come on, let's go join those worthless tequila girls and get out of this rain."

Conner left them to head over to broken leg zombie. "I'll be with you all in a second. I've got to finish this last one off."

Wait up," Lucha Libre called out to Conner. As he reached Conner, Lucha tugged at his elbow, pointing back at the gate. "The bar latching that gate? It's not all that sturdy. I don't know that we want to count on it if a bigger crowd of them gather out there anytime soon."

Thursday Friday Saturday Sunday Monday Tuesday Wednesday

Barbarians at the Gate

Just like that, the rain stopped.

At first, Bruce was pleased to free his face from the annoying, cold, wet pelting it was taking as he plodded along through the formidable open playa mud. A few minutes later, he was wishing for it to return.

Bruce wasn't certain if the rain had masked his scent or just cut down even further on the nighttime visibility, but he had advanced undetected into the open playa, up to this point. Without the rain, he could see and hear a small herd of z's converging toward him, their fuzzy silhouettes outlined by the lit art installations behind them in the distance.

Bruce had been careful to avoid the zombies thus far. He steered far clear of the multi-story Burning Man platform in the center of the open playa, which he could tell even from a distance was overrun – from the lurching movements he could see and the dwindling number of piercing screams he could hear from a distance.

Bruce came across a small art installation – a giant tetherball, with climbing pegs up the eighteen foot high pole. At the top were two chairs welded at the pole. He glanced up to see a man and a woman seated, both wearing just swimsuits. The man looked down, loudly making the 'shhhh' sound as Bruce passed by.

Bruce eyed the fuzzy outline of the zombie herd making its way through the mud toward him. He considered, from his Sunday television viewing, the selection of angles that NFL defensive players took at a receiver, running back or kick returner on a breakaway play. Bruce veered more to the left, so that the zombie herd wouldn't get the angle on him. He squinted and thought he could finally see the lit-up Alamo in the distance ahead.

Back inside the Alamo, all the coaxing and yelling of Lucha Libre, Catwoman, the tequila ladies, Cassie, Tess and Conner combined couldn't convince the crazed naked man on the balcony to drop the ladder. Conner and Lucha Libre attempted to lift one of the tequila girls, the most petite of the bunch, onto their combined shoulders, to climb onto the balcony, but couldn't quite make the required height, the tequila girl complaining continuously through the whole affair.

They tried to tear away material from the facades fastened to the side walls, in the hopes of concocting a makeshift ramp or platform to get to the second floor. The facades, unfortunately, were well constructed. Even the rebar wasn't helpful in their attempts to dismantle their surroundings.

The tequila ladies survived the prior zombie onslaught because their room was the only one equipped with a doorknob, and even better, one that locked. The bad news was that the doorknob wasn't a perfect fit to the pre-cut hole in the door. It had been adjusted to fit with shims, which loosened up after repeated pushing against it. The consensus was that the doorknob — locked or not — could end up being pushed right through the other side, if someone tried hard enough.

"We are going to have to make a decision about holing up in one of the downstairs rooms, even with the bad doorknob," Lucha Libre argued to the group. "The gates are not going to do the job as those things outside increase in number."

The cessation of rain drew more attention to the Alamo. The large z group that streamed out of the Alamo earlier, to chase the fleeing refugees from a stuck mutant vehicle, seemed to have returned en masse, and brought all their friends. They were loitering around the front gates, packing in and pushing forward, while they moaned incessantly.

"I just wish we could think of something to brace those gates better," Conner replied.

"I hear you. How about we grab that little naked man up there, and bolt him to the gates?" Lucha Libre vented, reaching inside his costume with his right hand to locate an inside pocket that held a small, thin but wide, flask. He pulled it out, unscrewed the lid, sucking down several gulps. "Aaahhhh," he proclaimed, "we might as well go out in style." Lucha held out the flask toward Conner. Conner instinctively grabbed it, pulling the nose of the flask up to his lips.

Conner caught sight of Cassie. He pulled the flask away, smiled and politely shook his head.

"Oh, come on, this is the good stuff, Crown Royal. It'll help warm us up," Lucha insisted.

Conner shook his head again. "I'm sorry, but I can't."

Lucha Libre smiled. "What, you're too good for Lucha Libre and his Crown Royal? You're just some lowly Stormtrooper. Don't get on your high horse just because crazy man up there thinks you're Darth Vader."

Conner laughed. "No, I just can't drink any more. I have a problem. I'm sure you understand."

Lucha Libre's face grew serious. "Hey, I'm sorry, man. Here I am shoving whiskey in your face. My bad. Lucha Libre's bad. Sorry about that."

Conner laughed again. "No worries, my wrestling friend. But come to think of it, we might want to keep our wits about us if the barbarians crash the gate."

"Huh?" Lucha Libre replied, not understanding, but then he got Conner's drift. He nodded his head, deciding to tuck his flask away back in his costume.

Conner looked up at the sky. There was already a small break in the clouds; a single star peeked through the night sky. Cassie came up behind Conner, the sound of her shoes sucking through the mud sounding like someone passing gas with each step. She pulled in next to his chest, taking his arm and wrapping it around her shoulder. They looked like quite a pair – Cassie in her mud-caked, billowy Jan costume, Conner in his mud-streaked Stormtrooper outfit. She was freezing, and tried to gather warmth from Conner's plastic-encased body, to no avail. "What's on your mind?" she inquired.

"Bruce," Conner responded in a concerned tone, still staring straight above. "We've been gone a long time. I hope he locked himself up with your neighbors in their car or found a way out of here."

Tess approached the both of them, shivering, huddling against the two, hoping to garner some body heat. "Did I hear you say Bruce? When do I get to meet this Bruce? When this is all over, and we get out of here, I want to meet Bruce."

Cassie giggled, happy to be talking about something pleasant, instead of the monsters outside the gate. "Tess, you little tramp, I'd think that you—" Cassie stopped mid-sentence. The sound of the gates rattling – the growth in intensity of the moaning on the other side – brought the entire group to silence. The gates started to surge forward and back like the tide. Cassie gasped.

"I think we might want to head into the room now," Lucha Libre called out.

One of the tequila girls spoke up. "Hey, sorry for not saying this sooner, but I don't think we want to go back to our room."

"What do you mean?" Lucha Libre raised his voice.

"Well, when we were all checking it out, if the doorknob still worked or not, someone must have left it locked, and we were just back there, and thought we'd test it again, and I shut the door..." the tequila girl explained.

"...and?" Lucha Libre interrupted impatiently.

"And it's locked. We're locked out. Unless you want us to push the doorknob through like you were all saying was going to happen anyway," the tequila girl's voice trailed off as she completed her explanation.

Catwoman grew quite annoyed. "And you couldn't have shared this tidbit right when it happened? Oops, we forgot to mention we've locked you out of the one place we might be safe from a truckload of zombies that are about to be delivered UPS to our front porch. You ladies are so not on my Christmas list right now." She shook her head as she made a beeline to check out the rooms, Lucha Libre joining her.

Conner, Cassie and Tess continued to eye the gate's ebb and flow. The crowd outside had obviously grown. Without the upstairs vantage point, Conner had no idea to what extent.

Catwoman and Lucha Libre returned. "She's right. Our best option is probably to go into the other room, and we all push against the door to hold them off," Lucha Libre suggested.

Conner sighed, shaking his head. "I know we may have no choice, but going in there really paints ourselves into a corner."

Lucha Libre walked over to Conner, commenting in a hushed voice, "I hear you, and there's going to be a lot more of them pushing on one side, than of us on the other."

"Do we have our weapons gathered up?" Conner asked.

Lucha Libre pointed toward the two-by-fours, bat and rebar in a small pile outside the door of the room they were now locked out of. "They're right there." Lucha headed back towards the door to pick them up.

"Well, I suppose we should go inside, and maybe they won't figure out for a while that we're hiding in there if they don't see us go in," Conner said loud enough for everyone to hear.

The gates surged even further forward, the zombie moans grew audibly more distinct. This served as a cue; everyone headed for the other downstairs room – equipped with no doorknob or lock.

Conner tuned out the screams of the annoying crazy naked man from above. Conner stood underneath the balcony, eyeing the gate, which seemed to have now stretched into the courtyard beyond its natural limits. Conner had no idea what was still keeping it fastened together. There appeared to be an endless sea of zombies behind it.

Just as Conner decided to turn around to head inside the room with everyone else, a ladder dropped to the ground immediately to his left. Startled, Conner took a couple of steps out, craning his neck upwards.

"Hey, I found this up here," Bruce hollered down to him, pointing at the ladder. "Don't you think you should be heading up to me right about now?"

Fess Parker and John Wayne

Bruce was holding court in the crowded room of an appreciative audience. "So, the Alamo just comes clearly into view. I try to sprint to it, I really do. Now and then I hit a patch where I can get a little traction, and I sail along for ten yards or so; then I just start sinking in the ooze, and every step you can hear the suction of the mud, the air and the water. This pack of zombies at my right, I've been eyeing them for the past several minutes. There are fifteen or so of them, and they don't ever stop to rest, they are like the Energizer Bunnies of zombies. They are matching me step for step. I just hope I have the angle on them. I get close to this damn place – which is lit up like a shopping mall – and there is nobody out back. I can see the edges of what looks like a rock concert crowd out front, so I know I don't want to go there. I get to the back, the zombie pack is right behind me at this point, maybe ten yards out. I see two bicycles against the wall, lit up by floodlights. Just above them is a ladder built into the wall that stops partway down...I climb up over the bikes, which wasn't easy, and I reach the ladder. I start climbing up it and look down. The zombie pack has reached the wall down below – they stumble all over the bicycles, knock them down to the ground – but they can't figure out how to use them as a footstool to get to the ladder, so they just hang around below me, snarling. I get to the top, slip in the open bay, hop over to the edge of the balcony, and see you all packing into the room downstairs; the zombie crowd pushing and shoving at the gates. I see the ladder lying below my feet on the balcony. As I start to grab it – the naked man here – races over, pushing at me, trying to stop me. I toss him aside, more than once – maybe I should have just tossed him over the balcony, I guess – and then I see Conner down below as I get the ladder situated, and the rest, as they say is history. Oh yeah, and apparently, we should all thank Cassie and Tess's neighbors for making me bring this duct tape here."

Everyone in the room was glad to put the surrounding horrors out of their mind, indulging again with gallows humor as a coping mechanism. They laughed guiltily, looking at the frail, naked man in the corner, duct tape sealed over his mouth and an ample supply used to construct handcuffs as well as more tightly wrapped around his ankles. "Your neighbor told me that there was a thousand things we might need duct tape for if I found you," Bruce turned, addressing Tess, who was seated cross legged immediately to his right. "Your neighbor could have been one of the doctors at the clinic I ended up at for a moment during my crazy journey over here. He could tell his patients, 'take two duct tapes and call me in the morning.'"

Conner had retrieved the group from the downstairs room, shepherding them up the ladder after Bruce set it down. The gates finally gave way as Conner and Lucha Libre were the last ones to step onto the ladder. Once everyone was up on the balcony, they apprehended the naked man before he could cause any more trouble. They all packed in tightly into the eastern upstairs room. They decided that the less they stepped outside the better, so they didn't agitate and motivate the zombie crowd below.

"But I haven't shared the big news with you here," Bruce announced. He stood up in the small crowded room. "Not only did I bring duct tape in one pocket, but I managed to bring this in the other." Bruce produced the M9 pistol, holding it straight up in the air. The room filled with audible gasps. "Now don't worry, the safety is on. But there are ten bullets left. So I'm sure our plan is just to sit tight here and wait this out, until sooner or later the authorities get control of the situation. But I tell you, right now, the zombies seem to be getting the upper hand. So if push comes to shove, at least we can fend a few of them off with this."

Conner's jaw dropped. "How on earth did you get that, Mr. Bruce?"

Bruce sat back down, leaving the pistol in between his legs. "Well, I had another roundabout journey to get here. I told you I stopped by the clinic in Center Camp, dropping off some poor soul who got electrocuted. Who do I bump into, Conner, but Alan Gorman? Can you believe it? He was serving as a doctor in the clinic – don't ask me how that came about. So he starts talking to me, and the military is there with him. Conner, they are looking for you and me. They want to interrogate us about everything we know about the zombies before they got to Burning Man, it seems. Which means, by the way, whatever Conner here might have told all of you about these zombies, you didn't hear it from him. You don't want to confess that you found out anything about these zombies from us, or they're going to want to talk to you, too. Anyway, they take me into custody, but the zombies start to overrun the area, so they decide to relocate. The guy escorting me got bit pretty badly. He gave me this pistol, so I helped him to their relocated headquarters and then I escaped and headed here."

Tess placed her hand back on Bruce's knee. "Wow, you are our hero, our knight-in-shining-armor, or should I say, knight-in-shining-duct-tape."

Bruce chuckled. "Yeah, I guess this is what it feels like to be Fess Parker, although I understand my man Conner here would be John Wayne, with his bat and everything." Tess was the only one who laughed. She rubbed Bruce's knee playfully for a moment.

"Who is Fess Parker?" one of the tequila girls asked, yawning, somewhat disinterested in the conversation and the company.

"I don't get it," the other tequila girl joined in. "Why is Conner John Wayne? I thought John Wayne was a bad dude."

Bruce laughed. "I guess we're getting old, Conner. Because I remember going to the Parker Creek cinema when we were kids for the Saturday matinee, I was little, but I remember seeing you there, too..." Bruce paused to explain. "Conner was a few grades ahead of me at Parker Creek where we both grew up. Anyways, they would show real old double bill movies on Saturdays for kids for just a buck, hoping you would buy popcorn and cokes, which we did. It was still bargain babysitting for parents wanting to dump off their kids for a few hours. Usually there was a theme for the two movies. On this particular Saturday it was Alamo day, so they showed the Disney Alamo flick with Fess Parker, and then the version of the Alamo with John Wayne."

Catwoman chimed in. "Wait, I thought the Alamo movie had Billy Bob Thornton, and who was it—that guy who was just on that network TV show— with the cowboy hat, and was the sheriff of Vegas a while back?"

"Yeah...true that," Conner laughed, "but it doesn't count. The only Alamo movies that we're going to talk about here had Fess Parker and John Wayne in them."

"Well then, what's all the deal here about Pee-wee Herman?" the first tequila girl asked in a negative tone of voice. "Why are there cut-outs of him everywhere? Was he in another Alamo movie?"

Tess was incredulous. She shook her head. "Wait, you don't know about Pee-wee Herman's first movie?"

"I really don't know much about Pee-wee Herman. That's a little before our time," the tequila girl shot back, a little snippy, insinuating that Tess was dating herself compared to the young tequila ladies.

Catwoman was growing impatient with the two young women who hadn't really held their own so far. "Oh, give me a break. Have you heard of Abraham Lincoln? Or Pink Floyd? They were before your time too. That doesn't mean you still shouldn't have heard of them. When I was little, man, Pee-wee Herman rocked. And I can't believe you wore a tequila costume and you don't know who Pee-wee Herman is."

"I don't get it..." the tequila girl replied, defensively.

"You do know the song 'Tequila' don't you? Saxophone going, guitar going, everyone shouts tequila. You know that, don't you?" Catwoman inquired in a sarcastic tone.

"I think that's a little before our time, too," tequila girl retorted.

"Before a lot of people's time, I'll bet," the other tequila girl added.

"Oh my God. Fine then, you two. I was going to enlighten you about Pee-wee Herman in his platform shoes and the tequila song, but never mind," Catwoman declared, dismissively.

Naked man apparently had a point to make about Pee-wee Herman, because he started to moan loudly through the duct tape. No one was willing to peel it off to find out exactly what was on his mind.

Zombies Gone Wild

Conner, Bruce, Cassie, Tess and the rest of their group were missing quite a show.

Close to two hundred zombies flooded the courtyard after the gates crashed. They were packed in, wall-to-wall, zombie-to-zombie.

The number of naked people at any given point in time at Burning Man was much smaller than reputation or imagination might otherwise conjure up as an estimate. Still, there were pockets within Black Rock City with a much higher concentration of nudity than others. Evidently, some of these pockets must have been especially prone to the earlier waves of zombie attacks during the day, or experienced a higher ratio on drugs that quickly progress to Stage II once infected, or perhaps some of them simply lost their clothes after becoming zombiefied.

Whatever the reason, there were a lot of zombies gone wild in the Alamo courtyard. There was a multitude of topless lady zombies ranging in age from their twenties through sixties, streaked with mud, many sporting tattoos, and sometimes, slight remnants of body paint. There were plenty of fully nude male zombies as well. Some of both sexes — but certainly a minority — one could tell were once hardbodies and quite attractive. But now, all were gray-toned, sporting open sores, caked mud, with various nasty odors wafting about them.

Everyone upstairs was mystified why so many z's were attracted to the Alamo, but attracted they were. The Alamo, at the moment, was the place to be for zombies gone wild.

The group continued to choose to ignore the zombie plague beneath them. They kept their door closed and delved into a raucous conversation regarding "which would you rather – become a zombie, or a _____," with everyone taking turns filling in the blank, followed by a vote – zombie or whatever filled in the blank. The zombie choice was winning more than half of the face-offs. Leading the list of professions less desirable than zombie was congressman, meth lab operator, reality television show star, and derivative mortgage securities investment banker.

Lucha Libre pulled out his flask and passed it around. Everyone but Conner and Cassie pulled a few sips from the silver-colored container. The conversation in the room fell silent, just as the flask was about to be forwarded for round two. The sound of Danny Elfman's "Breakfast Machine" started playing through the speakers again. Speakers were available throughout the installation, including in each of the rooms.

"How on earth...." Cassie let her question trail off.

Bruce looked around the room, confused, having not been in the Alamo when the music was playing before.

Lucha Libre provided enlightenment. "A very slight connection issue must exist with the iPod or whatever is producing this endless loop of Pee-wee music, and a receiver, or either unit and their power source. I doubt if it's the speaker wire, because there's a whole bunch of speakers, and they must be running off multiple speaker channels. It must be located downstairs somewhere, and the zombies bumped into it before, breaking the connection, and again just now."

Heads nodded. No one offered a counter theory.

"Well, it bears checking out," Conner remarked. "It's also time we took a peek at the back wall again. I'll go crawl on my stomach out there and see what I can see." No one offered any argument. The group previously debated escaping over the back wall, where Conner and Bruce had both entered via the built-in-ladder. The problem was, there were still too many zombies for their liking milling around outside.

Lucha Libre and Catwoman scooted away from the door. Conner, still in his Stormtrooper costume other than the face mask, crouched down, opened the door just enough to pass through, and slithered out on the balcony on his stomach. The choral-like moaning of the zombies could be heard over "Breakfast Machine" playing through the speakers. Conner raised his head slightly, stealing a glance at the courtyard below. It was packed with zombies – naked zombies, tattooed zombies, costumed zombies, painted zombies. They seemed more agitated; their level of activity was definitely increasing. Conner wasn't sure if it was because they smelled or otherwise detected him out on the balcony or the sudden return of the music set them off.

Conner proceeded to the back wall, where he was more out of view from the courtyard zombies. He rose up, just high enough to see a plentiful pack of zombies still pacing around the rear exterior. They certainly outnumbered the ten bullets Bruce possessed. Conner crawled back toward the room, disappointed.

Conner returned and gave his report. The increased noise level of the zombies below could be sensed by everyone upstairs. The room again fell silent as the balcony began to shudder, as it had earlier, before Bruce's arrival. This time, the shaking was more severe, producing an earthquake-like sensation.

"The zombies are up to no good down there," Cassie commented. "Who knows what they're knocking and banging into that might support this second level." A pall was spreading over the room.

Tess decided there was no need for that. There was nothing they could do for now about the zombies below. She would take things in a different direction. "Well, if we're sitting on top of the zombie apocalypse, I don't want to go down without saying I kissed, I mean *really kissed*, our hero, Bruce Kepner." Tess, still seated on the floor, uncrossed her legs, turned to Bruce, and placed a lip lock on him, stroking his goatee with her left hand, without any objections on his part.

Owning the Open Playa

The zombies ruled the open playa of Black Rock City. The surface was still far too muddy to accommodate vehicle traffic – even venturing out on foot was a real chore. Within the streets of the city, there was enough block-to-block chaos, as zombies wandered deeper and deeper within the confines of BRC, discouraging any notion of deploying the still available deputies, military personnel and Black Rock Rangers out into the open playa. They were becoming overmatched simply trying to secure the camp itself.

A small number of reinforcements had already arrived – a dozen Marines helicoptered in from the Mountain Warfare Training Center, plus forty-four officers from the Reno agency call-up had recently set foot on the playa. But with the Colonel focused on beefing up the perimeter patrol, the net gain inside the city was twenty-five. These new boots on the ground within the city merely brought the number of able-bodied personnel under the command of Chief Master Sergeant Carter back to the level it was two hours before. Carter would have to make do for the time being. He also had to contend with securing the array of vehicles stuck in the mud on the exit road, which had already been visited by the zombies breaching the perimeter from the other side.

Carter had given up on securing the open playa.

The zombie population continued to rise. While the vast majority of Black Rock citizens weren't doing drugs, there were enough taking something of adequate potency to provide a steady stream of easy targets for advancing z's, and once-bit, they progressed to full-zombie-mode in terms of minutes rather than hours. Added to the mix were those infected in the late afternoon and early evening that were just beginning to turn, as well as a growing number of infected persons meeting an early demise through accidental causes, as panic continued to spread through the camp.

Some of the new zombie population pillaged like pirates through the blocks of Black Rock City. Others were drawn to the well-lit art installations in the open playa, where zombies ruled. The pockets of uninfected citizens out on the playa rapidly dwindled. The various art installations didn't offer secure enough shelter. The mutant vehicles, by design, typically had some means of open access.

Zombies wandered aimlessly up and down the stairs of the Burning Man platform. They stepped all over the shipwreck protruding out of the playa floor. Zombies controlled the multi-storied Wall Street buildings, the mutant buses, sharks and pirate ships, the maze, the faux roller coaster and the banks of porta-potties.

The open playa was littered with infected citizens, lying on the muddy ground, passed out inside mutant vehicles, sprawled on the floors of art installations. They lay in states of agony, confusion, exhaustion, incredible thirst and semi-consciousness.

Only three open playa sites remained with the uninfected; all were encircled by a growing number of zombie admirers. A man and a woman sat fifteen feet high in chairs welded to a giant tetherball pole, nervously hanging onto their seats as zombies shook the poles below. A determined small group still defended the sacred pagoda temple from behind the closed temple gates. And far out on the open playa, the Alamo was surrounded.

Thursday Friday Saturday Sunday Monday Tuesday Wednesday

Tequila

The Alamo was not built for its current environment. The outer beams supporting the second floor balcony weren't rooted deep enough below the soggy playa mud; they were becoming unstable, shifting as the throngs of zombies pushed up against them. The locked door to the unoccupied downstairs room quickly was opened; the doorknob pushed through the ill-fitting hole. The downstairs rooms weren't constructed with an occupying zombie horde in mind, as they banged, clawed and even chewed into the walls.

The first support beam gave way shortly after midnight. The group upstairs could feel the shudder as the balcony sunk slightly towards the other side. Everyone rose to their feet. Conner peered out the door, seeking answers. He suggested everyone exit the room, to the ledge of the back wall of the balcony. A second support beam below them snapped as he spoke, the remaining beams supporting the balcony tilted as their anchors shifted further in the mud. A chain reaction swept across from left to right; the balcony platform separated from two of the three remaining beams and collapsed. A loud rumble filled the air, accompanied by sounds of cracking, as the "Breakfast Machine" music went silent for good. The track lights and floodlights, however, still illuminated the area.

The balcony platform, disconnected from all but one beam, listed like a sinking ship, taking the side wall of their upstairs room with it. Those seated against the inward wall – the two tequila ladies, Lucha Libre and Catwoman, were flung downwards as the wall collapsed. They slid beyond the collapsed wall onto the balcony platform tilting toward the ground below. Dust from the room and debris shot into the air.

The interior balcony platform now pointed down seventy-five degrees toward the ground, held up partially by the one support beam still connected to it. The remaining beam was leaning backward the same seventy-five degrees, its anchor popped out partway in the muddy morass that was no longer able to fully support it.

Conner had both feet out the front door when the platform gave way. The section of platform to his right, from the door to the Alamo outer wall, separated from the rest of the balcony. The section snapped downwards while still partially connected to the outer wall. The ladder that had been lying on the section fell at an angle. The ladder came to a rest, leaning against the outer wall and dangling section of the platform.

Conner's forearms caught the floor of the room on his way down. He rested his elbows on the edge of the floor, next to the open door, his body hanging out over the ledge. The door swung back into him, knocking him in the head.

The scene was this: the Alamo courtyard was packed with zombies, about half were lathered in mud. The two upstairs rooms were intact, except that the occupied room lost its interior wall when the balcony collapsed. The balcony platform split into two sections – a small section now was dangling from the outer wall with the ladder propped against it. The much larger portion of the broken balcony sloped down toward the ground, held up partially by a single remaining support beam that was unstable and tilting. The room's interior wall that collapsed came to a rest at an angle, touching the room at the upper end, and the balcony platform at the lower end. Conner was dangling out the room's door – which now led to nowhere. Catwoman, Lucha Libre and the two tequila girls were in precarious positions out on the collapsed wall and balcony platform.

One of the tequila girls, closest to the back corner of the inward wall, before it collapsed, slid the furthest. She lay perilously on her side, below the collapsed wall, in the center of the sloped balcony platform, reinforced only by the listing support beam below it, perhaps seven feet off the ground. Her tequila friend was hanging on for dear life to the edge of the collapsed wall, her feet frantically flopping around on the platform, next to the face of the first tequila girl. Lucha Libre was next in line, lying on his back, head facing downhill, near the second tequila girl's arms, his feet slowly slipping above him. Catwoman was caught in an awkward position, her legs hanging out in the open air, off the edge of the platform over the courtyard, holding on tightly with one hand to the base beam of the collapsed wall.

The second tequila girl panicked, screaming and kicking. Without looking behind, she launched her left foot directly into the face of her tequila friend below her, sending her friend sliding further downwards to the bottom edge of the balcony platform, the change in weight causing the platform to sink even lower, and the others clinging to it to shift further off balance. A mustachioed male zombie with a shaved head, loop earrings and wearing nothing but an orange Speedo swimsuit, started climbing up the tilted support beam that was keeping the platform from dropping all the way to the ground. His weight added to the drag on the bottom of the platform, gravity drawing the four above irresistibly toward the zombie masses.

Catwoman, Lucha Libre and the second tequila girl were in the process of losing their grips, when the weight at the bottom of the platform was relieved; the mustachioed zombie scaling the beam was able to stretch, reach the first tequila girl and drag her toward him. They both fell backward to the ground. A swarm of zombies descended upon her, as she struck the playa floor. Those above her turned their heads or closed their eyes as she was quickly ripped apart.

Conner could feel his elbows giving way, his arm muscles trembling from keeping his one hundred ninety pounds from dropping to the ground below. He looked for something to grab onto – but only a slippery door frame availed itself. Conner sensed his muscles tightening beyond acceptable limits. His left arm gave out first as he slipped back a couple of inches. Conner contemplated what to do when he hit the ground below.

Cassie's hands grasped his own. He looked up at her determined face. She was on her knees, with Tess hanging onto her. Slowly she began to tug him in, to the point where he could support his own weight.

In the back corner of the room, the naked man sat still for this first time, his mouth still sealed with duct tape, his arms and legs still held in duct tape bondage. Just behind Cassie and Tess, Bruce also dropped to his knees, stretching outward, trying to reach Catwoman. She had managed to reach up with her left hand and grab onto the base beam of the collapsed wall, so that she was now hanging on with two hands instead of one.

The remaining tequila girl lost her grip on the far edge of the collapsed wall. Screaming, she slid down to where her friend had resided moments before. Another zombie was already working his way up the beam, with a second one right behind it. She could see them slowly scooting up towards her. She began to shout "no" repeatedly. The tequila girl began kicking violently, even though the zombies were still a good distance away. The collapsed wall and platform began to sink further with each kick.

"Stop it," Catwoman yelled at her. "You're going to kill us all."

Just as Conner lifted himself back inside the room, he saw what Bruce was trying to accomplish. Without saying anything, he grabbed Bruce's ankles. Bruce stretched further downward, reaching Catwoman's hands. Bruce grabbed both wrists and held on tight.

The tequila girl continued to kick and scream. The wall and platform sunk again, sending Lucha Libre sliding head first into her. She grabbed onto him, pushing him beyond her, blocking the path between her and the oncoming first zombie.

"You bitch!" Catwoman yelled in fury at her, as she helplessly watched the scene unfold, fortunate that Bruce was grasping her wrists tightly, or she would be down there with her boyfriend.

The tequila girl used Lucha Libre as leverage to push herself upwards with her feet. With each kick, she sent him inches closer to the first zombie slowly scooting up the beam. Lucha hadn't been willing to turn over or make sudden movements for fear of knocking the platform further down, which might send Catwoman even more into harm's way. On his back with his head first, he could see that Catwoman was now safely within Bruce's grasp.

Lucha Libre quickly turned over. He thrust himself upwards with his hands. He felt around with his feet for leverage, hoping to push himself back up the platform a little, using his feet to help hold his position while he scooted up with his hands. Lucha wasn't counting on tequila girl taking advantage of his feet being placed a little higher. She again kicked against them as she climbed slightly higher, sending Lucha Libre downward and onto his stomach.

The first zombie on the beam stretched forward, trying to grab hold of Lucha Libre. Lucha rose to his knees, which sent him sliding even closer to the zombie. Lucha glanced up at Catwoman. "I love you," he yelled up at her, his voice trembling.

Lucha Libre decided to take the offensive. He scooted forward on his knees a foot or so, swung his arms from his side at the first zombie's outstretched hand, grasping them as he followed through, before letting go. He sent the first zombie off balance, sliding backward into the second zombie. Both fell to the ground. From above, Catwoman, Bruce, Conner, Cassie and Tess let loose whoops and cries of "yes!" as they watched him wrestle the two zombies off the beam.

Tequila girl stretched to reach the side of the collapsed wall. Moving rapidly, without caution or providing warning to others, she caused the platform to shift again. While she managed to hang onto the wall that was now within her reach, the movement sent Lucha Libre off balance. He slid down to the beam, his legs dangling below, while he hung on.

A group of zombies rushed forward, Lucha's legs now within their grasp. They began to bite away through his costume, tugging and pulling on Lucha until they dragged him down to the ground and piled on top of him.

Catwoman began to scream hysterically; Bruce almost lost his grip on her. "We've got to pull her in," he shouted back to Conner. Conner had Tess take his spot holding Bruce's ankles, while he quickly lay on his stomach next to Bruce. Cassie, not needing to be told, grabbed hold of Conner's ankles. Conner stretched and grabbed Catwoman's right wrist with both of his hands, allowing Bruce to release one hand to grab her left wrist with both his hands. The two men proceeded to reel her in, while Cassie and Tess anchored them. Moments later, Catwoman was safely returned to the floor of the room.

Below, tequila girl clung to the collapsed wall. She looked up at the group, all of them glaring below at her. "Okay. Now, help me," she commanded.

The Bridge Upstairs

Cassie and Tess each held onto one of Conner's costumed legs while he lay on his stomach, dangling out over the side, hanging onto Bruce's ankles. Bruce lay, stomach first, on the collapsed wall, reaching down to tequila girl with one of the two-by-fours. As they retrieved her, the wall and platform shifted again, only after this time, the surface felt stable. One minute later, everyone was back up into the room. Then, the fireworks started.

Catwoman slapped tequila girl across the face. "I ought to throw you right back out there and you can see what it's like, you slimy little snake of a slut," Catwoman slapped her again. "You killed two people just now, and you have this smirk on your face. What kind of evil bitch are you?"

Tequila girl backed away from her until she was standing behind Bruce. She started to cry. "I didn't kill anyone. Everyone saw that was an accident. You think I made this stupid balcony and wall cave-in? I just saw my friend die, so you just leave me alone, you freak."

Catwoman lunged at her. Bruce and Conner had to keep the two ladies separated.

"Stop," Tess directed Catwoman in a calm voice, gently taking her hand. "She's not worth it. When this is all over, when we're out of here, we can turn her in or whatever else we decide to do. She'll have her day of reckoning. But let's just get through this, for right here, right now."

Catwoman was almost hyperventilating, but slowed down her pace with each deep breath. Tess stroked her hand. The two hugged, both crying. Cassie started wailing too, standing next to Conner. Tequila girl strode over and sat on the floor next to the duct taped naked man. She looked up at Conner.

"What are we going to do about him," she asked, pointing at naked man, changing the subject.

Conner stepped over to naked man, eyeing him carefully. Conner turned around. "I guess we need to unleash him, before anything else happens, don't you think, guys?"

"Yeah, I suppose so." Bruce sounded reluctant. He took several steps forward, standing next to Catwoman and Tess. Tess kept her left arm around Catwoman, but wrapped her right arm around Bruce's waist.

Conner ripped the duct tape off naked man's mouth. Surprisingly, he made no sounds. Conner struggled to pull apart the duct tape hand cuffs and ankle cuffs. Conner leaned over, biting into the edges of the tape until a new tear formed in the hand cuff. After a minute, he finally worked it completely off. He then repeated the procedure with the ankle cuffs. Still, the naked man was completely quiet.

One-by-one, everyone sat down, no one talking. Cassie reclined next to Conner, planting gentle kisses on his cheek, his face being the only exposed part of his body. Bruce sat in between Tess and Catwoman, both placing their heads on his shoulder.

Tequila girl remained seated by naked man, staring up at the ceiling. She brushed her short, brunette hair from her forehead. She eyed how unkempt the others looked, disheveled and caked with mud. She looked down at her outer costume remnants, which hours before had been sown to a large faux tequila bottle; her friend sewn at the other side. They had planned to wear the same outfit each night on the playa, so that by the end of the week, everyone across Black Rock City would be talking about those tequila ladies.

She was twenty-six-years-old, confident she had a great body, particularly compared to her present company. She reached inside her costume, adjusting her sports bra. She decided to pull off her costume remnants, given that her right side was already ripped open when they separated from the tequila bottle. She stood up, yanked the costume off, sitting back down in just her black sports bra and black, tight gym trunks. She strained to catch out of the corner of her eye, if either Bruce or Conner were checking her out.

They were preoccupied. But the naked man stood up, much to her dismay. Just as she was about to chastise him for an untoward advance, he walked past her, lifting his right arm, pointing down at the collapsed wall, balcony platform and toppled beam. "Look," he simply said.

The utterance of a coherent declaration from the frail, naked man captured everyone's attention. They stood up, casting their gaze down below. The balcony platform had stabilized during the tequila girl's rescue. Now there existed a somewhat navigable path from the beam — to the exposed platform, to the collapsed wall resting on top of a portion of the platform – that led up to the upstairs room; serving as a bridge of sorts, from the courtyard to the upstairs.

Several zombies were scooting across the beam, towards the platform. Two ahead of them were already crawling up the platform toward the collapsed wall, working their way up the bridge to the upstairs.

Thursday Friday Saturday Sunday Monday Tuesday Wednesday

The Battle of the Alamo

Conner scanned the room, finding and donning his Stormtrooper mask. He was sweating profusely inside the costume. Conner grabbed his softball bat, advancing to the edge, overlooking the collapsed wall. Bruce grasped the length of rebar with his right hand, his M9 pistol with his left, joining Conner at his right side. The collapsed wall rose up to the edge of the floor on Conner's right, angling further down and away from the floor to the left.

Cassie, Tess and Catwoman each picked up a two-by-four, helping to form a line along the open left side of the room. Tequila girl remained seated at the back, glancing around nervously. The naked man stood up, pacing behind the front line.

Conner started to pound his bat against on the edge of the collapsed wall, hoping to dislodge it away from the floor. Bruce joined him with the rebar, putting the pistol on safety, and back in his rear pocket. Although they tried mightily, they made no progress in moving the wall away.

The first two zombies were on the final leg of their sojourn across the bridge upstairs. They were forced to crawl, due to the steep angle leading towards Conner and Bruce, grabbing onto protrusions poking out of the wall along the way, for leverage, to prevent slipping downward to the exposed balcony platform.

"I think you can save your bullets for now, Bruce," Conner suggested, while they gave up trying to propel the collapsed wall downward. "I'll take the lead, since I have this suit," he yelled through his facemask. The first zombie was crawling on all fours, almost within range, the second zombie right behind him. Both were covered with playa mud.

Conner turned his neck, making sure no one was directly behind him. He stepped directly up to the edge, swinging the bat just like a three iron golf club. He connected with the first mud-zombie's chin, knocking the z backward into the second one. Both slid downward, all the way to where the wall ended, coming to a rest on top of the exposed balcony platform. The two tumbling zombies landed at the feet of three more mud-plastered zombies working their way up the bridge.

The entire front line whooped to celebrate Conner's easy first defense of the upstairs Alamo. The celebration ceased, when they realized the process was going to repeat itself, only now there were five zombies working their way up, several more on the beam, and a seemingly endless supply of mud-caked z's in the courtyard crowding around, waiting their turn.

Bruce put the rebar at his right side, shifting his weight on it, like a cane. "I know we need to save my bullets, but we need to think of a way of putting some of these guys down, or this could go on all night," he said to no one in particular, gazing down into the courtyard illuminated by the track lights on the side walls and flood lights pointing up from the ground level.

"Maybe if I knock them hard right, and they fall to the ground, it will mess them up a little...break some legs perhaps," Conner suggested.

"Maybe, if you knock one our way, we could reach down with the rebar, and two-by-fours, and put one down for good, while you keep knocking the others back," Tess proposed.

"I like that idea," Bruce smiled, quickly stepping behind Conner over to Tess, rubbing her shoulders for a few seconds, before returning to Conner. "Let's give it a try, Connerman."

Conner did exactly that. The first zombie queued up was smashed by a swing from Conner's right to left, sending the z several feet left. Bruce leaned over, spearing the zombie through the neck with a deep thrust of the rebar. Bruce started to drag the zombie with the rebar further left, stretching to keep it within the reach of the ladies. Meanwhile, Conner swung his bat the opposite direction into the head of the next z, sending it tumbling over the edge of the wall, down onto the courtyard, landing on three loitering zombies below. Conner was disheartened to watch all of them rise up again.

Bruce held his zombie still with the rebar, while the ladies leaned over the edge, taking turns beating its head with their two-by-fours. Conner knocked the next approaching zombie backwards into the two z's next in line, sending all of them into the gathering crowd that just made it across the beam. He looked left, in time to see Bruce pulling the rebar rod out of the zombie with the freshly smashed head. It was sprawled down on the wall, several feet below the room's floor line.

No one celebrated the zombie's demise. They all noticed a growing number of z's working their way up in the queue through the bridge to the upstairs. Conner had an epiphany. "We can't keep killing them and leaving them over to the left like that," he hollered down the line. "We'll just be building steps for these things to crawl up that side."

Conner ceased conversing, whacking another zombie who just crawled up within reach. Conner sent it flying right, off the wall and down to the ground below. Conner looked below to see the zombie rise up after the fall, heading back toward the beam.

Bruce took stock of their situation. He could sense the sudden realization everyone on the line had just come to; they had just been placed in an endless treadmill in which they would wear out long before the zombies did. There was no longer time to talk through any great plan, the pace of the zombies working their way up was quickening.

Because the angle was more favorable for the zombies on Conner's right, Conner was seeing almost all the action. The ladies and Bruce closed in, ready to take on any zombies veering to their left when Conner was disposed with another. They were careful not to get too close, however, and get hit as Conner swung the bat.

More than five minutes into the continuous assault, Bruce could tell Conner was already tiring. "Connerman, we have to trade off for a minute. Let me take the bat and give you a spell," he yelled, just after Conner sent another z flying right.

Conner kept his eyes focused ahead, replying without turning his neck. "No can do, Bruce. I've got the costume. It's a lot safer for me to do it."

Bruce would have not of it. "Not if you get too weak to swing, Connerman. Come on, you have to rest your arms for just a minute or two. The ladies and I will cover it. Step back, and hurry and give me the bat before this next one gets here." Bruce crowded in on Conner.

Conner turned his head left. He handed Bruce the bat. "Okay, but just for two minutes." Conner retreated to the back wall, resting against it while standing up. His arms were tight and sore. He looked left at tequila girl, who smiled and scooted next to him.

She stood up, closing within inches of Conner, lifting her arms. She started to massage his neck, finding the small open spot above the back shoulder pads of his costume. Conner recoiled. "Hold still, Connerman, and let me help you here." Conner didn't like her using Bruce's nickname for him, and didn't want to have anything to do with her. Still he thought, her hands were soft, and it did feel good. After a few seconds of mental debate, he pulled away, worrying that Cassie would turn around. "Sorry," Conner apologized softly to tequila girl. Conner caught naked man staring at him from the room's other back corner. Conner wondered what on earth naked man was thinking at that moment.

Conner cast his gaze back at the line. There were two zombies side by side within range, the one to the right coming up to Bruce's chest level; the one to the left coming to the ladies knees – due to the wall angling down to the left. Bruce knocked the zombie back into several more approaching z's. The three ladies all worked on the other z; Cassie and Tess with two-by-fours, Catwoman with the rebar. Catwoman scored a direct thrust into the zombie's right eye socket, sending the zombie down. All three ladies reached below the room's floor level, pounding away at the zombie sprawled just above the other dead z. The ladies finished it off.

Another z advanced directly to Bruce. Bruce had been marveling at the ladies' handiwork, just noticing the new z at the last moment. He took a wild swing and missed, the zombie made it to the room's floor, pulling itself up into the room with its left arm, reaching for Bruce with its right. The zombie grabbed Bruce's ankle, positioning itself for a bite just as Catwoman speared it through the neck with the rebar.

Cassie and Tess stepped forward, bashing its skull with the two-by-fours. Bruce joined in with the bat. The zombie collapsed just below them, sliding left into the next dead zombie. Conner ran up to Bruce, hugging him from behind before he could raise the bat. "Brucemoose that was a close call. Now give me the bat," Conner insisted, hollering through his Stormtrooper mask.

Bruce didn't intend to give up the bat, but caught Tess's worried gaze. Conner relieved Bruce of the bat, while Bruce allowed himself to indulge in Tess's bewitching eyes.

Just as Conner predicted, the accumulation of three zombie bodies helped open the steeper left side for zombie traffic, as the live z's could use the dead zombies for leverage while they climbed up. Conner became tied up with a troublesome zombie who didn't fall back after being struck hard in the face.

Two zombies right behind Conner's nemesis both veered to the interior side, as Conner and the first zombie continued to battle. Both quickly made it to the floor, the one on the interior side aided by stepping on the dead z's. The ladies struck at them, but with no decisive blows. Catwoman had not given Bruce back the rebar. Without any other weapon, and seeing the two zombies at left about to enter the room, Bruce drew out his pistol. "Stand back," Bruce yelled to the ladies. They retreated. He removed the safety, pointed at the closer z, and fired at its head.

Bruce missed badly, overshooting too high. "Wait," Catwoman yelled at Bruce. The three ladies ran toward the two zombies climbing up onto the floor. Pushing with the boards and rebar, the ladies knocked them backwards.

Conner was still struggling with his foe. The zombie was larger, heavier and stronger than the others he had faced. Conner struck it repeatedly without much effect. Finally, Conner had the inspiration to allow the z to grasp the floor, to lift itself up. Conner struck the bat down hard on the zombie's left hand fingers, then the right. He repeated the process, breaking most of them. Unable to use its hands for leverage, the zombie fell back. The next time it advanced, Conner successfully knocked it right, sending it flying to the ground.

The zombies to Conner's left charged again. The one on the far left reached the floor first. Cassie and Tess teamed up, knocking its head repeatedly with the boards as it attempted to climb up. Catwoman stepped up to Bruce. "Trade you," she directed him, holding out the rebar with her right arm."

"What?" Bruce replied incredulously.

"You ever shot a gun before?" she asked, hurriedly.

"Well....no," he admitted, his voice trailing off.

"I have. Now quick, give me the gun," Catwoman commanded. Bruce complied sheepishly. Catwoman took the M9, stepped close to the other zombie, dispatching him with a center forehead shot. At the same time, Cassie and Tess managed to send their zombie far left, tumbling down to the bottom, missing the other accumulating dead zombies.

"But now we have one less bullet," Bruce protested.

"I needed a practice shot. And you're one to talk," Catwoman laughed, walked up and punched him in the shoulder, before heading left to high-five Cassie and Tess. Bruce sighed and returned next to Conner.

Conner pointed down to a particular zombie halfway in the queue, coming up the bridge to the upstairs. "Would you look at that," he exclaimed loudly, without turning around. Everyone on the line couldn't help but take notice. Heading their way was Santa Claus, or rather, Santa Z – a portly male zombie in full Santa Claus costume.

Requiem for a Z

They were mentally and physically exhausted. A half-hour under that constant fear of death, of inflicting violence on others – even zombies— of swinging bats, rebar and boards nonstop, of fearing for their friends next to them had taken its toll.

Cassie, Tess and Catwoman were sobbing, as they toiled on. Bruce and Conner were becoming resigned that sooner or later, they would slipup, and that would be that. The zombies were relentless. Send them flying down fifteen feet to the ground, they simply arose, working their way through the courtyard to queue up and have another crack at the uninfected at the top.

Naked man, on the other hand, seemed to be gravitating closer to reality with the passage of time. On several occasions, he shouted out words of encouragement to those on the line. More than once, when one of the ladies' two-by-fours flew backwards out of their hands, naked man bolted from his position to retrieve and return the board. Tequila girl remained secluded in the back right corner, pouting. Everyone had pretty much forgotten she was present, as the stress of the assault on the Alamo continued on.

But then everything fell apart.

The zombies had generally proceeded up the bridge to the upstairs in single — or sometimes double — file. They consistently progressed up the exterior side, where the angle wasn't as sharp. If traffic was backed up at the top, when they encountered Conner and his bat, they ventured inward – to find Bruce with his rebar, and Cassie, Tess and Catwoman with two-by-fours.

Catwoman also had Bruce's pistol in the small fanny pack she was outfitted with. After she and Bruce each discharged a shot, bringing the number of rounds remaining to eight, she had to fire once more when the ladies experienced a very close call.

This was the environment those on the front line had adjusted into a routine with. Then, inexplicably, everything changed.

The number of zombie corpses had grown considerably with the passage of time. The dead zombies were littered all over the collapsed wall. Whereas half an hour earlier, the angle was too steep for a zombie to navigate the interior end of the wall that rested on the broken balcony platform beneath it, the dead zombies now provided the means of leverage to continue upwards.

Previously, a zombie or two occasionally stumbled upon this interior passage, which the ladies handled admirably.

But now, whether a random happenstance, or due to some other confluence of events, a solid line of zombies advanced together up the wall, eight zombies across. Another nine zombies followed closely behind, in three rows of three each.

The five on the line in the room were bunched somewhat to the right, because the action had been occurring predominantly to on that side. As the eight-wide procession of zombies reached to the top, the group was outflanked to the left.

Conner dealt with the three farthest to the right, rotating bashing them over the head as they tried to climb into the room. Leaning too far over the edge, trying to inflict a blow on top of one of the z's he had knocked downwards, he was pulled by the ankles onto the collapsed wall below by the other two zombies on the far right. Conner landed behind them, and just in front of the next rows of z's.

The others on the line were too busy at first to notice Conner's downfall. Bruce was preoccupied, as he speared the next z over, impaling it with the rebar just below the Adam's apple. Bruce was trying to navigate the zombie into an object for leverage, so he could yank the rebar out, and then finish the z off.

The three ladies were engaged, each working on a zombie in front of them with their boards, trying to prevent the z's from climbing into the room. Two zombies on the far left remained unaccounted for. They reached the room, standing on a dead z below, grasping the edge of the room's floor at head level. Pulling themselves upward, they entered the room.

At that moment, Cassie saw Conner in his Stormtrooper outfit below her, on the collapsed wall, in the midst of a pack of zombies. She screamed, stepping backwards. Her outburst caused Tess and Catwoman to retreat a couple of steps as well. Their three zombies crowded forward, starting to climb up.

Tess turned her head to notice two midsize male zombies — both in blue Hawaiian shirts and swimsuits — were already in their room, rising to their feet. As she tensed up, the naked man, who had been standing in front of tequila girl in the back right corner, yelled something unintelligible while springing across the room. He plowed full steam into the Hawaiian zombie closest to Tess, taking the zombie with him over the edge, back onto the collapsed wall, rolling downwards.

The other Hawaiian zombie already in the room fixed his gaze on tequila girl. He made a beeline for her in the back right corner. As he started to close in, tequila girl bolted forward to Tess.

While Cassie lost focus on the zombies in front of her, yelling frantically at Conner down below, Catwoman could see that the two-by-fours weren't getting it done. Dropping her board, she pulled the M9 out of the fanny pack.

Bruce wrestled his zombie further right — into the area vacated by Conner — leading it by the rebar resting in its throat. Propping himself against the intact wall to the right, he pulled the zombie hard into the edge of the floor, dislodging his rebar from its throat. Bruce immediately advanced, sending his gray-ooze-soaked rebar into the zombie's left eye socket. Bruce leaned over the edge, pushing the zombie into the collapsed wall, driving the rebar beyond the eye socket into the skull.

Catwoman calmly positioned her pistol in her right hand, steadying it with her left. She proceeded to pump a shot into the forehead into each of the three zombies climbing up into the room. "Four shots left," she said softly to herself.

The Hawaiian z already in the room turned, as his quarry – tequila girl – ran behind Tess. Tess held the two-by-four horizontally, seeking to thrust it into the Hawaiian zombie's chest, intending to shove him into the back wall where she could corner him.

The Hawaiian zombie snarled as he stepped towards them. Tequila girl, concerned he would reach her, pushed Tess into him. The zombie bit hard into Tess's left shoulder upon impact.

With her remaining strength, Tess let the Hawaiian zombie have it with the two-by-four directly in the mouth. Several teeth went flying; gray ooze dripped from the zombies' mouth. The zombie fell backwards into the wall from the force of the blow. Tess collapsed where she stood, feeling faint.

Bruce saw it happen. He had just turned his head, after dispatching his zombie with the rebar. He screamed, sprinting towards the Hawaiian zombie at the wall. He pushed tequila girl to the floor on the way, out of spite. Bruce, charged with adrenaline, arrived at the half-erect Hawaiian zombie, its feet sprawled partially towards the floor, Bruce, thrust his rebar with all his might into the z's right eye socket, penetrating the zombie's skull, sticking the rebar solidly into the wall.

Bruce left the Hawaiian zombie pinned to the wall. Bruce dived down to Tess, grasping her left hand with his right. "Tess, he pleaded, "hang in there, you can do it." He examined her left shoulder, which was bleeding profusely.

Tess felt a sudden surge of energy. "Bruce," she exclaimed, smiling, "you rock." Tess rose up suddenly, confidently. Bruce embraced her, hugging her desperately. He couldn't believe his good fortune. She must be immune to these horrid things, he thought. Bruce released his tight grasp of her, ready to kiss her with the fervor she had let loose on him earlier.

But Tess fell to the floor. Her equilibrium felt terribly off-kilter. She felt nauseous, with a rushing sound in her ears. She could see Bruce's face directly in front of her, but she was having trouble understanding what he was trying to say. Her vision was blurred, her eyes bulging and aching, her hearing deteriorating. Tess wanted badly to get back up to her feet, to get back in the fight, to be with Bruce and get to know him better, a lot better. She rose to her knees, focusing on the ceiling. Her head started to throb and pound. Tess leaned over on her knees and vomited. Bruce glanced behind and realized he had no choice to get back on the line.

Conner thrashed around on the collapsed wall. He could feel the zombies climbing on him, clacking their teeth into his plastic outfit. He knew it wouldn't take long for them to find their way to his neck or several other exposed areas. He rolled to his left, then to his right. He kicked a zombie in the chest, who was trying to dive on top of him. Conner looked up, seeing the new crescent moon poking through, the illumination leaving a white ring and turning the surrounding retiring storm clouds into something out of a renaissance painting of the heavens. He brought himself to his feet, feeling most fortunate that the softball bat landed next to him, He grasped the bat tightly.

Conner jerked his neck right, then left. He knew he was done for, even with the bat. There was no way he could dispatch nine zombies by himself.

Cassie, screaming, started to lower herself from the room floor down to the collapsed wall. Catwoman rushed over to her, pulling her back into the room. "Hey, baby, you gotta stay up here. I got the gun." Catwoman jumped down onto the wall, dodging a zombie corpse as she landed.

Catwoman came up behind the group of zombies circling around Conner, who was madly swinging his bat, keeping them at bay, if only for a moment. She planted rounds into the back of the skull of both zombies directly in front of her. Another turned around, making one step toward her before she squeezed a clean shot into its forehead, dropping it in its tracks. Catwoman took a step back; three of the zombies lost interest in Conner and rushed upwards toward her.

Catwoman spent her last bullet judiciously, placing it squarely in the forehead of the z closest to her. She retreated toward the room, two zombies in pursuit.

Conner, energized by the improvement in his odds, decided to take the fight to the zombies. Facing toward the room above him, he charged at the two to his left. He swung at their torsos. In rapid succession he planted multiple hits to their sternums; the third swing for each sent them flying down to the courtyard ground.

Conner now had three immediate pursuers remaining. Standing close to the edge of the collapsed wall, he could see a stream of zombies working their way up the queue. Conner shifted his position up a couple of steps, taking a wide swing at the nearest z, sending it tumbling downwards where the other zombies had landed in the playa mud.

With his last swing, Conner slid further, teetering with his heels on the edge of the collapsed wall. The two remaining zombies were between Conner and the room, closing in as Conner struggled to keep his balance. Seeing no way out, Conner tossed his bat at their feet, reaching forward, grabbing the shirt of each with his hands. "This ends now," Conner shouted, propelling backwards, taking the three of them downwards into the courtyard playa floor.

Catwoman climbed back into the room. Bruce leaned over to help her up. As Bruce pulled her inside, he saw Conner disappear over the edge, leaving his bat behind. A new group of z's was approaching. Bruce knew Catwoman had spent the last of the M9 bullets trying to save Conner. He made a split decision to retrieve Conner's bat. Bruce jumped down.

It instantly dawned on Bruce that he might have made a mistake. The next zombies in line were closer to the bat than he was. Still, Bruce rushed forward. Possessing the advantage of heading downhill, while his opponents had to advance uphill, Bruce won the race to the bat. He turned around, panting, scaling up the collapsed wall toward the room.

After reaching his destination, Bruce tossed the bat up to Catwoman. Gasping for breath, Bruce reached upwards as he approached the room. Catwoman grasped his hands, pulling him inside. Cassie sat in the back, bawling and hugging her disoriented friend, Tess. Tequila girl was once again in the other corner of the room, crouched in a fetal position.

Bruce and Catwoman peered down at the new batch of zombies lurking their way upwards. Catwoman grabbed the rebar that Bruce had deposited on the floor, before he leapt down to save the bat. She turned around, calling out, "Cassie, I'm so sorry, honey, but you've got to get up here, baby. We need you, like right now."

Bruce turned around to see Tess sprawled on the floor attempting to rise up, then sinking back down. He spotted tequila girl and felt a rage that he knew he must control for now. Standing at the front corner near the edge, he searched below for his good friend. Bruce turned, trying to block Conner's demise from his mind. He focused straight ahead. There were just four z's at the lead. He felt a twinge of optimism. They could do this, at least for a few more minutes.

Thursday Friday Saturday Sunday Monday Tuesday Wednesday

Reinforcements

Doctor Gorman finished suturing up the left buttock, after removing a bullet resulting from friendly fire in the Green Zone. Chief Master Sergeant Carter stood next to Alan, paying a quick clinic visit to his injured man, as well as checking in with Gorman.

Carter's sat phone rang. Carter took a step back from the procedure table, taking a call from the Colonel. "I have good news, son," the voice on the other end announced. A transport armada with over nine hundred National Guard troops just checked in. They're well past Nixon; they'll start pulling into Gerlach within twenty minutes."

"That is good news, sir" Carter replied flatly.

"That's not all," the Colonel continued. "On their heels, are the hundreds of Reno contractors we procured, bringing the security fences. We can start sealing this place in, as soon as the playa surface is passable. Not only that, the next wave of National Guard is coalescing; we should soon have eight hundred more troops to help with mop-up, and to sweep the wider area."

"Has the outer perimeter been probed any further, sir?" Carter asked, eying Gorman, who was listening intently to Carter's end of the call.

"We had two recent incidents on the southeastern perimeter, plus a new Stage II was discovered near the Hycroft mine, but that's it. So far, we've dodged a bullet on this thing going wild into the wider population," the Colonel shared.

"Sir, now that we have the reinforcements' time horizon, can we consider sending even ten or twenty men in from the perimeter, just during the interim? We aren't even treading water, sir. Every minute, countless more are getting infected all around this city," Carter pressed his superior officer.

"Son, you're doing the best you can with the cards you have been dealt. You just hang in there just a little longer, because help will be on the way," the Colonel responded patiently. "Now, I did call for another reason. We've got a media problem. I know you took out that webcam broadcasting on the Burning Man website, you shut down the media mecca tent, but there was no way we could keep a lid on this thing with so many sat phones and camps with private bandwidth. This thing has hit CNN, local Reno stations, a bazillion Internet blogs and who knows what else. So far, the story is some viral outbreak has hit Burning Man and a riot is going on, with a big call-up of area law enforcement and even National Guard. We've managed to keep the military out of it so far. I'm getting big pressure from upstairs to veil the deployment of Air Force and Marine troops on U.S. soil. CNN is pressing for an interview, and I'm told we have to provide one. I don't know if we can trust this Black Rock Ranger to be a team player for an interview..."

Carter interrupted. "Ranger Rick – as he's called? He's out of the Green Zone now, sir. He's pulled a number of rangers into an initiative going deeper into the city, trying to sort out the infected from the uninfected."

"Well, that's good on both counts," the Colonel said enthusiastically. "We don't want to facilitate CNN talking with the Burning Man management; they aren't too happy with us, as you well know. Who I really would prefer to put out in front of them, is Alan Gorman. We can just say he's the attending physician in charge; we don't have to mention he's retired Air Force. With the viral outbreak story out there, having the doctor talk will be perfect. He doesn't have a sat phone. Can you send someone down to him, so that we can get this going?"

Carter emitted a half-hearted laugh, "Sir, that's where I happen to be at the moment. He's in the room with me right now. He's heard my half of the conversation."

"Wow! Put him on, son, but first, this reminds me, as we want to keep a lid on the extraterrestrial bit, about Gorman's friends. Are you sure that the one you had in custody got lost to the infected?" the Colonel asked Carter.

Carter was defensive. "Colonel, we don't have physical confirmation, but my assistant, who was badly bitten, was with him at the time they were overrun. My assistant was too far gone to converse coherently when I was brought to him, but we have to assume that fellow succumbed as well. And before that, when we had him in our possession, we were told his companion was out in the open playa. As you know, these things totally control the open playa right now, and I would think there is no way his companion would make it out of there, intact."

"Alright, son, but you keep pressing for their whereabouts, just the same. We can't be too careful."

"Yes sir," Carter replied dutifully. Carter turned towards Alan. "He wants you," Carter informed Gorman, handing him the phone.

The Colonel repeated his media dilemma to Alan. He secured Gorman's agreement to be interviewed. "Here are your talking points, Alan," the Colonel directed. "You can confirm a viral outbreak of unknown origin. The CDC is involved. You are really not at liberty to speculate regarding any detailed information. They will need to take that up with CDC in Atlanta. There is a temporary quarantine in effect, as well as the aftermath of a major thunderstorm preventing exit from the area for now. This situation has resulted in frustration and some rioting throughout Black Rock City, as reported. You do not have access to any detailed information to share in that regard, but you are aware the National Guard has been called in. You can confirm there have been fatalities, both from the virus and from the rioting, but you aren't at liberty to hazard a guess on specific numbers yet. They will want a death toll more than anything else for their story. You can keep repeating, you are aware of a number of deaths, but aren't yet in a position to report specific numbers. They will press you, and you want to be evasive. Just let them know more specific information will be forthcoming. Push to end the interview as soon as possible, letting them know you are needed back in the medical headquarters. Don't under any circumstances share with them you are retired Air Force; you will be presented simply as the volunteer physician in charge. Don't confirm any knowledge of on-site military involvement or presence. I'm sure you can appreciate the sensitivity, Alan..."

Gorman cut in. "I'm a civilian now. I'm not completely comfortable lying if I'm pushed on a direct question."

"You're not on trial, Alan," the Colonel replied confidently. "This is just a media interview. I know you have the skills to think on your feet, be evasive, and avoid having to lie. Now we're counting on you. CNN has a freelancer still in the green zone. He has his own video equipment. We'll find you a suitable room. Then, we're arranging supervised transport for him back to Gerlach. We have some vehicles in place that can navigate the mud. I know you are team player, and you understand the sensitivities and the big picture we are dealing with here. We're counting on you, Alan."

Thursday Friday Saturday Sunday Monday Tuesday Wednesday

Remember the Alamo

Tequila girl was becoming hysterical at the back of room. "We are all going to die," she screamed more than once, scratching her fingernails against the back wall as she shrieked.

Tess lay to her left, wanting desperately to muster the energy to rejoin the fight. "Just shut up," she reprimanded tequila girl, weakly. Tess's thinking grew fuzzy again, she fell silent.

Bruce turned briefly, tempted to fulfill tequila girl's prophesy, as long as it was in the singular, not the plural. The approaching zombie, however, demanded his attention. He wasn't able to engage the zombies quite as up close as Conner did, lacking the protection of Conner's plastic outfit.

Bruce looked quickly to his left — at what remained of their line – Catwoman and Cassie, in addition to himself. He pushed the inevitable out of his mind. He caught movement out of the corner of his eye, to his far left. Someone was getting too close for Bruce to do anything about it. "Cassie, look out to your left," he shouted.

Cassie was occupied, using her two-by-four to push back a persistent, petite lady zombie wearing a purple bikini. Her jaw dropped as she witnessed naked man crawling back up into the room, a zombie in pursuit on the collapsed wall. Cassie divided her attention between bikini zombie – who fell backwards once again, but was starting to return to her feet – and naked man, who had clearly been bitten on his left arm. 'How is he managing to get around after being bit?' Cassie wondered.

Catwoman and Bruce took time from dispatching their current adversaries to notice naked man's return. Both bore a puzzled expression as they stole a glance of him rushing to the back of the room. Cassie became mesmerized, forgetting momentarily that her bikini-zombie was once again working back up to the room as well.

Naked man proceeded directly to tequila girl. His left arm bore a nasty gash. He leaned over, reaching for her right hand, pulling her upright from the floor. "Come on," he commanded.

"Did you find a way out? You can get us out of here?" Tequila girl asked optimistically.

Naked man didn't answer. He simply pulled hard on her right hand, back towards the edge of the room. Tequila girl didn't resist, assuming he had a plan. Naked man stopped suddenly, as he reached the edge. He grasped tequila girl's wrist with both hands, flinging her out of the room. She screamed as she landed directly in front of the approaching zombie. The z stopped in its tracks, now focusing at the present naked man delivered to its feet. Tequila's girl's high-pitched screams rose above all other sounds emanating throughout the Alamo. The screams soon trailed off into whimpers that were lost in the surrounding din.

Naked man glanced around the room, smiling, before jumping over the edge onto the wall below. He wasn't seen or heard from again.

Something Conner had said back in Sulphur, on the roof, more than half a day before, popped into Bruce's head. Bruce felt it worth repeating. "This day is just too weird for words," he shouted over at Catwoman to his left.

They returned to the fight, Cassie sobbing, as she once again pushed the two-by-four into bikini-zombie. She tried to stop crying but could not. Conner was gone. Tess was going. She knew she would soon be next.

A loud thump on the roof snapped Cassie out of her melancholy. She, Catwoman and Bruce exchanged nervous glances. "How in hell can zombies get on the roof?" Bruce yelled out to no one in particular. Next, a sliding, scrunching sound came from above. The advancing zombies prevented Bruce, Catwoman or Cassie from checking out whatever was lurking over their heads.

The sounds from above ceased. Bruce prepared himself for the worst. Then, a voice called out from above. "Cassie! Brucemoose! Cassie, Bruce!" Bruce didn't understand; he recognized the voice.

Bruce tilted his head upwards. "Conner?" he hollered. "Conner?" he called out a second time. He had to stop there, focusing his attention on a new zombie stepping up to the room. Bruce swung from the left, catching it off-balance. The zombie went flying down to where Conner had fallen earlier.

"Conner?" Cassie cried out. "Is that you?"

"It's me, Cassie, for reals. Come on, we have to get everyone on the roof," Conner called down below, with some urgency.

After Conner tugged at the zombies while he teetered on the edge of the wall, the three went tumbling thirteen feet down toward the courtyard, Conner's arms and legs flailing through the air. The two zombies, one at each side, landed directly on top of another zombie below. Conner fell in between them, sprawled on his back in an open, muddy space. The soft mud absorbed some of the blow.

Conner sat up, assuming he must have broken some bones. He was extremely sore, but amazingly, everything seemed to work. The zombies on each side of him were tangled up with the z's they crashed into. Straight ahead, Conner spied the ladder which earlier resided up on the balcony, but was now leaning against the wall; part of the front balcony platform dangling underneath it.

Conner rose, bolting to the ladder. Halfway there, zombies closed in, grasping at him. More than once, he sensed the clacking of teeth on his Stormtrooper costume. He knew his only hope was to keep his legs moving forward, and above all, not to fall to the ground.

Pushing away at each zombie in his path, spinning whenever he felt arms clutching him, Conner raced forward. The zombies had difficulty containing the moving target. Somehow, Conner reached the ladder, starting upwards, kicking at the hands reaching for his legs and feet.

Conner won the race to the top. Several zombies were able to emulate Conner's movements, chasing him up the ladder. A two foot ledge lined the entire wall. Conner stepped onto the ledge, grabbed the ladder, shaking it until his zombie pursuers fell back below.

Carefully tight roping the wall's ledge, Conner worked his way back toward the room, dragging the ladder along after every few steps. He continually was forced to shake zombies loose from the ladder, as they followed his movements from down below.

Conner finally reached the room. Resting his back again the corner outer wall of the room, he used the leverage to lift the ladder, wrestling with it, until he slid it onto the room's roof. Conner grasped the roof, using the top of the wall above the ledge, as a step. He slowly raised himself up, scooting across the roof, attempting to avoid getting tangled in the mesh netting that he just discovered. Evidently the netting had been abandoned there, the result of a last minute decision not to include it in the art installation. Conner worked his way over the mesh netting, reaching the edge. He called for his friends below.

After getting everyone's attention, Conner learned Tess had been bit, and that tequila girl and naked man disappeared into the zombies below. Conner knew that it would not be an option to leave Tess behind. He adjusted the plan he'd been formulating the past several minutes. He removed his Stormtrooper mask.

Conner could see that the zombie line was evolving back to single and double file. Cassie could be spared from the line. "Cassie," Conner called out, "come over and open the door." Conner had to repeat his request, before Cassie headed over, two-by-four in hand.

Cassie opened the door that now led to nowhere. She looked straight up, finding Conner's head, facing upside down just above her; no longer hidden beneath the Stormtrooper mask. "Oh my God, Conner, oh my God... I love you, Conner."

Conner provided an upside down smile. "Hey Cassie, I sort of have a plan to get you all on this roof, coming up outside this door. First, I'm going to hand you some mesh netting. You're going to get Tess into it, and I'm going to pull her up. Then I'm going to reach down and lift you up. We're going to wait until the right moment, when there is a lull with the zombies. Then, we'll lift Catwoman up. After that I'm going to create a distraction. You and Catwoman will lower the mesh netting. Bruce will hop in and kick the door shut so the zombies hopefully don't pursue him. I'll join you, and the three of us will lift him. Do you understand all that?"

Cassie nodded her head enthusiastically, so thrilled that Conner was alive and someone had a plan.

"Okay," Conner continued, "go tell Bruce and Catwoman, and make sure they buy into it, and let's get this going."

Bruce and Catwoman might have agreed to any plan at that moment as the status quo didn't look too attractive as an option. Cassie soon was dragging a semi-conscious Tess across the floor. Moments later, Tess was in the mesh netting, being lifted up to the roof. Conner didn't dare disclose his motives to Cassie or Bruce, but among other reasons to lift her first, he thought it logical to test the mesh netting on someone already infected.

Tess and the mesh netting passed the trial run. Minutes later, he successfully lifted Cassie up above. He wanted Cassie first, both selfishly, as well as because Catwoman was a little taller, a little heavier, and he felt it safest for two of them to lift Catwoman up together.

Then the waiting game began. Conner stripped off his Stormtrooper pants. Cassie stroked Tess's hair. Conner and Cassie watched nervously over the edge, down at the bridge to the upstairs. They searched for a spot in the queue where a single file line formed, combined with sufficient gap to risk sending Catwoman up, leaving Bruce to fend for himself, momentarily. Cassie agreed with Conner on the best spot to target.

"Try to send the next couple of zombies over the edge to the ground, so they don't come back, and you'll be good to go," Conner hollered below. He and Cassie anxiously watched Bruce and Catwoman work together to dispatch the zombies as requested. After the second one went flying downward, Conner hollered at Catwoman to head to the door. One minute later, she was looking as relieved as someone could through a Catwoman mask, sitting on the roof next to Conner and Cassie, still holding the rebar rod.

"Okay," Conner explained, " Now what I'm going to do next is going to seem really weird, but it worked back at Bruce's place up on his roof, so I'm going to try it again. I'm going to tell Bruce to run now, so be ready to lower the mesh netting down to him, and hang on tight while he gets in. Be sure to remind him to kick the door shut. I'll be back to help you, when you let me know he's ready to lift up."

Conner rose, scooting over to the edge before Cassie or Catwoman had a chance to ask or say anything. Cassie grabbed the mesh netting; she and Catwoman crawled to the spot above the door.

Conner lowered his head over the edge. A zombie was getting closer to the room than Conner would have liked. "Go Bruce, go!" Bruce, bat in hand, retreated to the door. The lead zombie started to climb up into the room.

Conner unzipped his pants. He commenced urinating over the edge, as close as he could to the point where the lead zombie was situated. The zombie turned around, pushed himself down off the room's floor, back onto the collapsed wall. The z held its hands up into the air, letting the stream of urine spray all over him. Within moments, two more zombies arrived, all mesmerized by the urine falling from the sky.

Conner began to grow worried. His bladder didn't have much more than a few drops left, and still the ladies hadn't called for him. Then, try as he might, Conner had nothing left. The zombies stood still momentarily, snarling up at the sky, seemingly upset that there was no more pee forthcoming. It didn't take long for them to lose interest. The three of them proceeded back up into the room.

Conner dashed over to the door, sliding up on his stomach to the left of Cassie and Catwoman. "What's wrong?"

"Bruce's foot slipped through the mesh netting, his leg is poking out the other side," Catwoman explained.

"Well, we have to take him up anyway. Cassie, give me your end, and you help Catwoman," Conner shouted, so Bruce could hear. "Bruce, here we go, push that door shut, if you can."

Conner, gripping the left end of the mesh netting — Cassie and Catwoman gripping the right — began to lift up. Bruce's extra weight, compared to the ladies, made elevating the netting much slower going, even with three people pulling upward.

The door burst open. While the door lacked a knob, Conner hoped if the door was shut, the zombies might not figure out that they could push the door open – the door able to swing in either direction. Fortunately, the first zombie, launching through the door at full steam, sailed out into open air, arms flailing as he dropped to the ground.

The next zombie fell forward as well, but managed to grab onto Bruce's left leg, which protruded through the mesh netting. The z clung onto Bruce's ankle and foot with arms outstretched. The added zombie weight brought the ascent almost to a halt. The third zombie stood still in the doorway, but made a deliberate decision to jump out towards Bruce. The z almost missed its target, but was able to grab onto the mesh netting by its fingers, just below Bruce's back.

The additional weight almost caused Conner, Cassie and Catwoman to lose their grips. "Hang on," Conner shouted. Hang on, they did, but given the combined weight below exceeded the combined weight above, Conner and the two women began to slowly slide on their stomachs, toward the edge of the roof. "Bruce, we're losing you," Conner cried out frantically.

Bruce desperately shook his left leg, twisting and turning as best he could. The zombie clinging on finally started to slip, first losing hold of Bruce's ankle, then Bruce's foot. The z dropped to the ground.

Conner, Cassie and Catwoman's forward slide halted just as their chins passed over the edge of the roof. Unable to halt their movement with their hands that held on valiantly to the mesh netting, they instinctively used their feet to help drag to a stop.

With one zombie still hanging on by its fingers, the three were not able to lift Bruce any higher, they merely held their ground. Bruce knew he must take matters into his own hands, literally. Bruce fought off panic, as he saw the zombie trying to pull its mouth closer to the mesh netting, snarling, trying to take a bite. Bruce turned on his side, contorting as his left leg was still stuck in the netting.

Using both his hands, Bruce began to pry away at the z fingers clutching the netting. One by one Bruce worked each finger of the zombie's right hand free. The zombie hung on stubbornly with just its left arm. Bruce considered the softball bat he tossed into the netting when he jumped in. Cramped inside the netting, Bruce couldn't raise the bat to swing at the z's fingers. He could, however, poke the bat through the netting to push at the persistent z.

Bruce turned again until he could reach the softball bat lying at his side. Grabbing it by the narrow handle-end, he poked it through, ramming it again and again into the zombie's snarling face. The third attempt sent the zombie to the courtyard below. Moments later, Bruce was on the roof, exchanging hugs.

Thursday Friday Saturday Sunday Monday Tuesday Wednesday

Tipping Point II

Thanks to Ranger Rick, the zombies began to run out of targets. Out on the open playa, they virtually ran out of uninfected citizens to assault. Within the radius of the city, block after block, Ranger Rick launched an initiative with Chief Master Sergeant's blessing, to separate the infected from the uninfected, and to secure the uninfected citizens.

Ranger Rick had only a dozen rangers with him when he set out hours before, during the rainstorm. His gambit was to rely on a central tenet of Burning Man – participation. Underneath the awning of a theme camp, where he assembled his men, he held out a map of Black Rock City, assigning a segment to each of them.

Ranger Rick listed seven principles for his men to memorize and take with them out into the muddy city: 1) recruit someone suitable to be responsible for each city block and ensure you receive a report from each of them when they are finished; 2) convince them to recruit at least six persons to assist in their tasks; 3) have them gather all infected persons in an immediate area underneath an awning and mark each collection spot on their map; 4) have them demand that any uninfected person still outside directly head to any automobile, RV or trailer, and lock themselves inside – and assist such persons in getting someone nearby to take them in, if necessary; 5) insist they do not engage anyone with a Stage II infection — run away from Stage II cases, and revisit that area later; 6) insist they do not enter any area that doesn't provide multiple exits – do not paint yourself in a corner should a Stage II infected approach; 7) ensure all recruits memorize these principles.

Every one of the rangers was able to enlist their needed volunteers with relative ease, despite the rain, mud, and sheer terror that the rumors circling the camps had created. The zombies swept through the city inflicting casualties and havoc at will, but primarily in the portions not yet visited by Ranger Rick's recruits.

Not every person was safe in their vehicles. A few cars or RVs housed a Stage I infected person that subsequently turned on the other occupants. Some people panicked when surrounded by a pack of rabid Stage II cases, vacating their vehicles only to be apprehended by the infected. There were also the occasional instances of persons with Stage II, bearing an arm cast, prosthesis or enough jewelry and bling, being able to smash through a window or windshield.

But by the time the main thrust of the National Guard arrived, the city was fairly sorted through – uninfected locked away in cars, RVs and trailers; Stage I infected lying in misery in hundreds of collection sites; and Stage II infected wandering throughout the city with impunity.

The number of Stage I and II cases was staggering – way beyond what anyone had earlier estimated might have been the worst case scenario by the wee hours of Tuesday morning. The number of Stage II cases exceeded two thousand; Stage I cases were rapidly approaching nine thousand. The number of dead was in the hundreds.

The rules of engagement the Colonel passed down through the National Guard chain of command, were to only execute head shots on Stage II cases when necessary to securely evacuate the uninfected or in self-defense. The Colonel had already been impressed upon by his chain of command that the public might never fully know or understand the nature of the infection, but they would understand mass execution of thousands of U.S. citizens.

The Colonel's marching orders were to permanently seal off Black Rock City with security fencing, just beyond the existing orange perimeter fence, and to leave the infected inside the fences. The race against time the National Guard was up against was to evacuate the uninfected and work with the vendors to get the fencing erected before the existing Stage I cases turned en masse into Stage II.

The evacuation was set into two phases. Evacuees were to be herded into a staging area beyond the BRC airport; outside the security fencing being erected. Within the staging area, citizens were to be subject to inspection, followed by an orientation explaining the official version of what they had just encountered, before they could be released.

The National Guard proceeded into the city on vehicles that traversed the slowly-drying mud. The vendors commenced with fence erection. The open playa was left alone – the assumption being there was no one left to save, and priorities required that resources were better spent elsewhere.

Thursday Friday Saturday Sunday Monday Tuesday Wednesday

A Farewell to Art

They had been stranded out in the art installations on the open playa for over six hours. It was becoming more and more clear that help was not on the way anytime soon. The immediate concern, surfacing for everyone, was when would Tess turn?

Tess weighed in on the topic herself. Emerging out of a haze a half hour earlier, she begged the others to separate from her before she turned into one of those things. Since then, Tess had slipped back into unconsciousness.

From the rooftop, they could see a number of large trucks and other vehicles arrive beyond the perimeter fence. They watched a floodlight rise up, directed downward in that immediate area. A second floodlight was erected. Even from a distance, they witnessed considerable activity; however, there was nothing transpiring that gave any hint of hope of a rescue attempt. The goings-on did prompt Bruce and Catwoman to broach the idea of fleeing the Alamo, and make a run for it, to the crew with the floodlights.

"I don't think I can leave Tess all alone," Cassie objected, wiping tears from her face, "and I can't go along with tossing her aside." Catwoman suggested previously that they consider wrapping Tess up in the mesh netting, so that she would be restrained, and they could push her over the roof, if need be.

"So, don't you two have a better idea how long Tess has left?" Catwoman queried Conner and Bruce.

"We just didn't see anyone turn by themselves after being infected," Bruce replied. "Dax, he turned after he fell off the roof. All we have to go on is what Alan Gorman told us, and it sounds like it's not a definite, exact length of time."

Cassie scooted up next to Tess again, running her fingers through Tess's hair. Catwoman looked Conner in the eye, while pointing at Cassie. "You need to talk to her," she prodded Conner in a low voice.

Conner crawled over the ladder he previously placed on the roof to Cassie. "I'm not leaving her," she blurted out to Conner, before he had a chance to speak.

"Hey, I didn't want to leave my boyfriend, either, honey," Catwoman rose her voice, but kept her tone civil. "But some things we just have to do. We don't have a choice."

Conner inched right next to Cassie. "I'm so sorry. But.... you don't want to be here when she becomes one of those things. You don't want to have to defend yourself against her. You don't want us to have to do that either. You don't want to put her, or you, or us, in that situation," Conner spoke softly, patting Cassie's knee.

Cassie pushed Conner's hand away. Her tears resumed. "But what if she doesn't turn? We don't know for sure what's going to happen. Or if she turns, she might get better later on. No one knows what's going to happen to any of them, after more time passes," Cassie argued.

Conner replied patiently, in a pleading tone. "You're right. No one can say with one hundred percent certainty much about anything that's going to happen out here. But if we leave her on this roof, and we escape — if she doesn't turn— she'll still be safe from these zombies below. If she does turn, she's not going to get caught up in anything they're doing down below, so she should be safe no matter whatever happens to them. Cassie, we can't be with her when she turns. And you can say that might not happen, but you cannot argue that the odds are pretty solid she will. But the thought I'll leave you with is if anything happens to you, because you stayed with Tess, you're going to leave a teenage daughter behind. Now, I'm not leaving you, so if you want to do this, I'm with you for the duration, but I hope you think about what I'm saying."

Cassie fell silent.

Bruce, sitting upright with his palms pressed against the rooftop, seized the opportunity to make his case. "It does look to me like the zombies behind the wall have wandered off in the direction of those floodlights. So if we can somehow go down the back wall and we go wide left or wide right of the trucks and floodlights, we'd steer clear of the zombies. Then, we could jump the orange perimeter fence – it's just three feet high or so, and we'd be out of this mess."

"Amen to that," Catwoman added, seated next to Bruce.

"The question is," Bruce continued, "how do we get down from here? This ladder we're sitting on only reached a few feet above the balcony from the ground, and we're on the roof. And we can't reach that other ladder built into the back wall."

The group grew silent as they watched an ambulance, with flashing lights, pull up underneath the floodlights. The ambulance seemed to add to their sense of urgency.

Conner became engaged in the conversation. "I know....I know what to do....the mesh netting. We tie it to the ladder, and lower the ladder until we can position it below us. Then we tie the mesh netting off, and we climb down the netting to the ladder..."

Bruce interrupted. "Tie the netting to what?"

"The rebar," Conner exclaimed, grabbing the nearby rebar rod that Catwoman brought up with her. "We take the softball bat that you so kindly carried up with you, and see if we can pound the rebar near the edge of the roof here into the top of the wall of the room below. If it doesn't work, we can try a different plan, but why not find out if we can pound this rebar down far enough?"

Instead of answering, Bruce grabbed the rebar and the bat. He scooted to the back edge of the roof, holding the rebar over a couple of different locations, before settling on a final spot. Catwoman crawled up, taking a firm hold of the rebar.

"Pound away, Bruce baby, pound away," Catwoman called to Bruce, above her.

Minutes later, the plan was in place.

Cassie hadn't spoken since Conner had pleaded with her. Conner lowered himself to his knees, next to Cassie – still communing with Tess. Conner gave Cassie a hug. "Are we staying or going?" Conner asked, hopeful the answer would be the latter.

Cassie breathed in deeply, brought her index finger to her mouth, kissed it, and placed her finger on Conner's lips. She nodded her head slightly. "We're going." She turned to Tess. Cassie kissed her forehead, before putting her mouth to Tess's ear. "Goodbye Tess," she whispered. "I will always love you."

The descent went without a hitch. Conner discarded what remained of his Stormtrooper costume. At the bottom, Bruce retrieved the two bicycles still against the back wall, suggesting that Cassie and Catwoman try them, given the playa surface appeared to be drying out, and abandon them if they did get stuck in the mud. The two women acquiesced; the bicycles worked well enough, as long as they avoided certain spots. Conner and Bruce sprinted alongside them. Various zombies took off after them, but the foursome outpaced the z's with relative ease. They veered right, avoiding the zombies near the perimeter fence ahead of them.

A couple of minutes later, they reached the orange perimeter fence, ditching the two bikes. Conner and Bruce helped the two women to the other side, before climbing over the fence themselves. Zombies were in pursuit, but were still forty yards back.

Black Rock City was behind them. The clouds had dissipated. Stars dotted the sky, although only the brightest were visible, due to the ambient light from the floodlights. The sounds of power tools and chatter filled the air from the vendor work crew in the distance. "I can't believe we did it," Catwoman yelled excitedly as they sprinted, hard left towards the floodlights.

A shot rang out. Then another.

"What the hell?" Bruce screamed, as he noticed blood splattered on his arm after the person next to him dropped suddenly to the ground.

Thursday Friday Saturday Sunday Monday Tuesday Wednesday

Doctor Gorman, I Presume?

"Hold your fire!" A voice pierced through the darkness from the distance.

Another shot rang out. Everyone dropped to the ground. "Don't shoot, damn it!" Bruce screamed in the direction of the floodlights, "Don't shoot."

"I said hold your fire!" the booming voice repeated in the darkness. "They're not infected. They're talking and they're running too fast to be infected. Now get over there and help them out."

Bruce looked to his right. Catwoman lay on her side, blood oozing on the right side of her mask, running all over her ear. "Hey," Bruce called to her, leaning over, examining her bleeding head. She didn't respond. Cassie and Conner crawled up next to them.

"Oh my God!" Cassie cried out, seeing Catwoman was shot, lying limp in the drying playa mud.

Bruce and Conner looked ahead. Two National Guardsmen wearing headlamps were sprinting towards them with rifles in hand. "You shot her!" Bruce yelled at them angrily as they approached.

The Guardsmen didn't apologize as they reached the foursome. Both looked twenty-one years of age, if that. One told the group, "You're lucky we happen to have an ambulance here, and a doctor. We just had an accident, a pretty bad fall into the razor wire, putting up the big fence." He stopped to point back at the security fence being assembled. He pulled out his radio, requesting the ambulance to head over. "We'll watch your position here. Sometimes those things out there figure out how to scale the little fence. That's what we thought you were."

"God damn it! If you knew what we went through today, what she went through, to get here, only for you to shoot her," Bruce yelled at the two angrily, pacing around the fallen Catwoman.

Cassie tended to Catwoman, tearing off a piece of her billowing, mud-stained Jan costume pants from the bottom trousers, pressing the material against Catwoman's head wound to slow the bleeding. She removed Catwoman's mask, while Bruce and Conner gawked – none of them had seen her full exposed face before.

The ambulance pulled to a halt alongside them. A driver and passenger hopped out, opening the rear doors. Out stepped Alan Gorman from the back of the vehicle. Gorman, who had been sitting next to a patient, quickly hopped out, trotting over to his new patient.

Alan did a double take as he approached the group surrounding Catwoman. He beheld Bruce, then Conner. "I don't believe it... I just don't even believe it." Gorman knelt down, donning gloves, signaling for the ambulance paramedics to join him. They brought flashlights, a medical kit, and plastic sheeting which they lay underneath Catwoman's head.

Alan spent an agonizing minute with the small LED light, his face right up almost into Catwoman's ear. Finally, he emerged, turning to face Bruce, Conner and Cassie. "Well, this is one lucky woman – she's just been grazed. There's no point of entry. She's coming to already. I've got to suture her up, but she's going to be fine." Gorman went right to work. He spoke as he prepped and stitched her. "You guys just can't stay away from me, can you?"

"Last time I saw you—" Bruce started to say, but Alan interrupted.

"Hey, we'll talk in a minute here, let me just finish this." Alan dabbed ointment onto the wound, cleaned the surface one last time before turning to the ambulance drivers. "Let's load her into the back. Her pupils look fine, but you'll want to keep her for observation for now, at least until she gets another examination later this morning."

The ambulance men brought out a gurney. Catwoman turned her head to her three companions. "Hey, am I okay?" she asked in a weak voice. Bruce smiled and nodded.

"You're going to be fine," Alan Gorman answered for them, as the paramedics lifted her into the gurney. Catwoman looked up into the sky as they carted her away. The clouds had disappeared. The stars were in full force. She could sense quietness in the night sky.

"Hey, we're coming with her," Bruce called out to them.

"Sorry," Alan interrupted, placing his hand across Bruce's chest to stop them from following them to the ambulance. "There just isn't room. She's taking my place." Alan turned, calling out to the ambulance driver. "Hey, I'll catch a ride back...you guys get going."

"You sure, Doc?" the driver called back, as they loaded Catwoman inside the Horton Model 453 ambulance.

Conner, Cassie and Bruce rushed to the ambulance, somehow searching for closure with Catwoman, as she was unceremoniously being spirited away from them. They exchanged hurried good-byes, with promises extracted to see each other shortly.

Alan Gorman quickly waved the ambulance on. He promptly tugged at Bruce with his left hand and Conner with his right. "Come on, we need to talk." Alan turned around to address the two young Guardsmen. "You can go ahead and rejoin your unit. We're going to stroll over that way too." The two members of the Guard trotted back towards the floodlights. Alan, Bruce, Conner and Cassie headed that direction at a much slower pace, through the drying playa mud.

Alan smiled, nodding towards Cassie. "So, Conner, this is the woman you trekked all the way across the desert to save?"

"For reals, Dr. Gorman. She is, all that," Conner replied happily, continuing to use a teenager's slang for effect. Cassie held his hand, stroking his fingers with her thumb. She glanced back into the open playa, trying to make out the Alamo in the distance, wondering what would become of Tess.

"It looks like we're finally taking control of this place. You should see how many troops are entering the city now. The only spot still wild at this point is probably these art installations out in the open playa. It would appear you're the only ones to make it out of there unscathed." Alan stopped in his tracks, satisfied no one else would hear them, before continuing. "Listen, fellas. Bruce, when I saw you last, you were being taken into custody. And I'm pretty certain you both are still on the big Colonel's list. It seems they want to keep quiet – real quiet — the whole meteor thing I told you about. And they know I spoke to you about it. So they want to keep you two under wraps for now, I think, and most likely you, too, ma'am if they find out you're together, since I would assume you've shared whatever you know with her. Now, I don't know if they just want to make sure you'll keep things quiet, or if they will detain you for a few hours, days or weeks while they try and put a lid on the story of what's happening here, but I might suggest you downplay anything about what you know about how this virus originated."

"Are you serious?" Cassie asked indignantly, her hands on her hips.

"He's serious," Bruce interjected. "I experienced how serious they were firsthand earlier tonight. But what happened to you?" Bruce enquired of Alan. "Why are you out here and why were you at the clinic when I saw you last?"

Alan put his hand on Bruce's shoulder. "Hey, let's fill each other in on all the details in a bit – but the short story is, after I finally connected with the Air Force, and they coordinated a presence here, I was shuffled aside to a motel in Gerlach, so I volunteered to staff the clinic. Then, when the National Guard just showed up, they brought their own medical team, so I volunteered to go out on this ambulance run, and now I'm calling it a day. A very, very, long, long, day. But, now here's the deal, guys, on what happens next. They are processing everyone in a staging area by the airport, inspecting them, registering them, before they're cleared to exit. I could talk you through how to sneak out of here, but sooner or later, and I would bet on sooner, they will find you, and they'll treat it a lot more seriously, if they think you're evading them."

"They'd find me if I snuck home?" Bruce asked incredulously.

Alan laughed. "Well, yeah. I gave your location when I got rescued from Jungo Road out past your place. I need to share that story — about what happened out there after I left you — just like I'm sure you've got a story or two for me. But anyway, the BLM went to secure the Hycroft mine and your place, and I'm sure someone is standing guard there waiting for you, now that the Colonel is in charge."

"So what are you saying – we're fugitives?" Conner questioned in a defensive tone.

"Yes and no," Alan equivocated. "You haven't done anything wrong. It's just, right now it's all about controlling the story out there, about what happened here. They don't have to worry about me. I'm retired Air Force and they're comfortable I'm still one of them. But since I opened my big mouth and talked to you, they are going to want to keep a lid on what you might say. So I would suggest you downplay knowing much about anything, other than what anyone else trapped in Burning Man would know."

Bruce cleared his throat. "So, what do we say when they ask about what you told us?"

"That I hadn't slept in two days, and that I was mumbling about a lot of things, and you weren't paying much attention." Alan suggested.

"So, the meteor, the virus from another planet, they're not taking that seriously?" Conner wanted to know.

"I didn't say that. I just said that they want to control the story, and that chapter is not going to be in the story, if you get

372

my drift. And your lives, my friends, will be less complicated if you stick with their story," Alan responded firmly.

A chilly breeze whipped through the playa. Cassie began noticeably shivering. "Look," Conner said, gently pulling Cassie next to him as they drew closer to the floodlights, "I'm not going to take on the United States Air Force, are you, Bruce?" Bruce shook his head. "We're just happy that the National Guard is here, and you're evacuating everyone, and that you've got control of the situation. Thank God we beat this thing," Conner exclaimed.

"Beat this thing?" Alan responded skeptically. "If you were launching an attack on our planet, on the human race, would you pin your hopes on one drone meteor? What makes you think they didn't send another somewhere? Or there isn't another one coming? Or a hundred?"

The Burning Z

burningz.com

discuss The Burning Z

find out more about Sulphur, Burning Man and the Black Rock

check out the zombie library